Praise for the ||||||||||| W9-DJM-286
bestselling author Elizabeth Adler

Invitation to Provence

"This new novel shares with its predecessors a great sense of place, charming characters, and wonderful descriptions." —*Booklist*

"No one does travelogues inside terrific contemporary romances better than Elizabeth Adler. Her latest tour of the Mediterranean is superb as readers obtain a taste of Provence while also reading an interesting family drama . . . as she has done with *Summer in Tuscany* and *The Last Time I Saw Paris*, Adler provides a delightful tale for armchair travelers to enjoy."
—*The Readers Guild*

The Hotel Riviera

"Fans of contemporary romance with a touch of suspense will take much delight with a trip to the Riviera."
—*Under the Covers*

"Adler is well known for her charming stories of modern romance . . . an endearing novel." —*Booklist*

"Adler throws in enough twists and turns to make things interesting and keep the reader turning pages . . . [she] transports one immediately to the French Riviera and paints an enchanting picture of the Cote d'Azur . . . If you're looking for a novel to take you away from it all . . . this is the one for you!" —Bookreporter.com

More . . .

Summer in Tuscany

"Like Tuscany's beauty, this book is heaped with delicious words and literary creativity . . . thoroughly engrossing."
—*Bangor Chronicle*

"A very modern romantic comedy."
—*Stuart News*

"A deft hand in creating characters to cheer for and settings to dream over in this deeply appealing story of love, family, and the beauty of Italy."
—*Booklist*

"The tiny, sun-baked village of Bella Piacere is the stuff of dreams . . . [a] dramatic tale . . . sumptuous backdrop and colorful cast of characters . . . a delightful escape."
—*Publishers Weekly*

"The beauty and rich culture of Tuscany form a wonderfully romantic and compelling backdrop for this delightful novel. Ms. Adler's characters are complex and riveting, making this another must-read novel."
—*Romantic Times*

"Adler is superlative at making readers feel they know her characters . . . *Tuscany* offers satisfying summer reading."
—*Brazosport Facts*

The Last Time I Saw Paris

"A wonderful voyage depicting one woman's struggle to regain her sense of self-worth and identity . . . Adler always excels at bringing vivid and lifelike characters into being."
—*Romantic Times*

"The popular Adler gets the dynamics of a new relationship pitch-perfect . . . but it's the detailed, realistic description of the trip to France . . . that makes her latest great vicarious vacation reading." —*Publishers Weekly*

"Outward adventures lead to an inward journey of self-discovery."
—*Booklist*

"Cushy as an ermine throw, smooth as a ride in a chauffeur-driven Bentley, bubbly as Veuve Clicquot, this latest treat from Adler makes murder, thwarted passion, and inheritance disputes delightful."
—*Kirkus Reviews*

"Entertaining. Adler is expert at digging deep into her characters' psyches and showing what makes them tick. Her villain here is wonderfully portrayed—as are all the other characters in this well-plotted, entertaining work."
—*Publishers Weekly*

"Spellbinding. Adler is a true genius." —*Affaire de Coeur*

"Gifted storyteller Elizabeth Adler proves once again why she is truly a master of sweeping, intense, and dramatic novels."
—*Romantic Times*

The Hotel Riviera

Summer in Tuscany

The Last Time I Saw Paris

In a Heartbeat

All or Nothing

Sooner or Later

Now or Never

The Secret of the Villa Mimosa

Legacy of Secrets

Fortune Is a Woman

The Property of a Lady

The Rich Shall Inherit

Indiscretions (writing as Ariana Scott)

Fleeting Images (writing as Ariana Scott)

Leonie

ELIZABETH ADLER

Invitation to Provence

St. Martin's Paperbacks

INVITATION TO PROVENCE

Copyright © 2004 by Elizabeth Adler.
Excerpt from *The House in Amalfi* copyright © 2005 by Elizabeth Adler.

Cover photo © Paul Loven/Imagebank

Library of Congress Catalog Card Number: 2004048388

ISBN: 0-312-98642-4
EAN: 9780312-98642-1

Printed in the United States of America

St. Martin's Press hardcover edition / September 2004
St. Martin's Paperbacks edition / August 2005

St. Martin's Paperbacks are published by St. Martin's Press, 175 Fifth Avenue, New York, NY 10010.

10 9 8 7 6 5 4 3 2 1

FOR ANABELLE AND ERIC

ACKNOWLEDGMENTS

MY THANKS, as always, to my agent and friend, Anne Sibbald, and to the people at Janklow & Nesbit, who look after me so well. To my editor, Jen Enderlin, who is simply the best. To Richard, my husband, for a multitude of reasons. And to Victor and Carmen Bacigalupe; Francesca Bowyer; Warren and Betty Forman; Bill and Sandi Phillips; and Ross and Barbara Salamone—friends whose love and support I truly value.

All my past life is mine no more;
The flying hours are gone,
Like transitory dreams given o'er,
Whose images are kept in store
By memory alone.

—JOHN WILMOT,
Earl of Rochester,
"Love and Life" (1680)

NOTHING MUCH ever changes in the village of Marten-de-Provence. The terrace café now has plastic chairs instead of tin, and the awning is green instead of blue, but the Café des Colombes is the same, still owned by the Jarré family who've run it for decades, and the simple menu hasn't changed much in thirty years either. Allier's grocery shop under the arched arcade is still there, its fresh fruits and vegetables in wooden crates arranged tidily out front with hand-chalked price tickets. The fountain with the stone drinking trough drizzles lazily and a couple of dogs lounge in the shade next to the old men in berets, sitting on wooden benches, sticks clutched in their gnarled hands, watching their small world go by. The doors to the little peeling pink stucco church are open and a woman in a yellow summer dress climbs the worn steps carrying an armload of bright flowers. The village even smells the same, of coffee and roasting chicken, of crushed thyme and ripe melons and horses.

A long mellow-stone wall bordering the château grounds runs along the lane next to the square, from which small houses wind up the cobbled streets into the hot rocky hill-sides. And stuck on top of the loftiest hill of all is Saint-

Sylvestre, a *village perché*, a mini fortress of old, its walls dug deep into the rock. Now it's a haven for artists and the cultural tourists who come to its annual summer music festival in the former monastery, set among fields of lavender, and whose great bronze bell still tolls the passing of time.

Poplar trees line the lane that runs alongside the château's grounds, their branches forming a tunnel of green overhead through which sunlight filters like scattered gold coins. The big pillars topped with carved stone griffins marking the château's entrance are still there, their features worn from centuries of gusty mistral winds, and beyond them, through the big iron gates, is the long cypress-lined driveway that leads, straight as a die, to the Château des Roses Sauvages.

Tree-studded lawns sweep away to the left with a glimpse of the lake glittering silver in the sunlight, then the château comes into view, soft as an ancient fresco against its background of rocky hills, with the spiked ridges of purple mountains as a backdrop.

The house glows ochre-yellow in the evening sunlight, its tiled roof dipping and curving. Water spills musically from a fountain on the flowery terrace, and chestnut trees cast their welcome shade. Of course, in summer the big doors are always left open to catch the breeze, and also, once upon a time, to welcome visitors.

Now Rafaella Marten stands alone in the château's sunlit hall. A bird trills outside, then all is silent. Leaning on her cane, she stares out on the magical vista, at the *allée* of century-old chestnut trees that leads to the lake and the fantastical Japanese bridge, built by her great-grandfather, connecting to a small island. On hot summer nights when she was a girl, she would wander across that bridge to sleep naked in the little gazebo, safe from prying eyes, with a soft breeze to tantalize her restless young body.

Ah. . . . youth, Rafaella thinks, smiling at the memory, *so long ago . . . when everything seemed possible.*

It is a hot day but the faded parquet floor feels cool under her bare feet, for even now she still like to go barefoot. Her gypsyish red skirt swirls around her ankles as she walks, the very same skirt she had worn the day she met the man who became the love of her life and who most certainly was not her husband.

She glances ruefully at herself in the long gilt rococo mirrors spaced along the hall: at the mass of silvery hair pinned into a loose bun and the lined parchment-skin, at the strong nose that even in her youth had given her an arrogant look, and the soft, full mouth that gave lie to it. Only her eyes are the same, heavy-lidded and the blue of the Mediterranean, which is not so many miles away and where, once upon a time, she had swum every glorious day of summer.

Rafaella lives alone at the château now, with only Haigh, her English butler and dearest friend and companion, to look after her. Haigh is a little bantam cock of a man, short with spindly limbs and the thin, deprived face of a poor Cockney boy. He's been the Marten family butler for over fifty years and is almost as old as Rafaella.

There's nothing Haigh doesn't know about Rafaella. He'd been there when she was young and vital, commanding her small empire—the château and its vineyards. He'd been there through the good times and the bad. She has no secrets from him.

Once this house had rung with children's laughter, the splashes and happy shrieks coming from the swimming pool, the plop of tennis balls on the red clay court, the tinkle of ice in cocktail glasses as the sun set red as fire over the white stony hills. But now the doors are locked, the rooms behind shuttered, the lovely old furniture shrouded in dustcovers. The family is long gone, scattered to the four corners of the earth, shattered by scandals over money and women and by a mysterious death.

Rafaella leans on her cane, listening for sounds of the past. A grandfather clock ticks. A bee buzzes, trapped in the window. Loneliness hangs in the air along with the scent of the wild roses that give her château its name.

It seems to Rafaella that the château is dying of that loneliness. It needs youth and energy, love and laughter. It needs a family to overcome the past and to bring it back to life.

Her mind finally made up, she walks back through the house, whistling for the dogs. They come running, claws skittering on the cool parquet, the massive brown-and-white Bernese mountain dog she'd named Louis because his floppy ears and soulful eyes gave him the look of one of the old French kings. Mimi scrambles behind him, a miniature black poodle, a mere fraction of Louis's size, though she seems not to know it. By now, in dog years, they are almost as old as Rafaella.

"Come, my children," she says, smiling, for in her heart they are her children and they love her as her own real offspring never had. "It's time to take action."

She walks to her room, takes a seat at her desk. Louis flops against her, panting, while Mimi, attracted by her frivolous scarlet toenails, begins to lick her feet. From the drawer Rafaella takes the large square cream-colored cards with *Château des Roses Sauvages, Marten-de-Provence* engraved in dark blue. Then she picks up her pen and, in her now shaky script, she begins to write.

PART I

The Invitations

> *Passion is a malady. It's dark.*
> *You are jealous of everything.*
> *There's no lightness, no harmony.*
>
> —GEORGES SIMENON

1

WHEN THE INVITATION that was to change Franny Marten's life arrived in her mailbox on a leafy Santa Monica street that last day of July, she didn't even notice it. She was too worried about her long-distance boyfriend, Marcus. She was meeting him tonight. He'd said they "needed to talk." "So talk," she'd said, smiling into the phone, but then he'd said it wasn't the right moment and besides he needed to see her. Now Franny was wondering nervously if there was something ominous in those words.

She was leaving Your Local Veterinary Clinic where she worked, and she turned her head as she always did when the glass doors shut behind her, just to check that her name was really there. It still gave her a buzz to see those hard-earned letters after it that said she was a qualified doctor of veterinary surgery, and it always tugged at her heart that her father was not there to see it, too. He would have been so proud of the way she'd handled herself after he'd died, leaving her alone in the world at age seventeen. He'd have been proud of her struggle to put herself through college and med school, working all those jobs, baby-sitting, cleaning houses, waitressing, any work she could get to make ends meet, and even then it had been touch and go.

Franny looked like the typically blond Californian, but she was still a small-town Oregon girl at heart. Ten years had passed since she'd driven down the coast in a junky old car with that newly earned vet license in her otherwise empty pocket, in search of a new life. That dream life included success in her new career and of course love and marriage, which would lead automatically to children and "a family." She'd especially hoped for the family because it was something she'd never had. She sighed thinking about her dream. So far only the career part had come true. Still, maybe one out of four wasn't bad.

She opened the door of her dusty white Explorer Sport, flinching as the day's trapped heat wafted over her. Air-conditioning blasting, Kiss FM blaring, she gunned the engine and headed for Main. Of course the traffic was hell, but wasn't it always? Stalled at the light, she flipped down her mirror and checked her appearance. Hot, un-made-up, blond hair dragged back in a fat, untidy braid. Purple smudges of fatigue showed under the long, narrow water-blue eyes, an asset she owed to her Norwegian mother. She looked awful and she knew Marcus would notice and comment on it because that's the way Marcus was—he always found her weak spots.

Actually, other than the pale blue of her eyes and her blond hair and her name—her mother had been a great admirer of J. D. Salinger—Franny didn't owe much else to her Nordic mother, who had simply left them for "better opportunities" when Franny was three years old. She died a few years later, and lonely young Franny had felt nothing at all except, when she was older, guilt for not caring. But her mother had been someone she'd never known, someone who had never wanted to know her.

It was different when her father died. Then she was devastated. He had been her friend, her supporter, the rock on which the burden of her life rested, and suddenly with a car accident all that was taken from her. Somehow she found the strength to get on with life the way they'd planned it, because that's what her father would have expected of her. And what people saw when they met the nice small-town blond vet was not exactly what they got. There was a core of steel forged from hard times under that soft exterior. She'd needed it in order to survive alone in a big, tough world.

Sighing, she switched her thoughts to the beautiful German shepherd whose life she had—*fingers crossed, hope, hope, hope, please God, I'm praying for him*—saved today. Then she'd had the difficult task of trying to stabilize his distressed owner, a leggy L.A. girl in skintight gray biker shorts and a cropped T-shirt that showed her gold-stapled navel.

"It all happened in a moment," the girl sobbed. "He just ran after a ball, the car threw him into the air, it never even stopped. . . . He's all I've got." And Franny had mopped her tears with Kleenex and comforted her with hot coffee and an arm around her shoulders. Soft-hearted, sympathetic, gentle, she was always ready to listen and to offer help, and she always gave that extra time, which simply left no time for herself. And which meant, of course, that despite Marcus's complaints, after dinner she would make sure to go back to the clinic and check on the dog. If necessary she would be there all night. That's just the way she was.

Fretting in the crawling traffic, she finally turned right on

Montana, then left onto a leafy side street, stopping in front of the tiny 1930s Craftsman-style cottage that was her home. Her first *real* home. Well, hers and the bank's anyway, and small though it undoubtedly was, after the dingy furnished rooms in grim, gray parts of town that were all she'd been able to afford when she was putting herself through school, to her it seemed like a palace.

The house was set back from the street with a narrow paved path and patches of grass on either side. It was painted forest green with tan trim. Four steps led up to a sweet little front porch that just cried out for a rocker, the kind with a slot in the arm to hold your glass and a slatted rest for your feet, but Franny had never yet had enough spare money to buy one.

She found a parking spot and jumped out, stopping at her mailbox for the usual bundle of bills, junk mail, and catalogues. She didn't even notice the square cream envelope with the French stamps. She took the four steps up to the porch two at a time, then just two more strides to the front door where, as always, she tripped over the loose plank that she'd been meaning to fix for ages. She thought it was really quite dangerous and she'd better do something about it this weekend.

Sadly, though she loved animals, there was no dog or cat of her own to greet her because she didn't have the hometime an animal needed. Without their friendly barks and purrs, the small house seemed too quiet. She tossed the mail onto the kitchen counter already cluttered with leftover take-out cartons and bundles of half-dead flowers in pottery jars. Six days a week the house was a mess. On the seventh, a Sunday (what else), she cleaned it up. Today was only Wednesday and stuff spilled from drawers and cupboards, old coffee mugs sat around on top of piles of unread books and magazines, and a trail of discarded clothes led to the bathroom, where she was headed now, flinging more onto the heap as she went. She hadn't been born a slob—it was purely a matter of the proper allocation of time, of which there never seemed to be enough.

She barely had time to shower and throw on some clothes—jeans, a white tank top, a lacy blue crocheted shawl against the later ocean-night chill, turquoise flip-flops, and the dangly fake turquoise earrings she'd picked up at the drugstore and thought *so* sexy, though she certainly was not feeling sexy tonight. She was too worried about her meeting with Marcus.

Stopping just long enough to check her appearance in the mirror, she tugged at the tank top, hoping Marcus wouldn't give her that cool up-and-down look that said without words that he thought she looked as though she'd just thrown herself together. Which was the truth. She had. Still, she left her heavy, pale-blond hair loose and sprayed on a generous amount of the ginger-flower perfume. Her cheeks were flushed from rushing, and she looked about nineteen years old instead of thirty-five.

On her way out she quickly tidied the hodgepodge of flea-market bargain furniture, desperately plumping cushions, shoving old newspapers into a pile, because Marcus always came back with her, and he hated what he called her "squalor" and her cheap but eclectic and colorful furnishings.

She got back in the Explorer, heading down the California Incline and onto Pacific Coast Highway. The ocean glimmered on her left like an iridescent pewter bowl, joggers trotted along the beachside paths with their dogs running alongside, and small children dashed happily in and out of the waves, unwilling to call an end to the day.

She remembered clearly the night she'd first met Marcus, a classic tall, dark, handsome guy with a shy smile and bold eyes that had met hers across a table a year ago. It was at a birthday dinner for a friend, and he was with a pretty girl to whom he wasn't paying much attention. Instead, he kept looking at Franny, couldn't seem to take his eyes off her in fact. Franny had sipped her wine, trying to act cool, glancing occasionally at him over the top of her glass, wondering if she was misreading that message in his eyes. And she wasn't, because later he came over to her and said, "You know, you have the most magical blue eyes. I felt as though I'd gotten lost in them. It's as though I've known you for a long time, maybe even in some other life."

Now no man had ever said anything like that to her before and of course she was knocked out by it, so when he asked for her phone number, she gave it to him. There was a message waiting on her machine when she got home. "I can't stop thinking about you," he said. "Please say you'll have dinner with me tomorrow night."

Franny found him irresistible, like catnip—one sniff of him and she was crazy. Unfortunately, Marcus lived in Atlanta, where he was in property development, building new condos for singles. He came to L.A. twice a month, then he'd promised to make it over more often. And those first few months were heady. They made love all the time, or at least all the time he could spend with her. He sent her flowers and often called just to say goodnight. Lately, though, he'd been too busy to get out to L.A. so often and then he'd been distant, as though his mind were somewhere other than on her.

Franny still wouldn't face up to it, but in her heart she knew the writing was on the wall and she wondered whether it was better just to finish it right now and save her pride. She realized Marcus was behaving badly and that she was stupid to take it, but he was like a bad habit she couldn't shake. She kept hoping that she was wrong and that he really loved her.

She was so caught up thinking about Marcus, she almost rear-ended the Honda Civic in front of her. This time her sigh came from her gut. The only thing certain in her life was that, as usual, she'd skipped lunch—no time—and she was starving. She only hoped Marcus wouldn't be critical of her hearty appetite. And dammit, if he was, she would just tell him to get lost. Oops, she'd almost missed the turnoff. She quickly slid the Explorer across two lanes, eliciting a barrage of horn honking as she sped onto Channel Drive and made a jerky stop in front of Giorgio's.

Grabbing her beat-up brown bag and remembering too late that she'd meant to change it for something smaller and more stylish, she smoothed back her windblown hair, left the car with the valet, and went inside to meet her destiny.

2   THE ITALIAN RESTAURANT was intimate and crowded, with a buzz of conversation and the clink of wineglasses and the pleasant aroma of pasta and sauces and women's perfume.

"Mr. Marks's reservation," Franny said to the smiling hostess.

The girl checked her list. "Mr. Marks hasn't arrived yet. Would you like to wait for him at the table?"

Franny said she would, squeezing past the close-packed tables to one in the corner. She ordered a glass of Chianti and sat looking around her. She didn't come here often and she liked watching the smart people who treated this place as their neighborhood restaurant. She studied the young family at the next table. She thought enviously how perfect they were, so beautiful and happy with their two small sons and another baby obviously on the way. They were an example of everything young people were supposed to strive toward, while she . . . well, *she* was in limbo.

She sipped her wine, studying the menu and thanking god that at least this time she wasn't the one who was late. The hostess came toward her, escorting a lovely woman, tall and elegant in a black dress, dark hair pulled back, sleek as a cat.

"Ms. Marten?" the woman said. Franny nodded, looking up at her with a puzzled smile. "I'm Clare Marks," the woman said and a hot thrill of apprehension shot up Franny's spine. "Marcus's wife," the woman added calmly. "He thought it was time we met."

Franny could feel the blood drain from her face. "His *ex*-wife," she managed finally, not wanting to believe the truth.

"His *wife*, Ms. Marten." Their eyes met, Clare Marks's brown and curious, Franny's dark blue with shock.

Bewildered, Franny thought, This can't be happening to me. Just a couple of hours ago at work *she* had been the woman in charge, the strong one, the one with the comforting arm and the encouraging words. Now she was reduced to zero, at a loss for words. In an instant her love affair with Marcus was rendered meaningless. She stared at her hand clutching her wineglass so tightly it might break, unwilling to meet Clare Marks's eyes.

Clare pulled out the chair opposite and sat down. She signaled the waiter, asked for a glass of the pinot grigio, then turned back to Franny.

"Of course Marcus didn't tell you he was married," she said calmly. "He never does. He leaves it to me to work it all out. He's a shit that way but . . ." She shrugged. "Most men are, don't you think?"

Franny lifted her eyes and looked at Clare, wondering if she was going to scream at her, accuse her loudly in front of the entire restaurant of being "the other woman." She glanced wildly around looking for a quick escape but the tables were too close together to make it easy. Instead, for courage, she downed her wine in three big gulps.

The waiter reappeared to take their order. "I suppose we might as well eat," Clare said, glancing quickly at the menu and ordering the langostinos with fettucini.

The waiter gave her an approving smile—it was the house specialty. He turned expectantly to Franny, who took a deep breath. She couldn't just sit here and have dinner with Marcus's *wife*. Of course she couldn't. She was getting up and leaving *right this minute*. Suddenly anger simmered. Dammit, no! She refused to be outfaced by this bitch.

"I'll have the potato gnocci with the tomato sauce, please," she said in a tight little voice she barely recognized as her own. "And another glass of the Chianti," she added recklessly.

Clare Marks leaned her elbows on the table, hands folded under her chin, staring silently at her. The happy hum of conversation floated around Franny's head like confetti at a wedding. Her chest hurt. Well, of course it did, that was where her heart was. Her eyes hurt, too, from staring at this vision that was her lover's wife. The perfect features, the sleek dark hair pulled back to show her perfect profile, the perfect expensive little black dress, the perfect pearl earrings. And the platinum band embossed with diamonds on the third finger of her left hand.

Suddenly chilled, Franny hitched her blue crochet shawl over her shoulders. She felt unstylish and out of her league. She took another gulp of wine and the dangling earrings she'd thought so pretty clanked loudly against the glass.

"Cute earrings," Clare Marks said, and Franny glared at her. She knew Clare knew they were cheap and of course she hadn't really meant it as a compliment. She wondered bleakly why Marcus had even bothered with her when his wife was so beautiful.

"You're looking at me and wondering why he does it, aren't you?" Clare said. "I mean, I'm Miss America personified, right? And that's who I was. Well, Miss Georgia, anyhow. Huh, actually I was more like Miss Hick from Hicksville, an innocent just like you when I met him. Anyhow, Marcus and I have been married for seven years. And *you*, Franny, are the seventh woman I've had to say good-bye to. How's that for a record?"

Franny just sat there silently, stiff as a corpse in the throes of rigor mortis, aware that Clare was looking pityingly at her. Then Clare drained her glass and said, "The hell with it. Why don't we just get a bottle? After all, this is a kind of celebration. Freedom for you, and—since I've left Marcus— freedom for me, too. And this time I really mean it. I won't stay with that seven-timing, adulterous son of a bitch any longer. Not only that, Franny Marten, I'm gonna take him for every cent I can get, and trust me, honey, it will be *a lot*." A grin lit her lovely face. Her brown eyes sparkled and she suddenly looked like a mischievous little girl.

"Did Marcus really send you to tell me this?" Franny asked.

"He sure did. The prick never could do his own dirty work, but from now on he'll have to. *You*, Franny Marten, are my last assignment. I've quit."

Franny took a big gulp of the wine. "Well, fuck Marcus Marks," she said too loudly, and the young marrieds with kids at the next table turned to glare at her.

Clare was forking up her fettucini like a starving pro-footballer straight off the field after a hard game. "Tuck in," she said. "Love—or the lack of it—can make a woman hungry."

Franny took a bite of the gnocci. It tasted great. "Maybe you're right, Mrs. Marks," she said, choking on the name.

"Have a drink of water," Clare said helpfully, "and of course I'm right."

Clare had not been exactly truthful with Franny about her past. In fact, it was a past she didn't care to remember. But Franny was no dummy the way she had been. Franny was a veterinarian, educated, successful, dedicated, while *she* had had to learn on the job, so to speak.

She leaned forward, looking into Franny's eyes. "You and I hardly know each other," she said, "but somehow I feel as though I've known you for years."

"Oh my god." Franny gasped, shocked. "That's exactly what Marcus said when we first met."

"I'll bet he also said, 'We must have met in some other life,'" Clare said, and Franny stared at her. "Oh yes," Clare added. "He said that to me too. It's his usual come-on line. Marcus is nothing if not predictable."

She delicately pulled a crayfish apart, devoured it in a single bite, then licked her fingers. "So, what are you going to do now? You want to confront him? Marcus hates that you know. That's why he sends *me* to do the dirty work. He'll hide from you at every turn."

Tears clung to Franny's lashes. "Why did you stay with him when you knew what was going on?"

"For the same reason millions of other women do, honey. Sometimes we call it love, sometimes infatuation. Either way, a man can be like a disease—one you never recover from." Clare's smile was rueful as she met Franny's eyes. "All I can say is, I'm sorry."

"I *hate* him." Franny took another gulp of wine. "I *hate* him for deceiving me, for stringing me along, for being a liar and a cheat." That steely inner core surfaced now and she was facing the truth head-on. "Anyhow, I knew," she admitted. "In my heart I knew it was over."

Clare stared at her, surprised. "Well, bravo for you, Franny Marten. I took you for the doormat type. Obviously I was wrong."

Franny shoved the tears away with her finger, feeling suddenly better. "I think I need some tiramisu," she said firmly.

"Of course, something sweet, just the thing for a cracked heart," Clare agreed. "Trust me, it's not broken," she added. "Marcus does not have the capacity to break a woman's heart, only to cause a little damage. You need what's known as 'a soul' to break someone's heart, and Marcus definitely does not have 'a soul.'" She sighed. "And nor, I suppose, do I since I've yet to break *anybody's* heart."

Franny dug her spoon viciously into the creamy tiramisu, wishing it were Marcus's eyes. "Well, *I* certainly do have a soul, and I intend to keep it."

"Hmm. You do that," Clare said. "Keep your soul intact. In the end, it's all you've got."

They finished the tiramisu in silence as the waiter poured the last of the wine into their glasses. Clinging to the shreds of her dignity, Franny said, "I want to thank you for what you just did. I certainly never expected to be sitting here with Marcus's wife." She stared thoughtfully into the depths of her wineglass. "The odd thing is that . . . Well, you're honest and straightforward, and you were *kind* to me. To tell you the truth, Clare, I like you. In different circumstances, I think we might have liked each other."

Clare knew exactly what she meant. "Honey, it's just the contrast with the hard time Marcus has been giving you lately, always putting you on your mettle, always getting at you for being late or not looking right." She held up a hand as Franny gasped in recognition. "It's what he does with all his women. It's part of his control-freak sickness, his let's-play-get-the-girl. Let's tell her she's great, beautiful, sexy, fun . . . then let's bring her down to size. All the way down until she's somewhere way beneath him, leaving Marcus on top and in a very superior position. Which is exactly where he likes to be." She shrugged. "Of course then the game is over and it's time to find a new prey."

Clare's eyes softened as they met Franny's hurt look. She gripped her hand across the table, "Don't blame yourself, honey. I've been there too. He's just a bad guy and what you need, lovely Franny Marten, is a salt-of-the-earth kind of man, a man who will look after you, a man who cares about your happiness, a man you need never worry about cheating on you. Actually, I need a man like that, too." She sighed. "But where do you suppose women find them?"

"God knows." Franny glanced at the happy couple at the next table, collecting their kids and their belongings, ready to leave. "But they're obviously out there somewhere," she added wistfully.

Clare eyed her, relieved. "I thought this might turn out to be a massacre, but you took it really well. You know what, Franny? We're just a couple of innocent small-town girls at heart, right?" Under the table, Clare crossed her fingers. What she had said wasn't strictly true either, though it was where she had started out.

A sense of relief made Franny smile. She threw back her head and drained her glass. Watching her, Clare said, "Better let me give you a lift home." She knew how much Franny had drunk and how upset she still was. "I've got a limo waiting."

Franny couldn't remember the last time she'd ridden in a limo. It must have been at her high school prom. Still, she had her pride. She couldn't allow Marcus's wife to drive her home. "That's okay. I've got my car outside," she said.

"Yeah, I know, but we've both drunk a lot of wine and *my* car has a driver. Why not get your keys from the valet and tell him you'll pick up yours tomorrow?"

Franny was suddenly too tired to argue. She fished in her satchel for her credit card to pay the check but Clare got there first.

"This one's on Marcus," she said, and they both sniggered as Clare signed his name with a flourish. Then, arm in arm, with *ciaos* and *thank-yous*, they headed out the door.

3

A SHORT WHILE LATER, they were sitting in the long black limo outside Franny's house. As usual, she had forgotten to leave a light on and she thought the house suddenly looked very small and dark and kind of lonely.

"Well it's 'home,'" she said defensively. "My friends tell me it's more Oregon than L.A., which is probably because that's exactly who I am, still more Oregon than L.A."

"Cute," Clare said, reapplying her lipstick without the benefit of a mirror.

"So where do you live anyway?" Franny asked.

"Out of a suitcase right now, honey." Clare pointed to the collection of expensive luggage piled into the limo. She hadn't allowed the driver to put it in the trunk because she needed to know exactly where it was at all times. After all, it was practically all she'd got now. "I guess I'll just check into Shutters Hotel for the night. I'll think about what to do tomorrow."

Franny suddenly realized that because Clare had left Marcus, she was temporarily homeless. She had been so nice and understanding and it didn't seem fair to send her off alone into the night. After all, they were sisters in this experience, facing their futures together.

"Why not come in and have some chamomile tea," she suggested.

"Why not? 'The night is young and we are all alone,'" Clare misquoted, sliding gracefully from the limo, all long legs and high heels. "Though I'd prefer coffee," she added. She stood for a minute, eyeing the empty front porch, then she said a touch wistfully, "It's funny, but I've always longed for a little house with a front porch and a rocker."

"And I always longed for a little house with a husband," Franny said, and their eyes met and they collapsed into giggles as Franny struggled to get her key into the lock. At last she got the door open and they stepped cautiously over the creaking loose plank into the house.

Clare made herself instantly at home, exclaiming over the multicolored rag rugs, the fifties coffee table, the antique French armoire. She inspected the framed photos, sniffed the ginger-flower candles, put on a CD and turned up the volume, ignoring the general state of disarray.

Franny put coffee on to brew, decaf of course. She fished a bag of Pepperidge Farm Milano cookies from the pantry and put them, still in the bag, along with a couple of hastily rinsed blue pottery mugs onto a flowered plastic tray.

"Coffee's coming," she said, setting the tray on the buttoned red-velvet ottoman next to Clare's bare feet. She was sprawled across the sofa looking as though she belonged, stiletto mules off, eyes closed, toes wiggling in time to Rod Stewart singing "You Go to My Head."

"Like the bubbles in a glass of champagne," Clare sang along with him in a low sexy voice, smiling to herself and making Franny smile, too. Clare was different from the women she knew. Not only was she enviably gorgeous and chic, she was also down-to-earth, a small-town straight shooter at heart.

Clare sat up and took notice when Franny poured the

coffee. "Just what a girl needs." She smiled. "A good cup of coffee and Rod Stewart to curl up with." She glanced at the small pile of mail Franny had brought in with her, noticing one envelope with French stamps. "So who's writing to you from France?" She held up a hand, grinning. "If it's from another married lover I don't want to know about it."

Puzzled, Franny inspected the large, square cream-colored envelope. She didn't know anyone in France. She ripped it open and read the address out loud. "'Château des Roses Sauvages, Marten-de-Provence.' My great-grandfather Marten came from France," she said, surprised. "But I never knew exactly where he was from. There was a big family fight or something and he left and came to live here. I don't think he ever talked to his family again."

"So read it. Maybe you'll find out why," Clare said, but Franny was already reading it.

> Dear Franny,
>
> I am writing to invite you to a reunion of the Marten family here at my home.
>
> Of course you do not know me, but each of you to whom I am extending this invitation is related to me. You are cousins, perhaps many times removed it is true, but generations do not take away the fact that you are Family.
>
> I am asking you to arrive on September 20th for a stay of three weeks. You will be contacted by a travel agent and the necessary travel arrangements will be made for you.
>
> I will enjoy getting to know you and showing you your ancestral château, and I think you might enjoy getting to know one another, coming as you do from the far-

*flung corners of the world. Yet you have the same blood-
line, and I've always believed that blood counts.*

*I am an old woman now and it is my wish to reunite
what is left of this family. Please do not let me down.*

It was signed "Rafaella Marten des Sauvages." There was
nothing shaky about her signature.

Franny read it again. And then again.

"*Oh*," she said finally. "*Oh no!* I don't believe it. This is
ridiculous. Of course I can't go."

Clare wiggled her toes and yawned lazily. "Go where?"

"To a château in Provence for a 'family reunion' with a
family I never knew existed. Just listen to this, Clare," she
said, and read her the invitation. "I've never even heard of
this Rafaella Marten who says she's my aunt. All I know
about the Martens is that my grandfather hated them and my
father said it was with good reason. Dad never went to
Provence to meet his family, so why should I?"

"*Why?*" Clare sat up straight. "Well, for *the adventure*, of
course. Christ, just give me the opportunity, I'd be there in a
flash."

"You would?" Franny looked doubtfully back at the invitation. Rafaella Marten was an old woman. All she wanted was
to bring her family together again at her château, their "ancestral home," as she called it.

Franny slumped onto the sofa as her empty life flashed
before her eyes. *I have no one,* she thought, facing facts. *Only
the animals, and even* they *don't belong to me. Now Marcus is
gone and I'm a failure in the love department, too. I never had
a family—it was always just me and dad. There's never been
time to think about being lonely. Am I lonely? Was that why I*

allowed Marcus to take a piece of me, to take my life and twist it out of shape to satisfy his own need to control?

She sank into the sofa next to Clare, still clutching the invitation in her hand, staring blankly in front of her. *Who am I anyway, besides the nice young vet at your local clinic, the one everybody can rely on to take on the extra work and to come in on Sundays. . . . Don't worry, Franny will deal with it, they say. And don't I always?*

To be part of a family was what she had always wanted, though she'd never expected it to come long-distance like this. All of a sudden she had an aunt, she even had cousins. They were all to meet in some romantic old château in Provence, land of sunshine and olive trees and wine. *A family home,* she thought longingly, *a château where the Martens have lived for centuries.*

She looked at the beautiful Clare sitting expectantly on the edge of her sofa. She felt as though she'd known her forever, far longer than the seven-timing son-of-a-bitch Marcus.

"Okay, then maybe I'll go," she said cautiously, making Clare laugh.

"What have you got to lose?" she asked. "After all, your job will still be here when you get back."

"And Marcus won't," Franny said flatly.

"Damn right he won't, baby, and you can thank your lucky stars for that!" Clare looked at her, head tilted to one side, considering. "Just do it, Franny Marten," she said. "It's the opportunity of a lifetime."

And Franny beamed at her, relieved not to have to make the decision. Clare had already made it for her.

"Okay, so I'll go," she said, and for some reason immediately felt very lonely.

"Hey," she said impulsively to Clare, "why not just stay here tonight, the sofa's quite comfortable and I'll put on more coffee." She looked hopefully at Clare, who wrinkled her nose.

"Decaf?" she said.

Franny laughed. "Tomorrow I'll go to Starbucks first thing," she promised.

"You've got a deal," Clare said, "on one condition. No more talk about Marcus."

Franny laughed again. "Deal," she said, and went to put on more coffee and find a blanket and a pillow.

4

JAKE BRONSON STRODE into the bar at the Four Seasons Hotel in Manhattan and stood for a moment, taking in the scene. Quite a few female heads turned to look back at him, speculating on who he might be. Tall and hard-bodied, dressed in jeans, an old cashmere jacket, and a blue shirt, he wore life's experience on his handsome face. He also wore cowboy boots—his one concession to his boyhood dream of owning a ranch—and his thick, dark hair was rather too long because he considered getting it cut a waste of time, and he had a habit of raking his hair back with a large hand that knew how to punch out a man as well as how to gentle a nervous horse.

His light eyes narrowed in a smile, acknowledging an acquaintance across the room as he took a seat at the bar and ordered a Bud. He wasn't a man for fancy drinks in martini glasses. "Make that glass well iced, will you?" he added. It was a quirk of his—he liked his beer at freezer temperature.

He took the invitation from his pocket and read it again. He was forty-four years old, and the last time he'd seen Rafaella Marten he'd been sixteen and more than a little in love with her. For him, she'd been the perfect older woman—beautiful, charming, intelligent, sensual, filled with gaiety and love of life. And she was also his father's lover.

Up until then, Jake had been buried away at his father's hacienda in Argentina, where he'd run wild with no one to stop him. His father, Lucas Bronson, was an internationally famous polo player and playboy whose profession took him all over the world. Jake's mother, an American beauty from a good New York family, had died when he was young, after which his father had brought him back to live at the hacienda. An old woman he called Abuelita, or "little grandmother" (though in fact she was no relation and spoke only Spanish), had brought him up, and his only companions were the cowboys, the *gauchos* with whom he rode the horses culled from the pampas. By herding cattle, the little horses learned to be fleet of foot and to turn on a dime, which made them the best polo ponies of all. In fact, Jake could ride almost before he could walk, and his ambition had always been to own his own small ranch. But life had led him on a different path.

When he was sixteen, his father had suddenly summoned him to Provence and his whole life changed. He'd arrived at the château an ignorant youth with a single small suitcase containing nothing more than a couple of frayed shirts and his other boots. But Rafaella had understood the lonely boy on the brink of manhood. She'd taught him the civilized arts of polite society, made him part of her family, was like a mother to him. For a year his life had seemed complete, though his father had never really wanted him there. Finally, of course, he'd been forced to confront his overpowering father and had left to face life alone. He'd kept in touch with Rafaella though, and over the years, he wrote her about his graduation from Annapolis, about being selected for Naval Intelligence, about his youthful marriage to "a lovely girl, too beautiful to even describe, and probably too young to settle down with a naval officer who's always somewhere else other than with her." And as a wedding gift, Rafaella had sent the massive old silver candelabra Jake had always admired and which had been in her family for almost two centuries.

A couple of years later, when disaster overtook the young couple, she wrote to Jake offering him sanctuary at the château, but he turned her down. He wasn't fit for human company, he said, and he would get over it by himself. Just the way you've always done, Rafaella observed.

Life drifted on, there was an annual card at Christmas, a gentle reminder that the other was still there, but he never returned to the château that, for a short, happy period of his life, he'd called home.

When disaster struck, Jake left the navy and the intelligence service and eventually, after a year propping up bars and attempting to drown his sorrows, he opened his own risk management business, which is what the old-fashioned pri-

vate investigation biz came to be called after it became up-
dated with computers and databases and young people with
Ph.D.s in economics or science, rather than ex-cops with
guns. Somewhat to his surprise, his business had become
successful, and he now had seven hundred employees
worldwide. He was good at what he did. It wasn't what he
would have chosen, but it filled the gap in his life and for
that he was grateful.

Now he inhabited a spare, gray loft space in SoHo that
said almost nothing about him. In truth, he was rarely there.
He was always roaming the world on business, just the way
his father had. Every now and again, when the lure of the
wild became too strong, he would escape to the mountains,
where he'd built himself a rough log cabin, just two rooms
and a front porch with a rail for propping his booted feet
while watching the sun set through the lofty branches in a
dying red glow.

The only sound would be of birds calling each other on
their nightly way home to their nests and the soughing of
the wind in the tall trees, and the only thing of great value
he possessed was the eighteenth-century silver candelabra
given by Rafaella as a wedding gift that stood incongru-
ously on his plain wood-plank kitchen table. For Jake,
heaven on earth was right there in his few solitary acres,
ten miles from the nearest small town and the nearest bar
and light-years away from the tensions of his business
world.

He owned a '97 mud-spattered four-wheel drive that was
once green but now showed more rust, and a stray dog he'd
picked up on the road and named Criminal for his wicked

ways; and also a soot-gray gelding named Dirty Harry that nobody else had wanted. The dog and the horse both lived at the stables outside the small town when he was off on his travels. Of course they preferred being with him, but they accepted the rough with the smooth and greeted him as joyfully as Santa at Christmas when he came home again.

Jake thought the emotion he felt for Criminal, his shaggiest of shaggy somewhat-of-a-retriever, was probably the closest to true love he could feel now. Which didn't say a lot for his friendships with women, which were of the on-and-off variety, mostly because he couldn't spare sufficient time to put into a relationship. A dog would always wait for you. A woman would not.

He glanced at his watch. It had been exactly four hours since he'd called Rafaella and accepted her invitation. He'd rearranged his schedule for those weeks and delegated important work, so that he would be there in September, come rain or come shine. He was willing to bet that his life would never be the same. Rafaella always had that effect on him.

Meanwhile, he was on his way to L.A. The car would pick him up in ten minutes. It would take him to Teterboro airport in New Jersey, where his private jet awaited. He wasn't looking forward to the trip, but business was business.

He sipped his Bud. It was iced to the hilt, and he grinned his pleasure to the bartender. He was studying the list of invitees Rafaella had sent him. The only unknown was a woman named Franny Marten. He'd bet that Rafaella didn't know much about her either, other than that she was Paul Marten's daughter—Paul Marten was the only sibling of Rafaella's father. Which meant that this Franny

Marten might suddenly find herself heir to a château and a fortune.

Jake's office had tracked the details of her life in a matter of hours. Now he studied the bleak snippets of information that told him who the possible heir to the Château des Roses Sauvages might be. Franny Marten was alone in the world, a single Santa Monica vet who also did good works for rescued animals.

He could just picture her, a too-nice Oregon girl, a little bit gawky, a little bit country, addicted to jeans and peasant tops and lacy shawls, sort of like Ali MacGraw in *Love Story*, all big white smile and soulful dark eyes. He'd bet she was the kind of vague woman who'd button her shirt wrong and drink chamomile tea, and that she'd smell faintly of horses and disinfectant with a whiff of citrusy perfume.

Jake's researcher had also discovered there was a boyfriend. Marcus Marks lived in Atlanta and was married. Jake wondered briefly how supposedly intelligent women got themselves into these situations. Then, since he was on his way to L.A. anyway, he decided he'd better check out Franny Marten himself before letting her loose on Rafaella. Nice country girl or not, the promise of a château and a fortune could turn any woman into a predator.

5

THE NEXT DAY, Jake parked the rented silver Mustang in front of the undistinguished square building in a strip mall near Main Street in Venice Beach, California. YOUR LOCAL VETERINARY CLINIC AND ANIMAL HOSPITAL was inscribed in large gold letters on the glass doors. Underneath, in slightly smaller gold letters were three names. Franny Marten's was the last because, Jake supposed, she was the most recent partner to be taken on by the practice. He nodded his head, thinking she must be proud of that. It was quite an accomplishment considering the odds that were stacked against her, being left alone and without financial support at age seventeen. Maybe she wasn't so bad after all. He wouldn't bet on it though. The thought of inheriting money could do strange things to even the nicest folk.

Inside there was a line of chairs filled with people clutching disturbed-looking cats in carrying cages and anxious-looking dogs sniffing the floor and each other, growling uncertainly because this was unknown territory. The young woman behind the counter was named Lindsey—it said so on the badge pinned to her green polo shirt. She smiled nicely at him and asked how she could help.

Jake told her he was new to the neighborhood and he'd heard that Dr. Marten was a good vet. He said he really cared about his dog and needed to introduce himself and make sure they got along. "Make sure we understand each other" was the way he put it, and Lindsey smiled and said she understood and that Dr. Marten was almost finished with an emergency and would be glad to discuss his dog with him.

Jake took a seat next to a wheezing bulldog with bloodshot eyes. Flipping through a copy of *Cat Fancy* magazine, he wondered what the difference was between the pampered Persian in the picture and the feral black panthers that patrolled his cabin in search of food. Somewhere along the line of evolution they were related, but looking at this prize puss, he wasn't quite sure where or how.

"This way, please, Mr. Bronson," Lindsey said, showing him into a small room with the usual steel table and equipment. "Dr. Marten will be with you in a moment."

Jake leaned against the table, arms folded, waiting. The door to the next room was open and he could see an enormous orange cat and his equally huge and overstuffed owner.

"Look here," Dr. Marten was saying sharply, "a bee-sting on the tongue is very dangerous to any animal, especially a cat. Marmalade's tongue swelled and he almost stopped breathing. Fortunately, antihistamines took care of that, plus some oxygen. The swelling's gone down and he's able to breathe on his own. Right now he's moping and very sorry for himself, but he's taken a few tentative laps of water which, trust me, is the best thing that's happened to him today."

She had a low, sweet voice and Jake found himself leaning closer, trying to catch what she was saying. He caught a glimpse of her back view and smiled. His guess about her had been close. She was tall, long-limbed, and a little bit gawky in a doctor's white coat and jeans, but her hair was pale blond and not dark like Ali MacGraw's. She wore it pulled back in a fat braid, like a pony's mane in a dressage show, and a thin strand of silver and turquoise stones was strung around her neck. He'd bet anything she drank chamomile tea.

He was still smiling when she turned and caught his eye.

Surprised, she answered his smile. "Be there in a minute," she called and went back to her patient and his owner.

"The thing is," she told the owner in a sharper tone, "it's okay if you and the cat don't eat for a while. You both have enough body fat to get by, but water is essential and Marmalade will have to stay here until I'm satisfied he's okay."

"You're right," the owner said meekly. "Just do whatever is best for him."

"I will," she promised. "But I want you to tell me you're going to do what's best for you, too. You can't go on like this, Ronnie. You have to take yourself in hand, go to Weight-Watchers, go on a diet, go to the gym, or I'm afraid Marmalade will be needing a new owner before too long." She patted his arm and turned away. "Okay, call me in a couple of hours and I'll let you know how he's doing."

Jake raised his brows, surprised. Dr. Marten was not afraid to speak her mind.

She came into the room at a trot. "So," she said, beaming a nice-girl smile at him. "What can I do for you, Mr. . . ." she checked the card Lindsey had given her. "Mr. Bronson?" She fixed him with narrow eyes that were the dazzling clear-water blue of an early-summer Norwegian fiord. Her gaze was so direct, so unexpectedly candid, Jake was taken aback for a second.

"I'm new to the neighborhood. I just wanted to meet

you, make sure my dog will have a good vet. You know how it is."

She nodded, frowning earnestly. "I certainly do, and I only wish more people got to know their vet *before* that emergency happens. It always helps to know the man and the animal—as you probably saw from the little vignette in the next room." She laughed, shaking her blond braid out of her neckline. "Sometimes a little honesty goes a long way. You don't think I hurt his feelings though, do you?"

Her clear eyes clouded and Jake just knew she would hate to hurt anyone's feelings. "You did the right thing," he hastened to reassure her, "probably saved the owner's life as well as his cat's."

Franny Marten took the time to look properly at him, as a woman and not merely as "your nice local vet." He was attractive, offbeat, different from the usual California guys, and he was looking back at her with an intense kind of look that suddenly made her toes curl.

"That's not my job," she said hastily, "but Ronnie's a nice guy, I hate to see him going downhill. Besides, I know how much he loves Marmalade. So, tell me about your dog, Mr. Bronson."

"Jake," he said quickly.

"He's called Jake? Nice name." She leaned against the steel table, arms folded across her chest, interested.

"Uh, actually the dog's name is Criminal. I'm Jake."

She stared at him, shocked. "You named your dog Criminal? But that's terrible."

"Not if you know his wicked ways it's not," Jake said. "But he's the best dog a man ever had. I don't know what I'd do without him."

Franny put a hand on his arm and squeezed it gently. Her eyes shone with sincerity. "I wish everyone felt that way about their pets."

"Criminal's no pet—he's my best friend," Jake said, wondering if he'd suddenly gone mad. He never opened up about his emotions to anyone, especially a woman.

"I understand," she said softly. "And I'll be here for you and Criminal should the need arise, though I'm still not convinced you should have inflicted that name on him."

Then she gave him that bright good-girl smile and offered him her hand. "Just remember to bring Criminal in for his shots, Mr. Bronson. Got to keep things up-to-date, you know. And don't worry. I'll take good care of him." Then with a little wave of her hand she was gone.

Jake caught a brief whiff of something sweet that might have been ginger flowers, and that was it. He was just some guy checking out a vet for his dog. And she was just a vet doing her job. At least, that's what Jake told himself later, sitting in the car remembering the feel of her slightly rough hand in his and the sweet, ginger-flower scent and the firm note in her voice as she told the fat guy to get his act together. He laughed thinking about it.

He thought Doc Marten was okay. She was no fortune hunter, no girl on the make. She was what she was, a nice woman with the most amazing eyes that he'd bet could look right through you when she was mad at you.

6

JAKE WAS STAYING at the Peninsula Hotel. He liked it because of its gardens that led on little winding paths, past jungly greenery and splashing fountains to the cottages. If he closed his eyes and ignored the dull roar of the L.A. traffic, he could almost have imagined he was somewhere in the countryside instead of right here in the middle of Beverly Hills.

Avoiding the rooftop pool area, which was a hangout for Hollywood's young agents and wanna-bes, he went instead to the wood-paneled bar and ordered a Bud. It was quiet and he needed to think. Besides, the bartender knew him and his glass came straight from the freezer, as always.

"How's biz?" the bartender asked.

"Pretty good, thanks." Jake sank into a leather club chair, nursing his beer and thinking how thrilled Rafaella was going to be when she met her niece. And a "nice" niece at that. Perhaps it would make up a little for those two disappointing sons who might—or more likely, might not—show up for the family reunion. He'd have to do something about that, go see Felix and try to persuade him to come home and make peace with his mother. And then try to find Alain, though Alain as always was a mystery man—no one ever knew his whereabouts. Not that Felix cared. He hated his brother with an overwhelming passion, and Jake for one didn't blame him.

He took a sip of his beer. Outside the hotel, traffic hummed, birds sang, phones rang. The scent of the great bouquet of flowers in the hall reminded him of Franny Marten's flowery perfume. He found himself wondering what she would look like with her hair out of that braid and flowing loose, out of her vet persona and into her own life. He wondered what that life was like, what kind of place she lived in, who her friends were, whether she also had a dog who was her closest companion. And he wondered if she knew that she'd gotten herself involved with a married man.

He remembered her gentle touch on his arm, the genuine concern in her beautiful eyes. He knew this was no girl on the make, no Hollywood babe looking for success, no beauty looking to be a trophy wife, no eager heiress ready to grab all she could. She was who she was, which was totally unlike any other woman he knew.

He glanced at his steel watch. Like fancy cocktails in fancy glasses, he disliked fancy watches. Five o'clock. A bit late to ask a woman out to dinner but what the hell, nothing ventured, nothing won. He was smiling as he dialed the number of Your Local Veterinary Clinic and asked to speak to Dr. Marten.

"Dr. Marten here," she said in that sunny voice he felt he knew well, even though he'd met her only once and that for a scant few minutes.

"Jake Bronson," he said. "I came in to see you today about my dog."

"Criminal. I remember. Oh, I hope nothing's wrong?"

There was that touching note of concern in her voice again. "Nothing's wrong," he said. "It's just, well, Doctor, even though I told myself there was no chance a woman like you would be free for dinner tonight, I thought I'd call anyway, just to check. That is, if you would like to have dinner, of course," he added, amazed by how hopeful he sounded.

"Oh . . . well . . . hmmmm . . . dinner . . ." He could almost hear the cogs turning in her brain as she thought about it quickly: *a total stranger, he came in off the street, didn't even have the dog with him.*

"Don't worry, I'm not a stalker," he said. "Listen, how about Joe's in Venice. That's near you. We could dine on the patio with lots of other people around so you wouldn't have to worry."

"How'd you read my thoughts?"

"It's what every woman in her right mind should think when a total stranger asks her out."

"Well, thank you, I'd like to have dinner with you tonight," she agreed suddenly, as though if she waited any longer she might change her mind. "That would be really nice. About eight? Is that okay?"

"Eight o'clock then," he agreed, smiling as he clicked off his phone.

JAKE WAS STANDING UNDER a cool shower when he realized there was a flaw in tonight's plan. He'd met Franny Marten under false pretenses; he couldn't tell her that he was here to check her out, nor could he tell her he would be at Rafaella's family reunion. That was Rafaella's secret. He got out of the shower and, still dripping, grabbed the phone. He'd call her right back and cancel.

But what excuse could he give her? That something had

come up in the couple of minutes since he'd invited her out? That he suddenly felt ill? One excuse sounded lamer than the other. No, better just go through with the dinner and hope she would forgive him when the truth came out later. Meanwhile he'd keep his distance, make it short.

He also wondered if he should warn her about Marcus, but remembered he wasn't supposed to know anything about her private life. He guessed she would just have to find out the hard way. Anyhow, who did he think he was, the patron saint of innocents who didn't have the gumption to know they were getting involved with married men? Dr. Marten had made her bed and, as the saying went, she would have to lie on it, until, as they also said, the proverbial penny dropped. She was just another woman caught up in a bad affair.

JOE'S CAFÉ on Abbot Kinney in Venice was a small storefront place with a tree-lined patio in back and a young urban clientele who enjoyed the good food, the high-decibel chatter, and the sense of being somewhere special.

"Mr. Bronson is already here," the host told Franny, leading the way to a corner table out on the patio. Franny glanced anxiously at her watch. She was twenty minutes late.

Jake got to his feet when he saw her coming, a blond

gypsy in a flowing skirt, dangling earrings, and an armload of bracelets. He grinned—she looked as though she might tell his fortune any minute. Still, her hair swung loose in a silken curtain over eyes that struck blue sparks from his as she smiled at him.

"Sorry I'm so late," she said, offering him her hand.

He held onto it, smiling back at her, more pleased to see her than he had any right to be. "As a working woman, you're excused."

She pushed the slipping curtain of hair aside and stared gravely at him, no doubt comparing him to the loser boyfriend, Jake thought. He was an expert at reading people, and he discerned an unexpectedly strong woman underneath that soft blond exterior, like a soft peach with that hard kernel inside. Knowing her past, he understood that the inner strength was what had kept her going.

Franny felt as though he could see into her life, her soul. She was suddenly glad she was having dinner with Jake Bronson tonight instead of wrapping herself in her old patchwork quilt and huddling into her pillows, hiding from the truth about her relationship with Marcus.

He asked what she'd like to drink. "Something pink and girly," she said, surprising him. "And alcoholic." She grinned. "It's been a long day."

He called the waiter and Franny studied the menu, hoping he couldn't hear the hungry rumblings of her stomach; she'd missed lunch again. "I'm going to have the scallops with ginger to start, and then the lamb chops," she said, then glanced guiltily up at him. "I'm starving, but anyhow we're going dutch on this."

"It's good to see a woman with an appetite, and dinner's

on me." He held up a hand when she protested. "I asked *you* out," he said, "and besides I still need to prove to you that I'm a gentleman."

She took a sip of her drink. "And are you?"

"I've been called other things in my time, but I'm still hoping."

"Funny thing, I've never thought of myself as 'a lady.'" Franny laughed, "I suppose there was never enough time to practice being one. I've always just been the 'career woman,'" she said, mocking herself. "You know, making her own way in the world, that sort of thing."

"It seems to have worked," he said as the food came and the waiter poured the wine.

"So," she said, realizing she knew nothing about him except that he had a dog, "what do you do anyway?"

"I'm in the risk management business. Security," he added helpfully when she looked puzzled.

"You mean like . . . *a bodyguard!*"

"My company trains bodyguards for international celebrities and billionaires. We ensure their safety. And I investigate the backgrounds of their employees at the big companies, find out their problems."

"You're a P.I.?"

"Sort of . . ."

She sat back, flabbergasted. "I thought that was all Hollywood baloney. I never knew people like you really existed."

"Well, here I am."

"In the flesh and all," she said, awed. "I bet you get to travel a lot."

"I do."

"I'd like to travel," she said wistfully and Jake smiled,

thinking of the invitation. "Still, all those plane flights, all the delays, the long lines for security checks, you must find it tiring."

"I have my own plane."

Franny sat up straight. She pushed back her slippery hair and narrowed her long eyes at him. "You have *your own plane*?"

"It's not huge, you know. It's for my company and it's a few years old now."

"Oh my god. I never met anyone who owned their own plane. You must be very rich."

He laughed. "It's just necessary for my job. I can't always rely on commercial airlines."

"So," she said, forthright as always, "why haven't you been snapped up by some lucky woman already? Unless you are married of course?" She hadn't thought of that until now, hadn't remembered that married men had been known to ask women out on dates, too.

"There's been no one recently I've wanted to marry," he said, cool now.

Franny bit her lip, knowing she'd gone too far. She said, "I'm sorry."

He changed the subject. "What's it like being a vet? Do you get many customers like Ron and Marmalade, or do you normally just treat the animal?" And so Franny entertained him through the meal with stories of her patients. Then she told him about the poor German shepherd. "Oh, that reminds me," she said, looking at her watch, "I have to go back to the clinic after dinner to check on him."

"You're a dedicated doctor, then," he said, and she nodded in agreement. "I couldn't be any other way," she said simply, and she could tell from his eyes that he understood.

"So, tell me about *you* now, not your animals," he said, pouring more wine. He looked up at her and their eyes linked. "I want to know more about the *real* you."

"Well, I'm an Oregon girl. My father owned a little vineyard where he grew pinot noir grapes. He lost what money he had when phylloxera hit. Mom left when I was just a kid. I never knew her, so I didn't miss her when she died, though I'm still overwhelmed by guilt about not feeling anything." She glanced anxiously at him. Was she revealing too much? She didn't think so. Somehow she knew he understood. "Do you think that's terrible?"

He shrugged. "I never knew my mother, either. Like with you, she left when I was a child."

"Tell me about it," she said eagerly, leaning an elbow on the table and cupping her chin in her hand.

So Jake told her about his early life in Argentina and his relationship with his father. He described the sweeping acres of grassy pampas and the *gauchos* who were his only friends. He told her how much he loved the speedy little horses who would later become polo ponies and be sold to eager connoisseurs all over the world.

"Were you as lonely a kid as I was?" she asked suddenly.

He wasn't surprised by her question. He felt they came from the same lonely place.

He nodded, serious. "It's the kind of loneliness only those who have been there can know," he said quietly.

Instinctively she reached across the table for his hand, holding it unself-consciously in both hers. "But it worked out for you. You dealt with it, you became who you are."

He smiled. "And exactly who am I, Franny Marten? Who

do you see sitting here with you, drinking wine in a charming restaurant?"

"I see a nice man," she said simply. "You want to know how I can tell? It's the same gut feeling I use with animals. Somehow you just know when they are going to be okay, or you know they're potentially vicious and going to bite. I don't think you are going to bite me, Jake Bronson."

He smiled. "So," she said, "what took you away from Argentina?"

"Two women." Jake toyed with the stem of his wineglass. "And I fell in love with both of them. The first was very beautiful, a Frenchwoman full of *joie de vivre*. I was just sixteen and she was in her forties. She was my first love, and I love her to this day."

"How romantic," Franny said softly, "that you still love your first love. But then, who was the second?"

"Her name was Amanda. We were young. We got married. She died." Jake avoided her eyes, suddenly wary. He never talked about his past to women, and rarely even about his present.

But Franny closed her eyes, as though feeling his pain. "I'm so sorry," she said finally.

He shrugged. "It was a long time ago."

"And now?"

"Now? Oh, I built a little cabin up in the mountains. I keep my horse there, an old gelding nobody else wanted. Then there's Criminal and a couple of feral cats who come to visit whenever there's food around. There's true solitude, silence, peace." He shrugged again. "It's what makes me happy."

She nodded. There was a different man under his urbane, edgy exterior.

"What about you?" he asked.

"For a long time I never realized I was lonely. There was never time until my dad died. Then I knew I was Alone with a capital A. There was no family, nobody to look after me, nobody to care if I succeeded, or just"— she lifted a resigned shoulder—"ended up waitressing. So I pulled myself together and got on with life. I worked four jobs to put myself through college. I ended up a vet." She shrugged again. "And you know what? I'm *still* lonely."

He was looking at her as though he knew exactly what she meant. She met his gaze. Maybe she'd said too much after all.

"I have to go see my patients," she said, collecting her bag and her wits as he paid the bill.

They were standing outside the café, waiting for the valet to bring their cars, when Jake asked if he could go with her, and Franny said, "Why not?"

Back at the clinic they inspected the German shepherd, lying very still with a big ruff collar around his neck to stop him from licking his wounds. Jake watched as Franny knelt next to him. She stroked his fur and he rolled pleading brown eyes at her. "Don't worry, darling boy," he heard her whisper, "you're doing fine, you're going to be all right. I'll take care of you." The injured dog thumped his tail just once in acknowledgment.

Back outside, Franny called the dog's owner on her cell phone and told her he was doing great, and she thought he'd be fine. "Now what?" Jake said.

"I'm going home. I'm going to kick off my shoes and make

a cup of chamomile tea and think what a lovely time I had tonight." She ran her hand lightly down his arm, not in a sexy way, just friendly, nice-girl style.

"I could go for a cup of chamomile tea," he said with a touch of longing in his voice that hit home.

"Okay, so I'll make you some tea and then I'll send you home to bed because I'm really tired."

No nonsense there, Jake noted with a grin. She'd laid the ground rules, let him know where he stood all right.

 THEY PARKED OUTSIDE the little green house, then got out and stood looking at each other. She was suddenly hesitant, and he knew what she was thinking. After all, he was a stranger and she was about to ask him into her home.

"If you'd rather not, it's okay," he said, "I'll just head back to that Starbucks we passed and grab a take-out coffee."

She shook her head and her long hair rustled like silk. "Too much caffeine, you'll never sleep. No, I promised you chamomile tea and that's what you'll get. Come on in."

As usual, she'd forgotten to leave a light on, but she skipped unerringly up the steps. Jake followed her onto the unlit porch, hit the loose plank and felt his ankle twist agonizingly. "Jesus!"

She turned to look at him. He was balanced on one leg

like a stork. She wanted to giggle, but she could see he was in pain. "Oh god, I'm so sorry," she gasped. "It's that loose plank, I should have warned you."

"I wish you had," he said through gritted teeth.

She opened the door and helped him to the sofa, sat him down, knelt in front of him, slipped off his shoe, and ran her hand over his rapidly swelling ankle.

Jake looked down at her pale blond head bent over his foot. Her fingers were cool and firm, very doctor-like. He thought it was almost worth the pain.

She got to her feet. "It's definitely not broken but it's a bad sprain. If you like I can drive you to the emergency room, or I can strap it up for you. I'm pretty good at this sort of thing."

"I'd rather you did it," he said. "I feel like the German shepherd," he added, grinning, but she was all crisp medical efficiency.

"You'd better get that foot up on the sofa. Here, I'll put a cushion under it, and I'll get an ice pack and an Ace bandage."

While she was gone, he took a look at her home, at the sagging chenille sofas and the green-check throws that looked remarkably like horse blankets, at the tufted red-velvet ottoman and the fifties flea-market coffee table. Only the armoire in the corner was good, a fine French antique if he wasn't mistaken, and he wondered if Paul Marten had brought it with him to America all those years ago. Pottery jars spilled wilting flowers and scented candles were everywhere. Still, despite the general disarray, he thought it had a well-worn lived-in kind of comfort that wasn't too far removed from that of his cabin. He definitely liked it and thought it suited her.

She was back in minutes carrying a washbowl filled with

ice and water. She stuck his foot in it, grinning as he flinched. "I thought you were the tough-guy bodyguard trainer," she said mockingly, then she went off to the kitchen, where he heard her filling the kettle and rattling dishes.

When she came back she had her hair up tied in a black ribbon and a tray with two steaming mugs of tea, along with some pills and the Ace bandage.

"Drink the tea," she ordered. "It's very soothing, makes you nice and relaxed. And take these pills, they'll help kill the pain." She knelt in front of him again, took his swollen foot out of the ice water, patted it dry, and began to bandage his ankle tight enough to make him wince.

"All done," she said finally, sounding like the efficient vet she was. "Now I'll get you a proper ice pack and you'll be fine."

"Thanks," he said, meaning it, but also wondering how he would drive back to the hotel. And besides, he had to be in New York tomorrow.

Franny returned with a bag of frozen peas, which she arranged over his foot. Then she closed the shutters, lit the candles, and put a match to the kindling in the grate. As the flames began to flicker round the apple logs, the smoky scent swept her right back to her Oregon childhood. She kicked off her sandals with a satisfied sigh. "There," she said, beaming at him again with that easy smile. "*Now* we can relax."

"I'm sorry," Jake said, trying not to be distracted by the fact that her skirt was hitched up over her knees—rather pretty knees at that, showing her long, slender legs, "I'm keeping you up late. I know you have to work tomorrow."

She came to sit next to him and lifted his bandaged ankle

onto her lap, holding the frozen peas firmly over it. It was possibly the least romantic situation Jake had ever been in, but somehow that just added to her charm.

Her eyes linked with his. "Hi," she whispered.

"Hi," he whispered back and then somehow they were leaning into each other. *I shouldn't be doing this*, Jake was thinking as he moved closer. *She's gonna hate me when she finds out.*

I shouldn't be doing this, Franny told herself. *I've only just met him . . . I don't really know who he is.*

Jake attempted to put his arm around her but the position was awkward. Franny slid obligingly along the sofa and put her arms around him instead. He could feel her heart beating against his as they kissed, but strangely his head was swimming. Suddenly he felt like a man in a dreamworld.

"It's the painkillers," practical Franny said. "They've made you woozy. I'll drive you home if you like."

No, I don't like. I want to stay here with you, Jake thought. Besides, he couldn't let her drive him back to the hotel. She thought he lived in L.A., and this certainly wasn't the moment to tell her he'd been lying. And anyhow, by now he could hardly move.

Franny stared doubtfully at him. His eyes were closed and it was clear he wasn't going anywhere. She roused him, put her arm under his shoulder and helped him limp to her bedroom, where she lowered him onto the bed. He sank back against the pillows, groaning as he drifted off again. There was nothing for it but to undress him. She unbuttoned his shirt and somehow managed to maneuver his arms out of his sleeves and tug it off. She hadn't realized how heavy a half-asleep man could be. Next she unfastened his buckle and slid off his belt. She hesitated before tackling the zip. She'd never gotten a man out of his clothes before, they'd always done it themselves. Still, it was easier than she'd thought, and he looked cuter in his blue boxers than she'd thought too, hard-bodied, smooth-skinned. . . . She covered him quickly with her old patchwork quilt.

"Paradise," Jake was murmuring, "I think I've found paradise, Franny Marten." She laughed and dropped a quick kiss on his forehead.

Back in her tiny living room, Franny put on a CD of Diana Krall singing of lost love, then slumped back onto the sofa. Sipping the chamomile tea, she wondered what on earth she thought she was doing. She had a strange man in her bed, a man she'd only met that morning, a man she hardly knew. What was she, crazy?

Plus she'd kissed him. I mean, she'd leaned right over, snuggled right up there, and *kissed him*, showing about as much finesse as a raunchy high school girl on prom night. She smiled, remembering the way his mouth had felt under hers and the faint tremor that ran through his body. She almost wished she hadn't given him the painkiller—she would definitely have liked to kiss him some more.

The fire had settled to a dull glow and she was tired. She took off her skirt and top, turned out the lamp, pulled the green-check horse blanket over her, snuggled down and closed her eyes. Maybe there was life after Marcus after all.

9 FRANNY WOKE AT SIX, as she always did. She sat up and pushed back her hair, listening for any sound from the bedroom. Nothing. She tiptoed across and peeked in the door to make sure it wasn't all a dream. Jake was still there, lying peacefully on his back and not even snoring, the way Marcus had. He looked so good she almost climbed right in there with him. In the clear light of day she thought it was probably a good thing he'd sprained his ankle. Otherwise she might have made a real fool of herself.

She found jeans and a sweatshirt, dressed hurriedly, got in the car and drove to the clinic. The shepherd was sitting up and taking notice. She ruffled his thick neck fur and told him he was a good boy, remembering to thank god for answering her prayers as she did so. She checked his wounds, gave him an antibiotic shot, fresh water, and a little food. He wagged his tail gratefully. "Be back soon," she whispered, with a final pat, then got back in the car and drove to Starbucks.

She ordered a *grande* decaf low-fat latte for herself, and a *venti* regular with a double shot of espresso for Jake, because she figured he would like his coffee strong. On the way home she picked up a box of Krispy Kreme doughnuts, the plain glazed kind, and she was back at the house before he even awoke.

JAKE'S EYES were still closed but he could smell ginger-flower candles and coffee. He wondered where on earth he was, then he remembered that he was in Franny Marten's bed and, unfortunately, alone. He tested the ankle. He felt no pain. What was she, some kind of genius vet?

Then he opened his eyes and she was standing there with the Starbucks coffee in her hands, looking like a blond Oregon angel. For a second it disturbed him, knowing she'd been watching him sleep. He'd been off guard and vulnerable, a place he did not normally like to be. But there was a smile in her lovely pale eyes, her blond hair was in the pony-tail braid again, and she was un-made-up and barefoot. This was a great way to start a day, he thought with a surge of emotion that he seemed to remember was called happiness.

"Hi," she said, smiling that sweet enchantress smile, totally unaware of the effect it had on him. "Coffee?" She raised the paper cups invitingly.

He pulled himself upright, watching her as she sat on the edge of the bed and handed him the coffee.

"How did you sleep?" she said.

"Great, thanks. And you?" He clapped a remorseful hand to his head. "Oh god, I took your bed."

"I was okay on the sofa. I've done it before." She took a sip of her coffee. "Yours has a double shot of espresso in it. I thought that's what you'd like."

The coffee was so strong Jake almost choked on it, but he smiled anyhow and said it was perfect.

"So how's the ankle?" she said.

He'd almost forgotten that was the reason—the only reason—he was in her bed. He jiggled his foot under the blanket. "Pretty good," he said, wishing he could claim to be incapacitated so that he could stay another night, but he had to get back to New York.

"Think you can walk?"

"I'll give it a good try."

He glanced at his pants neatly draped over a chair, with his shirt hooked over the top. He checked. He was still wearing his boxers.

"You took good care of me."

"That's what I do," she said lightly, "take care of the wounded and injured."

"I don't think I'm exactly wounded."

"Well, injured then. You're certainly that. Oh, I almost forgot." She got up quickly, then tripped over his shoes, which she'd left in the middle of the floor, recovering before she spilled too much of her coffee. She grabbed the Krispy Kreme box from the dresser where she'd left it. "Plain glazed," she said. She looked doubtful again. "Or are you a chocolate man?"

"Never chocolate." He took a doughnut and wolfed it down.

She perched on the edge of the bed, nibbling on her doughnut. "Usually I can't manage breakfast," she said. "I'm always up too early. This is good though."

She held out the box and he took another. He didn't want to get out of this bed, he didn't want to move from this spot, he wanted to stay here eating Krispy Kremes with Franny Marten for a very long time. "I guess I'd better get up," he said reluctantly.

She hovered anxiously over him. "Let me help you."

Jake was sorely tempted to feign excruciating pain when he put his foot to the floor, but he resisted. "It's okay," he said. "I'll manage."

She slid her arm around him, ready to help anyway, and he turned to look at her. Their eyes linked and the room seemed suddenly very still. She leaned in to him and he took her chin in his hand, drinking her eyes in with his, drawing her face closer until he felt her sweet doughnut-scented breath on his mouth. And then he was kissing her and her lips were soft as cushions under his. He pulled her closer, wanting more of her. Now she was kissing him back and they were falling against the pillows, holding each other and kissing and kissing, unable to take their mouths away.

"Sweet," he murmured in between kisses, "you are so sweet, Franny Marten." Then, suddenly brought back to reality by the name Marten and remembering the reason he was here, he pushed her away. He held her at arm's length and she watched him with puzzled blue eyes that asked, without words, what was wrong. "Nothing," he murmured, unable to resist her, "nothing is wrong, Franny." He pulled her gently back to him, stroking her soft hair that had come undone from its braid and spilled over his chest in a silken fall as she slid down his body, smoothing her hands over him until his skin felt on fire.

"Here, here," he whispered, "come to me, my lovely Franny," and he held her hands in his, kissing each finger, sliding his tongue between them, kissing the soft, warm space under her arms, stroking her breasts, taking the jutting pink nipples into his mouth, then ranging down her body until he found the soft mound and her secret places and she whispered to him not to stop, oh please don't stop. He covered her with his body, delirious with her sexy scent, her sweet breath as her lips sought his. He pulled back, stopped for a moment, and her eyes followed him as he found his jacket, took a condom from his wallet. She watched him put it on, smiling at him as she said, "Oh, what a big boy you are," and they were both laughing as he fell back onto the bed and took her smooth loveliness into his arms again. And then they made long, slow love.

Afterward, Jake held her close, unwilling to unlink their bodies. She snuggled endearingly into him, dropping hot little kisses onto his face, his neck, anything she could reach.

"Beautiful," he murmured, recognizing that rare little thrill of happiness. "You are beautiful, Dr. Franny Marten."

"Oh! Oh my god!" She pushed him away, sat up, looked at him wide-eyed with shock. "I'm late for work!"

"Is it that important?" he said thoughtlessly, because all he could think about was making love to her some more.

"*Important?*" She stared at him as though he was crazy. "*It's who I am!*" She leaped out of bed and ran into the bathroom. She stopped and came out again. "I'm sorry, but I really have to go," she said, kissing him some more.

"I know who you are, Franny," he said quietly. "I understand." And she smiled trustingly at him.

"Here, you shower first," she said, pulling him to his feet. She showed him the bathroom, watching still worried as he hobbled off.

Franny was smiling as she went back to the kitchen and

began to tidy up, if you could call piling dishes in the sink and scraping the candle wax off the tables tidying. It was 7:30 and she hadn't even showered yet. She would be late for work for the first time in her life.

Minutes later, Jake emerged from her bedroom fully dressed. His hair was still wet from the shower, and he raked a hand through it and then along the rough blue stubble on his jaw, looking at her. Franny stood uncertainly, not knowing what to say. Did you say, Well, thanks for spending the night, glad I could help? Did you say, I loved making love with you? Or, See you again soon?

He saved her the trouble. He put both hands on her shoulders, tilted her face up to meet his, and said, "Thank you, Franny Marten. For everything. It was wonderful." For a second his lips met hers in the softest of kisses, then he let go of her and limped to the door.

She heard the loose plank splinter as he stepped on it again, heard him curse, and despite herself she laughed. She would see him again soon, she just knew she would. She had noticed that he had not said he would call her.

She hurried into the shower, flung on some clothes, and drove too fast to the clinic, where she temporarily forgot about Jake as she immersed herself in the work she loved.

That afternoon, a huge bouquet of Casablanca lilies, smelling like a tropical island in summer, arrived for her. The accompanying card read, "I couldn't find ginger flowers so I hope these will do instead. Thank you again, Jake."

Marcus was forgotten. She was walking on air, smiling as she remembered her night with Jake. It hadn't been the usual sort of encounter between a man and a woman, but there again, if it weren't for the ankle, she might never have really gotten to know him. She was sure he would call her later.

But Jake still hadn't called by the time she went to bed. She didn't change the sheets because, like a smitten teen, she wanted to lay her head on the pillow where his head had lain. Now she buried her face in it, seeking his scent, dreaming of him. She knew he would call tomorrow. But he did not. Nor the next day, nor the next. An unsmiling Franny thought about calling him, even though she knew she shouldn't. But when she asked the secretary for his number, Lindsey told her that Jake hadn't left an address or a number because he'd only come to the clinic to check out Franny as a vet for his dog.

"Criminal," Franny said, biting her lip.

"Jeez, what a name to give a dog," Lindsey added.

But Franny wasn't even listening. She turned miserably away. She had reached a new low. She was just a foolish woman who didn't know how to handle men. She always gave too much, and look what had happened to her. Again. She wished Clare were here, but Clare was back in Atlanta, picking up some more of her stuff. She decided she wouldn't tell Clare about Jake, though, because she just couldn't admit she'd made a fool of herself again, so soon after Marcus.

ALL THE WAY BACK to New York, Jake thought about Franny. He knew how much it would hurt when he didn't call, after how wonderful she had been to him and what had happened between them. But there was nothing he could do except send her flowers. And damn it, he missed her already. He wished he could tell her the truth, but he'd have to wait and trust he could work it all out when they met again at the château.

10 As RAFAELLA WALKED ALONG the path beneath the chestnut trees, with the dogs romping ahead, she imagined life as it used to be on hot summer days like this. In the old days there were always house parties, and she would gather friends around her and they'd ride their horses out to the vineyard for picnics or have long lunches at Café des Colombes. They would take up all the terrace tables, making a racket, capping one another's jokes and tall tales, laughing and drinking Pernod.

Then, there always seemed to be laughter and food and wine and glamorous clothes, because Rafaella had been a clotheshorse right from the age of three, when her notorious aunt, Marguerite (her mother's sister who was always said to be "no good"), brought her a winter outfit from Paris. It was a red velvet coat with a matching little hat trimmed in snow-white ermine, and for the first time she had seen herself reflected in those same hall mirrors as glamorous and gorgeous and feminine all at once. Of course her mother had said she looked like a cheap little Santa Claus, but her mother was like that. Maritée Marten could never have been called a free spirit the way her sister was, and besides, she never liked her daughter.

When Rafaella finally hit her stride in her teens, tall and too thin with a neck like a swan that looked so fragile it might bend under the weight of all that piled-up dark hair, she embarked on a lifelong love affair with clothes, buying from Dior, Yves Saint Laurent, Givenchy, and Valentino. She still had most of them stashed away in the cedar-lined attics set aside for just that purpose because she couldn't bear to give her beloveds away.

The young men in her crowd were all in love with her. They met her eyes with a sexy question, which of course she'd laughed at, thrilled with their attention and a little afraid of it at the same time. They told her she was a beauty, which she knew not to be true, but she liked it anyway and became an expert flirt, enjoying herself, enjoying being young, enjoying life.

Then she'd married Henri de Roquebrune, who had taken her name because of the inheritance clause in the Marten family trust. The Marten line had gone on unhindered by change from the time the first known one, a wealthy seventeenth-century burgher from Bordeaux, had purchased the bishopric and much of the land here—a common occurrence at that time, when rich men could buy their way into the clergy and own entire villages and even towns. It was he who had built the beginnings of the château and founded the Domaine Marten winery.

Rafaella never knew if she was in love with Henri or whether she'd just been dazzled by his older-man glamour. He'd seemed so much more mature than the young men she knew.

Henri had wined her and dined her and romanced her. He'd also taken her, with friends to chaperone—not too successfully as it turned out—on a summer yacht trip to the Aegean islands, where he also took her virginity on a white beach with the sound of the sea lapping in her ears and sharp pebbles sticking into her naked behind, and with the shrill night sounds of crickets in her ears, which from then on she would always associate with making love.

Her son Felix had been the result of that night, though knowing what she knew now, Henri should certainly have been more careful. After all, she was only nineteen years old and an innocent for all her big talk. It meant she'd had to walk down the aisle of the Saint-Marten village church draped in shimmering white satin with a long, heavy train that slid *plop, plop, plop* down the stairs as she descended, with an extra large bouquet of lilies to cover her bump.

She smiled now, thinking about what a little idiot she'd been. Henri had turned out to be a cold man and boring, something she'd never realized, enthralled as she was by his older-man experienced attentions, by the waiters at the smart restaurants who bowed to him, the doormen who saluted him, the elegant men and women he knew, and the Paris society he moved in, while she was barely out of the schoolroom and like a filly at the gate raring to go.

Of course Henri hadn't given her the Marten name back when she'd left him, but now he was gone, buried with her parents and the other Martens in the flowery little graveyard just outside the village.

When she'd realized that she did not love Henri and that he certainly had never loved her and had married her only for her money, she'd proceeded to live her own life, keeping the château filled with friends. She'd become something of a fixture in café society in Paris and on the Côte d'Azur, where the Martens owned a *pieds dans l'eau* villa, which meant it was right on the sea. You could step out from your bedroom onto the hot summer tiles of the terrace and run down the steps, through the gardens and directly into the cool blue sea that slid around your body like a thin silken nightdress.

She'd flirted, and there'd been a few *liaisons* of course, but nothing serious—until she met Lucas Bronson, that is. Then nothing she could have done would have stopped that tumultuous fall into love's darkest entanglement.

Rafaella thought what fun life had been then, how glorious those years. Did she regret any of it? Not a bit. Not even Lucas. Except now maybe, she regretted how careless she had been with time, all those wasted hours and frittered days, the long lazy weeks that led to irretrievable years. She had been a foolish woman with time, and now it had caught up to her.

And, at the heart of it all, had always been the château.

11

THE CHÂTEAU WAS HOME, the place where Rafaella's heart was, but it was the vineyards that were her true passion. By the time she was twenty-five, Rafaella's knowledge of wine making equaled that of the most prestigious male vintners—and this was in an era when few women were in "the business" of producing and selling wine.

Taught by her father, she had worked at the winery dressed like the workers in men's big bright blue overalls, though she'd had to roll them at the wrists and ankles and hitch them tight around her thin waist with a piece of string. Her dark hair was bound in a red kerchief, her pretty hands were stained purple with grape must, and her head swam drunkenly from the fumes as the grapes fermented in the great vats.

On cold, dark early-spring mornings she'd prowled the rows of vines with her father, drinking great gasps of air so cold and clean it was like the wine itself. The light of the moon illuminated the threads of a rare frost that her father told her could ruin the precious crop in mere hours, and she'd helped spray the young grapes to stop them from freezing.

It was Rafaella who had replanted the wild white roses that gave the château its name, at the end of each row of vines. The roses were important because they would be first to be attacked by pests, thus giving the Martens warning to protect the grapes. And she'd spent many long nights poring over orders and accounts with her father, who also taught her how to make a good deal with the bottlers, and had taken her with him to Portugal in search of a new source of cork.

Now, they said, there was nothing Rafaella Marten didn't know about wine. Personally, she thought it was a good thing she still enjoyed drinking it because her apprenticeship had been long and hard. She was the only Marten heir, and when her father died, the full responsibility for the business—and its workers, who were the village people she had known all her life—had fallen on her shoulders.

Though on the surface she seemed frivolous and carefree, Rafaella ran her winery in a most professional and creative manner. She opened up new markets in Asia and the United States, finding acclaim for her "supple, sensual red wine with a hint of flowers in the bouquet and a velvet heft to it that tingles on the palette like the scent of fresh pine on a winter mountain day." That's the way the reviewer in the *New York Times* acclaimed it on its first launch. Not bad, Rafaella had thought with a satisfied smile, for what was essentially a jumped-up Côtes-du-Rhône. Admittedly, it was of the first order, but it was still no smart Bordeaux.

Rafaella also took good care of her workers and her village, always there in times of crisis and of celebration. As a girl, she had gone to school with the villagers' children and was known to them as Rafaella. She knew every family by name, always knew who was sick or who was leaving the village to work in the city and who had come back, tail between their legs, because after all, the allure of home was too strong.

In fact, it was the château and her love for it that had come between her and the man known to everyone as "the Lover." Lucas Bronson was an arrogant, handsome nomad, a champion polo player, a world wanderer, always restless, eternally on the move in search of the next "main event" in life. Following the polo matches, Lucas switched countries and continents with as little thought as Rafaella put into planning a picnic. Of course she did not go with him because she had her work and her home to look after. Even love had not been able to tie down Lucas Bronson. And even after she left him, Rafaella believed—she still had to believe, otherwise she couldn't bear it—that Lucas had really loved her.

Ten years ago Rafaella had officially "retired," and Scott

Harris had come to run her vineyards, though she still couldn't resist keeping a finger in the pie, stirring the mix every now and again, just to see what would happen.

Scott was Australian. He'd grown up in the Barossa Valley and, like herself, he'd been in the wine business since he was a boy. Now she looked forward immensely to their weekly "business lunches" at the Café des Colombes. In fact, they were the highlight of her week—until the idea of the family reunion had taken over, that is. Now all she could think about, all she longed for, was that there might be a family again at the Château des Roses Sauvages. And that her sons would return to her.

12   JULIETTE LABOURDE had just spent an entirely satisfactory day shopping and lunching when she returned home to find the invitation in her mail.

Juliette lived alone on Manhattan's Upper East Side, in a large, colorful apartment crammed with old family bibelots and a flurry of blond Pomeranians. She was the kind of large woman who was built to last, and though she was Rafaella's age, time had not been so kind, although admittedly she had not started out gorgeous. But, oh, she'd been popular. All the men had adored her. Like Rafaella, she had that sparkle that brought life and excitement with her, and that she definitely had not lost. Her hair was still a flaming red, her eye shadow blue, and her mouth a glossy pink. With a flowery caftan hiding her bulk, she looked like a grandmother from hell en route to a Hawaiian vacation, but her smile and her warmth made you forget about all that in the space of a minute and just want to be with her.

When Juliette saw the large, square cream envelope with the French stamps and Rafaella's familiar writing, she gave a little cry of recognition, dropped her bags, and ripped it open immediately. She scanned the invitation, her head to one side, one hand clutched excitedly to her throat. *"Ma chère amie,"* it began.

> *Too many years have passed since we saw each other, too many lifetimes have disappeared into the past, too much water has flowed under too many bridges. We, who were once so close, lost touch, I retreating to my solitude here at the château, and you flitting around the world with your darling army officer husband, God rest his soul—a more decent man never lived. (Of course I'm referring to Rufus, not to husband number one who, like my own, is better off nameless!)*
>
> *You lived in so many places while I just stayed here, running my winery efficiently because, as you remember, it was always my passion (or one of them, the other being the Lover of course), and drowning my sorrows in a nightly glass of champagne with Haigh. (You'll be glad, no doubt, to know he is still here, still interfering in my life, still my friend—perhaps my only friend now unless I can still count you in that number? Ah, but I forget, there are two others. You remember Jake, the Lover's*

son? He spent a year here at the château in happier times. I love him still—certainly more than I do my own two sons who departed years ago. You will recall that story of course—how could you forget? Felix under a cloud of suspicion for murder, and Alain after having been caught robbing the winery until he almost bankrupted us. Just so you know, I have never heard from either one since Felix walked out and Alain was thrown out. I often wonder, Juliette, Was I wrong in the way I brought them up? Too indulgent? Too loving? Was I wrong not to believe either of them—though I tried hard—when they pleaded innocent? Perhaps I will never know the answer to that. Or maybe I will, since I am asking them to put the past behind us and inviting them here to the reunion in the hope that we can forgive each other and begin all over again.

Who else have I invited to this grand reunion? you must be asking yourself. Alas, there are not many left. There's a young American woman, descended from my father's brother, Paul, who ran off to America after a great falling out. The row was over who would marry Maritée—my father got her and so she became my mother, but it was really about who got control of the winery. Again my father won. Paul never returned. He married someone else, had a son, and that son had a daughter named Franny Marten. Then there's Jake, of course, because in my heart he's always been like a son to me. And then there's you, my dearest Juliette, because after all these years, you too remain in my heart.

Call me a sentimental old woman (and much as I hate to admit it, we are getting old), but I want to make *peace with what is left of my family, and I want to see my friends again.*

"Do not disappoint me, Juliette," she finished in her old commanding style, making Juliette laugh. And she signed it firmly, "Love, Rafaella."

Juliette sank onto a yellow damask sofa, arranging her flowery caftan around her ample body, gold bracelets clanking, Pomeranians clambering up, tiny paws plucking at her for attention. "Oh, sit down, you sillies," she said, giving them an affectionate shove, and they settled with disgruntled expressions next to her.

"Well, I never thought I would hear from you again, Rafaella," she said out loud, "and now here you are, all of a sudden rejoining the land of the living!"

She leaned back against the cushions, eyes closed, smiling as she remembered the good times they'd had together. They had been friends since they were girls, and in fact if it were not for Rafaella insisting on taking her to lunch at La Coupole in Paris, Juliette would never have met the man she eventually married.

It was long ago, when they were both young and glamorous and brimming with life and laughter. Rafaella had come up to Paris for a few days to stay with Juliette at her apartment in an old courtyard building in Saint-Germain.

Juliette's place was constantly abustle with friends dropping in, messengers delivering bouquets, admirers stopping by. Invitations to cocktail parties, costume balls, and other grand events were stuffed casually into the edges of the huge seventeenth-century mirror above the black-marble mantelpiece, and Juliette's first husband was stuffed into a tiny

boudoir just around the corner, where his mistress lived. Juliette's two young children were always dashing in and out,
chased by nannies, stealing chocolate bonbons from berib-
boned boxes and dropping them on the striped silk sofas,
where they left ominous little brown stains at which Juliette
just laughed, and an earlier batch of Pomeranians rampaged
everywhere, snapping at heels and yapping constantly.

Rafaella had never understood Juliette's miraculous ability to laugh at anything: a stain on a sofa, a bad haircut, an
ugly dress. Juliette also had no taste and inevitably chose the
wrong color or a fabric too clinging for her large figure. Un-
fashionable as she might appear though, she cut a swath
through Paris, leaving a felled legion of broken hearts behind. Until she met Major Rufus Thomas and, like Rafaella
with the Lover, gave him her heart.

Rafaella was with her that lunchtime in La Coupole. It
was in March, too many years ago to count, with the sun
struggling out of the clouds and a gusty wind whipping at
their skirts. They ran shivering through the large glass revolv-
ing doors, laughing and smoothing their ruffled hair, hugging
chubby little fox jackets around their throats, settling at the
bar and ordering glasses of champagne. Rufus was two seats
away, smart in his khaki British major's uniform, his brown
leather belt gleaming like his eyes.

"Like polished *marrons*," Juliette whispered loudly, the
way her whispers always were, and his eyes were in fact the
color of chestnuts. They were also shiny with hope and longing. Rafaella was looking beautiful, her dark curls all wind-
tossed and her blue eyes sparkling with fun, and at first
Juliette thought the army officer was interested in her. He
kept glancing at the two of them as they speared their oys-

ters, throwing back their heads and letting them slide down their throats with little moans of pleasure.

He was British though, and shy, so he said nothing. "I obviously have to take the initiative in this case," Juliette whispered. Then, giving him that big smile of hers, she said, "Welcome to Paris."

Rufus moved over the two seats, introduced himself, and said, "Now I feel right at home."

By this time Juliette had eyes only for Major Rufus Thomas, so Rafaella swallowed her twelfth oyster, drained her glass, and went shopping on her own. In fact, Juliette remembered that was the day Rafaella had bought the spectacular red chiffon dress from St. Laurent's second collection for Dior.

Late that evening, Juliette had drifted home with a soft look in her eyes that spelled trouble. Rafaella guessed that "trouble" had already taken place, and Juliette confirmed this in loud whispers in her bedroom as they changed for the party they were to attend that night.

"You wouldn't believe his body," she whispered, closing the door firmly against all comers. "He's like a Greek statue, hard as marble, only more virile." She giggled, with a reminiscent look about her that made Rafaella laugh, too. "Who knew the British were sexy?" she added. "I mean, all you hear is that they are cold and emotionally ruined at a young age by sadistic nannies and homosexual boarding schools. But not Rufus. He's warm as a brioche straight from the oven and loving as a new puppy, all over me with licks and kisses."

She took Rufus with her on her next visit to the château, and the two of them occupied the big room in the East Tower, hardly venturing out except when hunger became too much or Rafaella sent Haigh up to complain that she needed company.

Juliette smiled, remembering how she and Rufus had glowed pink from their exertions. Their eyes had sent secret sexual messages, and they couldn't keep their hands off each other. Love and sex had permeated the very air around them.

Then one day her husband showed up and there was a wham-bam knock-down, drag-out fight, with the husband confronting her with her indiscretions and she confronting him with his longtime mistress. Fortunately, Rafaella had managed to push Juliette out of the way before she could brain her husband with a raised wine bottle. "It's a good vintage, *chérie*," Rafaella protested. "At least if you are going to hit him, do it with a table wine." Then she'd sent Rufus out of the room and sat Juliette and the husband opposite each other. Because they were Catholic and divorce was out of the question, she'd brokered an almost-amicable separation with the appropriate financial settlement.

Meanwhile, Juliette and her children had moved in with Rafaella and *her* children. Rufus was a professional army man, as his father and his grandfather had been, but he was at the château as often as he got leave from his regiment. So, with Rafaella's own long-abandoned husband permanently living in Paris, they had become one big, happy extended family at the château, with parties for the little ones as well as the grown-ups, and long, lazy summer days spent at the seaside villa at Cap d'Antibes with a myriad of friends to join in the fun.

Later, after her husband died, Juliette had finally married Rufus, daringly wearing white, with Rafaella as matron of honor, splendid as always in the red Dior chiffon. Juliette had followed Rufus around the world on his army postings, and they were never apart until the day he died ten years ago, breaking her heart forever.

Ever since then, the East Tower room had been known as Juliette's room. "I wonder if Rafaella has forgotten that," Juliette said to herself now. "If so, then I'm about to remind her!" And she laughed a great, booming, jolly laugh. "Oh, the times we had," she said, delighted. "And now just think, it will happen all over again. In fact, it'll be quite the little Agatha Christie mystery, with everyone gathered at the big country house for a grand reunion, except this time they'll know for sure the butler didn't do it." She laughed again, thinking of Haigh, with his stiff upper lip, in the role of the killer. Still, she had wondered about the murder in the past, and if the killer was really Felix? Or was it Alain?

She picked up the phone and, regardless of the six-hour time difference, dialed the château's number, which she remembered clearly even after all these years.

Haigh answered, and when she said who it was, he said of course he knew it was her, nobody else ever called in the middle of the night and nobody else talked that loud, either. Then he put Rafaella on.

"Are you coming then?" Rafaella said, just as though they had seen each other last week.

"Of course I'm coming. You can't have a grand family re-union without *me*," Juliette said, grinning. She heard Rafaella's sigh of relief and added, "But I want my old room back, the one in the East Tower with the view of the lake, and you'd better have Haigh ice the good champagne and not try to palm me off with the nonvintage."

And Rafaella laughed and then their voices dropped into the soft, intimate tones of women friends who have a lot to talk over. Which they did for a couple of hours, despite the cost.

13

FELIX MARTIN INHABITED the forty-fourth floor of the great glass-and-steel office tower that dominated the Hong Kong skyline. If you were crossing the choppy bay on the little Star Ferry that chugged back and forth between Kowloon and Central, the setting sun that glinted off all that bronze glass almost blinded you. But inside, of course, all was cool and there was no glare, only a muted bronze silence.

Felix wondered about that. How could silence be bronze? Still, it seemed tangible, a combination of light and the absence of sound. Everyone was gone for the night, and he was alone with only the dim whirr of the air-conditioning and the soft buzz of the bank of computers beating out the pulse of the world's race for more money on the global stock markets. The computers flickered with a faint green glow, the tan leather sofas were hard-cushioned and uninviting for lounging, the steel lamps were sharp and angular and the light they cast was too dim to read by.

Who the hell had he paid to decorate this place, anyhow?

Felix wondered, staring out at the ferries and at the hurrying businessmen, small as ants below, on their way to the Tycoon Bar at the Mandarin Oriental for an evening drink to loosen up after the stresses of the day. Soon they would head home to face a new set of stresses—their wives who complained they didn't see enough of them, small children who tore up the peace and calm of the household, sullen teenagers who demanded more and more "things" they absolutely "needed."

Felix did not have a wife, though there had been two possibilities in his earlier years, both of whom had followed the same "wife path" he'd described above. Except for one, the women he'd known had always wanted more. Grander houses, more designer clothes, bigger jewels. What they'd really wanted was more of *him*. They'd scrunched his soul until it felt so tight he'd wanted to kill them. And that was the end of any thoughts of marriage for him.

Felix, the rich bachelor, was known as quite a catch in Hong Kong society. His black hair was streaked handsomely with silver, he wore immaculately tailored pin-striped suits, and his shoes were handcrafted in London. He could make good small talk at a party, knew how to treat a lady, and not only gave generously to all the proper charities, he also bought tables for their gala balls and dinners. And he actually showed up, usually with someone important as well as beautiful on his arm. The words *confirmed bachelor* were whispered, but Felix was not gay. It was just that he'd had it with women. Except for sex, which of course he could buy. All he thought about, all he dreamed about—when he had that rare couple of hours of sleep that fate and time now allowed him—was making money. And making *more* money.

Unfortunately, sleep no longer seemed to factor in the "living" equation. The more he made, the less he was able to sleep, until he was at the point of sleep deprivation where his hands shook uncontrollably and sometimes his head spun, and he missed his footing, or he missed what someone had just said.

The invitation lay unopened in the exact center of his oversized desk. He stared out the window, waiting for the blip from the concierge desk downstairs that would tell him Jake Bronson had arrived, winging in like Mercury, bringing a message from his past. A past he no longer cared to think about, though in those hard waking moments, that three o'clock in the morning dead zone when his life seemed suspended while everyone else's went rushing on, his mother, Rafaella, came to his mind as he'd last seen her, white-faced and trembling. It was not something he cared to think about now, and he wished he had not agreed to see Jake, though for a while there they had been almost like brothers.

Felix was in his early twenties when Jake arrived at the château. Alain had been there too, but Alain led his own secret life and wasn't around so much. Mostly it was just him and Jake.

The internal phone blipped and he pressed the ON button. "Mr. Bronson is here to see you, sir," the concierge said.

"Send him up." Felix went and sat in the big leather chair, safe behind his impressive antique desk, and waited for whatever was to come, toying absently with the letter from the Bank of Shanghai that awaited his attention.

The outer door buzzed and he pressed ENTER, hearing

brisk footsteps crossing the marble hall, then the polite tap on his door.

"*Entrez*," he said in French because that was the language he had always spoken with Jake. He did not get up as Jake walked toward him, and Jake stood a few feet away, looking at Felix.

Taking him in, Felix thought uncomfortably, and no doubt comparing him to the last time he'd seen him. Meanwhile, Jake looked good, still lean, still with that thick, dark hair and his father's big confident stride and those cool gray eyes that seemed to look right into your soul.

"How are you, Jake?"

"I'm well, thank you, Felix. And you?"

Felix nodded that he was okay and Jake grinned. "Still a man of few words, huh?"

"Like you, I prefer action." Felix picked up a silver paper knife and slid its silky blade through his strong fingers.

"I told your mother I had to be in Hong Kong. She asked me to see you." Jake eyed the knife through narrowed eyes.

Felix said nothing, looking warily at the cream envelope with the French stamps.

"You're famous here, Felix," Jake said. "In business circles, that is, though of course you also made a few headlines in your local newspapers when you were younger."

Felix said nothing and Jake pushed further. "A pregnant girl found dead at the foot of a cliff? And you suspected of being the father of her child? And possibly of giving her that fatal push?"

Felix lifted his eyes from the knife. "If you are here just to provoke me, Jake, this conversation is terminated."

Jake's shoulders lifted in an exaggerated shrug. "Of course there was no DNA in those days. Nothing could be proven, but you, Felix, were unable to account for your whereabouts, and Alain was. What was your mother to believe?"

"Mother never gave me a chance," Felix said angrily. "She never even listened to me. And why should she, when Alain was so convincing, placing the guilt on my shoulders. Mother could never see the truth about Alain, she was blinded by his charm, never saw the slime that was underneath. Until it was too late."

Jake said mildly, "Oh come on, Felix, a little sibling rivalry, a touch of jealousy, a girl you both fancied . . . loved even. So tell me, what *is* the truth?"

Felix sighed. He got up from behind his desk and walked past Jake to the floor-to-ceiling expanse of bronze-tinted windows, staring moodily out at the passing show below. "I said it to Mother then, and I say it to you now: believe what you wish. It will not make me any more guilty, nor will it make my brother any less guilty."

He swung around and stood, hands behind his back, a looming dark figure against the bronze light. "Tell me, why are you really here, Jake?"

"I come as a messenger from your mother. She's an old woman now, Felix. There's not much time left and she wants to see both her boys again."

Felix gave a short bark of laughter. "And I'm supposed to go trotting back like the prodigal son."

"That's entirely up to you," Jake said quietly. "Of course, do as you wish."

Felix turned away and Jake's eyes quickly scanned the desk, taking in the letter from the Bank of Shanghai. It was an acknowledgment that the monthly stipend paid to a Bao Chu Ching at an address in Shanghai was to be increased from thirty to fifty dollars. Jake memorized the account number and the address instantly. To him, it was the smallness of the sum that seemed significant. Thirty dollars was the average wage of the poorest workers, yet Felix paid it to this woman every month.

"I'll give the matter some thought," Felix said, still staring out the window, his back still to Jake.

"That's all your mother asks." Jake hesitated, then said, "I also have the same message for Alain. I need to find him, Felix."

"Hah!" Felix swung around with a great snort of anger. "Of course you do. *Mama's boy,* the *real* prodigal son. No doubt he'll want to return to claim his inheritance. Well, sorry to disappoint you, Jake, but I have no idea where Alain is. Probably dead by now, from being too smart for his own good."

Jake nodded. He walked over to Felix and held out his hand. "We were friends once, Felix," he said, meeting his eyes. "You were kind to a lonely out-of-place kid who knew nothing. I've never forgotten that, or you."

Felix looked at the hand outstretched in old friendship. He nodded somberly. "And I have never forgotten you, Jake."

The two men shook hands, then Jake turned and made briskly for the door. "Think about it, Felix," he called over his shoulder. "It means everything to your mother. And perhaps to you, too. I hope to see you there."

As the door closed behind him, Felix stared at the envelope. His mother's writing looked shaky, like an old woman's. Of course that was exactly what she was now, an old woman.

He ripped open the envelope, withdrew the invitation, and read it. Then he began to laugh. "Oh, Mother, you old fraud," he said, still laughing. "You just want to reunite the family because blood is thicker than water, right? Well, too bad, Mother, because I am not coming. You can have your family reunion all on your own, which is the path you chose all those years ago. This son is not coming *home*."

IT WAS MUCH LATER that night that Felix Marten's body was found in the service alley behind the giant bronze-glass building. Apparently he had fallen from the open elevator used to haul heavy freight. He'd been killed instantly, still wearing his custom pin-striped suit and his handmade shoes, though both had come off in the fall. He'd landed head down, and his face was smashed to smithereens. Of course it was suicide, everyone agreed at first. But then, maybe not. Like many rich and powerful men, Felix had enemies. The rumors flew fast as wildfire around Hong Kong. Was it an accident? Felix had been noticeably uncertain on his feet recently. Had he been pushed? Was it murder?

Whatever the case, Felix Marten had found the final bronze silence. He slept at last. And he definitely would not be attending the family reunion.

14 JAKE WAS ALREADY IN Shanghai when he heard of Felix's death on television. He was in a spacious, air-conditioned high-floored room at the Grand Hyatt Hotel, the tallest building in the city and the second tallest in all Asia. He had been sipping green tea brought immediately on his arrival by a diminutive floor waiter in a white Mao jacket.

Jake had been looking forward to a night's sleep. It seemed a long time since his feet had touched ground for more than a few hours, and he was in dire need of a massage to take the crimps of air travel out of his spine, then a shower and a night's sleep in a real bed for a change. Of course Felix's shocking death changed all that.

Jake immediately got on the phone to his contacts in Hong Kong and found out what he could, frowning when they said it was suicide. An autopsy would reveal more of the truth. Meanwhile, he had not yet told Rafaella he'd spoken to Felix. Now he had to call and tell her he was dead.

He dropped into a deep leather chair, his chin sunk onto his chest. Felix had seemed an angry man, a tired man, a vengeful man, but he had certainly not seemed suicidal. Of course, that didn't mean he hadn't killed himself. Jake had known many men who, on the surface, appeared day-to-day normal and who underneath suffered from an overwhelming depression. He wondered about Felix. He wondered exactly where Alain was. He wondered about the woman named Bao Chu Ching, who lived right here in Shanghai at number 27 Hu Tong Road, Apartment 127, and who'd been receiving thirty dollars a month from Felix Marten for ten years, a sum that had just been increased to fifty.

He glanced at his watch. It was ten in the morning in France. He sighed as he dialed the château, hating his role as the bringer of such terrible news.

Haigh answered, sounding irritable at being disturbed. "I was just about to take Rafaella into town to do some shopping," he told Jake. "She says she needs new shoes, though lord knows she has enough to stock a shop already."

"It's a woman thing," Jake said, smiling despite himself. And then he told Haigh the bad news. He heard him gasp, then a long silence. He knew Haigh had helped raise Felix, so this was a terrible shock to him, too. "I'm sorry, Haigh," he said. "Are you all right?"

A sigh gusted down the phone. "Yes, I'm all right. It's a good thing I'm here though to tell Rafaella. She won't take this easily. She had such hopes that Felix would come home again. And now he will, only it'll be in his coffin."

"You want me to tell her?" Jake asked.

"No, it's my place to do so," Haigh said, sounding solemn and dignified at the same time. "It's better not on the phone, you know, better if I'm there to help her."

Jake promised to call later, then he put down the phone and sprawled in the chair, staring blankly at the wall. He thought again about the woman, Bao Chu Ching, who had received Felix's money every month, wondering if she was a clue to something in his past, something that had caused

Felix to kill himself. Or perhaps caused somebody else to kill him.

Forgoing the lure of the soothing massage, the relaxing hot green tea, and the soft bed, he took a long cool shower, put on fresh clothes, and got a taxi to Hu Tong Road.

15   JAKE PAID OFF the cab and looked around. He was in one of the poorest parts of the city, certainly not a place frequented by tourists and travelers. The lowest of workers lived in these tumbling cinder-block apartments propped up with bamboo scaffolding and linked by drooping strings of wires. The bluish light of TV screens flickered in the darkness, and the odor of sewage and decay seeped from the gutters. Here and there small, open-fronted stores filled empty niches, and the arc lights of a motorway circled the area in blinding yellow halogen, silhouetting the jagged buildings and sending the inhabitants scuttling into the shadows. Over all filtered the sounds of poverty: the snarl of a dog, the wail of a child, the angry shout of a woman, and the impenetrable high whine of Chinese music.

He checked the address again. Apartment 127 was on the ground floor, to the left of the entrance to the four-story building. As he watched, the door to the apartment was pulled open and a child stepped out. She was about ten years old, small and thin and wearing what appeared to be a school uniform, a gray skirt and a short-sleeved white shirt. Her black hair was cut in a short fringed bob that emphasized the skinniness of her neck. She didn't even notice him, just sped by him on sneakered feet, folded money clutched in her hand.

Jake followed her to one of the storefront businesses, a Chinese medicine shop, and saw her speak to the owner. The man took her money, unlocked a safe, took out a small packet, and gave it to her. She sped back, and this time she glanced up at Jake as she passed. He caught the look of surprise on her face at the sight of a non-Chinese in these parts. Then she was gone, back down the shadowy street, back through that malodorous doorway, into the poor home that Felix Marten had paid for.

Jake had seen her face clearly under the light over the medicine shop door, though. Sweet, startled, and wide-eyed. Wide blue eyes, the blue of the Mediterranean on a sunny summer day. They were Rafaella Marten's eyes. He smiled. There was some good news for Rafaella after all. She had a grandchild.

The question was, Was she Felix's? Or Alain's?

16 RAFAELLA STOOD AT THE door of Felix's old room over the front portico, staring at the polished brass knob, unable to bring herself to turn it and open the door. The tears seemed stuck behind her eyes. She could not cry and she wondered, the way mothers always do, where she had gone wrong.

This room contained Felix's entire life up until the time he'd left the château at the age of twenty-three. His clothes were still hanging in the closet with his shoes arranged in rows beneath. He was always a neat boy and he'd grown into a fanatically neat man. His room had a military spareness about it that, when he was seventeen, had prompted Rafaella to suggest the army as a career for him.

"Don't be ridiculous, Mother," he'd said, with that contemptuous little line about his lips that had always worried her. "Of course I'm not going in the army. I'm going to run the winery."

And Felix would have run it well, Rafaella thought now, leaning tiredly against his door. Of course he would have alienated everybody, that was the way Felix was, but he would have produced good Marten wine efficiently enough.

Finally, she gathered her courage and opened the door. Haigh had been there before her. He'd taken off the dust-covers, made sure the room was thoroughly cleaned, laid out a suit of clothes on the bed ready to dress Felix for the last time. She looked at the formal morning suit, the gray jacket and striped pants, the immaculate white shirt and gray silk cravat. Even the correct socks and shoes awaited Felix's final dress engagement, and her heart brimmed with grief for the son she had lost so many years ago.

"But why would he kill himself?" she asked Haigh, "Felix was always so strong."

"Too strong for his own good," Haigh answered grimly.

Looking now at the remnants of Felix's life, Rafaella wondered how her chubby, sailor-suited boy had come to this sad end. This son who had deserted her, who'd accused her of believing he'd killed the girl, when all she asked from him was the truth. "I'm your mother," she'd said. "I'll help you. Just tell me it was an accident. I know that's all it could have been." But in her heart she had not believed his story, and somehow Felix had known that.

She sank into the big green leather chair by the window. The sun illuminated every line on her weary face and finally the tears came, racing down her powdered cheeks, leaving little tracks, extra new lines, but of grief this time. Outside the door the dogs whined miserably.

Rafaella was remembering when she gave Felix this room. He was just seven years old. "Let's go take a look at your new room," she'd said, and he'd stared at her surprised. Holding his hand, she'd walked, barefoot as always, along the broad chestnut-floored hallway, past the pairs of exquisitely painted double doors leading to various rooms, past the great sweep of the staircase with its polished banisters and gleaming brass stair rods, around the corner to this big room immediately over the front portico.

"Here?" Felix asked, amazed, because this was the finest guest room in the house.

"You're my eldest son," she explained, smiling. "It's only right that you have the best room."

"My desk will go under the window," he'd decided, marching around the room, lifting the beautiful curtain fabrics, testing the bed with his hand, stamping his feet on the Beauvais carpet, hating its softness. "And my green leather chair."

"And which green leather chair is that?"

"The one in Papa's study," he said sharply. "After all, he never uses it. He's never here."

"Right," Rafaella agreed meekly, because it was the truth.

And, just the way he was to be for the rest of his life, Felix took charge, changing the room from a beautiful boudoir to the spartan masculine space where he allowed no one entry except the housekeeper and then only because he wanted his place to be spotless.

Of course Felix never allowed his brother into his room. He kept his door locked, with the key on a chain attached to his belt. But anything "forbidden" was fair game to Alain. He'd found the housekeeper's key and one afternoon when Felix was safely on the tennis court, he'd sneaked in.

The inevitable happened and Felix had found him "going through my stuff," he shouted, outraged and Alain, the little blond angel, had stared him down, daring him to do anything about it. So Felix hit him, sending blood spurting from his nose and down his shirt-front. But no tears had spurted from Alain's eyes. Instead he punched back. In no time they were rolling on the floor, yelling at each other, and then the grownups came running, screaming at the sight of all that blood.

Haigh had separated them by means of a good kick on the rump for each one. They'd rolled off each other, glaring up at the new enemy. "*Je vous emmerde,* Haigh," Alain had cursed, and Haigh had given him a whack and set him on his feet, thrusting a towel into his face. "Go to your room," he said, while Rafaella ran to Felix's side, not knowing how injured he was.

"I don't have to obey you," Alain yelled.

But Haigh stood his ground. "Oh, and what are you going to do about it?" he'd demanded, hands on his hips.

With a sidelong glare at his mother, Alain had slunk through the door and along the hall, back up the stairs to the nursery.

Haigh had inspected Felix, still lying on his back covered in blood. After making sure the blood was Alain's he said, "Get up, Felix, and clean yourself up." Turning to Rafaella, he said, "Alain's nose is probably broken. I'll drive him to the hospital, Madame, while you take care of Felix."

Now, sitting in Felix's green leather chair under the window in the room that had been his, Rafaella thought how alike her two sons had looked, even though Alain was blond and Felix so dark. Both had her blue eyes and both had the slightly hooked nose that she swore came from their father's family and not hers. Yet they were completely different in temperament, as was proven to her later, the day after the murder.

17

AFTER HE'D FINISHED his studies at the Sorbonne, Felix had come home ready to learn from his mother how to run the winery. Rafaella thought he'd changed, and it was definitely a change for the better. He was gentler, easier to talk to, sympathetic. It was all too good to last, she thought nervously, and of course she was right.

One evening a few weeks later, a rare summer storm spattered hail against the windows where they sat having dinner together, safe in the small dining room with its decorative celadon-green paneling. The bunch of yellow lilies Rafaella had picked that morning dropped amber pollen onto the polished table, and a couple of creamy candles flickered in the dusk.

They were eating Haigh's special fresh tomato-basil soup, one of Rafaella's favorites, and its warmth was comforting on the cool night. With it they were drinking a vintage Château Marten that she thought too heavy and too dry, but Felix said confidently it was still round on the palate and the dryness was perfect with the soup.

Though they disagreed on the bottle of wine, they saw eye to eye on the winery. Rafaella's passion for it was matched by Felix's. He was like her father that way.

"I have a surprise," Felix said. "I have plans to expand our local winery." Then he told her he wanted to buy a small vineyard that had come unexpectedly onto the market in the Saint-Emilion area, near Bordeaux.

"It's not a first growth," he said, "but there's room for improvement. It's been neglected and the name has downgraded, but with my expertise and energy we'll have it back on its feet in no time."

Rafaella knew only too well that investing in a vineyard cost a great deal of money—and that it took years to establish. "And exactly how long is 'no time.'" she asked.

Felix considered. "There'll be a lot of grafting to be done, new rootstock . . . four, five years maybe."

"More like ten," she said.

Just then Haigh arrived with a steaming platter of risotto. Rafaella handed him her glass of wine to taste. Haigh sniffed it, then took a sip, allowing the wine to roll around his palette, savoring it slowly.

"Too dry for my taste," he declared, "a little harsh, and certainly all wrong with this meal." He shrugged. "Of course there are those who prefer their wines this crisp. Personally, I prefer a little more fruit."

"Right on the mark, Haigh," Rafaella said, smiling sympathetically at Felix because she knew he still had a lot to learn. Felix scowled because he hated to be proven wrong about anything.

"Why do you have to make everything a challenge?" he said, back to his cold voice again.

"A challenge, Felix? We are talking business. *Your* business."

"The *family* business," he retorted, and the familiar frown creased his brow.

Rafaella sighed. "This is really about Alain, isn't it?" she said, reaching across the table for his hand. "No, don't move away from me, Felix. It's right for a mother to hold her son's hand when he's troubled. You and Alain are so different—it's not surprising you don't get along. But no matter what, *you* will be the one in charge of the Marten winery. It will be yours to run, Felix."

He raised bitter eyes to hers. "But not alone, *maman*. Never alone. Alain will always be there. He'll be half owner after you're gone and he'll make my life hell. He'll wreck everything you and great-grandfather and grandfather worked for, and he'll do it just for the hell of it and to get even with me."

Rafaella sighed. She hated the discord between the brothers, but she couldn't simply give Felix the winery and leave Alain out—that was the law of the land.

"You are both my sons," she said. "We are a *family*, and you will have equal shares. Besides, you are men now, not schoolboys. It'll be up to you to work things out."

Felix pushed back his plate and stood up. He took his wineglass and drained it, just to show her that the wine was good after all, Rafaella thought with a small sigh at how competitive he was, even with her.

"Of course, you always take Alain's side," he said as he strode angrily from the room. "You always have."

The front door slammed hard enough to rattle the windows. She heard the car start up, then in a swish of wet gravel, Felix was gone.

Rafaella heaved a bigger sigh this time. So much for their new relationship, she thought, getting up from the table and leaving her food untouched. She went to stand by the window, looking out at the tossing trees and the rose petals drifting in the wind along the terrace. A lawn chair caught in a gust rolled across the grass, and gray clouds scudded in a lowering sky. She wondered where Felix had gone. To the winery, she supposed. He worked there most nights. And Alain was hardly ever home—he was either in Paris, where he was supposed to be studying, or at the villa in Cap d'Antibes with some girl or other. Or several. She never knew with Alain, but just thinking about him made her smile. Alain brought a kind of *joie de vivre* with him that always made her laugh. Poor Felix, she thought sadly, will you never learn that it's yourself you are battling, not your brother?

She did not hear Felix come home that night, though she sat up late, reading in bed, waiting for him. And he was not at breakfast the next morning. She supposed he was in his room and didn't want to disturb him, so it came as a shock when he arrived home an hour later, wet and disheveled and limping badly.

"What is it? What happened?" She ran to him, fearing a car accident, but he waved her away. "It's nothing," he muttered as he limped up the stairs to his room. Worried, Rafaella ran after him, but he shut the door in her face and she heard the key turn in the lock.

Haigh ran up the stairs and stood next to her. "Better leave him alone, Madame," he said. "Whatever it is, he'll get over it."

But Felix did not get over it nor did Rafaella because later that day the *gendarmes* arrived to question him about a young woman they claimed he knew. She had been found dead at the bottom of the Saint-Sylvestre gorge, a place popular with tourists, where the walking path circled the highest point and where they always took their pictures. The dead woman was pregnant, but Felix denied he'd been with her. There were no witnesses and no evidence against him. Alain knew the girl, too, but he was in Antibes so there was no need to question him.

Rafaella knew something was wrong, though, and when the police had finally gone, she questioned Felix about what had happened. He accused her of believing he'd got the girl pregnant then killed her. He said she should give his charming brother a closer look, ask him a few questions. When she attempted to put her arms around him, he flung her away. "Believe whatever you want, *maman,*" he snarled. "You always will."

And then he'd packed his bag and left, never to return.

RAFAELLA MOPPED HER TEARS on the hem of her skirt, thinking she was like a child herself, never with a handkerchief when she needed it. *Ah, Felix,* she thought, *you were a hard, prickly little boy who grew into a difficult young man. You had a surface that was hard for love to penetrate. I only hope you eventually found some happiness in your life.*

She walked across to the bed and ran her hand over the suit Haigh had laid out in readiness for Felix's burial. "My poor, poor little Felix," she said softly, then left the room, closing the door gently behind her.

18 JAKE CAME "HOME" for Felix's funeral, but he also came to tell Rafaella the wonderful news that she had a granddaughter.

He stopped the rental car in the shade of the plane trees in the village square and got out to take a look. Nothing had changed, not even, he'd bet, the old boys and the dogs. Even the air had that same winey aroma. Life went on serenely in Marten-de-Provence, light-years away from his own busy and sometimes brutal existence.

He drove on, following the lichen-covered wall until he came to the great iron gates, and then his past life unfurled before his eyes in a sudden onslaught of memories. Jake thought of himself as a hard man who now gave his love to no place and no one, but *this* place was his soft underbelly. The year he'd spent here had been so perfect he had never been back, afraid to disturb those memories.

He drove on and as the château came into view, he stopped to look. How could he have forgotten that the house was the ochre yellow of evening sunlight? That the many tall windows led out onto the terrace? That the roof slanted steeply over the gabled attics and that in summer the big doors always stood open to let in the breeze and to welcome visitors? It all came back to him in a rush and he sat for a moment, taking it in. It was, Jake thought with a smile, a perfect picture of life as he knew it when he was young and a little in love. And one to which despite the tragedy of Felix's death, he felt sure he was now about to write a new chapter.

He strode up the low stone steps to those open doors and walked right inside, as though he were coming home. And there she was. Rafaella.

The dogs heard him first. They dashed at him, barking madly, leaping at his outstretched hands. Rafaella swung round to see what all the commotion was. She clutched a hand to her throat, shocked because looking at Jake was like looking into the face of the Lover. And like him, Jake Bronson filled the château with his strong, masculine presence, bringing life and vigor to the long-silent rooms.

Watching Rafaella, Jake noted the changes in the beautiful face that he remembered like a photograph kept in the breast pocket of his jacket, close to his heart. He saw the silver hair that was once a luxurious dark tumble, the passionate mouth now crisscrossed with fine lines, the slender fingers now crooked with arthritis. Only her eyes were unchanged, still that same brilliant Mediterranean blue. And then they were in each other's arms, holding each other close, and for the moment, time disappeared. Tenderness overwhelmed Jake as he bent to kiss Rafaella's soft cheek and smelled her familiar perfume—mimosa, wasn't it?

"You came," she said, smiling.

"I promised I would always be there for you." He smiled. "You're still as beautiful as my father would have remembered, Rafaella," and she smiled back, acknowledging his gallant lie.

Haigh came fluttering toward them, a white apron was

tied around his middle and he was wiping his hands on a cloth. "Sorry, Madame," he said, flustered. "I was in the pantry cleaning the silver. I didn't hear the bell."

"That's because I didn't ring it," Jake said, grinning and holding out his hand. "Remember me, Haigh?"

Haigh's thin, sun-brown face lit up in a huge smile. "Indeed I do, Mr. Jake, though you were nothing but a young whippersnapper when I last saw you. If you'll excuse me being so personal, sir, you are the spitting image of your father. Isn't that so, Madame?" He threw Rafaella a sharp glance, assessing her reaction to the Lover's son.

"I scarcely noticed the resemblance," she said, biting her lower lip to stop from smiling. She had a long-running one-upmanship game with Haigh that had started when they were both young. He still had that know-it-all attitude and it still irritated her, but she adored him. In fact, she wouldn't know what to do without him.

"Your old room is ready," she said to Jake, "but first come sit with me on the terrace. We'll have some champagne to celebrate our meeting again after all these years—twenty-eight, isn't it?" She laughed. "Of course I know exactly how long it is. I've been counting." She took his arm, and with the dogs running ahead, led him out, past the sparkling fountain to the shaddy loggia under the Chinese wisteria.

Haigh watched them walk arm in arm along the sun-freckled terrace, then he went to fetch a bottle of the '91 Krug from the wine cellar. He noted there were only half a dozen left but thought the way things were now, this would probably see them out. He put the bottle on ice, polished a couple of fragile crystal champagne flutes, and placed them carefully on a silver tray. He toasted slices of brioche and slid them in the silver toast rack, alongside a dish of *crème fraîche* and an iced crystal bowl of the Beluga caviar he'd been hoarding for the special occasion that had finally come. Then he filled a silver basket with "rose" biscuits, those sweet, crisp, sugary pink ladyfingers that were a specialty with champagne.

Pleased to be back in the role of butler, even if only temporarily, he untied his apron, put on his white jacket, straightened his silver-gray tie, and adjusted his accent from pure Cockney to upper-crust English. Haigh also spoke perfect French, something he used to do with foreign guests just to enjoy the look of bewilderment on their faces as they struggled to understand. Haigh was a little bit wicked that way. Power, he thought smugly, was a wonderful thing.

He wheeled the tea cart onto the terrace. "Madame, the refreshments," he said at his most formal.

19 RAFAELLA KNEW HAIGH was enjoying himself by the superior tone of his voice. She watched as he pulled the champagne cork with barely a sound and poured two glasses. He also set a tray with a silver teapot on the table in front of her.

"Just in case you or Mr. Jake fancy a little Earl Grey, Madame," he said. Positioning the trolley with its exquisitely arranged delicacies next to them, he made a polite little bow and left them to their conversation.

Even though he was dying to hear what went on, Haigh did not lurk behind the wisteria to eavesdrop because he was certain to hear it all from Rafaella herself later. Instead, he went back to his kitchen and poured himself a glass of the Scotch whiskey that bore his name, although with a slightly different spelling, and to which clan he sometimes, in moments of grandeur, claimed to be related. Then he settled down with the daily newspaper to wait.

"To our meeting again after all these years," Rafaella said, lifting her glass.

"Champagne like this is a small miracle," Jake said, tasting it.

"I can't think of anyone I would rather share it with." She rearranged her wide-brimmed straw hat so it shaded her eyes properly from the sun and also softened the lines on her face, because after all, she was still vain about her looks. "So, Jake, first tell me about *you*. Is there someone new in your life? Are you married again? Children?"

Franny came instantly into Jake's mind, blond, innocent, smiling at him with those blue-jeweled eyes. It was the only time he had not thought of Amanda first, and he was shocked by the power of his feeling for Franny. Still, he shrugged. "No one special," he said, "and certainly no children. And anyhow, you know I'm still in love with you, Rafaella." And she laughed with him, enjoying the joke.

"You'll find her, one day," she promised.

Looking around him, Jake heaved a sigh of pure pleasure. "To a boy who never had a real home life," he said, "you

Martens were my ideal family. You had everything, and for a while you let me be a part of it. It was the happiest year of my life and I've never forgotten it."

"Ah, yes, we Martens with our château in Provence and our famed vineyards, our apartment in Paris and the villa on the Côte d'Azur. But we were also a family with a history of too much pride, and you know that old saying, Jake? 'Pride goes before a fall'?" She heaved a deep sigh. "Sometimes I wish I'd never heard of the word *pride*. In fact, that's why I finally buried my own and decided to ask my sons to this family reunion. Not that there's much 'family' left, especially now with Felix gone. Poor, poor Felix, I think he broke his own heart as well as mine." Her voice trembled but she was determined not to cry in front of Jake.

Then Jake said, "There's good news too, Rafaella." She glanced at him, brows raised. "You have a granddaughter," he said, smiling.

She looked at him, stunned. "It can't be true!" she said, but looking into Jake's smiling face she knew that it was. The despair over Felix that was like a stone in her chest lifted a little and she smiled.

It was that same joyous smile Jake remembered from the old days. It lit up her face and suddenly she was ageless, beautiful again. "A granddaughter!" she exclaimed. "But where is she? Whose child is she? Tell me all about her." She was already making plans. "She must come here to live of course, so I can spoil her and teach her how to run the winery." Still smiling, she looked expectantly at Jake.

"She is Chinese and her name is Shao Lan," Jake said. "It

means Little Blue—and she was named that because she has your blue eyes. There's no mistaking she's a Marten. She's ten years old and she lives with her ailing grandmother, in very poor circumstances, in Shanghai. The only thing we don't know about her is which of your sons is the father. Felix was helping out minimally, but he certainly wasn't keeping her in luxury, and definitely not the way you'd expect a man to look after his daughter. And Alain, of course, did nothing."

Rafaella nodded. She understood her sons. "Felix was always a snob," she said. "He'd rather miss out on the joy of bringing up his own child because he was too ashamed to admit he had a relationship with some poor Chinese woman. Ah, Felix, just look what you missed." She smiled at Jake again. "But now I reap the benefit. I have a granddaughter to welcome home to the château."

Haigh was back again, hovering behind the wisteria arbor. He'd heard Jake tell Rafaella about the new granddaughter and he heaved a big sigh of relief, thanking god for giving his friend a break because, with Felix's death and Alain missing, it had looked like Rafaella's family reunion was going to be a disaster.

He cleared his throat as he approached, letting them know he was there. "More champagne, Madame, Sir?" He took the Krug from the ice bucket and wrapped it in the white linen cloth, then he refilled the tall glasses and presented them to his employer and her guest.

"Pour yourself a glass, too," Rafaella said, smiling. "This is a celebration, Haigh. We have a new granddaughter!" Then Rafaella said she would send her an invitation welcoming her to the château right away.

After that she looked Jake in the eye and said, "So now, Jake, tell me the bad news."

Puzzled, he said, "But how did you know there's bad news, too?"

She smiled. "I know you too well, Jake Bronson. In some ways you're exactly like your father. So now, tell me, what is it?"

"I don't believe Felix committed suicide," he said. "I think he was killed."

Rafaella gasped. "Are you telling me that Felix was *murdered*?"

"That's the way it looks right now. Only time and good detective work will prove me right or wrong."

"But what about Alain?" she said, subconsciously linking the thought of murder to her other son, something Jake spotted immediately, though he said nothing.

"Felix lied to me about Alain. Of course he'd kept track of him all these years. My contacts followed Alain's trail of self-destruction through Vietnam and Cambodia, but he's disappeared from the face of the earth. We may never find him, never know what really happened."

"But . . ." Rafaella began.

He knew she was going to ask how he knew Felix was murdered, and he put up a warning hand.

"Better not ask," he said. "Just let sleeping dogs lie." Yet even as he said it, he knew that he would not. He would not rest until he found Alain and discovered the truth about Felix's death.

20 WHEN SHAO LAN'S INVITATION arrived by special delivery, at first she refused to open the door, afraid it was the landlord about to throw them out again. The "apartment" was only a single small room that Shao Lan had divided with a screen made from bamboo poles strung with red cloth. It gave a false air of gaiety to the place, which pleased her, but now she ignored the knocking and hurried into the sleeping part of the room with her sick grandmother's supper—a bowl of chicken broth and a rice cake and some hot tea in a small, blue-patterned egg-shaped cup. She stood the tray on the rickety table next to the bed and said in Shanghainese, "Look, Grandmother, here is your supper and your pills."

Shao Lan spoke Shanghainese because that was her grandmother's only language. But Shao Lan also spoke Mandarin and Cantonese, as well as some English, which she had learned in school. She could also curse fluently in all of these languages, as could every child in the poor neighborhood where she lived.

Bao Chu wafted away the soup with a limp hand. Struggling upright she took the packet of pills, swallowed two and washed them down with the tea. Then she lay back again, eyes closed, her breath rasping harshly.

Poverty hung around the Ching household like a cold shroud of despair. The meager room was as clean as Shao Lan could keep it while also attending school, trying to keep up her grades, and looking after her sick grandmother.

That same despair had carved a stamp of seriousness on ten-year-old Shao Lan's heart-shaped face. Her large, round blue eyes, with just the slightest tilt at the corners to say she was Chinese, were solemn and she never smiled. There was nothing to smile about—she just took care of things.

All she knew was the daily juggle with money. Shao Lan never got new clothes, only second- or third-hand school uniforms from charitable societies who also chipped in with a present at Chinese New Year. The present was never what she'd dreamed about though, so she had given up dreaming and just got on with the harsh business of living, relieved when every month the letter arrived from the Bank of Shanghai containing the few dollars that paid their rent and their small expenses. Because of her grandmother's illness their expenses were soaring, terrifying Shao Lan, who wondered where they would ever get the money to keep her grandmother alive.

She often thought of the unknown man who was her father, wondering if he knew about her, and if so why he had never come to see her. Her mother had died when she was born, and the only family she had known was her grandmother, who had named her Shao Lan, or Little Blue, because of her startlingly blue eyes, rare in a world of brown-eyed people. Bao Chu's own name meant Precious Pearl. This was so far from the truth, because she had no monetary value whatsoever in this world, that even Bao Chu herself laughed at it.

The knocking at the door had stopped. Shao Lan lingered

by the bed, wanting to ask Bao Chu about her father, but she was afraid of the harangue that came whenever she tried to bring up the subject: She had no daddy. There never was one and never would be one, and she had just better get used to it. Sometimes Shao Lan wondered if it were true and that, like the Madonna, her mother had a virgin birth and she was some kind of freak.

She sighed as her grandmother started to cough. She coughed for what seemed to Shao Lan like a long time as she hovered over her with the tea. *Oh god, please don't let her die,* she prayed. *Don't let her leave me all alone.*

Visions of herself in an orphanage with bars on the windows, a place where it was always cold and there was even less food than here, flitted through her mind. She shivered, facing the truth. More likely she would end up on the streets, sleeping in a cardboard box and begging for a living, along with the other homeless. It was that or doing bad things with men.

When the knocking started again she went to peek through the door crack and saw a man holding an envelope. She flattened herself against the wall but he rapped even harder. "Hey," he shouted, because he knew she was there and knew the fears of the poor, "this is no summons to court. The landlord isn't after you for the rent. It's a letter from France, that's all."

Shao Lan hardly dared breathe in case he heard her. They didn't know anybody in France and she hoped he'd just go away. Too curious to let it go though, she finally opened the door a cautious crack. The messenger thrust the envelope through the gap. "Sign here," he said. Terrified, she cursed at him and flung the envelope back at him and made to shut the door in his face again.

He cursed back in rapid Shanghaiese, telling her she was a foolish child and all he was asking her to do was to sign this paper saying he had delivered it and she had received it. Still reluctant, Shao Lan opened the door again and signed the paper. She hoped she had done the right thing.

The letter was addressed to Bao Chu, and she took it into her. "Look, Grandmother," she said. "Here's a letter for you," but Bao Chu wafted her away with a limp hand.

"It's from France," Shao Lan said, and Bao Chu lifted her head, suddenly alert.

She struggled upright against the sweaty pillow, pushing her black hair from her hot face. "Open it," she said. Shao Lan did. "Read it to me," Bao Chu commanded. Shao Lin did.

"Oh, Grandmother," she cried, her face alive with a big smile. "Imagine, we are invited to go to France for a *family reunion*. You never told me we had a *family*."

"And I never would have, if it were not for this letter," Bao Chu said, leaning back against her pillows because she knew this invitation was the only hope for her granddaughter and it meant that she would lose her. "You will go to France, Shao Lan," she said. "And you will go alone," she added firmly.

She might as well have been sending her to the moon. Shao Lan's jaw dropped. "Alone," she whispered, afraid, because her own little section of Shanghai was the only world she knew. "But why?"

"It's time for you to meet your father." Bao Chu began to cough again. And Shao Lan knew her grandmother was too ill even to leave the house, and she cried because she was afraid to go to this strange country alone. She also knew that if she went, she might never see her grandmother again.

PART II

The Preparations

Life is a maze in which we take
the wrong turning before we have
learned to walk.

—CYRIL CONNOLLY

21 CLARE HAD RETURNED from Atlanta, where she'd gone to pick up more of her possessions, and now she had taken up residence in Shutters Hotel, on the beach in Santa Monica. The two had spent all their time together after they'd met, and Franny thought there was nothing she didn't know about her new friend. In fact, she'd never had a woman friend she felt so close to.

She and Clare were attempting to establish some order from the current chaos in Clare's room. Looking at the clothes overflowing from the closet onto the bed, the chairs and even the floor, Franny said, "You're going to need a huge apartment for all this stuff."

Clare stopped arranging a couple of dozen pairs of shoes around the perimeter of the room and, hands on hips, surveyed the scene. "I should open a shop," she said with a grin, "except I'm nothing without my clothes—just another woman on the downside of a divorce."

Franny looked at her.

"Oh, let's just leave it." Clare shrugged, dismissing all her worldly possessions with a grin. "Come on, hon, I'll buy you some lunch."

In Shutters beachside café, they were surrounded by cool L.A. women with the latest L.A. look. "Check them out," Clare said, eyeing Franny through squinted lids, mentally making her over. "You too could look like that."

Franny laughed and sipped iced lemonade through a bendy straw. "I'm not like them and I could never look like them," she said.

"That's exactly your trouble." Clare tackled her chicken Caesar salad with her usual hearty appetite. "You don't look like the woman you are *now*. You still look like the girl you were ten years ago."

"The Oregon girl, that's me," Franny agreed comfortably. "Come on, Clare, give it up, why don't you. You'll never make an L.A. woman out of this vet." She pointed a finger at her chest. "*This* is reality."

"Honey, you are a *grown-up* now, you're *a woman*. You just don't know it."

"You bet I do! I've had to be grown-up since I was seventeen. In fact a therapist would probably tell me I'm just longing to stay the little girl I used to be before my father died."

"Well, you can't go to a château looking like this," Clare said. "At least the Heidi pigtail has to go."

Franny clutched a protective hand to her blond braid. "I've had this hair for years and I'm not going anywhere without it."

Leaning over the table, Clare swept the braid up on top of her head. "*Now* you look like the woman you really are," she said, but Franny shook her head so her hair tumbled free onto her shoulders.

"Even if you changed me, I'd still be the same under-neath. I'd still be the tomboy in the hiking boots and the cut-offs and the T-shirt, I'd still be the vet in the white coat, and the woman in the flip-flops and the dangly earrings from the drugstore." She sighed. "No dress, no haircut can ever change who I am at heart."

Clare sighed too, mentally canceling the proposed shop-ping trip to Fred Segal, where she just knew that with the wave of her magic wand and a fairly large amount of money she could have turned Franny into a new woman.

"Besides," Franny said, "I don't want to give the family the wrong impression. This is who I am, this is who they get." She tethered her braid using an elastic band with a plas-tic flower on it. "See, I'll never be a sex kitten," she said, laughing.

Clare sipped her mango tea. "Hmm, *sex kitten*. Is that what you were for Marcus?"

"Clare!" Franny was shocked. Marcus was a taboo sub-ject.

"Of course you know he could get quite kinky," Clare said mischievously. "Marcus liked to try whatever was going."

"And you went along with that?" Franny was saucer-eyed with curiosity. Her sexual experiences with Marcus had been okay, but never anything out of the ordinary.

"We tried everything," Clare admitted, "including three-somes." She laughed at Franny's shocked expression, lifting an elegant bare shoulder in a little shrug. "Marcus liked it. I tried to think of it as a porn movie. You know, the kind where they always seem to be having a much better time than you ever do when you have sex." She shrugged again, slurping up the last of the iced tea. "Huh! It turned out to be just 'movie dust'—all sparkle and no content. For me anyhow." Franny still looked uncertain. Clare grinned and said, "Fact is, Franny, I like a man in my bed, not a woman."

"Oh thank God," Franny said, letting out a breath of relief, and they dissolved into gales of laughter.

Clare signaled the waiter for the check. "Trouble with men is, after a few weeks of putting up with them and their foibles I tend to say what I really feel—and bang! There goes another relationship."

"I know exactly what you mean." Franny eyed her new friend doubtfully, then said, "Oh, Clare, I did it again!"

Clare didn't have to ask what Franny had done again. She could tell by the guilty look on her face. She sighed, wondering when Franny would ever learn. But then God only knew it had taken *her* long enough. "He's married," she said.

"He was. He said she died."

"Huh, that's a new one!"

"Oh no, I believe him."

"Why?" Clare was at her firmest.

"Well," Franny hesitated, remembering Jake as he'd told her about it. Exactly how did she know? "It's like with the dogs," she said finally. "Somehow you can just tell when they're basically good."

"So if he's good, why haven't I heard about him before? And where did you meet him? And what happened to him anyhow?"

"He came into the clinic. He called later, asked me to dinner. I went. He came back home with me and I asked him in for tea. He tripped on the loose plank and sprained his ankle."

Clare groaned. "You've got to get that fixed or someone'll

be suing you for something." Alarmed, she said, "He isn't, is he? Suing you?"

"Nope. Well, not so far anyway. The thing is, Clare, well . . ." Franny broke off, blushing.

"You slept with him on a first date?"

Franny nodded.

"And is that what happened with Marcus?"

She nodded again and Clare sighed.

"Bad habit, girl. You've got to stop." She held up her hand as Franny started to speak. "No, don't tell me. . . . He never called, you've never seen him again. Hey, honey, what d'you expect? A lifelong love affair after a dinner and a little nookie? Come on, Franny, you're just asking for heartache."

"He sent flowers," Franny said defensively.

"Oh, big deal. 'Hey, thanks for keeping me warm in bed. . . . See you around.'" Seeing Franny's miserable face, Clare stopped her lecture. "Okay, so just promise me one thing. Next time you'll stop and think before you jump into bed with a stranger. Trust me, you'll be a happier woman. And if it makes you feel any better, I speak from personal experience. Besides," she added thoughtfully, "nobody wants to be considered a slut, now do they?"

"I'm no slut," Franny said indignantly.

"Then, honey, try not to give the wrong impression by behaving like one. I speak as a friend."

"I know you're right," Franny said humbly. "And I've got my pride back now. No more men unless I pick 'em, and no sex until I say so."

They looked at each other in silence. Franny's thoughts drifted to the trip to France and how much she would miss Clare.

"I'll miss you, y'know," Clare said, leaning across to pat Franny's hand. "I feel like we're comrades in arms, in battle against the enemy—Man!"

"Man!" Franny agreed, and that lonely feeling swept over her again, a feeling she couldn't bear. "Clare," she said hesitantly, "Would you . . . I mean, why not? . . . Well, why don't you come with me?"

"You mean to France? Well, for one thing, I'm not invited."

"I'll bet Aunt Rafaella would love to meet you," Franny said. "I can send her a fax, ask if it's okay."

"You'd do that? For me?" Clare was so touched there was a lump in her throat.

"Just say yes," Franny pleaded.

"I'm the fastest packer you ever saw," Clare said, and they laughed so loud people turned to look.

Suddenly the château in Provence gleamed like a good-luck token for both of them, and they talked and talked about their new plan until Franny said she had to go.

Clare watched her walk to the exit, in a hurry as always to get back to her animals. Her long, loping stride put a sexy swing in her hips of which she was totally unaware. Clare thought Franny was like a well-kept secret: there was a lovely woman under that pigtail.

She had to admire Franny's integrity, though. No Cinderella makeover for her. Franny believed in who she was, even though she still wasn't exactly certain who that might be, except as far as her vocation with animals was concerned. She certainly was not sure when it came to men. This uncertainty hadn't got her far with Marcus, but then,

Clare had not gotten far either, and she had put years of effort into it.

The waiter refilled her glass with mango tea and Clare stared moodily into space, thinking about her past and her indefinite future. She hadn't been exactly truthful with Franny, and it bothered her, but it was too late—or perhaps too soon—to do anything about it now.

D-I-V-O-R-C-E. The word spelled itself in her mind. Dolly Parton wrote that song. Now *there* was a woman who knew about men—Dolly knew what she was talking about all right. Clare thought you had to admire her spirit. Only a woman who knew exactly who she was could pull off that look.

Clare had turned thirty-five a few months ago. The realization that life was speeding by and there was a lot she was missing out on because she was still hooked on that unfaithful asshole Marcus had prompted her finally to leave him.

There were other lives to be lived, she'd decided, instead of the Marcus trap. At the time, marrying Marcus had seemed safe, and it had saved her from an increasingly hard life.

Clare sighed. She was just a dumb kid from a small Georgia town and all she'd ever wanted was what she'd advised Franny to look for: a salt-of-the-earth guy who'd always love her, a guy who'd be faithful, a guy who'd look after her.

And what, Clare wondered, would she give him in return? What had she to offer a man like that? A great wardrobe? A nice line in "I don't care about anything," when the truth was that at heart she was just another divorced woman licking her wounds.

She drank the last of her mango iced tea then paid the bill, leaving a big tip because she knew most waiters were marking time working for a living while waiting for real life to start, and besides, she believed in karma, small acts of goodness. What if I were to tell them there is no "real life"? she thought as she sauntered to the exit, waving thank-you. What if I said, "Look, girls, this is all there is, better make the most of it." She wondered if they'd believe her or just keep holding on to their dreams.

She pressed the elevator button and stepped in, alone. Alone in her room, she decided to pack for the trip to Provence. She did not like "alone." The very word sent shivers down her spine.

She thought about the château and the old woman who wanted to reunite her family. She wondered who she might meet there. Her spirits rose—she'd always loved adventure and this was something special, new faces, new places, new everything, and about as far from her past as she could get.

"It's the simple life for me," she sang, flinging clothes into an expensive suitcase.

Then she threw herself onto the bed, kicking her feet in the air. "Wow!" she yelled. "Oh, wow! This time next week, I'll be in *France*!"

ON HER WAY HOME, Franny thought about what Clare had said, and she stopped off at a small boutique, where she bought a pretty silk skirt, yellow with a pattern of tiny blue flowers, and some T-shirts. She also bought a couple of pairs of shorts and some turquoise-beaded thong sandals. She popped across the street to a shop called Only Hearts and picked up some cute underwear—just in case I get run over, she told herself with a grin. The purchases would cut into her small savings a bit, but Clare was right. She couldn't go to meet her aunt looking like the poor relation. And what the hell, she was going on the first real vacation of her life. Next week, she was flying to Paris!

22 RAFAELLA WAS WAITING AT THE Café des Colombes for Scott Harris to show up for their weekly business lunch, a pleasure she always looked forward to. He knew as much about wine as Rafaella did, if not more, since he'd been brought up in a famous wine-growing region of Australia. Ten years ago, when she had finally "retired," he'd come to run the Domaine Marten for her. And he'd done it most successfully.

In addition to his knowledge of wine, Scott was an attractive and amusing man, something to which she had always been partial, and besides he managed to make her feel young again.

She sat at her usual table by the French doors leading onto the vine-shaded terrace with the view of the church and the sandy *pétanque* court under the plane trees where, in the cool of the evening, the village men played highly competitive games. The dogs flopped, panting beside her, and the sun cast deep shadows under the arcade where Allier's greengrocery was already closed for lunch. The bronze bell in the monastery in Saint-Sylvestre tolled the hour. Life in the village of Marten-de-Provence was the way it had always been, slow and ponderously sweet.

Laurent Jarré threw a pink cloth over the table and brought a bottle of his own rosé, which he plunked on top, along with a fresh baguette and a saucer of new olive oil for dipping.

Laurent was the son of the original proprietor of the café. He was a big, flamboyant-looking man with olive skin, a full head of thick black hair, a bristling mustache, and eyes like shiny black olives. He always wore a collarless white shirt and black pants, with an immaculate white apron slung loosely around his hips.

"The gypsy," Rafaella called him, and he agreed there must certainly be Romany stock somewhere in his bloodline. With his fierce expression, he looked a man to be reckoned with, but Rafaella knew he was at heart a gentle man. Laurent's wife had died some years ago and he was without a lady in his life.

As she did every week, Rafaella asked him if he was seeing anyone from the village or the neighboring town who might make him a suitable wife.

"After all, you're still a young man," she told him sternly. "You need a woman in your life."

Jarré said there was nothing doing, nobody he fancied. "I might just have to take a trip to Paris and find myself a wife there," he said gloomily.

"But you've never been to Paris," she said astonished,

knowing that he'd never been farther than Marseille in his life and that not for many years. "How will you meet anyone? Whatever will you do with yourself all day?"

He looked back at her with mystified black-olive eyes. Such a problem had not occurred to him. "Then maybe I won't go," he said uncomfortably, and Rafaella said that perhaps it was better to stay put and keep trying his luck locally.

Jarré went off to get meat for the dogs. Hearing the *clip-clop* of hooves on the cobblestones, Rafaella turned to see Scott on his black mare, riding into the square. She watched admiringly as he dismounted with the practiced ease of a true horseman. Scott Harris was lean and fit, with sandy-red hair and hazel eyes, creased at the corners from too many years in the sun. In jeans and a soft blue chambray shirt he was, she thought appreciatively, very good to look at.

Scott tied the mare in the usual spot under the plane trees, within reach of the fountain and the water trough. He pulled a carrot from his pocket and gave it to the horse, who crunched it loudly, snorting her pleasure. Louis and Mimi dashed over to greet him, and he fished in his other pocket for the chew bones he knew they liked.

"G'day, how are ya, Monsieur Jarré," Scott said, shaking the patron's hand. Scott had only been in the village ten years and was not yet on the level where he could call Monsieur Jarré by his first name.

He bent to kiss Rafaella and said, "Mmm, you smell so good, like summer flowers."

"Mimosa. I've been wearing it for years. Besides, you say that every time." She patted the seat next to her. "Come, *mon cher ami*, sit here and have some wine."

Jarré poured Scott a glass of rosé, watching him intently as he sniffed the fruity bouquet, then tasted. The wine came from Jarré's own mini vineyard on the small hill down the road to the west of the village, and he was anxious for Scott's professional opinion.

"Monsieur Jarré, you make the best rosé around here," Scott said. And Jarré puffed out his cheeks in a pleased smile.

Rafaella had dressed for the lunch in a white linen skirt and a fitted jacket with wide lapels that dated from the 1970s. With it she wore strappy blue sandals that showed her red-painted toes, and a blue glass necklace she'd bought in Venice more years ago than she cared to remember. Her silver hair was pulled back from her face, and despite her years, she looked very beautiful.

"You're looking pretty darn gorgeous today, boss," Scott said with a grin.

"You're not so bad yourself," Rafaella replied, smiling. The truth was, there was no real need for their weekly meetings, she trusted Scott implicitly, but both of them went through the ritual pretense of keeping her informed on the business. He asked her opinion on the planting of new rootstock, on whether to try Chardonnay next year on the east hill, on why the grapes were so late to ripen (was it because of too much spring rain?) and she gave her expert opinion.

The vine arbor over the café's terrace filtered the sun's glare into a soft, pleasant glow as Jarré brought out a plate of tiny young asparagus for them to try. Then Rafaella ordered her usual mushroom omelette, while Scott ordered his usual *steak-frites*. Being Rafaella, though, as well as talking business, she had to ask Scott about his love life.

"You mean lack of it," Scott said with a grin.

"Now, a man like you," Rafaella said thoughtfully, picking up a thin stalk of asparagus and nibbling on it, "good-looking, intelligent, knowledgeable, a powerful man in the wine trade, now I would say a man like you, Scott, is a catch."

"Oh yeah, I'm just not catchable. I'm far too busy for any woman to tie down."

"But aren't you ever tempted by the thought of a pretty woman waiting for you in the evening? A companion? A lover? How about a proper home with a bunch of children swarming around your knees, calling 'Papa' when you walk through your front door at night? Dogs barking in greeting, music coming from the salon, wine being poured, the smell of something good cooking in the kitchen? Now, surely that must appeal?" She stared thoughtfully at him. "Unless you're gay, of course, and even if you are, then there are some very charming men around here. Surely you must have met some of them?"

Scott put down his glass. He leaned across the table, in her face. "Rafaella, I am not gay," he said sternly. "Nor am I in the market for a wife and certainly not kids. I'm a free man and that's the way I like it and that's the way I intend it to stay. Anyhow," he added as he speared a piece of steak, "I already have the dogs and the horses. That's enough for me."

Rafaella glanced at the black mare tethered under the plane trees in the square. As she watched, the horse took a great slurp from the water trough and shook its head violently, scattering drops on the sleeping village dogs, who lifted complaining heads before subsiding again. She knew Scott never drove his Jeep when he could ride a horse. "You and that horse are joined at the hip," she grumbled.

"More like the arse, I'd say," Scott agreed amiably. "Anyhow, are you all ready for the grand family reunion? The whole village is abuzz with it, and with the news that Jake Bronson will be back."

She sighed. "I suppose there's nothing this village doesn't know about me. And a lot of them knew Jake's father."

"The Lover." Scott helped himself to more *pommes frites* and filled Rafaella's glass.

Rafaella stole a *frite* from his plate. "I suppose I'll never live down that scandal."

"Why should you? Sounded like the perfect love affair to me."

"I'm glad to hear it from such an expert. Why don't you follow my example and have one of your own?" She smiled into his eyes.

"I'm not celibate, you know," Scott said mildly. "I'm just not the settling-down sort. It's kinda like the wild west, where I come from, and I'm still that wild west kinda guy."

"All the good ones are," Rafaella said, laughing. "But you promised you'd come to the reunion," she said, anxiously. "You *are* 'family,' Scott. You're the one who's always there for me, always helping, keeping me and the winery alive."

A grin sparked his hazel eyes. "Perhaps I should call you *maman* instead of Rafaella."

"Call me whatever you like, as long as it's not a fool."

"Never that," Scott said, suddenly serious. "And you know I wouldn't miss it."

When lunch was over, Haigh drove up in the small Peugeot. He rarely allowed himself to drive Rafaella's Bentley, which dated from 1962 and was reserved for very special occasions. He personally kept it polished to a lacquered gleam, and the last time they'd used it was for a reception at the winery two years ago.

"How're you, Haigh?" Scott said, getting to his feet and shaking hands with the butler, who looked quite different in a pink shirt and white linen pants, his summer, off-duty uniform. "I'll be on my way, Rafaella," Scott said, dropping a kiss on her soft cheek, leaving her with a sheaf of production notes to mull over and a smile on her face.

She watched him walk away with that nonchalant outdoorsman swagger, admiring how easily he swung onto his horse, thinking how attractive he looked with the sun glinting off his red hair. Sometimes she wished he were really her son instead of the pair she'd ended up with.

When they left, Laurent Jarré stood outside his café watching them drive away. He wondered sadly if Rafaella was as lonely as he was.

And outside her little store, Mademoiselle Doriteé, her frizzy hair spiraling out from her head, her green eyes soft behind pebble-thick glasses, still unmarried at age forty-five, also watched them go. She unstraddled her *moto* and propped it against the wall, gazing admiringly after Haigh. What a fine husband he would make for some lucky woman, she thought innocently.

23 JULIETTE HAD NO PROBLEMS packing—she just took everything. Bathing suits, pareos, beachwear went into one bag, linen shifts into another, silk cocktail dresses another. A suit or two, just in case she needed to pop up to Paris for a few nights, a couple of ball gowns in case Rafaella went the whole hog and threw a really grand celebration. Hats—she always needed a hat in Provence to keep the sun off her face and hide the wrinkles, as well as to stop that pesky wind from blowing her hair around. Then there was the special case for shoes, and the satin-lined velvet pouches for lingerie, and the beauty case for the necessary creams and lotions that glued her face back together in the morning. And of course the three special Vuitton travel containers in which the Pomeranians would fly luxuriously, if complainingly, to Marseille on Jake Bronson's Gulfstream IV—because thankfully, he'd called and offered her a lift.

Next, Juliette went shopping for gifts because she enjoyed giving much more than receiving. She headed straight for Barneys, where she chose a couple of cashmere sweaters for Rafaella, in a blue that matched her eyes. While she was there, she also bought a sweater for Jake, in red this time because she felt that after all these years, Jake Bronson probably needed bringing out of himself. He needed to be taken out of his lonely rut and brought back into real life, and red was surely the color to do that.

Next, she stopped into Tiffany, where she found a silver bracelet with heart-shaped charms for little Shao Lan, plus a pretty pair of long, slinky silver earrings for Franny. Jake had told her she was a little bit flower child, and she thought they would suit her. Plus a silver pen for her friend, Clare, whom no one seemed to know.

Next stop was Dunhill, where she picked out a bright paisley silk vest for Haigh, who she assumed was still as rail-thin as he'd always been, and also a nice striped silk tie for the Aussie vintner.

Strange bunch for a "family" reunion, she thought in the cab on the way home, surrounded by her packages. A distant American niece, her friend, an unknown Asian grandchild who might or might not be Felix's, the "Lover's" son, Rafaella's young winemaker, and herself, the old friend. Plus Haigh, of course, whom she knew could put them all in their places—and keep them there. She sighed, hoping for Rafaella's sake that it all worked out.

24

SHAO LAN SAT by the hospital bed where Bao Chu Ching lay tucked to the neck in crisp white sheets, looking smaller than Shao Lan remembered. Her grandmother's eyes were closed, but her face was strangely free of the tight lines of pain. Shao Lan thought, mystified, that she looked almost like a little girl.

Shao Lan looked very neat in her gray skirt and short-sleeved white shirt. Her old coat was folded on top of her small plastic case on the floor next to her. In the case were a couple of changes of underclothes, one clean shirt, and two pairs of white socks. Her shiny black hair had been newly shorn by a kindly neighbor and now it stuck out peculiarly around her ears. She held a bunch of red flowers she'd bought for her grandmother, and frightened, she tightened her grip on them.

Footsteps approached and she turned her head reluctantly, knowing what was to come.

"There you are, Shao Lan," said the man from the travel agency, smiling. "All ready to go?"

Shao Lan just gripped her flowers tighter until a nurse in a crisp white uniform removed them from her cramped fingers. "I'll put those in a vase for your grandmother to see when she wakes," she said. "And now you must say good-bye. It's time you were off to catch that flight to Paris, you lucky girl."

Lucky, Shao Lan thought, and she bent over to kiss her grandmother good-bye. *I wish it were the nurse who was lucky. I don't want to go to France. I don't want to be with those strangers who call themselves my family. I don't want to leave grandmother.*

But, "Good-bye, Grandmother," she whispered obediently, letting her hand be taken by the man from the travel agency.

She sat silently next to him on the drive to the airport, staring terrified at the great planes swooping overhead. She had never seen a plane before except as a dot in the sky. The man parked the car, then took her bag and her hand and walked her into the departure area. At the check-in desk he hung a laminated plastic card on a black cord around her neck with her name and destination written on it in big black letters.

"There," he said jovially, trying to cheer her up, "now everybody will know you're Shao Lan and that you're going to Paris."

They walked to the departure lounge and he looked uncertainly at her frozen face. She had not said one word, not looked at him in all this time. "Wait here," he said, hurrying into the gift shop.

He came out a few minutes later carrying a bag. "This is for you, Shao Lan," he said, "enjoy your vacation." Then he handed her over to a woman in a blue uniform, and, his responsibility over, with a sigh of relief he turned and hurried away.

Shao Lan was left on a seat near the departure gate by the uniformed attendant who was now in charge of her and told not to move until she came back. Although she wanted very much to go to the bathroom, Shao Lan held her breath and her bladder and looked around her. People hurried past but nobody looked at her. Feeling very alone, she opened the bag from the travel agent. A rare smile curved the corners of her mouth as she took out the soft white woolly lamb. It was the kind of toy you bought for babies, but Shao Lan had never been "a baby," and she had never had toys.

She held the lamb to her face, feeling its softness, smelling its newness, touching the blue ribbon around its neck, smiling into its vacant blue eyes. "I'll call you Baby and I'll never leave you," she whispered. She planted a kiss on the woolly lamb's pink nose and hoped the woman would come back soon because she really had to go.

25 JAKE WAS AT HIS cabin in the mountains. He'd been trying for some time to get Dirty Harry into the horse box, but the horse wasn't having it. He reared and kicked out at Criminal, who was acting like a sheepdog, slinking behind the horse, nipping at his heels, trying to herd him into the box.

Jake sat on the fence, loose and relaxed, a blade of sweet grass between his teeth, watching the pair of them. It was an old game they played, Dirty Harry being the uppity stallion and Criminal the trusty shepherd. They enjoyed it and in the end the horse would allow himself to be subdued, and, hooves clattering, he'd edge meekly into the box. Then, knowing the game was over, Criminal would leap into the cab of the old green pickup, to which Jake had already attached the horse box. He'd wait for Jake to lock the horse in and get into the driver's seat, then he'd woof importantly, as though saying, "Okay let's go then," and they'd drive off.

Of course both animals knew where they were going, back to the stables near town. And of course they didn't want to go there and they didn't want to leave Jake, but they had learned to take the good with the bad.

Criminal's mission finally accomplished, Jake slid off the fence, checked the horse, locked its box and got in the driver's seat. The dog leaned his head out of the window, ears flapping in the breeze, scanning the woods for wildlife as they descended the winding route to town.

"This is going to be some party, Criminal," Jake spoke out loud, sharing his thoughts the way he always did with his dog. It was one of the perils of living alone, you talked to your animals, but the bonus was they didn't give you any lip.

"Yes, sir," he said, glancing out of the corner of his eye at the dog, who eyed him back. "Quite a scene, huh? Rafaella will be back on form again, beautiful and charming and winning all hearts, including mine all over again. Franny Marten will be the odd girl out, my flower child lost amid the splendors of her ancestral home." He sighed. "Trouble is, boy, I really care about her. Silly, I know, after only one night and all those years alone, but hey, that's where I'm at. And will she ever speak to me again? I'll have a hard time explaining myself, but y'know I couldn't tell her I was just checking her out before letting her loose on Rafaella.

"Then there's her friend, Clare Marks—well, now, she's the mystery player in the pack. And Juliette—well, Juliette will be Juliette, loud, raucous, generous, and funny.

"Then of course there's Haigh, who'll put us all in our place with a few short, sharp words. Plus the handsome Aussie winemaker—I wonder if Rafaella's hoping to set her grandniece up with him, keep the winery business in the family. If so, I'll have to put a stop to that!

"And then of course there's little Shao Lan, the unknown granddaughter who will make Rafaella a happy woman again. And of course, hanging over us all," he added thoughtfully, "will be the shadow of my dear father, 'the Lover.'"

Sensing Jake was finished, the dog turned and hung his head out the window again, watching the woods for jackrabbits, though if he saw one, all he would do was bark. Criminal was a well-behaved dog, which was quite different from being a well-trained dog in that Criminal did exactly as he liked, which was almost always exactly what pleased Jake. The arrangement worked out very well for both of them.

Jake wondered if Rafaella would put him in his old room, the one on the third floor that used to be her father's, well away from the one used by her icy mother, whom nobody had liked. And well away, too, from the room overlooking the lake that Rafaella had later shared with his father, a room made dark in spring by a giant magnolia tree that flung its flashy, waxen blooms to the moon and that, according to Rafaella, smelled like the Garden of Eden. But of course that was because she was in love then.

Jake thought his old room was the most beautiful room in the entire château. It had a giant sleigh bed covered in dark gold velvet, narrow Tiffany lamps shaded in amber, and odd pieces of Biedermeier and Louis XVI furniture, all found by Rafaella's father, who was a keen *antiquaire*. The two windows overlooked the terrace where the Chinese wisteria drooped, heavy with purple blossoms that changed color with the evening light to a showy pink. Jake could recall clearly the sounds and smells of the nights when he was sixteen and would lay awake wondering what life was about.

Nights at the château were almost tangible, heavy with the scents of nicotina and maquis. Hit by the sprinklers, the grass flung its scent in the air, the reeds rustled in the lake, the fountains smelled green and mossy, the crickets hummed, and often nightingales sang.

Happiness struck Jake like a jolt in his stomach. He was beginning to get used to this new feeling. "Damn it, Criminal, I'm going home," he said, smiling. "And I'm going to see Franny again." Remembering that hard kernel he'd discerned at the heart of his peach, he added, "Better keep your paws crossed for me, boy. I'm going to need all the luck I can get."

Remembering Juliette's three Pomeranians that were to accompany them on the jet, he looked at Criminal. "Why don't I take you with me, boy?" he said. "You can make friends with Louis and Mimi. Besides," he added, patting the dog's big head, "I know Franny will love you." And the dog looked back at him with those sharp, intelligent brown eyes and gave him a woof.

"I knew you'd say yes." Jake said.

26 ALAIN WAS THE ONLY one who would not be coming home for the reunion, and Rafaella stood outside his old room. Mimi and Louis sat next to her, waiting. Downstairs, the ancient longcase clock in the hall ground its gears creakily before striking six times. Evening sunlight beamed through the tall southwest-facing windows, showing up the cracks on the black double doors, which had been painted with skull and crossbones by Alain himself in an act of rebellion at the age of fifteen.

The fact that the doors dated from the eighteenth century had not deterred him. He'd said he was sick and tired of "old." Alain had always wanted the here and now, he'd wanted fast cars and slick women and city life. He didn't want to be stuck in the country at the château. He needed to be in Paris or on the beach at the Côte d'Azur, sniffing out bikini-clad girls who might think he was at least eighteen and rich and smart as well as handsome.

Rafaella had always thought of Alain as her "wounded bird." He was quieter than Felix, always thinking, always plotting revenge against his brother, demanding Rafaella's attention and crying at the drop of a hat.

Alain had cried when he brought her the baby birds he

said he'd found dashed from their nests. When he discovered Rafaella's favorite pug drowned in the lake, he'd carried the poor little body all the way home himself. He'd been soaking wet and shivering from diving in, trying to rescue it, he'd said, because he knew how much his mother loved her pet.

Felix was always locked away in his room, but Alain was always hanging around. Sometimes he'd be sunk into the corner of the big gold brocade sofa in Rafaella's room, hiding beneath the cushions. Spying on her, Haigh said.

"But I didn't mean to hide, *maman*," Alain explained when she questioned him. "I just wanted to be near you." Later he'd made up a poem for her, apologizing for being bad. Now Felix would never have written her a poem, but then Felix would never have hidden in her room, either. Yet Alain endeared himself to her as Felix never had, and much later, when they both abandoned her and each other, it was the loss of Alain that hurt her the most.

Trouble was, Rafaella thought, running a finger over the chipped skull and crossbones, Alain got away with everything because he had the kind of charm that could get him into trouble anywhere in the world—and also get him out of it unscathed.

Alain was the handsome son, tall and too skinny in his early days but whip-thin and muscular as he grew, with sun-streaked blond hair falling shaggily over his blue eyes and sun-brown skin stretched tautly over his high cheekbones. With his full mouth and sexy stare, he set her friends gossiping. Watch out, they said, he's trouble, and they'd kept their daughters carefully away because they knew Alain was exactly the kind of "bad boy" a girl would fall head over heels for. And they also knew that with Alain it was no holds barred. God help Rafaella, they said to one another, he'll be the death of her one day.

Rafaella still hesitated, her hand on the brass doorknob. She knew that, unlike Felix's room, Alain's was not exactly the way he'd left it. After he'd gone, Haigh had made order out of the chaos. He'd cleaned it, put everything in its place, which was certainly never the way it was when Alain was in residence. She would find no trace of her younger son's personality here, except perhaps a leftover hum of energy in the air.

Alain had lived in an aura of light and movement. A hedonist, he drew people to him, then crushed them, turning away when he was finished with them. Which is what people said must have happened with the young woman from Marseille, except it still seemed more likely that Felix was the culprit, because Alain had witnesses who said he was in Antibes. Anyhow, Rafaella still believed it was an accident because whatever Felix might have been, he was no murderer.

Jake had still not been able to find Alain, however. He was gone from her life as surely as Felix was. Resolutely, Rafaella turned away from Alain's door. She would never see her younger son again, but she still wondered if he was really the father of her new granddaughter.

27 LATER, LYING WIDE-AWAKE in her big four-poster with the curtains pulled back to let in the cool air and the soft flutters and scurryings of a country night, Rafaella was still thinking about her younger son, pinpointing the time when her life changed.

Jake was gone, she had lost her lover, then Felix, and then she also lost her best friend when Juliette and Rufus moved suddenly to Australia, where Rufus had been posted as an aide to the governor-general. Rafaella missed Juliette terribly. She missed the yapping little Pomeranians, missed the joyous boom of her laughter, missed her loud, confidential whispers and the exchanged secrets between women, but Australia was far away from Provence and life had to go on.

The château was no longer crowded with happy faces, and laughter no longer rang in the hallways. She spent her days alone with her dogs. In the hope that Felix might come home, she even purchased the little vineyard in Saint-Emilion for him.

It would be her gift to him, something of his own and nothing at all to do with his brother. Then, to her surprise, Alain had suddenly returned to live at the château, between jaunts to Paris, that is, and for the first time he'd shown an interest in the winery. He'd also talked constantly of Felix, undermining him subtly to her. He hinted at how sullen Felix had always been, how unrewarding as a person, how self-contained and dangerous.

"Dangerous?" Rafaella had repeated, alarmed.

And Alain had turned and looked at her, his blond hair flopping boyishly over those Marten-blue eyes. "Well, he turned out to be a murderer, didn't he?" he said, and Rafaella thought it was odd that he was laughing as he said it, as though it were all one great, marvelous joke.

She remembered grabbing him by his shirt, her eyes blazing with anger. "Don't you dare say that," she'd cried. "Felix did *not* kill that girl. He told me so, and Felix does not lie."

Alain simply raised one elegant dark brow. "He *told* you that, *maman*? I *don't* think so. From what you said, he told you to 'believe whatever you want,'" and he'd laughed at her again, because it was true, and he had her and he knew it.

Then, looking suddenly repentant, he'd put his arms around her and hugged her. "There's nothing you can do about him, *maman*. You must just face the facts."

In the end, though, it wasn't just the facts about Felix she had to face, it was the facts about Alain.

A few months later, when Alphonse Giradon, the winery manager, along with her accountant and her head enologist, asked for a meeting at the château, Rafaella was surprised. Alain had taken over two years ago and she had left the running of the winery to him.

She had known Alphonse for forty years, but now he stood stiffly in front of the long table in the grand dining room, refusing to sit down. Then Haigh arrived with cold drinks and sugar biscuits and the espresso she thought by now must surely flow in their veins.

"Madame," Alphonse had said hesitantly, "we have sad news to relate. It is not easy to tell you this story, Madame, especially after . . ."

He had not said the name, but Rafaella knew he meant "after Felix" and also "after the Lover," because there was nothing the villagers and her workers did not know about her life. It was part of the price she had to pay for being their *patronne* and a price which, until now, she had not regretted.

"Yes?" she said. "Please go on, Alphonse."

The other two men stood silently by his side, lending moral support, while her old friend Alphonse told her that Alain had been systematically siphoning off money from the winery accounts. Alain claimed to have ordered thousands of expensive new growth-stock, but instead he'd pocketed the money. He'd found a dozen different ways of filling his pockets. And he'd left the Marten winery devastated.

Alphonse had hung his shaggy gray head. "I am distressed to be the bearer of this bad news," he'd said finally. "Your son has been very clever. We never knew until the audit that he robbed the winery. Every penny we made over the past years has gone into his pockets. Everything you and your family and the village have worked for centuries to build is in jeopardy. Madame Rafaella, we are looking at the end of the Marten winery." He'd lifted his head to look at her, and Rafaella saw the tears in his eyes. "What can I say, Madame, to comfort you, to comfort all your workers who now face unemployment. All is in disarray, Madame, and I only wish I had known and come to you earlier."

It was a blow to her heart, but Rafaella knew she had to take charge—it was her duty, her responsibility to her family name and to her workers. She took a deep breath, gathered her strength.

"My friends, please sit down," she'd said gently. "I understand how difficult this was for you, and I appreciate your honor in coming to me." She turned to Haigh, standing arms folded by the door, his eyes black with anger. "Bring a bottle of champagne for us, Haigh," she said, managing a smile. "We are about to drink to the rebirth of the Marten winery. No one here will be unemployed, and no one will go without because of my son. I will make sure of that. And I will make sure that the winery gets back on its feet, even if it means selling off all my assets and working twenty hours a day."

And that is exactly what she did. It cost her another son as well as most of her money, but she'd honored the Marten family's commitments to her employees and to the business.

Of course Alain had denied it. He'd yelled and screamed at her, his eyes full of fury. He'd blamed Felix, he'd blamed Alphonse, he'd blamed the accountants, he'd even blamed her for not taking care of the winery herself, the way she always had.

"You are a liar as well as a thief, Alain," she'd said finally. "And you show no remorse for what you have done. You've humiliated me and the Marten family and everything we stood for and now you can get out." Her heart was breaking as she said it, but she knew it had to be done.

"I'll get back at you for this," he'd said, throwing a venomous glance back across the room at her. "I'll get you, *maman,* one of these days, and perhaps in the way you least expect."

Rafaella had not cried when Alain left. It was as though all her tears had dried up. She was alone at the château with just Haigh to help her and listen to her when she was exhausted and didn't see how she could go on. But gradually she'd built up the winery until the Marten name meant something again.

The château became even more silent and empty. Haigh covered the furniture in the unused rooms in dust sheets and closed their doors. Because of her arthritis, Rafaella moved out of the bedroom that held so many memories for her, into the downstairs library where she read and wrote in her journal about the past glorious days at the château.

She'd worked hard for many years until Scott Harris came to take over, and at last she was free of the day-to-day stress. And she finally knew she was a lonely woman.

Solitude became a habit until that day, standing in the hall with the dust motes floating in the golden beams of sunlight, with silence all around her, when she realized that because of her, the château was dying. And that's when she'd planned her invitations.

She would bring the Château des Roses Sauvages to life again.

28 IN THE MARTEN-DE-PROVENCE village square, men were up on ladders stringing tricolor buntings between the plane trees and Laurent Jarré was supervising the erection of a handpainted banner that said, BIENVENUE A LA FAMILLE MARTEN. Welcome to the Marten family.

The youth of the village congregated near the fountain, giggling and pushing each other, arguing about whose turn it was to man the helium pump that blew up the balloons, shrieking with laughter as they took gulps of gas, causing their voices to rise to a wild pitch. A firm stop was put to all that by Father Jérôme, in his dusty black robes, on his way to the church to check that all was in order for the celebration service that was to be held later that week.

At the local store and post office, Mademoiselle Doritée, with her gray hair spiraling wildly and her pebble glasses glinting in the sun, hung her cross-stitched sampler of a village scene, inscribed with the slogan BIENVENUE AUX MARTENS on the glass door, while across the square Philippe Allier hung up orange, green, and yellow buntings that matched the colors of his fruits and vegetables. The old boys on their benches in the shade leaned on their sticks, watching with rheumy eyes, wondering vaguely who was arriving that caused so much stir, and the dogs, galvanized from their usual sloth by the excitement, chased their tails and each other before wading into the fountain to cool off.

The sun beat down and beads of sweat trickled over Jarré's broad forehead as he hurried back to his café. After their hard work the men would be crowding in, demanding a cold Stella, and the youngsters would head over to Mademoiselle Doritée's, sifting through the freezers for ice cream, grabbing cold sodas from the vending machine, and generally making a racket. Poor Mademoiselle Doritée could never keep track of them. Bewildered, she would push back her springy gray hair, adjust her glasses, and demand to know who had taken what and who had paid and who had not, and the kids would just laugh and tease her until she grew purple in the face with frustration. Then Allier would have to leave his store and hurry across the square to sort it all out.

At four o'clock the Dépôt de Pain would open its doors and the aroma of freshly baked breads and baguettes to be eaten with supper would waft across the square, sending housewives scurrying. The fish truck had already rumbled in, flinging open its sides to reveal an iced display of gleaming silver John Dory and coral red rascasse, mounds of green-bearded mussels, miniature eels, and small pink shrimp that smelled as sweet and briny as the sea itself. Jarré had chosen his fish for the all-important "dish of the day" and he'd placed his special order for the even more important lunch to be served next week to Madame Rafaella's new family.

He already had tiny banon goat's-milk cheeses marinating with herbs in the beautiful deep-green olive oil, pressed from olives from his own trees. He grew the herbs in his small back garden, along with his various lettuces: escarole, lambs, rocket, miniature romaine. Jarré was particular about his produce. He liked his vegetables small and fresh, and his carrots and squash were miniatures of perfection, as were his tomatoes that came in green and yellow and even striped, as well as the usual robust red. These he served sliced thinly on a large white platter drizzled with a soupçon of his best olive oil and a hint of lemon juice, plus a grind of fresh black pepper. He'd scatter fresh basil over them, ripped between his fingers of course and not cut with a knife or scissors because that bruised the delicate leaves and turned them black. His *petite symphonie*, he called it proudly whenever he served it, which was throughout the summer months, in fact well into October if the sun kept up its good work.

But the tomatoes were just the start of the special lunch he was planning for the Marten family. He intended to make Madame Rafaella proud, see that her smart city guests were not insulted by his simple village cooking. Jarré had learned to cook from his grandmother, but in his youth he'd also done a stint in a grand restaurant in Marseille where he'd learned, among other things, how to present a beautiful plate, one that pleased the eye as well as the palate. Now, with the family reunion, he would have a chance to really show his caliber as a chef for the first time in many years.

Up at the Domaine Marten winery, Scott Harris was inspecting the new labels he had designed for the special Cuvée Famille Marten that was to be his surprise to Rafaella.

The winery had the look of an old monastery, and this was the image on the original Domaine Marten label. It was drawn in black ink by an earlier Marten and had hardly been changed since its inception, except for special events, like jubilees and the celebrations marking the end of conflict in the two world wars, and of course for the wedding cuvée when Rafaella got married. But this new label was special.

Scott had changed the old black ink drawing to a flamboyant red, Rafaella's favorite color, and the lettering, now intertwined with vine leaves in the shape of a garland, proclaimed this to be the Cuvée Réunion de la Famille Marten. Not only had Scott designed the label, he had also personally blended the wine, using the grapes from the stoniest of the hills to give a hint of the *garrigue*, a flinty undertone overlaid with softest satin and fruit. Scott thought his description of the wine matched Rafaella, flinty undertones with a smoothly satin exterior and the soft heart.

Pleased with his work, he sent the labels down to the bottling plant near the town with word that they must be completed right away. Meanwhile, up at the château, a team of village ladies in flowery wraparound aprons ripped off dustcovers and brandished mops and feather dusters in a major spring clean. Haigh had told them that every window and shutter was to be washed, every brass doorknob polished till it glittered, every gilt picture frame whisked over with a chamois cloth. Teetering on stepladders, the women chattered as they worked to bring the reopened rooms back up to Haigh's high standards.

"The family is not coming here to find a run-down old house, Madame," Haigh told Rafaella, who grinned and said, "And what do you plan to do about its run-down old mistress, then?" Haigh replied, "There's not much to be done there, but how about we go up to the attics and look through your wardrobe, pick out something for the first meeting. After all, you need to make a good impression. There's the gala dinner the whole village will attend, and of course, Jarré's luncheon at the Colombes. Plus, the grand finale."

"The grand finale," Rafaella said, surprised. She had only anticipated their arrival, hadn't thought about the fact that, at the end of the three weeks, they would return to their own lives.

In the attic closets, Rafaella gazed at the rows of garments on satin hangers, all neatly encased in transparent bags. "Just look at this, Haigh." She pulled a fluffy gray fox jacket from the cupboard and held it to her cheek. "I wore this the day Juliette met Rufus at La Coupole, the same day I bought the red Dior. Oh, Haigh, I absolutely must wear the Dior. It's my all-time favorite. Do you think it will still fit?" And she found it and held it against her, frowning doubtfully into the mirror. Then, at the back of the closet, she spotted a fall of creamy satin. "Oh, here's my wedding dress. Remember, Haigh, *maman* wanted me to have it dyed black so I could wear it as an evening dress, but the satin was too heavy—it weighed me down. And so did my husband," she added with a grin, recalling her husband's face as she walked down the aisle toward him, with an extra big bunch of lilies to hide her pregnant bump and her heavy satin train going *plop-plop-plop* behind her down the stairs. Proud, unsmiling, her husband, Henri, was a man who was getting exactly what he'd set out to get—a meal ticket for life.

The fact that his bride was young and charming and in love—or at least infatuation—meant nothing to him. Rafaella had read it in his face and knew she had made a terrible mistake. In church, holding the lillies over her bump, she'd prayed that her baby would not be like him, but of course Felix had turned out to be exactly like his papa. That's the reason she'd loved Alain more, she supposed, because he had her gaiety, her zest for living.

She rummaged through the men's suits hanging on broad wooden hangers in yet another closet and took out a jacket, a dark blue velvet *smoking* with satin lapels cut narrow in the Edwardian style. "Look, Haigh. This used to be *grandpère*'s," she said, "I'm sure it would fit you. Oh Haigh, you would look wonderful in it. Do try it on."

"Madame, I don't need *grandpère*'s *smoking*," Haigh objected. "I have no occasion to wear it."

"You do now. Come on, Haigh, you can wear it to the celebration gala." And she held the jacket against him approvingly. "Very *comme il faut*."

AFTER A COUPLE of hours sorting clothes with Rafaella, Haigh went back to his kitchen to inspect his new jacket. He rather liked the pointed cut of the lapels. He would give it a good brush, hang it outdoors to get rid of the smell of mothballs. He thought it would look quite smart for the gala party.

Meanwhile, he had to keep track of the women cleaning the house and check on the young kitchen helpers. The larder was stocked, caterers hired, the menus prepared, the parties arranged. Haigh and Rafaella had chosen the wines, the dining room table already had its leaves pulled out, ready to be set with the finest china and silver. Later, the gardeners would cull the grounds for every perfect flower, which Rafaella would arrange in tall vases, and the château would be filled again with their sweet fresh scent.

Haigh inspected his kitchen one more time. The black-

and-white tile floors gleamed, as did the big steel range and the dishes and crystal in the old-fashioned glass-fronted cupboards. Still nervous, he hurried back upstairs to check the guest rooms again, even though he'd already checked earlier that day.

And Rafaella, content at last, sat under the wisteria bower on the terrace with Mimi on her knee and Louis sprawled panting beside her. Their beloved château breathed again, and tomorrow life would once more flow through its veins.

PART III

The Family Reunion

Falling in love is the greatest
imaginative experience of which most
human beings are capable.

—A. N. WILSON

29 FRANNY AND CLARE EMERGED from the neutral cocoon of the plane into the vast mysteries of Charles de Gaulle airport, where they stood in line to show their passports, then waited a long time for their baggage. Of course Clare's five suitcases came out last, just when they were thinking they'd been lost. Next, they stood wearily in line for a taxi, breathing in real French air—well, petrol fumes and cigarette smoke anyway, then hurtled down the *Périphérique*, the motorway that encircles Paris, shooting off at a charming neighborhood with open-air cafés and dozens of little restaurants, boutiques, perfumeries, and pastry shops. This, the cab driver told them, was Montparnasse.

"Montparnasse," Franny repeated, thrilled. "Clare, we're in the real Paris, the city where Picasso lived and girls dance naked at the Folies Bergères, and artists and writers drank absinthe at Le Sélect and too much wine at the Closerie des Lilas." Thrilled, the two stared out of the windows, absorbing the Parisian atmosphere along with the petrol fumes and the cigarette smoke.

The Gare Montparnasse teemed with people who all

looked as though they knew exactly where they were going, which was more than Clare and Franny could say for themselves. Bewildered, Clare pushed a cart loaded with her luggage while Franny clutched her only bag firmly in her hand. She'd been warned to beware of pickpockets and bag snatchers as well as French con men who were only using their Gallic charm to get hold of her traveler's checks.

They hurried to the platform from which the superfast TGV train to Avignon would depart. Just as the train slid smoothly and quietly alongside the platform, a tall, chic young woman dressed all in black came rushing toward them, dragging a small reluctant Chinese girl by the hand.

"Which of you is Franny Marten?" she demanded in heavily accented English. *"Oui? C'est vous?"* She glared at Franny. *"Eh bien,* I am the Marten travel agent here in Paris. I am supposed to travel with this child to Avignon but I am sick with the flu. I cannot possibly go." She paused to cough, fanning herself with her free hand. "You are in charge of this child now. She belongs to you." And she pushed the child at Franny, then turned on her heel and walked away rapidly.

It all happened so quickly that Franny and Clare had no time even to question her. Stunned, they followed her with their eyes as she made her way rapidly through the diminishing crowd. They saw her hurry to the station café, make herself comfortable at an outside table, order coffee, and light a cigarette. There she sat reading a newspaper, her obligation and her flu over.

"Bitch!" Clare exclaimed, astounded. Then, "Ooops, sorry." She bent to pat the little girl's head. "I didn't mean that."

Shao Lan stared down at her new shoes, shiny black and

very stiff. They hurt her feet. The plane journey had seemed endless, no one had talked to her, no one had even seemed to notice her. She'd sat bolt upright all the way, not daring to eat or drink, wondering how it all would end and if she would ever see Bao Chu again. She was frightened of the noise, frightened of being alone in a strange place, frightened of what would happen to her, a poor child nobody even noticed.

The woman who'd met her had grabbed her so firmly by the hand it hurt. "Come with me," she'd said brusquely, whisking her past policemen and officials. They had looked for a long time at the papers she carried in the plastic envelope strung around her neck, and she'd hid her face, clutching the woolly lamb closer. Now the woman had left her with more strangers. She didn't know where she was or who they were or what was to happen, but she was determined not to cry. She did not want to lose face.

Franny looked at the small girl staring down at her shoes. She was wearing a skimpy coat that looked as though she'd grown out of about a year ago, and her shiny black hair had been lopped into jagged bangs. She looked exactly like one of her hurt, bewildered animals at the clinic. Suddenly, the child threw her a quick, darting glance and Franny saw that her eyes were bright blue. Her name was written in bold letters on the plastic packet around her neck. SHAO LAN CHING, it said, and in brackets after it (MARTEN).

"Poor baby, she looks like a little refugee," Franny said.

"She's no refugee. Don't you realize she's another Marten, heading for the family reunion."

"Oh my god, then of course she must be my *cousin!*"

Franny hunkered down and took the girl's chin in her hand, lifting her face so she could see her properly. "Hello, Shao Lan," she said gently. "I'm your cousin Franny and this is your new friend, Clare. We'll take care of you now. Don't worry about anything. Okay?" But Shao Lan looked silently down at her shoes.

"Do you think she speaks English?" Franny asked doubtfully, and Clare said she'd bet she didn't understand a word.

Taking Shao Lan by the hand, Franny picked up her little plastic case, shocked by how small it was, barely big enough for a doll's clothes. They boarded the train and sank into their comfortable seats, glad to be on their way at last. Shao Lan ignored them. She closed her eyes as the train sped through the countryside. All she wanted was to be back home with grandmother in their room on Hu Tong Road. She thought about running away.

FRANNY WAS WONDERING what the Château des Roses Sauvages would be like and whether her Aunt Rafaella would like her, and what it would be like living in a French village. It's just a dream, she reminded herself. In a few weeks it'll all be over and you'll be back to being the nice Dr. Marten, the kindly vet in Venice Beach, California, paying your mortgage on time and loving other people's animals because you don't have time to spare for one of your own. And avoiding men so as not to make another mistake.

30 WHEN THE TRAIN FINALLY pulled into Avignon, the skies were gray, rain threatened, and a cold, gusty wind whipped at their legs. Franny buttoned Shao Lan into her skimpy overcoat, then she pulled on her sweater, hunching her shoulders against the wind. She watched Clare, who was pacing like an irritated panther, her black hair blowing horizontally, searching for the car that was supposed to meet them and take them to the château.

"It's no good," said Franny, shivering by now. "They must have forgotten us or got the wrong date or something. We'll have to rent a car and drive there ourselves."

At the car rental a stern woman in a crisp white shirt and a silk scarf printed with the firm's logo informed them brusquely that no cars were available.

"But there must be cars," Franny said frantically, because by now she was frozen as well as worried. "Please check your computer again."

The woman checked. "Well," she said reluctantly, "perhaps there is something. A car was just returned, but it hasn't yet been examined and cleaned."

"We'll take it," Clare said, "just show me where I sign," and she winked at Franny as she handed over Marcus's credit card.

Half an hour later they were in a too small red Fiat that smelled of French cigarettes and heavy perfume. It was so small they had to stack most of Clare's suitcases next to Shao Lan, squashed into the backseat. Franny drove and Clare read the map. It took them an hour to find their way out of the maze of one-way streets. All the signs seemed to say TOUTES DIRECTIONS, and whichever road they took just seemed to lead them deeper into suburbs. By some accident or miracle—depending on which way you looked at it, Franny said, disparaging Clare's map-reading abilities—they found themselves on the right road, but by now the rain was slicing sideways across and the windshield wipers were struggling just to keep afloat.

"Shit," Clare said, then clapped a shocked hand across her mouth, glancing back at the child. "Do you think she heard?" she whispered.

"We'll never know. That child is never going to speak," Franny said, peering wearily through the murk. She didn't know how it could get any darker, but somehow it had. She braked at a stop sign and felt the car pull to the left. "Uh-oh," she muttered as lightning illuminated the sodden landscape and thunder rolled. Then Shao Lan screamed and they turned, surprised, to look at her.

"At least now we know she has vocal cords," Clare said, turning back and holding a flashlight over the map, praying they were on the proper route because they hadn't passed a gas station in forever and there wasn't even a house along this godforsaken road.

The car gave another little jiggle, pulling to the left, and again Franny straightened it out. Then suddenly the engine stalled and they were aquaplaning, teetering on the edge of a ditch before the car finally settled, with a *whoosh* like a relieved sigh, the right way up but on the wrong side of the road.

There was a long silence. Franny had the wheel in a death grip. She stared terrified through the windshield. "Jesus," Clare said, shaken. "I didn't bargain for this. Are you sure this *is* Provence?"

Franny thought of the much-anticipated blue skies and sunshine, the scents of the famous countryside, the wonderful old château, the food and the wine. She glared at the gloomy reality outside. She was jet-lagged and exhausted and in the middle of nowhere in a storm. "Our cell phones won't work here," she said. "We'll just have to wait for a passing car and thumb a lift." She took two Snickers bars from her bag and offered one to Shao Lan, who simply turned her head away. "It's okay, baby," Franny said persuasively, "it's just good American chocolate."

Clare bit angrily down on the other Snickers bar. "God, Franny you sound like a forties movie," she said, "the victorious American troops winning over the foreign kids with chocolate bars and the women with nylons!"

"First child I ever knew to turn down chocolate," Franny said. "Do you suppose she's not feeling well?"

"I hope she's not going to throw up." Clare licked the chocolate off her fingers, feeling better.

Lights flickered through the rain and they almost fell out of the car in their hurry, jumping up and down in the middle of the road and waving their hands over their heads. "Stop. Stop! Oh please stop!" they yelled. Lightning flashed again and thunder crashed right after it and they clutched each other screaming.

The pickup truck slowed to a cautious crawl and a man with thick gray hair and a round, lined face stuck his head out the window. A sweet aroma drifted toward them from the back of the truck. "*Qu'est-ce qui se passe?*" he yelled over the wind.

"*La voiture—arrêtée.*" Franny said, finding a couple of words of schoolgirl French.

"*Merde.*" The driver got out and stood in the pouring rain, arms folded, regarding their car with a frown. *Vous avez de la chance. Vous auriez pu finir dans un fossé.* You're lucky not to end up in the ditch. *Où allez-vous?* Where you go?" he added in English.

Franny shoved the sopping hair out of her eyes. "We go to Marten-de-Provence," she said, and all of a sudden he beamed at them.

"*Ah, eh bien, vouz êtes les Martens, n'est-ce pas?*" He held out his hand and Franny shook it, praying he would just say, Please get in my truck. But instead, while they stood with the rain streaming down their faces, he introduced himself.

"*Je suis Philippe Allier, marchand de fruits et légumes dans le village de Marten. C'est un plaisir, mesdames, de vous rencontrer. Et pour Madame Rafaella, j'ai l'honneur de diriger la famille au château. Eh bien, mesdemoiselles, venez vite.*"

He darted across the road, plucked Shao Lan out of the car, carried her back and installed her in the truck's passenger seat. He fastened the seatbelt, wiped the rain tenderly from her face, and closed the door. Then he ran back to their car again and began pulling out the luggage.

Clare winced when she saw her expensive suitcases sitting in the puddles in the middle of the road, but she said nothing. They helped Monsieur Allier load everything into the rear of the pickup next to the Cavaillon melons.

"Okay, *mesdames*." Allier dusted his hands and held up the tarpaulin. "*Montez avec vos valises, puis nous irons vite au château.*"

Franny and Clare didn't need to understand French to know that they were to ride under the tarp with the melons in the back of the truck. They climbed in, hunkering down behind the cab out of the wind, then Monsieur Allier covered them with the tarp and they were off.

31   CLARE SHOVED THE TARP away, gasping for breath, almost asphyxiated by the sweet smell of the melons that rolled and bumped against their legs.

"Classy way to arrive at the ancestral château," she yelled over the sound of thunder as Monsieur Allier drove up a hill into a dark little village. Franny's heart sank. Plastic chairs and tables were stacked under the café terrace, the festive buntings dripped sadly, and the welcome sign dangled forlornly.

Then they left the village behind and were driving under an avenue of trees. Wet leaves shaken by the wind splattered down and stuck to their faces and their hair. "Like

Babes in the Wood," Clare muttered through chattering teeth.

Then Monsieur Allier made a sudden left along a lane studded with pointy trees so tall their tips disappeared into the mist. A brilliant blue flash of lightning zigzagged to earth near a steel gray lake and in front of them sprawled a large, dark house.

Monsieur Allier opened the window to the back of the truck. *"Alors, le Château des Roses Sauvages,"* he said, circling the parterre garden and coming to a stop in front of the stone steps leading to the massive front door.

Franny stared doubtfully at the house. It was in complete darkness. Her eyes met Clare's, and she knew they were thinking the same thing. Could this really be the right place? She glanced at Allier, busy unloading their luggage. Maybe he was a madman. He could have brought them here to kill them.

"Les lumières ne fonctionnent pas à cause de l'orage," Allier explained. They looked dumbly at him. *"L'électricité . . . Phut . . ."* He flung his hands in the air. *"Demain tout va marcher."* He piled the luggage on the steps and opened the passenger door, bowing courteously as he offered Shao Lan his hand. To Franny's surprise, she took it and descended daintily onto the gravel driveway.

"Bien, ma petite," Alliers said, patting her head fondly. *"Je ne veux pas déranger Madame Rafaella et ses invitées."* He shook their hands politely. *"Bonnes vacances, mesdemoiselles, et bonne chance. Je vous verrai à la soirée."* Then, rain dripping off his long nose, he climbed into the pickup and, with a quick wave, swerved around the turning circle and jolted, melons bouncing, back down the drive.

Franny took Shao Lan's hand. It felt cold. "What if no one's here?" she whispered to Clare. "What if we've come to the wrong place?"

"Why are you whispering?" Clare whispered back, then she giggled.

"Well, I guess there's only one way to find out." Franny put her finger on the bell and pressed hard.

32   THUNDER CRACKLED AS FRANNY leaned on the bell again. No one came, so she banged on the door, thinking, What if no one is there? What would they do? Even the village looked deserted. It was all too spooky.

Behind her, the others huddled under the portico. Even the silence seemed dark, with only the beat of the rain and the cypresses creaking in the wind.

The door was thrown open so suddenly she took a quick step back, staring at the cadaverous-looking man, holding an enormous candelabra.

"Oh my god," Clare whispered, "it's the house of Frankenstein."

"*Ah, maintenant,*" Haigh deliberately spoke French to put them on their mettle. "*La Petite Bleu, Mademoiselle Franny, et Madame Clare, je présume? Mais vous êtes très en retard,*" he added disapprovingly. Then, peering behind them into the night, he said in perfectly normal English, "What happened to the car?"

Nervously Franny explained that there was no car, that the rental had broken down and Monsieur Allier from the greengrocery had given them a lift in his pickup.

"I thought I smelled melons," Haigh said, sniffing as he waved them inside. "Welcome to the Château des Roses Sauvages. I am the butler and my name is Haigh." He closed the door behind them and the draft blew out all the candles. A slow wheezing creaked through the darkness, followed by a terrible grinding. Clare shrieked and clung to Franny just as a clock tolled the hours in a flat, dead tone.

"It's only a clock," Haigh told them, "an antique eighteenth-century clock to be exact."

"I knew we should never have come," Franny whispered, dripping rainwater, as the butler relit the candles and turned to look at them, tut-tutting when he saw the puddles on his newly polished parquet.

Holding his silver candelabra high, he said, "I'll show you to your rooms," and walked to the stairs. He stopped and looked back. Shao Lan had not moved. "Follow me, child," he said sternly, but she stood her ground. She wasn't going anywhere. Head lowered, shoulders hunched, she only glared at him, a deep blue Marten glare. "Fuck off," she said clearly.

Clare stifled a giggle. "Baby's first words," she whispered.

The butler stared down his long, thin nose at Shao Lan, one hand on his hip, head tilted to one side. "Well now, *aren't* we being the Little Madam," he said, then he turned and swished his way up the stairs. "Follow me please, and bring that child with you," he said, hiding a grin.

They followed him up the beautiful curved staircase, peeking at the large gilt-framed paintings and the marble statues in the dim niches, feeling the sumptuous softness of the carpet under their bare feet, still nervously aware that the big house was completely silent.

Haigh stepped in front of a pair of tall double doors. With a flourish he threw them open. "Shao Lan," he said, stepping back to let them see the beautiful candlelit room with its red damask—draped four-poster and heavy red silk curtains, "your grandmother wanted you to have the Red Room because she knew red was the special Chinese color for happiness and good fortune."

Shao Lan understood what he'd said but she didn't understand why he spoke of her grandmother. She wondered, Was Bao Chu here? Would she see her soon? Hope flickered.

Franny took her hand and led her into the room. She showed her how comfy the bed was, then knelt so she could feel the fluffy white rug, but Shao Lan's face showed no reaction. Then Haigh and his candelabra moved on to the room next door.

"This was Madame Rafaella's own room," he said proudly as they looked, awed, at the delicious green-and-white boudoir. "Madame wanted Miss Franny to have it. She said to tell you she hopes you will be as happy here as she once was."

Walking into the room, Franny thought she caught a sweet hint of mimosa in the air. The striped silk taffeta curtains rustled in a sudden draft. A strange thrill rippled up her spine, a tiny, soft stroking. She could swear she *knew* this room.

They followed Haigh's candelabra again and went next to

a fantastical white-on-white art deco bedroom that seemed to have been preserved intact from the twenties. "This is to be Miss Clare's room," Haigh said. "It was Madame's mother's room, and she was hoping Miss Clare would help dispel its ghosts."

They stared at him at the word *ghosts* and he smirked knowingly. "Only in a manner of speaking, you understand. I knew Madame's mother well, and I doubt she would want to haunt this place. She's more likely to be found in the casino in the Hôtel de Paris in Monte Carlo."

"Satin," Clare said, walking to the bed and running her hand lovingly over the embroidered spread, "and all these mirrors. Just look at the silver and the chrome. Oh my god, it might have been made for me!"

"Dinner will be served at nine o'clock," Haigh informed them from the doorway. "Madame Rafaella always dresses for dinner. Please be on time." Then, his duty apparently done, he took his candelabra and left them to sort themselves out.

33 SHAO LAN REFUSED to go into the Red Room. She sat on the edge of Franny's bed, her feet dangling. Clare had already gone to her own fantasy room to get ready for dinner. Outside, the wind still roared through the trees and thunder rumbled close by.

Franny talked encouragingly to the silent child as she helped her undress, then stuck her under the shower and made sure she washed. When she was done she wrapped her in a towel and the girl went and huddled on the bed again.

Franny sighed. She knew what to do with animals but not small children. She dressed quickly, left her hair loose, and gave an extra little spritz of the ginger-flower scent. She looked at herself in the mirror and thought with a sigh that perhaps she should have let Clare take her shopping after all.

Then she opened Shao Lan's tiny suitcase and stared, shocked, at its contents—a few pairs of tired underwear, some socks, and a clean shirt. Sighing again, she helped Shao Lan get dressed, then wrapped her in her own blue crochet shawl, hoping it might add cheer to the kid's awful outfit. It didn't help much.

Clare bounced in, brimming with excitement, chic as always in the perfect little black lace cocktail dress. She stared at the child in her blouse and crumpled gray school skirt, then at Franny. She raised her brows despairingly. "It's all we've got," Franny explained, thanking god there was no time for Clare to argue. In fact, the antique clock tolled nine as they walked back down the curving staircase to the hall where Haigh was waiting for them. Franny held Little Blue's hand, feeling suddenly nervous—after all, she was about to meet the only other member of her family, her real true family.

THOUGH SHE HEARD the clock strike, Rafaella remained sitting in front of her dressing table mirror. It was a myth about candlelight, she thought scornfully. It was just like any other light. Too much sent shadows under your eyes and mouth, too little gave you a featureless moon face. A woman needed to be lit with a soft pink or amber tint at exactly the right angle to look really good. Especially at her age.

But the women she was about to meet were young enough to look beautiful whatever the light. Haigh had told her they looked like a pair of drowned rats, but that they had "promise." Coming from Haigh, she took that to mean they were good-looking girls.

She had laughed when he'd told her Shao Lan's only words. "The poor child is obviously frightened," she said, but Haigh said he'd known right away she was a Marten by her sparky temperament.

"I never heard those words cross your lips when you were young, Madame," he said.

But looking at her reflection in the mirror, Rafaella thought, Ah, Haigh, if only you knew what I said to Lucas in bed on those long moonless nights, entwined in his arms in the sultry summer darkness.

She shook her head. This was no time to be thinking about the Lover. Her guests were waiting. Tucking a bright red hibiscus flower into her silver chignon, she secured it with a ruby clip, dabbed a little of the mimosa scent at her throat, and went to check her appearance in the tall mirror.

The red chiffon Dior swathed her shoulders and bosom, falling in a soft fluted column to her ankles. She ran her hands over it, liking the way it felt, pleased that it fit her as perfectly as the day she'd bought it. She had on a pair of Roger Vivier pointy-toed silk shoes from the 1960s. Despite the pain, she was determined to wear them tonight because they made her feel young again.

"Vanity is shameful in an old woman," she said to her mirror, "but it's a vice I can never give up." She wrapped a long strings of rubies around her neck, arranged the sweeping magenta satin shawl over her shoulders, picked up her cane, and walked slowly to the door.

The great moment had arrived. She would finally meet her new family. She hoped they would like her.

34

WEARING *GRANDPÈRE'S* BLUE VELVET *smoking*, Haigh looked like a character in an Austin Powers movie as he watched the guests descend the staircase.

"Bonsoir, mesdames, mesdemoiselles," he said, reverting to the pretense that he spoke only a little English, in the hope they might say something indiscreet so he could find out what they were really thinking. Then he escorted them into the main salon.

Fires blazed high in the two enormous limestone fireplaces at each end of the long, beautiful room, with its celadon-green paneling and amber taffeta curtains. Dozens of candles, reflected in the huge Venetian mirrors, sparkled like tiny rainbows of light from the crystal chandeliers. The

French doors leading onto the terrace were firmly closed against the storm, but the wind still rattled at them fiercely, sending little drafts that made the heavy curtains tremble.

Secure in the candlelit warmth, with the storm and the wind safely shut out, Franny felt suddenly content. This was the first place she had ever been that really felt like "home."

"May I offer you some champagne?" Haigh said, presenting the bottle, wrapped in a white linen napkin, making sure they clearly saw the name Krug and the year, wanting to impress them. Of course Franny didn't know a good year from a bad, never having had much opportunity to drink champagne, but Clare knew all right and she smiled her appreciation at Haigh.

They stood silently together by the blazing fire, sipping the champagne. Franny thought it was the most delicious thing she had ever tasted. How small and insignificant her own little house and its precious flea-market finds seemed compared with this grandeur. Yet her grandfather had been born here, and had things been different, this would have been her father's home, perhaps even her own. Curious, she examined the silver-framed photos of laughing groups from long ago standing on the front steps of the château, and she wondered which one of them was her great-grandfather.

Everything in this house must have a memory, she thought, touching the exquisite little rosewood table inlaid with garlands of a pale wood—every chair, every table, even the faded green brocade sofas. If only walls could speak, these surely would have quite a story to tell, of family gatherings, birthdays, christenings, weddings, fights, and love affairs. She wondered what could have happened to divide such a family.

Haigh had left them alone, the wind had dropped, and in the silence they heard the clatter of hooves. Suddenly the French doors burst open and the wind shrieked in again, sending the curtains billowing and snuffing out all the candles. In the swirling gray mist a black horse with a caped and hooded rider galloped past.

"I'll bet it's a ghost," Clare said, hurrying to shut the doors. "This place is like Sleepy Hollow."

A moment later the doors from the hall were flung open and their "ghost" stood there, dripping water from his long Drizabone-oil-proofed cape, the kind Australian ranchers wore to keep out the rain. He swept off his broad-brimmed hat, sending a small torrent onto the Aubusson rug, and gave them a beaming smile.

"Hi," he said in a very unghostly Aussie accent. "I'm Scott Harris, Rafaella's winemaker. I hope you're all okay. This is quite a storm."

Franny and Clare took a second look. He was tall and lean, with a tanned face and sandy hair that stood up in damp spikes where he'd pulled off his hat. Clare grinned and nudged Franny. "Hey girl," she whispered, "salt-of-the-earth type, remember?"

"Sorry ladies," Scott said with that sunny smile, "but the power won't be reconnected till morning. It's candlelight for all of us tonight."

Since Franny seemed to have been struck dumb, Clare introduced herself. "I'm Clare Marks," she said, shaking his damp hand, "and this is Franny Marten, and the little one is Shao Lan Ching Marten."

"The family reunited," Scott said, as Haigh appeared to take his wet coat. "I'm very glad to meet you all," Scott added, going over and shaking Franny's hand. Shao Lan hid her face in the toy lamb. He knelt next to her and took her hands gently in his. "Hey, pretty girl, don't be afraid. It's just a storm," he said. Over his head, Franny's eyes met Clare's, and they smiled.

Unnoticed, Rafaella stood in the doorway, watching them. The dogs crouched next to her, stunned into silence by the unusual sight of people in the salon. The child was the first one to notice her. She stared at her with those deep-blue Marten eyes, sending a thrill through Rafaella. Her granddaughter was so small and skinny and frightened, and she loved her already. She smiled back at her, but again Shao Lan hid behind the woolly lamb.

Rafaella looked at the tall woman with the long blond hair and knew she must be Franny. But what a beauty she was with that sweep of pale gold hair and her lovely peachy skin. There was an otherworldly quality about her too, a vulnerability and an unexpected gentleness. She was tall and lean, like the Martens, but her lack of style was definitely not inherited.

And the dark woman was her friend Clare. An interesting face, Rafaella thought, studying her, a sleek, self-assured, modern beauty, or at least that's the impression she gave. But beneath that smooth veneer Rafaella caught a hint of something else. Sadness, perhaps? They were young though and lovely, and with all of life in front of them, and she sighed, remembering how quickly those years went by.

Refusing to lean on her stick, she stood tall and proud, gorgeous in her red chiffon and her rubies, with the flowers in her hair. "*Bonsoir, mes chères amies,*" she said in her low, sweet voice. "Welcome to the Château des Roses Sauvages."

They swung round to look at her and she smiled. "I must apologize for the terrible storm and the lack of electricity. Meanwhile, I trust Haigh has been looking after you."

Scott hurried to help her with an arm under her elbow. He kissed her cheek and whispered, "You look drop-dead gorgeous," making her laugh as she walked into the room.

Her eyes met Franny's and it was as if a bond stretched between them, across decades, centuries, continents, a recognition of two souls, united by a past Franny had never known. Rafaella gave a soft sigh of relief—it was going to be all right after all. "I'm so happy to meet you, Franny," she said.

"And I am happy to meet you, Aunt Rafaella," she replied.

"Then kiss me, child," she said, putting her arms around her and holding her tight.

She stepped back and took Franny's chin in her hand, searching her face. "You have your grandfather's smile," she said. "He was a handsome man, you know, and you, *ma chérie*, are a lovely woman."

Blushing, Franny introduced Clare. "Another beauty," Rafaella said, smiling. "Welcome to my home, Clare. I hope you will enjoy your stay. When the storm is over you will see how fortunate I am to live in such a lovely place."

Finally, she turned to her granddaughter. Shao Lan had dropped the lamb and was staring back at her, looking very puzzled. "Shao Lan," she said gently, "I am your French grandmother, here to welcome you." But the child's eyes darted anxiously past her and somehow Rafaella knew she was looking for her "real" grandmother.

She took her hand and went to sit in the big leather wing chair by the fire. She knew Shao Lan spoke some English, and she turned her to face her. Speaking slowly and clearly she said, "Look at me, Shao Lan. I know your grandmother Bao Chu is in Shanghai and that you love her very much. But every little girl has two grandmothers. Bao Chu is your *Chinese* grandmother and I am your *French* grandmother. Your papa was my son. Do you understand, *ma petite*?" The child stood silently, apparently not understanding. Rafaella continued, "I am going to call you Little Blue and you shall sit next to me at dinner. You may eat whatever you choose and leave whatever you do not like. Do you agree to that?"

Little Blue stared silently down at her shoes again, and Haigh sighed. He thought this was hard going and he poured champagne for Rafaella and Scott and also for himself. He went to stand next to Rafaella, regarding the guests with his regal glare.

"Welcome, my new family," Rafaella said, raising her glass to them. "I want to thank you for traveling all this way to make an old woman happy. I will do my best to make your stay at the Château des Roses Sauvages a memorable one."

35

THERE WAS A SUDDEN commotion out in the hall. Dogs barked, the front door banged, and the wind roared through the house, snuffing out all the candles again. "Mimi, Louis," Rafaella called warningly, but they were already racing to the door

Seconds later they heard a growl and also a shrill yapping and snarling.

"It's those bloody Pomeranians," Haigh said resignedly, going out into the hall.

Louis and Mimi were lying on their backs, felled by a rage of tiny blond Pomeranians, who snapped triumphantly at them. A fourth dog stood by the door watching them with the bored expression of a street mutt who knew what a real fight was about.

"Oh, get *off* them, darlings." Juliette's voice came clearly from the darkened portico. "Don't worry, Haigh." she added, "It's all show, they won't kill them."

"It would make them very unpopular around here if they did," Haigh said. "Welcome, Madame. You have arrived in your usual style, I see." And Juliette's jolly laugh boomed across the hall as she swept inside, stopping to kiss Haigh on each cheek, adding a third kiss, a true sign of affection.

"And I'm glad to see *you* have not changed either, Haigh. You're still the same crotchety old despot," she said as he went out to deal with what he knew would be a mountain of luggage. "Now, where's my Rafaella. Ohhhhh . . . there you are, *chérie*."

She paused at the door, assessing her friend in the firelight. "You have not changed one iota," Juliette said loyally.

"And nor have you, my old friend," Rafaella said, wrapping her arms as far around Juliette as they would go. "Except in circumference," she added and Juliette grinned. "Too much good living and not enough good loving," she whispered and they laughed, remembering the secrets they had shared.

"Could that ugly hound possibly be yours, Juliette?"

Rafaella said, noticing the mutt still sitting calmly in the corner.

"Mine? Oh no, that's Jake's dog, Criminal."

Standing in the background, Franny looked up, startled. Then she decided she must have misheard the name. She smiled looking at Juliette, who lit up the silent house with her flame red hair and her emerald caftan and her yapping Pomeranians.

"And now, my dear," Juliette said in a whisper that the others heard clearly because even Juliette's whispers were loud, "where are the granddaughter and the niece?"

Franny stepped from the shadows. "I'm Franny, the niece."

"And I am Juliette, the old friend." Juliette sized her up in one long glance. "Do you have any idea what a little blue shadow would do for those wonderful eyes of yours?" she said. "I have just the shade. Remind me to lend it to you to-morrow." She touched Franny's hair lingeringly. "And such wonderful hair, completely natural of course, whereas mine is in the high-maintenance category now. I suppose I should be like Rafaella and let it all go silver, but I'm far too young at heart to allow that. Besides, it wouldn't suit me the way it does her. Rafaella was always elegant, you know. Dark hair or silver, it doesn't matter, she's still a beauty. As you could be too, *chérie*," she added thoughtfully, and Franny blushed and quickly introduced Clare.

Juliette assessed Clare's dark chic. Now here was a woman who had seen life, she thought, a woman who knew who she was, but perhaps not what she was looking for. An interesting woman, in fact.

And then it was Shao Lan's turn. "And here is my grand-daughter, Little Blue," Rafaella said, taking her by the hand and beaming.

Juliette bent to inspect her. "She's a little thing, but there's no mistaking she's a Marten," she said, "and *another* beauty." She sighed. "Do you know how lucky you are, Rafaella? My own grandchildren inherited their grandfather's looks instead of mine. They're Labourdes down to their little buckteeth that are going to cost me a fortune in orthodontist bills. They all have large heads and lanky limbs—I swear they look just like a bunch of little squid flopping around in the sea in Hawaii. While you, Little Blue," she kissed the child's cold cheek, "you promise one day to be a dazzler, de-spite those awful shoes that must be killing your poor little feet. Here, sweetheart, let *Tante* Juliette take them off." And she got on her knees and unbuckled them.

"Thank you," Shao Lan said politely.

Franny and Clare jumped. "*She spoke!*" Clare said just as Haigh came in, bent double under the weight of two enor-mous Vuitton suitcases.

"Does she not normally speak, then?" Juliette asked, sur-prised.

"I believe the only other thing the child has said so far was to tell me to f— off, or words to that effect." Haigh dropped the bags with a thud.

"Whoever told you that was probably right," Jake said, striding into the hall behind Haigh and dropping two more bags on the floor.

Franny's eyed widened. The world stood still. She stared at Jake, feeling the heat crawl up her back, sting her face.

What was *he* doing here? Numb, she watched as Jake clasped Rafaella in his arms.

"I know I'm in my usual room," Juliette boomed, heading for the stairs, as though she had been here just last weekend instead of twenty years ago.

"Of course," Rafaella said, "and you'll notice that the good champagne is being poured."

"Glad to see nothing has changed," she yelled, already prancing up the stairs on her small high-heeled feet, closely followed by the Pomeranians and Haigh, with Mimi and Louis, obviously in love, bringing up the rear. But Franny wasn't looking at them.

Jake came over to her. He held out his hand. She ignored it. "Well, hello again," he said.

She stared at him through narrowed eyes. There was steel in those eyes.

"What are you doing here?" she said coldly.

"Rafaella invited me. When she told me you were coming and that she didn't know you, I decided I'd better meet you first."

"Of course." Franny said, "You needed to check me out, make sure I was good enough to meet the Martens, that I wasn't a gold digger after the family money. Well, at least you didn't lie about the dog," she said, then she turned and walked away on legs that trembled.

She didn't know whether to run away or scream or just punch him and have done with it. In fact, her fist was all balled and ready, and she knew how to punch all right from being a tomboy.

How *could* he, how *dare* he make love to her, when all the time he was just checking her out, the way he did employees for giant companies. *Bastard*, she thought, fighting back angry tears, but dammit she wasn't going to cry for him. *Dammit, she just would not cry.* Totally humiliated, she walked back into the salon and stood by the fire, trying to warm her suddenly icy hands.

Still standing in the hall, Clare stared after her. Astonished, she turned to Jake. "What was all that about?"

He held out his hand. "You must be Clare. I'm Jake Bronson. I hope at least *you* will shake my hand."

"Clare Marks." She clasped his hand lingeringly. Looking into his eyes she thought, What a good-looking guy, a bit battered maybe, but she liked them that way.

"Ah," Jake said, remembering Marcus, "then, you're . . . you must be . . ."

"The other woman." She finished the sentence for him and they both laughed.

Clare tilted her chin, smiling, flirting with him. *Uh-huh, this one's trouble*, she told herself. *What happened to the salt-of-the-earth guy you promised yourself? Here you go again, Clare.* But she was beaming as she said, "I'm happy to meet you, Jake."

"Shall we join the others?" he said, offering his arm. She slid her hand through it, feeling like a bride as they walked into the salon.

Back in the salon, Haigh was pouring fresh champagne while the smiling village women, in their best black and frilly white organdy aprons, offered platters of Haigh's splendid hors d'oeuvres. But dinner would be even more splendid.

36 THE LONG MAHOGANY DINING table was set with the best ancestral china, a Limoges pattern bordered in coral and green, and with glittering Baccarat stemware. The starched linen napkins were monogrammed with an elaborate M, and the silverware was so old the pattern had almost worn off. Down the center of the table wild white roses, the *roses sauvages*, that Rafaella had picked from the garden were arranged in low silver bowls entwined with long garlands of greenery. A five-tier silver epergne overflowed with bunches of luscious purple and green grapes from the Marten vineyard.

The room was filled with the scent of roses and the waxy smell of the candles guttering in the drafts that still rattled the windows. They were locked now and the heavy silk curtains drawn tight, and inside all was firelit warmth.

Haigh went around the table pouring the Famille Marten Special Reunion Cuvée, showing each person the beautiful label that almost brought Rafaella to tears because there hadn't been a celebration cuvée since her own wedding. She said, delighted, that it tasted the way wildflowers smelled, silken on the tongue with a faint, flinty afterbite, and she complimented Scott on his blend.

Rafaella sat at the head of her table, smiling in a way Haigh had not seen for many years, as though for once she was thinking of the here and now and not of the past. Little Blue sat on her left, staring blankly at the plates of food, her inscrutable face giving no clue to the turmoil going on in her head.

Rafaella caught her doomed expression, guessed what she was thinking, and immediately sent Haigh to the kitchen to find the chopsticks he used whenever he got Chinese take-out from town. The child's eyes lit up when she saw them, and she even smiled when Haigh cut up her meat.

Jake was on Rafaella's right, with Clare next to him, while Franny sat opposite next to Scott, and Juliette dominated the other end of the table. The Pomeranians were milling around her, and Mimi and Louis parked themselves behind Rafaella's chair. Criminal, however, lingered edgily by the door, looking like a dog ready to make a fast escape.

Across the table tension crackled like lightning between Franny and Jake. He tried to catch her eye but she avoided him and he knew he was in deep trouble. Suddenly he wished he'd never met her, that their night together had never happened—at least then he could have started out even. Dammit, he'd been avoiding relationships all these years, and as soon as he succumbed, look what happened.

Suddenly Scott said to Clare, "I'm sure I've seen you somewhere before," and the formerly radiant and relaxed Clare froze.

"I've never been to Australia," she said in an ice-tipped voice.

Scott looked at her, surprised. "Perhaps we met in San Francisco," he persisted. "I worked in Napa for a couple of years."

"Sorry, I'm a Georgia girl," Clare said curtly, cutting him

off so coldly he turned away, embarrassed, and concentrated on his food.

Watching them all, Haigh thought with satisfaction that this party was beginning to feel like old times. Intrigue was in the air.

Juliette was talking with Franny about dogs and about Franny's work. "Of course I couldn't live without my own little darlings," she said, allowing a Pomeranian to jump on her lap and sniff her plate while the other two clamored in back of her, clawing at the brocade chair.

"Juliette, must we have the dogs for dinner, too?" Rafaella sighed, but Juliette just laughed her warm, booming laugh.

"Don't be so stuffy, *chérie*. They're only interested in what their mama is eating. It's quite normal. Besides, they've been to all the great restaurants. Why can't they do the same thing here?"

"Because that's my brocade chair they're wrecking."

"Chairs come and go. Friends last," Juliette said. "What counts is how fortunate you are to have these lovely young people around your table." And Rafaella leaned her chin in her hand, smiling, because Juliette always got straight to the point, and as usual, she was right.

Jake tried again. "So how are you, Franny?" She gave him that steely look and he wished he hadn't bothered.

"I'm well, thank you," Franny said, so coldly he could have chipped the ice off her.

"I hoped you liked the Casablanca lilies."

"They were beautiful. However, I didn't get an opportunity to thank you."

"Nor I you," he said pointedly.

"I didn't know you two had met," Clare said, astonished

because Franny had never mentioned Jake, and besides she needed to know whether he was free territory or if Franny already had claims on him.

"Briefly," Franny said.

"I see," Clare said, not seeing at all and wondering what the hell was going on.

Oblivious to the flying sparks, Rafaella sat at the top of her table, smiling that old smile Haigh loved to see. "And now I must propose another toast," she announced. "To Haigh, my old friend without whom I would not have survived all these years."

"To Haigh," everyone said, smiling just as the great doors flew open. The wind rushed in again, blowing out the candles and sending great drafts of black smoke down the chimney.

They heard footsteps crossing the hall, then the doors to the dining room were flung open. A man stood there, looking at them. He was wearing a custom-tailored pin-striped suit and handmade shoes. His hair was streaked with silver and brushed smoothly back, and his hawk nose gave him an arrogant look. There was no smile in his eyes, though a faint mocking one pulled at his lips.

With a little cry, Rafaella sank back into her chair. For a moment she'd thought she was looking at the son she had buried just a few weeks ago.

"*Mon dieu*," Juliette said softly, "the prodigal son returns."

"Well, Mother," Alain Marten said, "aren't you going to greet your long-lost son? I heard you'd sent Jake looking for me, so I came home."

Jake was on his feet in an instant, standing beside Rafaella. Haigh flanked him, staring at Alain, daring him with his eyes to make a move.

"Odd, isn't it though, how Felix and I got to look more alike as we got older?" Alain said, with that tight little mocking smile. "As you can see, we had the same expensive tastes, the same custom-tailored suits, the handmade English shoes. There's nothing Felix had that I don't have, *maman*. Are you not proud of me?"

Rafaella was silent as he embraced her. "Welcome home, Alain," she said at last. And over her shoulder, Alain smiled mockingly at Haigh and Jake. He had won.

37 FRANNY CAUGHT ALAIN's triumphant look. Something odd was going on and she knew instinctively it wasn't good. Jake knew it too. That's why he'd leaped to Rafaella's side, the knight in shining armor ready to defend her. It must be nice to have Jake Bronson so completely on your side, she thought with a twinge of envy. Then she suddenly realized that Rafaella was Jake's first true love. Of course, that's why he was here at the château, that's why he was protecting her. It all made sense now.

Alain offered Jake his hand and Jake stared coldly back at him. Alain grinned. "Surely you can't refuse to shake my hand. Can't you see all is forgiven and forgotten?"

"I'll never forget," Jake said. "Nor would Felix."

"But Felix is no longer with us to complain. Only you, Jake. And Haigh of course." Alain turned to the butler who was standing poker-faced next to Jake. "And how are you, Haigh? Still ruling the roost no doubt. Well, of course now that I'm home all that will have to change." He did not offer Haigh his hand and anyway Haigh had turned away before he'd even finished his little speech.

"*Maman*, you really must teach your staff better manners," Alain said with that irritating grin that had Jake tight-lipped. "And now, who else do we have here? Well, Juliette of course." He strode to the end of the table and stood behind her chair. He put his hands on her shoulders, squeezing them. "Still missing Rufus, I'll bet."

She shrugged him away. "You haven't changed much, Alain. Still the great games player, I see."

"What? No 'welcome home, Alain'? Come on now, Juliette, you were always my friend."

"I was your mother's friend. I saw what she had to put up with from you."

"And here's the new winemaker," he said, offering Scott his hand. Not knowing what was going on, Scott shook it. "Now that I'm back, we'll have to make a few changes," Alain said to him. "I've become quite a connoisseur, you know. I think you'll find out that I know exactly what I'm doing, Scott, when I'm in charge of the winery again."

His gaze fastened appreciatively on Franny. "Ah, and you must be the long-lost family member," he said, his voice silky. "Franny, isn't it?" He looked deep into her mesmerized eyes, then he lifted her hand to his lips and kissed it lingeringly.

Franny wondered, Why all the tension? Why was Jake

watching Alain through narrowed hawk eyes? Why was Haigh's glance laser-sharp?

"Franny, you're beautiful." Alain was still holding onto her hand. "As all the Marten women were. Why bother working as a mere vet when you could easily catch a rich man, someone to lavish you with jewels and furs, grand apartments, and private planes."

"I prefer my work," she said coldly as he walked around the table to Clare.

Clare watched him warily. He put a hand under her chin, tilted her face up to him. "Clare," he said softly, "I know you. We must talk later." She stared at him, surprised.

Next Alain turned to the child, who seemed frozen in place, watching him through frightened blue saucer-eyes, the chopsticks still gripped in her fingers.

He turned her chair to face him, and with his face just inches away, studied her carefully. There was something unpleasant about the way he ran his finger over her small nose, the curve of her short upper lip, the length of her slender neck, in the way he traced the outline of her closed eyes, touched her blackbird's-wing hair.

Then he laughed. "*Maman,*" he called, "I want you to meet my daughter. Oh yes, she's mine all right. See how proud I am of her? And I'll make you proud of the Martens again, too. I promise you that, *maman,* on my honor."

Jake wasn't the only one there who knew that honor was an asset Alain had never possessed. But Alain was her son, and Rafaella still loved him. She still wanted to believe him, and now she put her arms around him and welcomed him home again.

38 AFTER THAT, the party came to an abrupt end. Everyone went quickly to bed—except Rafaella, who was sitting on the sofa in the old library, talking to her son. In the candlelight Alain looked young and very handsome, and very much like Felix, but there were lines on his face now and a bitterness in his eyes that had not been there the last time she had seen him.

"I'm glad you finally came home, Alain," she said, remembering that Felix had come home in his coffin. "I needed to see you . . ."

"Before you die." Alain finished the sentence for her. "And are you planning on doing that sometime soon?" He laughed, making a joke of it, but he wasn't joking and she did not smile.

"I hope not, now that I've discovered I have a family again."

"My daughter."

"And a niece."

"Ah yes, the niece. I always liked a pretty woman."

"I remember," she said dryly.

He leaned back against the chintz cushions, as at home as if he'd never left.

"Actually, it wasn't that I wanted to see you before I died."

Rafaella's voice was so unexpectedly firm that he turned, brows raised, to look at her. "I needed to see you once again to make sure I had done the right thing when I threw you out. Where have you been all these years, Alain? And what have you been doing? Where did you make the money you claim to have?"

She looked hard at him, but Alain had been interrogated before and he was an expert at avoiding issues. "Where have I been? Oh, not so far away from Felix, running around Asia, like him. We saw each other from time to time, you know."

Jake had come into the room unnoticed. He leaned against the door, arms folded, watching, listening. Now he said, "And when *exactly* was the last time you saw Felix?"

Alain glanced up at him and sighed. "I might have known you'd still be around."

"Did you really think I'd leave you alone with your mother? You're the crazy one, Alain, not me."

"Why is this any of your business anyway?"

"Because I asked Jake to make it his business," Rafaella said sharply. "I asked him to find out what he could about you."

Alain glanced up at Jake. "And did you?"

"Enough to know that you are under suspicion for drug dealing, that you were in league with some of the toughest cartels in Asia, that you left a trail of debts and violence behind you . . . that you were in Hong Kong the night Felix died."

"Felix killed himself. He was always a coward," Alain said coldly.

"But it was you who killed that poor young girl." Rafaella realized the truth all of a sudden. "I never knew for sure until now, though Jake did. Unlike me, he could always see through you. And poor Felix suffered for it. He couldn't bear that I believed you and not him. I shall never forgive myself for that."

"Felix left because he couldn't stand being around Alain, not because of you, Rafaella," Jake said. "And in the end, Alain killed him because he couldn't stand the thought that Felix's child would inherit everything he considered rightfully his."

"Of course I didn't kill Felix, or that girl," Alain said calmly. "You know there's not a shred of evidence. Besides, Shao Lan is my child. I challenge you to prove she's not."

"I already have." Jake turned to Rafaella. "I was going to tell you tonight but I didn't have the chance. DNA taken from Felix's body matches with Shao Lan's, and in his will, Felix left everything he has, which is considerable, to his daughter."

Confused, Rafaella said, "But why didn't he acknowledge her before? Why did he allow them to live like that?"

Jake shrugged. "I suppose Alain knows the answer to that."

Rafaella stared at her son, lounging on the sofa, smiling as though nothing was wrong. She knew he was a man with no moral rules and boundaries, a man who lied when it suited him, a man who could kill a pregnant girl rather than face his responsibilities, a man who could kill his brother because he wanted his money and wanted to take over his life. How ever had she borne such a son?

"You can't prove it of course," Alain said confidently to Jake. "And besides, the authorities have closed the case."

It was true, there was no evidence against Alain, not even

any witnesses to say he'd been with Felix that night. If there were, then Jake would not legally be able to do what he was about to do, because then the police would have had to be involved. He glanced at his watch. It was three in the morning. He had to protect Rafaella. He had to get Alain out of here. He had to bluff.

"You're wrong," he said. "I personally have evidence, but because of your mother I will not use it. That is, if you get up and leave right now. I'll make it easy for you. My plane is at Marseille's Marignane airport. You can drive to Marseille and be out of the country in a few hours, on your way back to Vietnam. If you don't"—he raised his shoulder in a shrug—"then I'll call the *gendarmes* right now. The choice is yours."

Alain eyed him uneasily. He knew Jake was clever, he was good at his job, an expert they said. He'd believed he'd left no evidence but now he wondered. . . . Goddamn it, you never knew, and if they nailed him he was a man looking at a death sentence, or at least life in jail. *Fuck Felix and fuck his mother and fuck Jake to hell.* He didn't dare risk calling Jake's bluff.

He got to his feet. "So once again you are throwing me out, *maman,*" he said, "but let me tell you something: this time you'll live to regret it. *Both* of you."

Rafaella looked sadly at him. "My only regret was that you never told me the truth."

Alain stepped closer, his face in hers. "But I *always* told you the truth. It's just that you chose to believe the others. Now you leave me no choice." Jake took Rafaella by the shoulder and pulled her away. Alain strode to the door, flung it open, then turned and glared contemptuously at them. "I won't say good-bye, *maman*," he said with that mocking tone again. "You never know when you might see me again."

They heard his footsteps ringing on the parquet as he crossed the hall, the sound of the door opening, the shuddering as it slammed. A car started up. There was the spurt of tires on the gravel . . . and Alain was gone as suddenly as he had appeared.

Rafaella's shoulders drooped as she turned to Jake. He took her in his arms and held her tenderly. "I'm so sorry," he whispered. "I wish it could have been otherwise. I'm just so sorry."

And he stroked Rafaella's hair and held her for a long time while she cried on his shoulder for Felix and for Alain.

39 IN BED THE NEXT MORNING, Franny felt the warm pressure of a small body next to hers. She rolled over and saw Little Blue, her eyes still shut tight. She must have been afraid in the night and come into her room. She studied her innocent face as she slept, admiring her delicate prettiness, seeing the true innocence of childhood that still lurked beneath the hard veneer that poverty had given her. She felt about her the way she did about an injured animal: she just wanted to look after her, make her well again, and heal her wounds. She vowed to do exactly that. Whatever happened, she would always take care of her new little cousin.

Sliding from under the sheet, she walked to the window, pushed open the shutters, and looked out, astonished, on what she thought must be the very first morning God had ever made. Soft, cool, early-morning air stroked her cheek, bringing with it the scent of many flowers, and right outside the window a rare magnolia tree thrust a few perfect waxy cream blossoms to the sky. Below, a stone terrace led onto a parterre garden where tiny formal hedges of deep green box, no more than a foot high, enclosed miniature gardens of herbs and shrubs, their leaves still sparkling with last night's rain. To the right, an avenue of chestnut trees towered over a grassy walkway, dotted here and there with little iron tables and chairs. Beyond that, a lake sparkled silver in the sunlight. She saw a narrow wooden bridge, red as nail polish, arched like something from *Madama Butterfly*. Peering through the magnolia, she could just make out that it led to a small island with a filigreed white wooden gazebo.

To her left was a great sweep of lawns and banks of wild white roses, with hills beyond covered in arrow-straight rows of vines in their full leafy glory, in a million shades of yellow and green, red and purple. The stone buildings of the Domaine Marten curved into a far hill, and farther and higher, sticking into the sky like something from a book of fairy tales, perched what she thought breathlessly looked like an ancient castle.

Their arrival in the storm at the dark, sinister château was forgotten. *This* was heaven on earth. *This* was Provence. *This* was the way she'd dreamed of it.

Turning back into the room, she saw a note pushed under

her door. She wondered warily if it was from Jake, but discovered it was from Haigh, informing her that the evening's festivities would begin at six with cocktails for the family in the grand salon. The gala party itself would begin at seven. Dinner would be served on the terrace at eight. Cocktail dresses and black tie were the appropriate attire. And punctuality was expected.

Cocktail attire! The nearest she had to cocktail attire was the new yellow-and-blue flowered skirt and a tank top. Oh well, it would just have to do.

She glanced up and saw Little Blue, knees hunched under her chin, the woolly lamb clutched firmly to her chest, staring at her, big-eyed and uncertain.

"Hi." Franny smiled and Little Blue gave her a cautious smile back.

"You hungry?" she asked, and the child nodded.

"Okay, so why don't you and I take a shower and get dressed, then we'll go and see if we can find some breakfast."

The hall clock went through its wheezes and grindings, then slowly struck the hour. Franny counted along with it. Only six. Would anyone even be awake yet? No matter, she and Little Blue would explore the kitchen alone.

Ten minutes later, in jeans and T-shirt and with Little Blue in her blouse and school skirt and the awful hard shoes, they were downstairs exploring the vast black-and-white-tiled kitchen.

In the little courtyard outside, Haigh was drinking his morning cup of tea and reading the newspaper when he heard them opening doors and chattering softly. He was on his feet in an instant. *Didn't they understand that in houses like this tea and toast would be brought to their rooms promptly at seven? And that breakfast would be served on the terrace from eight on?* Come to think of it, with all the turmoil last night he'd forgotten to mention it. Damn, now they were invading his kitchen and he didn't like it.

"*Bonjour, mesdemoiselles,*" he said, frostily, tying on his apron. He was wearing his "morning" butler attire, which consisted of white shirt and black pants, and a haughty expression that melted just a touch under Franny's beaming smile.

"*Bonjour,* Haigh," Franny called out. "I thought we were the only ones awake around here."

"Not at all, miss," he said, relenting just a little and speaking in English. "I'm always up early, but especially today because we have the gala party."

"Ah, the gala party."

Franny's eyes sparkled but Haigh resisted her smile because that's just the way he was. Damn it, he thought, she reminded him of Rafaella when she was young. "The entire village will be here, Miss Franny," he said. "Madame has known them all her life. When she was a child she went to the local school with them and she worked in the fields with them, picking grapes. Many of them still work for her now at the winery."

Franny tried to imagine last night's chic *Vogue* vision out on the stony hills picking grapes under a hot sun, but somehow could not. "Must be fun, picking grapes," she said.

"You're likely to find out. Mr. Scott told me last night the harvest will be an early one. Any day now in fact."

"You mean we can all help? We'll do it together, sweet-heart," she promised Little Blue, who didn't understand but who nodded anyway.

"And now, if you will permit me, Miss," Haigh said, "I will arrange breakfast. It will be served on the terrace at the big table under the Chinese wisteria arbor. You can't miss it." He eyed Little Blue disapprovingly. "And this afternoon, Miss, I think it might be a good idea if you and I took a little trip into town and got that child some appropriate clothing."

"Absolutely." Franny beamed at him again, and Haigh felt his hard old heart melt just a little more.

As they walked along the sunny terrace to the wisteria arbor, just for a second Franny allowed herself to wonder where Jake was. She noticed Criminal wasn't around and thought maybe Jake had taken him for a walk. Or maybe he'd gone off somewhere with the "prodigal son." It had been the most almighty family row last night, though she still didn't know what it was all about, only that Clare had said Alain was bad.

"He's even worse than Marcus," she'd whispered to Franny as they wound their way, jet-lagged, exhausted, and bewildered, up the dark stairs to their rooms. "This guy's not merely bad, Franny, he's *evil*." And Franny believed that somehow Clare knew what she was talking about.

She asked herself why she was even thinking about Jake anyway. She didn't want to get involved with another bad guy who thought she was just ready to get into bed with him. He had humiliated her once, but now she had her pride and her values straight. Never again. She had finally learned her lesson.

40 CLARE ROLLED OVER IN her big satin bed, checking the time on the pretty little mother-of-pearl clock. Its filigree gold hands pointed to ten. She'd slept late, but what the hell, she had good excuses—jet lag, the family feud that took place at dinner, that creepy son, Alain . . . *and* Scott Harris, emerging like an unwelcome glimpse from the hard, rough past she would prefer to forget.

She pushed back the covers, swung her long legs over the edge of the high bed and walked to the window. Like Franny, she flung it open, then pushed out the shutters and took deep breaths of air. It was as though she were drinking wine, clean, clear, delicious. Who knew oxygen could be so intoxicating? She smiled as she took in the gardens and the grapes growing on the chalky hills and the rocky landscape leading to the massive cliff on which perched a fairy-tale village. She thought Provence was going to be okay after all.

Ten minutes later, showered, dressed in white shorts and a cute blue T-shirt that said WE LIED, SIZE MATTERS in sparkling letters on the chest, she followed the aroma of coffee to the kitchen.

"Oh, hi, Haigh," she said as he turned to look at her. "How're things?"

"Things are progressing, Miss Clare, thank you." He wondered testily what was wrong with these American women, invading his kitchen like they belonged. Didn't they know this was his territory?

Clare gave him a big smile, helped herself to coffee, then drifted back into the hall and out the open front doors onto the terrace. She perched on a stone lion, swinging her long legs and sipping coffee, which was all she ever needed in the morning to get her going. And this was *good* coffee. She wondered if Franny was up yet. *Of course* she was. Franny was an early riser, she'd always had to be, working those zillion jobs she'd held as a student, and now of course, because she performed surgery on the animals at 7 A.M. Clare was a night person, which was the way it had always been, holding down the zillion jobs she'd had, though most were a little different from Franny's.

The long stretch of driveway with its guardian cypress trees tempted her. She hopped off the lion, left her cup on the front steps, and wandered down the drive to see what was at the end of it. She'd reached the gates when she saw Jake coming toward her with his scruffy gray dog, as well as all the Pomeranians and Mimi and Louis.

"Hi." She waved. "You look like the Pied Piper, only with dogs instead of rats."

Jake laughed. "I hope that message on your T-shirt isn't true," he said, stopping to kiss her on both cheeks, French style.

"That shouldn't worry you," she said, and they grinned at each other. "Hey, I didn't know you were a friend of Franny's," she added, inquisitive as always.

"I wish I knew her better," he said, "but it's kind of a problem."

"So, what's up?" Clare leaned against the flaking stone pillar by the gate, arms folded across her chest, while Jake explained what had happened, though he skipped the sex bit. But remembering Franny's confession over lunch at Shutters Hotel, Clare guessed what had really happened.

"I can't say I blame her for being angry—and for not trusting you," she said when he'd finished. "You don't exactly come off as Mr. Honorable, though I understand your asking her out and all. I mean, there's something about Franny that's irresistible to men, even though she doesn't know it."

"That's what I like about her," Jake said, and she nodded.

"Yup, that's our Franny. So. Where do you stand now on this issue?"

He gave her a puzzled glance. He hadn't asked himself that question. "Beats me." He shrugged.

"Beats you, huh?" Clare unfolded her arms and drew herself to her full five-ten. "Then let me warn you, Mr. Bronson, if you are *not* serious about Franny, you stay away from her. She's too good to be messed around again and I won't stand for it." She poked a hard finger into his chest. "Get it?"

Jake got it.

"See you later. Take care now," Clare said, and she strode off down the leafy lane bordered with cow parsley and tall grasses and chalky white rocks that led to the village of Marten-de-Provence.

LAURENT JARRÉ WAS SETTING up his terrace tables when he saw the long-legged woman in the white shorts heading his way. He arranged the last of the place settings on the rose-colored cloths, positioned the glass salt and pepper shakers, straightened up and adjusted his low-slung apron as she came closer.

"Hi," Clare called, leaping up the couple of stone steps, and he was forced to notice how prettily her breasts bounced under her T-shirt.

"*Bonjour, madame*," he said politely.

"*Bonjour* to you," she said, taking off her sunglasses and smiling into his eyes. "You got any croissants? They didn't feed me at the château and I'm starving."

It took a few seconds for Jarré's brain to filter that into French. "*Pardon, madame, mais nous n'avons pas de croissants.*"

Clare sank into a chair, chin in her hand, pouting prettily. "*Quel dommage*," she said in such a terrible accent that Jarré laughed. "So laugh at me, at least I tried." She shrugged.

Jarré understood and he laughed with her. "All I can offer is a fresh baguette," he said, looking apologetic.

She slammed an enthusiastic fist on the pink table. "I'll take it. And the biggest cup of coffee you've got."

"*Bien, un grand café*," he said, his Provençal accent making *bien* sound like *bieng*.

"I'm Clare Marks, a friend of the Marten family," she said. She wasn't sure he understood, but she liked him, she liked his black eyes and his black hair, his solidity. She patted the seat next to her. "Why not join me? I could do to learn some French."

Jarré stared at her. Already under her spell, he sat down. "*Eh bien*," he said, beaming, "we will begin our lesson. I am Jarré."

"Glad to meet you," Clare said, smiling. She was beginning to enjoy Provence.

41   JAKE HAD NOT SLEPT, but he was used to that. There came a point when you were over the fatigue boundary and into second, then third wind, when the body just kept on moving and the mind ticked even faster. Thank god his bluff to Alain had worked. Of course he could have tried to make a run for it, but France was a small country and not an easy place to disappear in, especially when you were on the wanted list. He'd banked on the fact that Alain would seize the opportunity to get out of the country and not face prosecution, and he'd been right.

The plane was fueled and the crew ready and waiting, as was Oscar, the biggest and toughest bodyguard out of Marseille, ready for any trouble Alain might give him.

Oscar had called from the plane to say they were en route to Ho Chi Minh City, and that the "prisoner" was angry because they wouldn't give him alcohol or food and was threatening all kinds of trouble, but not to worry, he had it under control. Jake doubted Alain would ever risk returning to France.

Early this morning he'd taken a long walk, trying to figure out what he could say to Franny to try redeem himself, and now he wondered hopefully if Clare might put in a good word for him. He also wondered if Franny was up yet, what

she was doing, what she thought of him? He guessed he
knew the answer to that one. Franny had made it only too
clear last night that she'd put him in the same cheat-and-liar
category as Marcus Marks.

He thought of how she'd looked last night, sitting demurely at the dinner table in her prim white shirt and flowered
skirt. He remembered the swing of her sleek blond curtain of
hair as she turned away from him, as well as the wariness in
her eyes. He knew she was right—she didn't know who he was
or what he was, she only knew he'd made up a story about
Criminal, and that they'd ended up in bed together.

He sighed, thinking about what to do. He decided the
first trick was to get her to listen to him. The second was to
tell her the truth. The third was to explain that he could not
have betrayed Rafaella's trust, and the fourth was simply to
throw himself on her mercy. Remembering that steely core
under the soft blond exterior, he didn't think he stood much
of a chance. Unless, of course, she still felt the same electric
pull between them that he did.

He walked past the fountain and sat on the front steps.
Leaning back against the stone lion, he waited for Criminal
to catch up to him. At least the dog was enjoying himself,
keeping aloof from the yapping Pomeranians and the snooty
Mimi and Louis. "Street dogs rule. Okay, Criminal," he said,
grinning as the dog came shooting up the drive. He trotted
toward Jake, panted to a halt and dropped a bloodied rabbit
at his feet, then he sat on his haunches and gazed triumphantly at him. Jake didn't know whether to say "bad dog"
or "good dog." He finally settled for "clever dog," then took
the morning newspaper he'd picked up in the village,
wrapped the poor rabbit in it, and took it to the kitchen.

Haigh frowned when he saw the bloody parcel. "Damned dogs," he muttered, then added, "You'll never see Mimi or Louis do that. That pair couldn't catch a fly." He permitted himself a small laugh. He stopped and looked up at Jake. "Thanks for last night," he said. "Only you could have got rid of that bastard."

Jake shrugged. "By now he's back where he belongs."

"Never to darken the château's doors again," Haigh said with a grin. "I always knew he was the one who pushed the girl over the cliff, despite the alibi. Alain always had an alibi for everything. He was a rotten kid and he grew up to be an evil man. Thank god Rafaella has finally faced up to it."

Jake nodded. He was thinking about Felix. He believed he knew what had happened but he couldn't say because he had no proof yet, though he was working on it.

"Anyone else up yet?" He helped himself to a cup of coffee and leaned against the counter, sounding as casual as he could.

Haigh gave him a sideways look. He knew who he meant. "Madame took breakfast in her room. And Madame Juliette has not yet emerged, though god knows those bloody little Poms must be bursting to pee, I only hope not on my Aubusson. And Mademoiselle Clare took off for the village, I believe."

"The bloody Pomeranians came with me for a walk so you needn't worry." Jake waited for him to tell him where Franny was, but Haigh was fussing over his trays of canapés for the "cocktail" that evening, humming an off-key little tune to himself that Jake recognized as the old classic "As Time Goes By." He heaved a sigh. "Okay, Haigh, so tell me where she is," he said at last.

Haigh lifted his head momentarily. "And who would that be, Mr. Jake?" His face was so studiedly innocent Jake had to laugh.

"Okay, I confess," he said. "I'm looking for Franny."

"Hummph." Haigh went back to arranging triangles of phyllo pastry on a wooden chopping board. "You interested in her, then?"

"Let's say we have some unresolved issues."

Haigh snorted again. "Call it what you will, the result is the same. Anyhow, she's taking a stroll around the garden. You might find her out by the lake."

Jake gave Haigh a hearty slap on his back that sent his bits of pastry flying and brought irritated curses down on his head, but he was smiling as he jogged down the grassy path to the lake. The sun was high in the sky by now and the sweeping chestnut branches cast fluttering shadows at his feet. At the end of the shady tunnel the lake glittered green, and he recalled when he was a boy, running down here to catch a glimpse of Rafaella, hoping to spend time in her company, to listen to her stories of the Marten family, to hear her silvery laugh, to bask in her life-giving glow, and to melt inside when her Mediterranean-blue eyes looked into his.

Yet the woman he had married had been completely different from Rafaella. Amanda was a shy girl, quiet and delicately pretty, an academic with aims to become a professor of English, preferably at someplace like Princeton.

Jake stopped. He put his hands against a massive tree, stretching his tight hamstrings. He was a good runner, could still do a marathon with ease, though he no longer finished in the first dozen. Still, not bad for forty-four.

He straightened up and saw Franny on the red bridge,

leaning over the rail, gazing into the greenish water. He walked the last few yards and stood beside her. She glanced over her shoulder at him, then went-back to studying the carp darting under the bridge. For a long minute neither of them spoke.

Finally he said, "I'm sorry, Franny. I know what you think, but I was caught in a dilemma. I couldn't tell you the real reason I wanted to meet you because I would have been breaking Rafaella's trust. The invitation was to be her surprise." Franny turned her shoulder away from him. "I apologize," he added humbly. "I know what you must be thinking, that I used you, took advantage of you, but that's not the way it was. I liked you, Franny Marten, the minute I saw you telling off Marmalade's owner. I liked your spirit, I liked your independence. I knew how tough your life had been, how dedicated you were. And when I found out how deeply you cared about your animals, I liked you even more."

He sighed, not knowing if she was even listening. "When you took such good care of my ankle, I felt just like the German shepherd whose life you saved. And I liked it, I like the way you were concerned about me, the way you cared."

He put his hand on her shoulder but Franny shrugged it away. She moved two steps along the bridge. He followed. She frowned and walked briskly over the bridge to the gazebo, where she slumped onto the old blue sofa, twisting her head round so she could gaze at the water.

Jake pulled up a chair. He sat opposite, leaning forward elbows on his knees. He held a white rose he'd picked from the bushes that grew so lavishly around the gazebo.

"Franny," he said after a few minutes of tense silence, "are you ever going to speak to me again?"

"No," she said.

Baffled, Jake stared at the back of her blond head. He couldn't blame her. After all, she barely knew him, and certainly knew nothing about him, except what he'd told her about the cabin and about Criminal. To her, he was a man who'd conned his way into her life and into her bed. He thought he'd better do something about it, even though he hated talking about himself. He'd never revealed his wounds and his fears to anyone, but if he wanted her, that was what he had to do.

42 HE SAT QUIETLY looking at her, wanting to stroke her long hair back so he could look into her face, but he knew she wouldn't allow it. All he could do was try to explain who he was.

"When I was sixteen," he said, "I came to live here at the château and met Rafaella. She was my father's lover and the most beautiful woman I had ever seen. I was the most bitterly lonely kid you'd ever meet, living in my dreams and hopes of escape from the hacienda, rekindled every time Lucas, my father, came home. But he didn't come to be with me, he only came to rustle up some fresh polo ponies for his rich customers.

"Then when I was sixteen, Lucas finally realized I was ignorant. I guess he thought he'd better do something about me, and typically he dumped me on Rafaella, then left us both to get on with it while he traveled the world playing polo. And he played well, a ten scorer, the highest, one of the best in the world. Of course I can't blame him for wanting to pursue his career, but I do blame him for forgetting he had a son, and also for what he did to Rafaella."

Jake eyed Franny's indifferent back. He wasn't even sure if she was listening, but he needed to tell her. And he was telling her things he had never told anyone else, not even Rafaella, who knew who he was in his soul. Nor Amanda, whose personal philosophy had been that the past was the past, never to be retold, and they should live for the moment.

"Rafaella saw a lonely boy who didn't know who he was or where he was going in life," he said, speaking quietly. "The first time she saw me, she opened her arms and kissed me. I tell you, Franny, I thought I would die from that kiss, though it was nothing more than a gentle, affectionate embrace. I was in love with her from that moment on. I would have done anything for her, died for her, even. And I still would. Which is why I kept secret about her invitation and also why I had to let her know the truth about Alain and finally get him out of her life."

He shrugged. He still couldn't tell if she was listening but he'd gotten this far so he figured he might as well tell her the rest. "Anyhow," he said, "Rafaella taught me to be a civilized human being, she taught me how to behave in society. After all, I knew nothing except how to chow down with cowboys and ride a horse. She found me tutors, found out what I wanted from life. She knew I was in love with her, and I knew she was crazy about my father. There was a sort of neutral ground between us, an acceptance that this was the way things stood and the way they always would, but that didn't stop us from loving each other. She was like a mother to me, and I was the callow youth in the throes of first love.

"Things between her and my father came to a head after another year. He took it out on me, told me to get out and make my own way in the world instead of living off him. So I packed my few things and I went. I never saw him again."

He looked at Franny. She had buried her face in her arms. "Rafaella kept in touch," he said. "Years passed but I never saw her again either, and then a couple of months ago she invited me to the reunion. At first I wasn't sure. I was afraid today's reality would not live up to my perfect memories, but then I knew I had to come, I had to protect Rafaella. I admit I wanted to check you out. I needed to know you weren't some grasping woman who'd be out to take Rafaella for everything she could get, because Rafaella came first in my life. But then I met you and everything changed." He stared anxiously at Franny's indifferent back. She said nothing and he sighed and carried on.

"I went to Hong Kong to ask Felix to come home. He refused. I found out that later that night Alain had come to see Felix, probably to ask for money. Felix refused and I believe Alain killed him. So you see," he said quietly, "why it was necessary for me to check out all the guests, even Rafaella's own sons. And now you know the reason for the ugly scene last night."

He thought he saw a softening in Franny's back, a relaxing of the shoulders, a droop of her neck, but still she said nothing.

"Via Felix, I traced Little Blue," he said. "I knew as soon as I saw those eyes that she was Rafaella's granddaughter. I followed up the background, found out that Felix was definitely the father. I arranged for her to come here to meet her French grandmother, and I'm hoping she will bring back at least some of the joy to Rafaella's heart."

He heaved a sigh. "And what about coming back to the place I'd always called home in my memories?" He shrugged. "My fears were unfounded. Rafaella was exactly the same, still beautiful, still vibrant, but she was a lonely woman. My father had left her years before. I never knew the full story, though I knew he'd died. I never really had a father so it was no loss to me, but I never asked Rafaella how she felt. That's her secret, and no doubt one she'll take to her grave."

Franny looked at him over her shoulder. "How awful," she whispered. "What on earth did you do when you left the château?"

He leaned forward, his elbows on his knees, staring at the rose he was twisting in his big hands. "I joined the navy, got accepted at Annapolis. After graduation and a few years on nuclear subs I was recruited for Naval Intelligence. I loved the life, loved the comradeship and its 'clear and present danger.' I was a risk taker *par excellence*, and ultimately that became my downfall.

"I want to tell you about my wife, Franny. Her name was Amanda and I met her at Harvard, at the Widener Library of all places. I was there taking some courses and she was studying for a master's degree in English. She was brainy, kind of an intellectual prodigy, still only nineteen and already with a B.A. in her pocket. And god, she was beautiful."

He put his head in his hands, staring down at the floor. "I can still see her sitting at that desk with the reading lamp flashing a green glow over her pale face. She was petite, very slender with long dark hair and brown eyes that I always teased her were like a spaniel puppy's, soft and warm and intelligent all at the same time. She wore skinny black turtlenecks and short skirts and black tights with clompy black boots. I told her she was a throwback to the old Beat Generation, the Juliette Grecos and Simone de Beauvoirs of this world, and she agreed she probably was."

He sighed. "We were married before the semester was over. I wrote Rafaella to tell her because I knew she was the only one who would really care. She sent us a wedding gift, a magnificent old silver candelabra I'd always admired. I have it still, up at my cabin. I never look at it without thinking of her."

"And of Amanda," Franny said, understanding.

He nodded. "Amanda knew I was in Intelligence but she didn't know the risks. We never talked about them. Two years after we were married she told me she was pregnant. I didn't know how to react. What did I know about babies? You'll learn, she told me, laughing at me, and I knew I wanted to have a daughter exactly like her.

"We were in Tunisia, taking a little vacation and we went out that night to celebrate. My guard was down because I thought there was no need to worry. I wasn't even on a mission. We drove round a corner and I saw the roadblock, a barrier with gasoline poured all around. We skidded on the gas, hit the barrier . . . and the car exploded. It was deliberately planned by counterintelligence to kill me. Instead they killed my wife and my unborn child. And I was barely alive when I should have been very dead. And believe me, Franny, I wished I was."

He looked bleakly at her, a man reliving a nightmare. He felt her hand on his, stroking him gently, the way she'c stroked the injured dog.

"I still blame myself," he said. "I've gone through all the permutations of how I should have been more alert. Amanda trusted me so completely and I failed her. There's no way to find forgiveness for that."

He shrugged. "I was strong. I pulled through and after a year of tough physical therapy I considered myself ready to be back in the game. But not those in authority—they knew I burned for revenge and because of that I was dangerous. So they offered me the usual desk job given to 'disabled' person-nel. I chose retirement instead."

He got up and walked to the edge of the gazebo. He shoved his hands in his pockets and stared blankly across the lake. "I hung around the bars for a year," he said, "drinking too much and not caring where my life was going. Then I pulled myself together and bought my twenty-acre retreat or the mountain. I built my cabin there, every bit of it with my own hands. I let no one else touch it, allowed no one up there. The hard work, the solitude, and the simple goodness of the animals, Criminal and Dirty Harry, saved my sanity. Eventually, though, I needed more and so I set myself up ir Manhattan as a P.I.

"Because people knew my father's name, knew who I was I got the big society scandals, the divorces, the probate squabbles and disappearances—wives running off with an-other man, that kind of thing. Then, because I was good at the game, came the corporate clients, pharmaceutical com-panies, and manufacturing giants worried about industria spies. Then requests for guards and special security from foreign statesmen afraid of assassins and Hollywood royalty afraid of stalkers. I recruited Mossad-trained security personnel for billionaires living on the Riviera, and I still worked closely with Intelligence, searching out potential troublemakers and terrorists. And all the while I was looking for Amanda's killers."

He turned to look at Franny, who was sitting with her legs curled under her, watching him, wide-eyed. "I know a lot of people in high places," he said, "and a lot more in lower ones. I know a lot about almost everybody whose names you are familiar with, and therefore everybody is my friend. But my *real* friends are the guys I was in the service with. They are the men who work with me now. Them, I know I can trust."

He shrugged again, finally meeting her eyes. "And that's why I am who I am, Franny Marten."

He picked up the rose from the floor where he'd dropped it and held it to his nose, breathing in its wild, mossy scent. Then he held it out to her. "It's not a bouquet of Casablanca lilies," he said softly, "but again, it comes with my apologies."

"Thank you," she said softly, and he came and knelt before her. "We're alike, you and I, Franny," he said, taking her hands in his. "Two warriors against the war of loneliness."

Then she slid to the ground next to him and he took her in his arms and he kissed her. Properly this time, with all the passion in his warm lips, in his long, lean, hard body, in his encircling arms, that any woman could want.

43 JULIETTE PERCHED on the edge of Rafaella's bed, just as she'd done so many times in their youth, but then they had been gossiping about men and clothes and children. Now there were no men to gossip about, and for Rafaella now there were no longer even any children.

Louis and Mimi sprawled at the foot of the bed, exhausted after their long walk with Jake, snoring and twitching and smelling of the woods they'd been digging in, but Rafaella didn't mind. She lay back against the pillows, the white wicker breakfast tray on her lap, not even touching her coffee.

Juliette looked worriedly at her. "It's better you know the truth, *chérie*," she said. "Having children is one of life's great joys, but it can also be heartrending. Believe me, you did not fail Alain, unless it was to give him too much love. And because you loved him so much, you closed your eyes to his faults. Now, my dear, you must unload yourself of this great guilt because Alain's choices were his own, not yours."

Impulsively, she put down her coffee cup and climbed into bed, snuggling up next to Rafaella, the way they used to in the old days. She said, "Remember, you have Little Blue now, and Franny, as well as Jake and Clare and Scott. *Life* is for them, Rafaella. You must move on, *chérie*, and I am here to help you do that."

Rafaella looked gratefully at her. "Tell me, how have I managed without you all these years, Juliette?"

"You managed because you never needed to go shopping. If you had, then you would have called me," Juliette said, making Rafaella laugh. It was the best sound Juliette had heard that morning. "Now," she said, "what are you planning on wearing for tonight's soirée?" It was what they had always done, discussed who was wearing what so they could present the perfect picture together.

Rafaella forced herself to think. "The midnight blue lace, I believe. You remember the Saint Laurent? You were with me when I bought it."

On the surface life was back to normal and Juliette thought that was all she could expect for the moment.

44 LITTLE BLUE SAT at the square scrubbed-pine table in the kitchen. The woolly lamb was perched on a chair, carefully wrapped in a washcloth in lieu of a blanket. There was a glass of milk in front of her and she was counting the black-and-white floor tiles, thinking there must be enough to cover dozens of rooms like the one she shared with Bao Chu. She was missing Bao Chu very much.

Haigh emerged from the pantry with a single chocolate chip cookie on a plate. He put it in front of her along with a napkin. "Old American custom," he said, "milk and cookies, only here we keep it to single digits. One cookie only, they're bad for the teeth."

Little Blue looked blankly at him, she didn't know what he meant by digits and customs.

Haigh took the chair opposite. He leaned toward her, elbows on the table, hands clasped. She was such a skinny little thing, so tired, so wary, so pathetic. For once there was softness in his eyes as he said, "Tell me about Bao Chu. I'd like to know her."

The child's eyes came alive. "You would like to know Bao Chu?"

"Well, she's your grandmother, isn't she? I want to know all about you, Little Blue. Where you live, what it's like in Shanghai, about school . . ."

"My two favorite things are school and my grandmother," she said eagerly. "I love them both."

"Hmmm, got good teachers at that school?"

She nodded enthusiastically. "I learn English there."

He raised a skeptical eyebrow. "What kind of English?"

Little Blue blushed and hung her head. "I learned *that* English on the street from the others."

"I thought so. And I'm sure Bao Chu would not like to hear you say those words."

"Oh, no, never," she said, shocked. "I *never* said that to Grandmother."

Haigh grinned. "Better not say it in front of *this* grandmother, either."

"Oh, I won't, I won't, I promise."

"We need to go shopping soon, before the stores close," he said. He was wondering where Franny and Jake were when Juliette wafted into the kitchen amid a racket of yaps and yelps.

"Did I hear the word *shopping*?" She dropped a kiss on Little Blue's hair. "*Bonjour, mon petit chou*," she said, squeezing her in an enthusiastic hug. "And if it's shopping, then I'm your girl."

Haigh gave her one of his pointed looks. "Hardly a girl, Madame."

"Age is a state of mind, Haigh, you'd do well to remember that. Anyhow I'm younger than you, aren't I?"

"I don't remember, Madame," Haigh said loftily. "And Miss Franny was supposed to accompany us to town, but she seems to have disappeared."

"She's at the lake with Jake," Little Blue said, and they looked at her in surprise.

"Is she now?" Haigh said drily.

"*Et alors*," Juliette cried, "drink the milk, child, and let's go. You need a party dress for the grand soirée."

45   IT WAS SIX in the evening and Rafaella had yet to emerge from her room to join her guests. She sat by the open window, in the old ground-floor library that since the advent of her arthritis had become her boudoir, surrounded by the oaken shelves of leather-bound books her great-grandfather had bought to impress his bride and the silver-framed photos of beloved dogs through the years and pictures of aunts and uncles and her mother and father. Mementos of her long life were scattered all around: a favorite rose-colored silk shawl bought in Kashmir on a long-ago trip to India; an elaborate beaded lamp of many colors from Morocco; an English silver box containing her children's first soft curls. Lucas's gift still stood on her dressing table, a scrolled and flowered Venetian mirror that she still used.

They'd been lovers for only a few months when he'd bought her the mirror, as a gift after a long absence—playing polo, she assumed. She was never sure that was all he was doing, but she was too proud to go looking for him, and she knew Lucas was just not the faithful sort.

She'd forgiven him everything when he gave her the beautiful Venetian mirror. He set it in front of her and showed her her reflected face, tracing her features with his finger. "How could I ever forget you," he murmured. Then he'd kissed her and the mirror had reflected that kiss. In fact, there was little, Rafaella thought now, that this mirror had not seen.

The hall clock groaned and creaked and struck 6 P.M., its tone a half-beat flat, as it had been for decades. But tonight was different, and the château was no longer silent. She could hear water gurgling in the old pipes as her guests took their baths. A TV blared the news—that would be Juliette, always a TV addict. A child's footsteps sounded on the stairs, and her high voice excitedly called for Franny. Those noises mingled with the *clip-clop* of high heels on the parquet, the yapping of the Pomeranians, and Haigh's authoritative voice giving orders to the waiters recruited from town because tonight all the villagers were invited guests. The band hired for the evening was testing the microphones on the terrace. There was the rattle of trays and silverware as tables were set, and the smell of flowers was everywhere.

The silence of loneliness was banished. Rafaella lifted her head. She took a great draft of the sweet air, filling her lungs, smiling, imagining that the château breathed with her. It was alive again and tonight was a new beginning.

LITTLE BLUE was taking a shower in her very own bathroom. She had never had a bathroom or even a real shower before, and she spun under the warm jets, shaking her head like a puppy under garden sprinklers. She'd had a wonderful time. Juliette had found the most beautiful dress she had ever seen, and she'd also picked out more things, shorts and T-shirts, sundresses, bathing suits, cute sneakers, and the softest little sandals. When they got back to the château, Juliette had simply thrown the cruel black Mary Janes into the garbage. Then she'd kissed her and said, "Go see Franny, *ma petite*. She will help you get ready."

Little Blue had run upstairs, stopping to do an excited little jig on the landing, then she'd paused to think. Some things puzzled her. If her papa was really *grandmère* Rafaella's son, then he must be rich. So why, she wondered sadly, had he not taken care of her and Bao Chu? Why had he never come to see her and brought her here to meet her *grandmère*? And why, oh why, had he not *loved* her?

She'd run back downstairs to ask Haigh the important question, knowing instinctively he would speak the truth, but Haigh simply told her it was complicated. He'd said that later Rafaella would explain everything and she would just have to be patient. Then, speaking slowly so he was sure she understood, Haigh had said, "Your *grandmère* Rafaella loves you. You can trust me on that." And for once in her life, Little Blue trusted.

Now she jumped out of the shower and, wrapped in a towel, danced around her own Red Room, examining the old dollhouse and its intricate furnishings, inspecting the altar tables where she paused to bow just in case any of the ancestors Bao Chu had told her about happened to be around. She pirouetted to the window and climbed onto the cushioned seat, leaning out and comparing the view with the one from their small Shanghai apartment, of the desolate street with the garbage blowing in the gutters, the sagging buildings propped with bamboo poles, and the halogen glare that turned faces into alien masks. She wished so badly that Bao Chu were here to share this lovely château with her, to experience this wonderful freedom, these green places alive with flowers, and these people who loved her. Happiness was a new emotion, and she savored it like a rare good meal.

She cried out in surprise when she noticed the small blue box tied with white ribbon sitting on her pillow. *A small treasure for you, Little Blue, to bring you happiness at your* grandmère's *party tonight. Love, Tante Juliette,* the card read.

She read it again, then picked up the box, hitched up her slipping towel, and sped next door to show Franny, who was sitting in front of the mirror, brushing her hair.

"Look, look. It's *a present*," Little Blue cried, showing her the box.

Franny smiled and showed her an identical box on the

dressing table. "How lovely of Juliette to think of us, Little Blue," she said, just as Clare wafted through the door in a cloud of perfume and little else. In one hand she carried her dress on a hanger, and in the other a blue Tiffany box. "From Juliette," she said, amazed. "Do you *believe* her? She's just so wonderful I want to grow up and be like her."

Little Blue couldn't wait. She opened her box first and stared at the silver bracelet with the heart charm. "Is it really mine?" she asked, looking at Franny, and when Franny told her it certainly was and that she must wear it tonight for good luck, a big grin split her face. Then Franny and Clare opened their own boxes, exclaiming over their gifts.

Franny glanced anxiously at her watch as they quickly dressed Little Blue in her new sugar-pink cotton dress that tied on the shoulders with satin bows. Little Blue put on her new soft pink suede sandals and Clare painted her nails a matching pink while Franny brushed her short black hair until it gleamed. They stood back, admiring her as she perched the sparkly little tiara Juliette had found in the street market on top. "You'll be a princess tonight, *ma petite*," Juliette had promised, and looking amazed at herself in the mirror, Little Blue thought that it was true.

Clare slithered hurriedly into the strapless white taffeta that showed off her olive velvet skin; black satin mules; a black satin clutch; black hair pulled back in a chignon; a splash of red lipstick. She looked at the result in the mirror, hitched up the top and said with a grin. "The virgin sacrifice is ready."

Then she turned and saw Franny in her yellow-and-blue flowered skirt and a yellow tank top and she groaned. "Oh no, no, no, no, and NO! You should have *listened* to me, Franny!" she said.

"Too late now," Franny said, knowing she looked all wrong.

"You're just not grand enough for Rafaella's grand soirée," Clare said, exasperated. "Wait here, I'll see what I can do," and she disappeared, mules clacking on the parquet floors, back to her room.

Little Blue and Franny sat on the window seat and waited. Franny glanced worriedly at her watch. The minutes were ticking by. Little Blue swung her legs. Franny frowned. She had no style, that had always been her trouble, and she worried about what Rafaella would think of her. And what about Jake? She looked awful. She groaned and Little Blue patted her hand anxiously.

Then Clare dashed through the door with an armload of clothes. "Take that off," she commanded, and she hooked Franny into a black silk and lace bustier that pushed up her breasts prettily, though Franny complained they showed too much, and into a fuchsia silk skirt that flared around her knees. Clare's red suede mules were a size too small but she said it was too late to care about such minor details. She took off Franny's small pearl studs and put on Juliette's gift of silver dangly ones, then she swept Franny's hair hastily on top and anchored it with a dozen bobby pins, letting it half fall in a casually sexy tumble. A deeper lipstick, a flush of pink on her cheeks, and a tiny silver mesh bag on a long chain completed the outfit.

Clare stood back to check her handiwork. "And Cinderella *shall* go to the ball," she said, grabbing Franny's hand to stop her from looking at herself in the mirror and protesting she was showing too much skin and that anyway she didn't look like herself. She shoved Little Blue out the door in front of them, just as the old clock groaned the witching hour, and together they hurried down the stairs.

IN HIS PRIVATE QUARTERS behind the kitchen, Haigh shrugged his arms into Juliette's extravagant Dunhill multicolored brocade vest. He buttoned it, then tugged it properly into place. He thought Juliette didn't miss a trick—she'd always known how to please a man. He put on Great-Grandfather Marten's dark blue velvet *smoking* with the pointed satin lapels and admired himself in the mirror. It looked good with the vest, and the crisp white shirt, black silk bow tie, and black pants made the whole outfit look suitably formal. Hmm, he thought, not bad, considering.

Considering what? Well, considering he was knocking-on in years, and considering this was his first party in more than a decade, and considering . . . well, considering that tonight he was a happy man. There was even a smile on his face as he emerged onto the terrace, ready to boss around the hired help and anybody else who might cross his path.

JULIETTE, in a silver lamé sheath and a lot of diamonds, shimmered down the stairs, heading for Rafaella's room. For once in her life she was on time because she needed to be sure her friend was all right. The Pomeranians were shut in her bedroom, their silver food dishes piled with fresh chicken. Later, when the party was in full swing and nobody would notice, she'd let them out because she couldn't bear them to miss the fun.

"Rafaella?" she called, tapping on the door, then going in without waiting.

Already dressed in the long midnight blue lace, Rafaella was sitting in front of the Venetian mirror the Lover had given her, staring blankly at her reflection. The delicate scallops disguised her sharp collarbones and the long chiffon sleeves made her look very graceful. She'd clasped a pair of enormous emerald bracelets around each wrist and wound her hair into a simple chignon that showed off her long neck and the heavy emerald and diamond earrings that swung almost to her shoulders.

Juliette caught her breath. There was something almost barbaric about the way Rafaella looked tonight, and for a moment she saw her as the Lover must have seen her all those years ago, a sensual, exciting woman who could stop any man's heart with her beauty.

"My dear," she said, rushing to embrace her, "you are truly the belle of the ball. *Chérie*, if we both live to be a hundred you will never lose that magic, while I"— she ran her hands over her plump figure—"well I shall just get fatter and louder and will have to rely on my charm."

"My, aren't we the lucky ones?" Rafaella said. "Beauty *and* charm. Not bad for two old *femmes du monde*."

Juliette paused and looked searchingly at her. "You know," she said, "you never told me what really happened between you and the Lover in the end."

A flicker of sadness misted Rafaella's eyes, but she just shook her head. "One day, I will," she said. Then, trailed by Mimi and Louis, the two old friends walked arm in arm to the grand salon where the guests waited.

46 JUST AS THEY ARRIVED, Jake came running down the stairs, handsome in his tuxedo, then Scott dashed in the front door wearing an old dinner jacket and blue jeans which he said were the most he'd been able to rustle up from his meager wardrobe. Jake took Rafaella's arm and Scott took Juliette's and they walked to the salon, where the "family" waited, and where Haigh, a peacock in his colorful silk and velvet plumage, was already serving the last of the Krug.

Rafaella paused at the door to look at her new "family." "How beautiful they are," she whispered to Jake. "And just look at my grandchild. She's transformed."

But Jake's stunned eyes were on Franny, a stranger with tumbled hair and a sexy décolletage, all long legs and high heels. Was this the same woman he'd kissed only hours ago? Franny looked up and saw him. Their eyes linked across the room and, seeing this, Rafaella and Juliette exchanged knowing glances. The château was working its old magic, just the way it had done for them.

Little Blue ran to her grandmother and Rafaella took her hands and held them wide, admiring her new pink dress and her sparkly tiara. "Your grandmother Bao Chu would be proud of you tonight," she said. "And so am I."

Then everybody was kissing each other in greeting and

there was a smile under Haigh's aloof expression as he poured more champagne and summoned a white-jacketed waiter to bring the special hors d'oeuvres that, despite the many interruptions in his kitchen, he had made himself. And then Juliette presented Jake with his gift of a red cashmere sweater and Scott with his striped silk tie, delighting them, and Franny gave Rafaella her gift, a photograph of her father and her grandfather, framed in silver, that once again brought Rafaella close to tears, but she pulled herself together and called for a toast.

"Nothing will spoil tonight," she said, lifting her glass and smiling. "Tonight is for the young. And for the château that you've brought back to life." And they all drank to that, laughing and chattering together, all tensions gone, as though that first terrible night had never happened.

Scott went over to Clare and invited her for a private tour of the winery and, flirting with him under her lashes, Clare said she would like that. Jake stood next to Franny, not touching, though they might as well have been from the heat generated between them.

"You look wonderful," he said. "I like your dress."

"Then you must thank Clare. It's hers."

"It shows more of you than usual."

He sounded a bit put out and she smiled impishly. "Perhaps you remember, there is more."

"Now, now, stop flirting you two and come and greet the guests." Juliette detached them from each other as the first cars circled the parterre garden and the villagers, dressed to the nines, stepped out, astonished to find their vehicles whisked off to be parked by young men in red jackets.

Then Mademoiselle Doritée arrived on her *moto*, her skirt

hitched up to thigh level, something Haigh considered an unfortunate sight. She wore a long dark green silk dress, cut low over her bosom, which thankfully was masked by a white lace collar. A yellow flower was tucked into her wild, springy hair, though the town stylist had flattened the curls as best she could, but as the night wore on, her hair would revert to its old corkscrew self. She beamed with delight, shaking hands and accepting a glass of champagne, as comfortable as if she went to these kind of elegant affairs every week, because after all, like the others, she had known Rafaella and the château all her life.

"It's like old times," the villagers said, beaming and greeting Rafaella with kisses. They said how honored they were to meet her new family, and how lucky she was to have such beautiful "children." Of course nobody mentioned Alain, though via the village grapevine—meaning the ladies who'd served dinner the previous night—everyone knew what had happened. But they would allow nothing to spoil Rafaella's soirée.

Jarré jolted up the drive in his old Citroën with the wooden trailer attached. It was the same one his father had used to go to the daily markets, and he'd never seen the need to replace it and still did not. He was wearing his best black suit, dressed up with a dashing red bow tie. Buttoning his jacket, he strode up the steps, greeting people he knew, which was just about everybody except the young man who, to his surprise, parked his vehicle. Rafaella greeted him with affectionate kisses and introduced him to her new family. He bowed respectfully over their hands, but his eyes sought out Clare. Elegant in her white dress, she was as unattainable as a woman from another planet, and he quickly turned away.

Then he heard her voice behind him. "*Bonsoir*, Monsieur Jarré, the famous chef," she said as he turned, and she deposited quick kisses on both his cheeks.

Jarré felt himself turn a hot red. He said good evening and he was happy to be here, then edged away, accepting a glass of champagne from his old buddy, Haigh, who was right behind him.

"Pretty woman, isn't she," Haigh said, with that knowing little smile. As usual, he hadn't missed a thing.

The Alliers arrived with their ten-year-old daughter, who immediately took Little Blue's hand and led her out to the terrace to show her where the toad lived in the fountain. Even the old boys from the square were dressed up and had been ferried to the party in a minibus. They sat on a row of gilt chairs, dressed up in ancient suits that were now too big for them, their usually grizzly chins shaved pink and smelling of some citrusy lotion purchased from Mademoiselle Doritée's store, looking like wallflowers at the ball. Franny went and shook their hands, telling them she was Rafaella's niece. They smiled and nodded, and some even kissed her hand.

A great deal of champagne was quaffed, as well as lots of Stella beer, and out on the terrace the band, which consisted of keyboards, violin, an accordion, and a guitar played a medley of tunes that always made Franny think of Paris and Edith Piaf.

Haigh checked his watch, then strode to the kitchen to check the caterers, then back into the hall, where he struck a booming note on the brass gong and announced that dinner was being served. Everybody rushed at once to check the seating plan and find their seats.

The single big table ran the length of the terrace, spread with crisp white damask and many brimming pots of white roses, with swags of bay leaves intertwined with sage, rosemary, and lavender and smelling the way heaven surely must. Colored lanterns hung from the trees, and tiny lights were twirled around the Chinese wisteria and curled around the balustrade along the terrace. As night fell, the lights along the façade of the château sprung to life, bathing the house in a soft golden glow, while in front the fountains played and sparkled.

Looking at all the beauty around her, Franny stored the memories. It was the most wonderful evening of her life, here with her own family at her true family home.

Rafaella took her seat at the center of the long table. In the place of honor on her right she had put the mayor of Marten-de-Provence, a farmer who tilled Rafaella's own fields as well as his own. On her left was her old friend Jarré, and next to him sat Juliette. Franny was farther down, between Monsieur Allier and Jake, while Clare was at the other end, between Scott and the town *notaire*, the lawyer who took care of everybody's small problems. The old boys were lined up in a row opposite Rafaella, and Little Blue sat next to her new friend, Mireille Allier, while down the table Mademoiselle Doritée had tucked her napkin into her lavish bosom and was already looking around to see what was going to be served.

Bottles of water, as well as Domaine Marten, were lined up in silver coasters. The chargers at each place setting were a pale pink glass dating from the 1920s. The service was vermeil, and the glasses the finest long-stemmed crystal, all unused for many years. Even Haigh was finally satisfied. He had not let Rafaella down, everything was perfect. The smart caterers from Avignon had done a good job, and he gave a nod of approval to the entrée, a luscious lobster ravioli in a buttery coral sauce embellished with a single spiky pink crayfish.

Music drifted over the terrace, more wine was poured, conversation flowed fast, and laughter rang out. Little Blue and Mireille Allier giggled and held hands—the language barrier held no problems for them. The ravioli plates were mopped with chunks of baguette, then replaced with a new dish, containing exquisite little fillets of sea bass wrapped in lettuce leaves and simmered in white wine. After that came a fricassee of chicken in a green sauce made from fresh sorrel, parsley, and tarragon, served with a delicate squash flower stuffed with a mushroom mousse. The guests murmured their pleasure and dug in heartily while Haigh prowled the terrace like a drill sergeant, inspecting plates, making sure everything tasted as good as it looked. As the evening wore on, the guests helped themselves to even more wine, and the music got a notch louder.

Clare glanced at Scott, sitting next to her. There was no doubt he was an attractive man, plus he had that old salt-of-the-earth allure she was looking for. She sighed as a waiter put a salad in front of her, a delicate mix of tiny leaves with an ethereally light lemony dressing. "Can I *really* eat *more*?" she asked Scott. He grinned and said, "You'd better. Haigh is heading our way on an inspection tour."

Clare looked up at him under her lashes. "Do people in Provence eat like this every night of the week?"

"Certainly not me. A ham and cheese sandwich is all I get

in the evening. Sometimes I have lunch at the Café des Colombes, though. Jarré's a good cook. He knows what he's doing. Straightforward and yet not so simple."

"Hmm," Clare said thoughtfully. "Like the man himself."

Scott gave her a surprised glance. "You know Jarré?"

"We met this morning. He told me his life story and I told him part of mine." Scott's brows raised and she added, "Mine was a little more complicated. Besides my French wasn't up to it, nor was his English."

Scott refilled her wineglass. "I didn't meet you in San Francisco," he said quietly, "but I saw your photograph."

Clare swirled the deep red wine in her glass. "And?"

"I think you are even more beautiful in person."

She met his eyes. "And I think *you* are a very nice man."

"A man who's just met a very nice woman."

"Always an interesting situation," she agreed demurely. They heard Juliette's roar of laughter and glanced down the table to see the guitarist was serenading her. Then Juliette was on her feet and immediately Jarré was up and she was in his arms as they swung away in a perfect waltz.

Haigh frowned. Dinner was not yet over. Dancing should come later, but it was a lost cause, because by now most of the guests were on their feet and the band had revved things up another decibel.

Allier waltzed by clutching Mademoiselle Doritée, whose beatific look Haigh suspected had as much to do with the amount of wine she'd consumed as the fact that she was dancing with her neighbor. Then Scott bowed to Clare and she slipped into his arms as easily as a melting snowflake in her white dress. Jake was dancing with Franny, holding her lightly, not crushing her as close as he wanted because this was not the moment. "I need to see you alone," he murmured in her ear, and she nodded.

Rafaella held out her hand. "Shall we," she said to Haigh, and they danced together, smiling into each other's eyes.

"This is wonderful," she said.

"Of course it's wonderful. I've been working at it for weeks." Haigh laughed. "And it is all going to be wonderful for you from now on, Rafaella."

He only called her Rafaella when he was deeply emotional, and she squeezed his hand gratefully. "I know."

The waiters had replaced the salads with platters of cheeses and the dancers flocked back to the table. Chairs were pushed back and new groups formed, the women on one side of the table, the men on the other. The women clustered around Rafaella, complimenting her on the fine meal and on the beauty of the illuminated château. "It's just like in the old days," they said, their eyes gleaming with pleasure. And they praised her beautiful grandchild, and the charming and clever veterinarian. And of course many of them remembered Juliette and said it was so good to see her here again, and they asked after her children.

After that came dessert, a sweet pastry tart crammed with wild strawberries and raspberries with two sauces, one a melting swirl of vanilla crème, the other bitter chocolate. With this Haigh poured a very special pink champagne, a Piper-Heidsieck Rosé Sauvage, in honor of the Château des Roses Sauvages. Then the toasts began, with everyone complimenting Rafaella and her new family and the château, and Rafaella complimenting her "family" and her guests.

By now, Little Blue was drooping in her chair and Franny was so full she could hardly move, but Clare still sat upright, the perfect lady, not a hair out of place. Juliette was merry, but her blue mascara had smudged. Rafaella was beautiful and still smiling, her long emerald earrings swinging as she bowed her head to the tributes and the applause.

Then the music started up for real and people got up to dance again. Haigh broke out the *Marc*, the good stuff scouted from the very back of Great-Grandfather Marten's cellar. "When else would we get a chance to share it with so many friends?" he said, pouring liberally.

Jarré did not drink the *Marc*. Instead, he straightened his bow tie, buttoned his jacket, and smoothed back his hair. Fortified by the wine, mustache bristling, he strode over to Clare.

"Mademoiselle Clare, will you please dance with me?" he said. Clare said of course, and excused herself from Scott and slipped into Jarré's big arms with a sigh that sounded very much like contentment.

The moon lifted higher over the château, lightening the sky to a milky dark blue that almost matched Rafaella's dress. Her granddaughter came and sat on her knee, and she felt herself melting with tenderness. She looked around at her friends, true friends all of them, dancing and enjoying themselves, at her lovely niece and at Jake, who was obviously falling for her. And at Scott, whom she'd been so lucky to find, and whose eyes followed Clare a little jealously as she danced with Jarré. She looked around for Haigh, smiling when she saw him. He'd taken off the *smoking* and was sitting with a group of the local men whom he'd known as long as she had, sipping the good brandy and recalling old times. And then she looked at Juliette, twinkling with diamonds and complaining loudly that her feet were killing her—until she just slipped off her shoes and danced barefoot. The Pomeranians, released from their luxury prison, yapped and snapped and Mimi and Louis watched them adoringly, while Criminal surveyed the scene with an air of disdain, then slunk off down the driveway on business of his own.

Rafaella could remember many nights like this, when the Lover was still here, but she pushed those memories away and hugged her sleepy grandchild closer. Tonight she would only live for the moment.

It was almost two o'clock before the last of the stragglers wound their way back down the driveway, depositing many kisses as they went, assuring Rafaella this was the best party of their lives.

And a while later, standing at her bedroom window, Rafaella saw Franny and Jake walking down the chestnut allée. Jake's arm was around Franny's shoulders, and her body inclined instinctively into his. Rafaella sighed. She could not imagine anything more perfect than the young man she'd loved as a son falling for the young woman she had just acquired as a niece. It was the perfect ending to a perfect night. Even if, like Juliette, her feet were killing her and even though Mimi and Louis were already snoring on her bed, accompanied by a couple of traitorous Pomeranians, too exhausted even to wait for her to climb in next to them.

4 7

THE LIGHTS illuminating the château dimmed, then went out. The lanterns and the strings of fairy lights were extinguished in a sequence of receding stars, leaving only the moon, low now in the midnight blue sky. It shed a softly filtered light onto the trellised gazebo where Franny sat with Jake.

Crickets chirped, quieter now that it was so late, and the birds disturbed by the lights and noise finally retreated to their nests and settled down. The château was a dark silhouette against the sky. Everyone was asleep and they were the only two people left in the world. The night air was thick with the perfumes of the garden and the reedy green smell of the lake. Breathing it in, Franny thought it was like the Marten wine, sensual, alive, delicious.

"Franny?" Jake was holding her hand in both of his.

She turned her hand palm up in his, trustingly. "What is it?"

"It may sound ridiculous," he said, "I mean, we hardly know each other. . . ."

"But I *know* you," she said, "I know who you are. That night at my house, I warned myself against you. I told myself I was already having trouble with another man. I said all the proper things to stop myself from falling for you. And then you didn't call me and I knew it was too late. I'd already done it."

Jake studied her palm as though he were reading his future there. "I've made some decisions these past few weeks," he said in a low voice, and Franny bent her head to catch his words. "After Amanda died, I used my work as a way to stop from thinking about what had happened. It kept my mind occupied. I always had to be alert, always one move ahead. Not only did I have to think for myself, but I had to put myself in the bad guys' heads, know how they would make their next moves. Sometimes, it was a dance with death but I didn't care—live or die, it was all the same to me. I even enjoyed that dance. Other times I couldn't stand it and then I'd take off for the cabin, collect my dog and my horse and hole up for a few weeks, talking to no one, thinking of nothing except about one day maybe buying a real ranch, having miles of nothing but pasture and woodlands between me and the nearest human being. I enjoyed my isolation. I wanted to share it with no one. And then I met you, Franny, and my life changed."

She put her hands on either side of his lean, tanned face, feeling the early-morning stubble under her fingers. She looked into his gray eyes, pale in the moonlight, then leaned closer and slowly, softly traced his lips with her tongue. She lifted her mouth just long enough to say, "I know. And I love you." And then she kissed him.

He caught her to him. "God, oh god," he whispered, "I thought you were going to tell me you couldn't take the responsibility of a man like me, a man with a wounded past."

"Remember at dinner, the night I first met you? You asked me who I saw. And I told you I saw a *good man*. It was the truth, Jake. That's why I was so hurt when you didn't call That night I slept with my face on the pillow you'd used, like a dopey teen in the throes of first love. And you know what? It *was* first love. Nothing else counts."

"About Amanda," he began, wanting her to understand how he felt about his late wife, but she silenced him with a raised finger.

"You'll always love and remember Amanda and the baby you never got to see. You *must*. You have to face up to the fact that life goes on."

She lay back against the cushions and opened her arms and took him to her. His body trembled over hers. "Franny," he said, and there was that tremor of desire in his voice, "I want to make love to you."

Her long, narrow eyes widened as they met his. "I know," she said as he stopped her mouth with kisses, and at last, naked as those earlier lovers in the gazebo, they made love.

48 LYING IN BED, Rafaella thought the old gazebo was a fine place for making love on a soft late-summer night. She remembered the first time Lucas kissed her on the red Japanese bridge, how her knees had turned to jelly and nothing else in the world had mattered.

It was strange how destiny worked, she thought. If she had not been overcome by loneliness that afternoon in the silent château with its sad, shuttered rooms with the furniture covered in dust sheets, she would never have dreamed up the family reunion, never have got in touch with Jake. Then he would not have met Franny and their lives would have taken a different path. She thought how wonderful fate could be sometimes, when it played into your hands.

And she also thought of how, if she had not been in Cap d'Antibes on that beautiful summer evening, more years ago than she cared to remember, she would never have met Lucas Bronson, and her own life would have been different, too.

She was forty-one years old and alone that day at the Hôtel du Cap when she noticed the handsome man by the deserted pool overlooking the Mediterranean. It was a warm summer evening when all the world seemed to have been tinted blue; a blue haze hung over the indigo sea and the sun had hidden itself behind a blue-black cloud. Perhaps she should have recognized that dark cloud as an omen, but of course she didn't. She just heard the thump of her own heart as she sat watching him.

He was the most graceful man she'd ever seen, long-limbed with a tight, hard body. His skin was tanned a light gold and his too-long black hair was still wet from his swim and tucked back behind his ears. Tiny rivulets of sweat trickled into his dark springy chest hair and of course she noticed—what woman wouldn't—he was wearing one of those skimpy bathing suits that left little to the imagination.

She had been married for half her life to an older man who didn't give a damn about her. Other men had flitted in and out of her life, nothing serious, just a fling here and there, but now her heart gave an unfamiliar leap. Behind her in the bar, a man was playing the white baby grand and singing a soft love song, "A kiss is just a kiss" . . . and she knew she would remember that tune, "As Time Goes By," and that soft, husky voice for the rest of her life.

The man turned and gave her a long, lazy look over the top of the chaise. She smoothed her red skirt guiltily and sat up straighter, giving him a haughty glare that said she certainly had not been staring at him.

"I knew somebody had their eye on me," he said.

"You were right," she admitted, blushing, "I did," and they both laughed.

He came over to her table. "I'm Lucas Bronson," he said, "and I'm happy to meet you. Did you know your eyes match the blue of the day?"

She thanked him for his compliment, feeling strangely lightheaded, as though somehow she knew fate had come calling on her. His hand was firm as he took hers and still cool from his swim, and he did not let go. He just looked at her for a long moment, taking her in. He was so close she could smell the salty sea on his skin.

Finally he said, "I like you Rafaella Marten, and I like your wine. It is yours, isn't it, the Domaine Marten?" She nodded and he said, "I've heard all about you, someone told me you would be here and that we should meet each other."

He let go of her hand and returned to his chair, picked up his towel, and slung it around his neck. "I'll see you again," he said, looking at her the way no man had ever looked at her before, a deep, dark look full of sensual promise that turned her to jelly. Then he sauntered off down the path to the hotel, leaving her feeling as though Zeus himself had descended from the heavens.

"You must remember this . . ." The piano player was still singing. "As Time Goes By."

After that, she'd hung around the bar every day for a week, expecting to see him, to hear from him—a call asking her to lunch in Antibes, to dinner in Cannes, to a rendezvous on the moon. . . . She would have taken anything. But she got nothing.

Devastated, she went back home to the château, telling herself she was ridiculous to feel let down by a man she'd met only once and with whom she'd exchanged only a few words. But she knew those words hadn't expressed what was going on between their linked eyes. What she didn't know was that this was Lucas's usual *modus operandi* with women. Of course she'd heard he was a famous polo player, but now she discovered he was also famous for his love affairs, usually with rich society women.

It didn't matter. She was sick to have him, so she wrote inviting him to the château for a weekend house party along with a half dozen other guests. Then she moped around nervously, waiting for his reply. Two days later he telephoned.

"How are you, beautiful Rafaella in the red skirt?" he said, completely ignoring the fact that if she hadn't sent him the invitation he might never have called her. She reminded herself that she was forty-one years old, certainly old enough to know what she was doing—and certainly old enough to know better. Lucas was dangerous, but that didn't stop her. He said he would be happy to spend the weekend with her . . . "alone" his voice implied, and so of course she immediately canceled all the other guests. "Wear the red skirt for me," he said as he rang off.

A friend had warned her that Lucas Bronson loved both horses and women—in that order. He loved horses for their beauty, their strength, their intelligence, and the responsive way they felt between his legs when he rode them. And he loved women for their beauty, their ability to amuse, and the responsive way they felt under his body when he made love to them. The same "friend" also told her it was Lucas's proud boast that he'd made love to many women and that he'd loved them all, some for a few hours, some a few days, some for a few months, which of course left her wondering exactly which category he'd put her in.

The Friday afternoon he was expected at the château, she was standing at the window watching as he drove up. The top was down on his pearl gray Lagonda and the crisp scent of the cypresses hung in the air. He leaped out of the car without even opening the door, and Haigh, standing on the front steps to greet him, gave him a sideways look that implied a gentleman did not behave this way. And Lucas gave him a smile back that said of course he knew that and he didn't give a damn.

Unobserved, she watched from the library door as he looked around. The hall was bathed in late-afternoon sunshine and smelled delicious, the way it always did, of beeswax and lavender and the mimosa that was bunched in the crystal vases on the console tables and reflected a hundred times in the tall mirrors.

She was wearing her red skirt, as he had asked her to, with a chiffon peasant top, and she'd bound her hair with the strings of rubies she'd had all her life. She thought she must have looked like some Provençal gypsy from Arles, standing there, watching him. Then he saw her. He came over and took her hand. He kissed the palm and closed her fingers tightly around the kiss. "You can't know how happy I am to see you," he said softly, and surprised, she knew he really meant it. She could feel Haigh's skeptical eyes on her, but she ignored him and asked Lucas to join her on the terrace for cocktails.

Recalling the scene now, Rafaella sighed, lost in the feel of the past, remembering as though she were still there, standing with Lucas under the arbor of Chinese wisteria. The long stems of fragrant lavender-colored blooms drooped over her head. The breeze sent their petals flying, one by one, and the small velvety disks fell like kisses onto her bare arms. And there Lucas was, lean and dark and handsome, looking so coolly at her that all of a sudden she was afraid to be alone with him. She needed other people around so she wouldn't do something crazy, like leap into bed with him right away. Instead, she decided they would go to the café in the village for dinner.

She was aware of other diners glancing at them, half hidden in their lamp-lit corner. The locals smiled and nodded at her, and the tourists and travelers who had come for the music festival up on the hill stared curiously at them, she barefoot as always in her red gypsy skirt and Lucas, a handsome famous face they felt sure they knew from the newspapers. But Lucas was unaware of them, relaxed, easy, telling her about the exotic life of an international polo player and how he handpicked his ponies from his ranch in Argentina where his son lived.

His son! Rafaella was jolted out of the dream world he'd just conjured up. She sat up very straight because if she hadn't she might simply have crumbled from shock. She hadn't known he was married.

Lucas looked at her and laughed. He knew she was wondering about his wife. He told her she was American, that they'd split up after the child was born and that at first Jake had lived with her in Connecticut. He was two years old when she died and then he'd gone to live with Lucas—or at least to live at the hacienda. "You know how it is with a polo player's life," Lucas said to her. "I have to be wherever the game is, wherever it happens to be in the world. After all, that's what the sponsors pay for."

Rafaella's heart beat again. There was no wife, though the thought of the boy alone without his father bothered her. "Your sponsors?" she said because she knew nothing of the polo world.

"The multimillionaires who pay for this expensive game. Transporting forty horses around the world is not cheap, you know. All I can afford is my little hacienda—"

"Where your son lives," she said.

"Where Jake lives, yes."

She said she thought the boy must be very lonely, but Lucas just shrugged and said all Jake wanted to do anyway was ride horses. Then he changed the subject back to her, teasing her, making her laugh.

She did not usually go to the café alone with a man, she always ran with a crowd. Behind the *zinc*, or bar, she was aware that old Monsieur Jarré had his eye on them. She knew he would discuss it with his wife later, after the café closed, and no doubt Madame Jarré would discuss it with her neighbors in the grocery the next morning, and the neighbors would discuss it up at the winery, and by noon it would be all around the village that Raffaela Marten was in love. But she didn't care.

Now, an old woman lying alone in her bed, remembering how happy she had been that night, Rafaella sighed. Her memories seemed to produce sighs of nostalgia for the sweetness of the way life used to be, and the next memory was the sweetest of all.

They'd lingered late over their glasses of wine, and it was almost midnight when they got back to the château, where they went for a walk to the lake. The sky was a milky, moon-hidden blue, and a white mist curled from the moist earth. The grass, crushed under her bare feet, smelled like warm hay and there was magic in the air.

Lucas exclaimed with delight when he saw the red lacquer bridge, and she told him the story of how her great-grandfather had been in love with a geisha. She explained that of course the relationship had not worked; they could never have married, with her culture . . . and his. In those days you couldn't take a woman away from that life. Perhaps it was the same even now, she didn't know. When the affair was over, her despondent great-grandfather had built the beautiful bridge to remember his beautiful geisha by.

Lucas put his arm around her shoulders. She stiffened, afraid even to touch his hand as they walked across that lovely little red bridge together.

"Rafaella," he said, turning her to face him. "Rafaella," he said again. His lips were cool and unexpectedly gentle on hers, savoring her, tasting her as he might a piece of fruit. Then he buried his face in her neck and Rafaella flung back her head so that her long dark hair swung behind her. He twined the strands around his fingers and ran his lips up along the angle of her jaw, planted drifts of tender kisses over her closed eyelids, ran his hand over the high curve of her cheekbone. Then his lips fastened purposefully on hers, drinking in her mouth, her tongue, her sweet breath of rosé wine and fruit.

Rafaella's arms were around his neck, pulling him close so that not even the breeze could have found access between them. Her head swam. She felt that sexy slipperiness between her legs again, felt her nipples harden, felt a flush of heat that she had never known in her life before. She was tumbling into an abyss.

She pulled away from him. "Come with me," she whispered in a voice so low and throaty she hardly recognized it as her own. Taking his hand, she led him onto the grassy island to the little white gazebo, half hidden by roses and jasmine. Inside were a couple of couches, a table and chairs, an old painted cupboard with drinks and glasses.

They sank onto a sofa and Lucas slid the gypsy chiffon blouse down her shoulders to her waist. He held her away from him for a moment, a look of wonderment on his face. "I never expected you to be so beautiful, Rafaella," he whispered, and then his mouth found hers and she wanted him so badly that nothing else mattered.

"Oh god," Rafaella cried out as he entered her, but what she meant was *Oh Lucas*, because this was different from the beach in Greece with the pebbles sticking in her back and Henri breathing heavily all over her. This, she thought wildly as true sexual rapture lifted her over the edge into a chaos of many pleasures, *was what loving a man was all about*.

Lucas had come for a weekend. That weekend turned into a couple of weeks, then a month. In the end, except for his polo-playing activities, it was more than two years before Lucas Bronson left the château—and Rafaella—forever.

49 THINKING BACK, Rafaella saw that she had lived through those two years in a haze of sensuality. Her skin was more alive to the touch, her hair more glossy and silken, her breasts more taut, and her belly full of yearning. She remembered the times Lucas's eyes would catch hers across the dinner table, holding them with that deep, dark, hot look that turned her molten with silken juices. They would leave their guests still at the table, drinking wine, talking, and laughing, and slip away to her lamp-lit bedroom and its great bed, where they slid into each other's arms, murmuring with pleasure, unable to get enough of each other.

When Lucas was away (which, now that she thought about it, had been most of the time), she'd kept that special glow of a woman in love, and she'd kept her home filled with her friends and the friends of her boys. Though her sons were grown—Felix was twenty-three and at business school and Alain was nineteen and studying at the Sorbonne—when they were home she'd devoted her time to them as she always had.

She did her best to make sure they were happy, though with Felix, she never knew what really made him happy, if anything. But Alain kept her company and kept her amused. He was always laughing, always teasing, always had a girl or two around. She told Alain he was like his aunt Marguerite, a flirt and naughty to boot. He grinned and said, "So what's wrong with that?" "Not much," Rafaella had said, laughing too. She hadn't realized then that there was another side to Alain, and she would find out about it later, the hard way.

Lucas had been living at the château for about a year when he came home from playing polo in Argentina, bringing his son with him.

"This is Jake," he said. "He's just turned sixteen. I thought it was time he learned there's more to life than cowboys and cattle and a thousand acres of pampas."

Looking at Jake, Rafaella had seen a handsome, shy young man, tall like his father and with Lucas's light gray eyes. He wore jeans and scuffed old cowboy boots and a shirt that was rapidly becoming too small for his wide shoulders. He looked warily back at her and she'd smiled, wondering what he saw with those intense eyes, what he thought of her—after all, she was his father's mistress.

"You're very beautiful" were Jake's first words to her.

"*Et alors, vouz êtes un homme du monde,*" Rafaella had exclaimed, laughing. "You are a man of the world. You already know how to pay compliments." And Jake blushed and bit his lip, not knowing what else to say.

"Come, Jake." She'd put her arm through his. "Let me show you the château. Now you are going to live here with us you must choose your room, whichever one you like. Even if there are already guests in it, we'll throw them out, move them somewhere else. I'll simply tell them, sorry, but this is Jake's room now." And Jake lowered his head, overwhelmed with shyness.

As they walked through the big old house he'd glanced around him, stopping to admire the old silver candelabra on the polished rosewood dining table. He touched it, loving it with his eyes and his hands. "I've never been anywhere like this before," he said. "This house has a history. It's wonderful. It feels happy here. Alive."

Rafaella nodded. "That's the way I've always felt about the château. Later I'll tell you its story. Then I'll show you the winery and explain how we make wine and I'll show you the stables, and we'll get you a horse because I think perhaps the ones we have, except for your father's own horse, might not be up to your standards. And then you will meet my sons."

She had turned to look at him and he'd gazed back into her eyes. He had that same intense, unsettling look his father had, and she knew that one day he too would have the ability to be a heartbreaker.

"You make me very welcome," he said awkwardly.

She reached up—he was a tall young man—and gave him a kiss on the cheek. "You will always be welcome, Jake," she'd said.

Of course Rafaella knew that Jake had fallen in love with her. How could she not, when his eyes followed her everywhere and he somehow always seemed to be where she was, lurking within sight, throwing the ball for the dogs, grooming his horse, hanging about on the terrace? Rafaella thought he was as adorable as a puppy.

Alain, home for a couple of months for the holidays, made no bones about the fact that he resented Jake, but then he also resented Lucas. Rafaella understood, but as always, Alain lived his own life. On the other hand, Felix liked Jake. He went out of his way to make him feel at home, though not exactly his "friend" because Felix did not have friends, and besides he considered Jake just a kid. But he didn't talk down to him and he took him around the winery and explained how the *vendange* worked. He even allowed him into his room to see his collection of model race cars. Jake and Felix always respected each other, even though they did not understand each other, and Rafaella had appreciated that.

Jake never asked Rafaella about her relationship with his father. He never asked whether they would marry, but then Rafaella had never asked that question, either. She thought now, as she fell asleep, that perhaps she'd been too afraid to find out the answer.

AND NOW LIFE HAD come full circle. Jake was "home" again, and the filigree white gazebo was welcoming a new pair of lovers.

50

CLARE WAS FIRST UP the next morning. She threw on a short denim skirt, a white shirt, and sneakers then stepped outside into the corridor. Both Franny and Little Blue's doors were shut and she decided she'd better not wake them.

Downstairs everything was silent, though she suspected Haigh was up, after all it was after ten o'clock. She decided against disturbing him too, figuring he'd be in one of his huffy moods after the late night, and headed outside instead.

She ambled down the long straight driveway, her sneakered feet crunching on the gravel, sniffing the sharp cypressy scent that reminded her of the pinewoods back home. Soon she was out in the narrow lane that followed the perimeter wall of the château's grounds. The banks were high with wildflowers whose names she did not know, blue and purple and the yellow of the sun itself and she picked a few, feeling like a kid again, when she would pick field flowers and put them in a jam jar of water and watch them rapidly wilt. Birds sang and the morning air was clean and winey, the way city air never was.

She told herself it was mere coincidence that she ended up in the village square, waving good morning to Monsieur Allier who was busy attaching hand-chalked price tags to his *courgettes* and melons. "*B'jour, mademoiselle,*" he called, "*ça va bien?*" Smiling, she called back, "*Bien, merci, Monsieur Allier, et vous?*"

She headed purposefully across the cobblestones to the Café des Colombes. A good strong cup of coffee was what she needed, and also, hopefully this morning, a couple of croissants. A chat with Laurent Jarré would be kind of amusing too, or was he the *real* reason she was there?

Putting that stray thought to the back of her mind, Clare bounced up the steps onto the terrace and strode into the café, a smile already on her face. But Jarré wasn't there. She walked around the back of the *zinc* counter, inspected the coffee machine and poured herself a cup. She helped herself to sugar which came wrapped as tiny sausages in fancy pink and white paper and strode back onto the terrace, picking up a well-thumbed copy of yesterday's French newspaper as she went. Installed at a shady table under the awning with her feet propped on a chair, she sipped the coffee, flicking through the incomprehensible newspaper, waiting.

She didn't have to wait long. Jarré appeared from the garden behind the café carrying a straw basket piled with greenery. He stopped in his tracks and his dark eyes grew even darker when he saw her. Clare leaned back in her chair, looking over her shoulder at him, one eyebrow cocked.

"*Bonjour, Monsieur Jarré,*" she said, but there was an impish curl to her lips as she emphasized the *Monsieur*. "That is, if I can still call the man I danced with so many times last night '*Monsieur.*'"

Flustered, he said quickly in French. "It is the polite way in our village, *mademoiselle.*"

Clare unraveled herself from the chair. "Well then, we'll just have to change that, won't we? How about I call you Jarré? I like it better than Laurent. And you can call me Clare. Okay?"

Jarré nodded solemn as ever. "Okay," he said reluctantly.

"As you can see, I helped myself to some coffee."

"I'll make you some fresh." He hurried in to the bar.

"Jarré," she called after him, and he popped his head out again and looked questioningly at her.

"What do I have to do to make you smile?"

Jarré was smiling as he turned back to the coffee machine and prepared a *grand crème* for the beautiful woman sitting at his table. He also prepared one for himself then he took them and went and sat opposite her.

"You dance very well . . . Clare," he said.

"And so do you . . . Jarré," she said.

"You looked very beautiful last night."

"And you looked extremely handsome."

"How long will you stay here?"

"I thought a couple of weeks, but now . . . it depends . . ."

"It depends?"

"It *depends*."

He nodded, looking at her in a way no man had ever looked at her before. Clare was used to admiration, to lust even, but Jarré's eyes trusted her.

"I will do everything I can to make your stay happy," he said.

The idea came to her in a flash. "Then I know what you can do. You can give me cooking lessons." She flung her arms wide, shaking her head in astonishment at her brilliant idea. "Jarré I cannot even boil an egg, I *failed* mashed potatoes in home ec., I'm a disaster in the kitchen. Do you think you can change me?"

He shrugged, "*Bien sûr*," he said, looking a little doubtful.

"Then it's settled," Clare said happily. "*I'll* show up every morning and help in your kitchen and *you* will teach me how to cook." She held out her hand, "Deal?"

He took it. "Deal," he said, and this time he was smiling.

51

THE TOUR of the Domaine Marten winery was to begin at six, followed by dinner at the Moulin d'Argent in Saint-Sylvestre, the *village perché*.

As usual, Clare was first to be ready, sitting on the stone lion by the front steps, legs swinging. Little

Blue and Franny came next, quickly followed by the exuberant Pomeranians and Juliette, elaborate in a flowery caftan, bead necklaces, and many clanking gold bracelets. Jake appeared, walking up the driveway from the village, hauling Criminal tied with a piece of rope in lieu of a lead, something he'd never previously needed.

"He spends more time in the village than at home," Jake said, unconsciously reverting to calling the château "home," which was the way he'd always thought of it.

"It's the lure of the wild," Juliette cried out cheerfully. "Criminal must be in love with one of those *méchant* dogs that linger by the fountain all day. Trust me, there's some little French *mademoiselle* he can't resist."

Clare didn't need to look at Franny, she could practically feel the sexual electricity sparking between her and Jake. She wondered worriedly about Jake Bronson; he had a special and sometimes dangerous job, and he was a man with secrets— and probably a past. She only hoped Franny would make the right move this time. "Salt-of-the-earth type, Franny. Remember?" she reminded her, looking pointedly at Jake.

"Oh . . . oh *definitely*." Frannie beamed and Clare crossed her fingers. Meanwhile, she wondered what her own "right move" was to be.

Finally Rafaella and Haigh came out onto the portico. Little Blue, pretty in a yellow cotton sundress rushed to greet her. "*Grandmère* Rafaella," she cried, "I was missing you."

Rafaella stopped in her tracks—at that moment she knew true happiness. Beaming, she kissed her grandchild, "And I missed you too, and I want you to ride with me in the Bentley. Juliette too, I think. And Franny and Clare, you'll drive with Jake."

Sitting next to Jake, driving up the road that wound its way through soldierly-straight rows of vines loaded with bunches of overstuffed grapes, Franny wondered how it was possible that a place could get even more beautiful. But then Jake told her she should see the different beauty of the vineyards in winter, leafless and cut back into small witch-like branches.

"Sometimes it rains so hard," he told them, "and then the mistral comes and knocks down trees and tiles from the roofs and makes everybody bad-tempered. Around New Year's Eve, the cold creeps in, though it's still possible to eat lunch out on a sunny sheltered terrace. The night air feels sharp in your lungs and so clean you can almost drink it and you shiver as you pile on jackets and sweaters and go to Jarré's to dine on his hot *soup au pistou* and his hearty venison stew, and maybe drink a bottle or two of the wine we're going to taste now." He sighed happily. "I'll tell you, life does not get much better than that."

"But how can you remember it so clearly from all those years ago?" Franny said, astonished.

"How could I ever forget?" he said simply.

At the winery, Scott was waiting for them. The stone arches behind him glowed honey-color in the evening sun and the old monastery bell in Saint-Sylvestre tolled the hour.

"Right on time," he called, opening the door of the Bentley. "Welcome, ladies," he said, though with his Aussie accent *ladies* sounded more like "liediss." He got to Jake's car just in time to open the door for Clare.

Knees demurely together, she swung her long legs out. She looked up at Scott and her heart leaped. God, he was cute, and *truly* salt-of-the-earth. . . . He was everything she was looking for.

"You've come just at the right moment," he told Rafaella. "Harvesting on the west hill begins tomorrow. Everybody's geared up, the migrant workers are here, ready to go, plus the locals of course. We should be able to start the first crush to-morrow night."

Rafaella always enjoyed the *vendange*. It was exciting to see the grapes roll through the huge machines that removed the stems, then watch them tumble into the giant crusher. It was intoxicating to smell the sweet juice, and later taste a thimbleful to assess its sweetness. Too sweet? Too acid? Too green? Then see it cascade into the huge, freshly scoured fermenting vats from where, several weeks later, it would emerge as the beginnings of a new Domaine Marten wine. It was then that Scott's expertise would come into play. He was the "nose," the only person to blend the Domaine wines, us-ing his knowledge and experience and his instinct to add or subtract, to sniff and taste, to correct until he was satisfied with the new vintage.

Scott explained the process to them as they toured the big stone sheds, inspecting the tall steel vats and the huge ma-chines. Then he took them down to the cool dim sixteenth-century *caves*. The stone walls were arched and banded with old beams, and the aroma of wine made them giddy. On a stone table in the center of the largest cellar waited an array of glasses and a half dozen bottles of wine ready for the tasting.

Scott opened the first one and poured a small amount into each glass. "This was a great Domaine Marten vintage," he said proudly, demonstrating to the novices how to first swirl the glass to release the aroma, then take a sip, let it slide over their tongues, then allow it to rest for a second on the palette. "Then you spit it out," he said.

Little Blue stared at him, shocked. Of course Chinese peasants spat but she had never expected to see her elegant French *grandmère* do that. Still, they all sniffed, swirled, and sipped obediently, though Clare and Franny drank theirs instead of spitting. "Too good to waste," Clare told Scott with a grin.

After their tour, they drove up to the historic *village perché*, past old farms clinging to the rocky hillsides and the strange little conical stone buildings called *bories*, believed to be ancient shepherds' huts. The very walls of the *bastide* grew out of the rocks, and cobbled streets wound through the small village that still looked the way it had hundreds of years before.

Jake held Franny's hand, Rafaella held Little Blue's, Juliette held the Pomeranians (for once on their leashes), and Scott fell in step with Clare. She was instantly aware of him, his lean body, his easy outdoorsman stride. "Tell me, did we dance together last night?" she asked, pretending not to recall.

"We did."

"Hmm, if it was that good surely I would have remembered?"

She was flirting with him and he was enjoying it. "Don't you remember I told you how beautiful you were?"

She tilted her head, looking at him under her lashes, "And do you still think that?"

"I do," he said, sounding as though he were taking marriage vows, making her laugh.

"I like a guy I can laugh with," she said, linking her arm companionably through his as they walked.

They went to the sprawling outdoor café in the square, where they dined on roast chicken and the best *pommes frites* while the first stirrings of a mistral tugged at the umbrellas and sent their hair and napkins flying. Holding hands with Jake under the table, Franny hardly dared believe she was here in this paradise with a man she loved. *A man who loved her. A man whose bed she couldn't wait to share tonight.* The veterinary practice in Santa Monica suddenly seemed a long way away.

The monastery bell was tolling eleven as they drove back down the winding road to the château, and this time Franny, too, thought it was like coming home.

52 THAT NIGHT Little Blue could not sleep, for worrying about Bao Chu. She thought of her grandmother's cough and the way it shook her whole body, and the sweat streaking down her exhausted face. Terrified, she realized that Bao Chu might die soon, and that was why she'd insisted Little Blue go to France alone.

She got up very early the next morning and went and sat cross-legged, outside Rafaella's door until she saw Haigh carrying her breakfast tray. Then she asked if he would please ask Rafaella if she could speak to her.

"Of course, come in, *ma petite*," Rafaella called and Little Blue slipped into what was to her, her grandmother's magic kingdom. Her eyes roamed the tall shelves stacked with more books than she had ever known existed, taking in the many paintings, the tables with the photos, the silk shawl spread across a comfortable chair by the window and the huge four-poster bed where Rafaella lay propped against lacy pillows, watching her.

"Well? Do you like it?" Rafaella smiled at the child's stunned expression.

"All the books in the world must be here," she said, amazed.

Rafaella laughed. "Maybe not quite all of them, but there are thousands. Come here, *ma petite*, and kiss your *grand-mère*, and then tell me what you need to discuss."

Litle Blue climbed into the big bed, where she curled up unself-consciously next to her grandmother. "I am worried about Bao Chu," she said in a small, trembly voice.

Rafaella sighed. She knew from Jake that Bao Chu was in bad shape, though at least now she was receiving the best medical care. "I can't tell you not to worry, *ma petite*, because your grandmother has been ill for a long time," she said gently.

Little Blue lifted her head, fixed her large blue eyes on Rafaella, and said, "*Grandmère*, how do you die?"

Rafaella took a deep breath. She could hardly tell the child that the true answer to that question could only come from personal experience, though sometimes she'd wondered if you did not die little by little from life's blows. She thought about it, then finally said, "We believe that when you die, you go to sleep. Sometimes it's sudden, an accident per-haps. Sometimes it takes a long time to get there, like with Bao Chu. And sometimes it's peaceful and sweet and gentle, and you have time for a long good-bye with a smile in the eyes. My own father died like that, as though he were happy finally to go."

"Will Bao Chu die like that?"

"I hope so, child."

"And you too, *grandmère* Rafaella? Will you die with a smile in your eyes?"

Rafaella thought again about dying, as she had many times these last few years. "I will now, Little Blue," she agreed.

"And then will I see Bao Chu and you again?"

Rafaella thought about that. "It is said that if we believe, we shall all be reunited in heaven." Little Blue heaved a sigh of relief and said thank-you. Then together they ate Rafaella's breakfast of boiled eggs and toast, and for the moment the subject was forgotten.

53 EVERYONE WAS UP EARLY, dressed in shorts and T-shirts with their hair tied back, ready to pick grapes—except for Rafaella and Juliette of course, though they promised to come inspect the work at lunchtime and bring some of Haigh's "refreshments."

Scott met them at the base of the west hill, which was already crawling with itinerant pickers, their big scissors glinting in the already hot sun as they snipped off the fat bunches of grapes and laid them carefully in large straw baskets.

Scott was all business this morning and he barely gave

Clare a glance. He simply took them to a row of vines
demonstrated how to cut a bunch of grapes, and showed
them the perfect, round, ready-to-burst fruit that needed to
be cut, and the other lesser bunches they should not cut
Then he warned them to be careful of the wasps that were
always a scourge at the *vendange*, wished them luck, and left
them to get on with it.

Clare looked at Franny. "It's back to my roots," she said
tying up her hair, "right where my family started, in the
fields, only then I was picking onions not grapes. Doesn'
seem like there's much difference to me—hard work is hard
work."

And it was. After an hour Franny's back ached and Clare
had been stung twice. Two hours later even Little Blue had
slowed down. Three hours and they were sweating under the
grilling sun, praying that Haigh and the refreshments would
arrive soon. They stopped to gulp sun-hot water from plastic
bottles, then hauled their baskets to the trailer, where the
grapes were inspected and trundled off to the *chai*, ready to
be destemmed and sorted. Then it was back to the hot hill to
pick more.

Franny knew she would never feel the same way about a
bottle of wine again. She wiped the sweat from her face and
thought longingly of quitting and a cold shower. She could
see Jake farther up the hill, working methodically along his
row. He was already much farther than she was, and she
sighed and got on with it.

When the château's car finally wound its way slowly up
the hill, Scott called a lunch break. The workers scattered
into the shade to eat their cold potato omelettes and sand
wiches with a good slug of red to wash it all down, and the

party from the château straggled wearily back to the courtyard, where trestle tables covered with a red-and-white-
check oilcloth were set up under the stone arches. Hands
and faces washed, wasp stings taken care of, the new workers dropped thankfully into their chairs, watching hungrily as
Haigh laid out his offerings: a crisp *salade niçoise,* the same
cold potato omelette the migrant workers were eating, long
baguettes, and huge platters of ham and cheeses.

"So how do you like manual labor?" Scott said to Clare.

She grinned and bit into a slice of the potato omelette. "I
like the reward," she said. "This is wonderful. I'll ask Jarré to
show me how to make it."

"Jarré?" He looked at her, surprised.

"He's giving me cooking lessons. I start tomorrow. Maybe
when I go back to California, I'll get a job as a chef."

"You're going back then?"

The thought of leaving made Clare suddenly sad. "Let's
not talk about it."

"Okay. But you know I'm getting used to having you
around. I wouldn't want to have to move that into the I'm-
missing-you category."

"You wouldn't, huh?" She was doing that flirty thing with
her lashes again.

"Look," he said, "the harvest and the crush are my busiest
time. I never know when I'll be able to break free, but when
I do, will you have dinner with me? Please?"

"You mean you and me? Alone?" She was laughing at him.

"Alone," he said firmly and she nodded and said okay. After lunch, it was back to picking. Franny found it hard going,
but Little Blue, fueled by the food, had found new energy.
Jake was on his third row and Franny still hadn't finished her

first. She thought her arms would break from lugging the heavy basket that the itinerant North African pickers, who roamed the south each year for the grape harvest, carried so easily on their heads. Soaked with sweat, her hands stained purple with juice, her hair a tangled, sticky mess from constantly sweeping it back under her hat, filthy and tired, she was glad when Scott said the château workers could call it a day, though the rest of them would keep on until the hillside was finished.

Back at the château, a shower had never felt so welcome, and the thought of a quiet night spent with her man never more inviting. Franny just wanted to curl up in Jake's arms. She wanted to feel the heat of his body, to smell his skin and run her purple-stained hands all over him. She wanted to sleep with him, spooned around his body, loving him.

LATER, AFTER a simple dinner, Rafaella and Juliette settled down to play Monopoly with Little Blue and Haigh. Explaining that she had to be up early because she was going to help Jarré prepare the special lunch tomorrow, Clare went off to bed, while Franny and Jake went for a walk.

His arm was around her waist as they strolled back to the lake in the blue half-light. Criminal snuffled in the reeds, yelping when he slid into the water and got his paws wet, scaring a squadron of ducks who took off squawking. They sat on the grass to watch the returning ducks dunking their heads in the water and waving their silly yellow feet in the air as they scoured for whatever it was ducks ate. A swan patrolled the far shore, aware of the dog and on guard for its mate and her young. The same wind that had sprung up the night before suddenly raked through the treetops. Jake said it was the mistral blowing all the way from Siberia, down through northern Europe, then channeling through the mountain ranges to end up in Provence. "Scott had better get his grapes in quickly," he added, "or he's in trouble."

They lay together on the soft grass, kissing occasionally and talking about nothing and everything. Then, tired, they made their way back to the quiet house. At the top of the stairs, Jake took Franny's hands in his. His eyes asked a question, and she smiled as she nodded and walked with him, through the now silent house, to his room. There, curled up next to him, she fell asleep almost before her head touched the pillow. It had been another of the happiest days of her life. How many more could life offer her? she wondered.

54

CLARE WAS UP with the sun, dressed for work. She jogged down the lane to the village and arrived at the café just as Jarré was opening his shutters.

"*Bonjour*, Jarré," she called. He turned to look at her, surprised.

"I'm here to start work," she said. "Don't you remember?"

"But I didn't think you meant it," he said, astonished.

"Well, here I am, ready for action, sir," she said, snapping to attention.

Jarré looked doubtfully at her, still not quite believing. He decided he'd put her to the test, see if she was just bored and playing around, maybe showing off for him.

"*Et bien*, first the vegetables need to be scrubbed," he said, showing her into the tiny kitchen that was just barely big enough to accommodate both of them at the same time. "Then the salad will need to be prepped, tomatoes, lettuces, cucumbers. The red peppers must be toasted and blackened, cooled, and their skins pulled off, then diced small. And the mussels must be scrubbed clean."

He showed her her workstation—a wooden chopping block next to a deep porcelain sink, with a stack of metal bowls and an array of lethally honed knives. "Take care with the knives," he said brusquely, and left her to it.

Clare stared anxiously after him. This wasn't quite what she'd expected. She'd thought she'd be busy at the stove, sprinkling some delicious fish with fresh herbs, arranging it on a pretty dish. She picked up a knife and inspected it warily. She thought, you could easily kill a person with this knife. Next she looked around for rubber gloves, but there were none. Apparently Jarré didn't worry too much about his hands. Anyway, after the grape picking her own were already covered in nicks, plus a couple of wasp stings and a few broken nails, and were past worrying about. She picked up a brush and started scrubbing the tiny vegetables. She grinned—she was back to her poor-kid sharecropping roots all right.

When Jarré returned half an hour later, the vegetables were clean and in bowls, the greens were washed and spun dry, and the red peppers were toasting on the grill. Clare glanced up from the chopping board where she was carefully dicing tomatoes. She gave him a smile, missed with the knife, and neatly sliced open her finger. "Oh, hell," she said as the blood spurted. "Now, I've ruined the tomatoes."

With an alarmed cry, Jarré leaped to her side, examining the finger, stanching the blood. His face was agonized as he ran cold water over the wound. Clare smiled. She thought it wasn't all that bad, but she was enjoying the attention.

"It's all my fault," Jarré groaned, "I should not have let you, an amateur, use those knives. I should have known there would be an accident."

"It's okay," Clare said gently, watching his face as he bent over her finger. "It's really not that bad and it doesn't hurt at all."

"Ah, but you are just being brave," he said, meeting her eyes. Their faces were so close, just inches away, and Clare couldn't resist. She moved an inch or two closer and kissed him on the lips.

"There, now I'm all kissed better," she said, giving him her flirty under-the-lashes look as he blushed. It was amazing, she thought, smiling, a man who actually blushed instead of grabbing a girl when she kissed him. She really was in the land of milk and honey. She wondered if he'd liked that kiss as much as she had. She'd liked the way his bristly mustache tickled her face and she'd liked the firmness of his lips, the musky scent of his aftershave, and the clean smell of his skin.

Flustered, Jarré hurried to fetch a Band-Aid. He came back and wrapped it round her wounded finger. Then they sat in the bar together, silently sipping hot coffee. "You shouldn't have done that," he said finally.

"Done what?" she asked innocently.

"The . . . *er* . . . the kiss," he said, avoiding her gaze and sipping his coffee instead.

"Oh? And why not?"

Jarré sighed. "I think you are a woman who always does exactly what she wants, are you not?"

"I am," Clare agreed, nibbling on a hunk of buttered baguette because Jarré had no croissants again.

He was serious as he said, "But then how does a man cope with you? How can he know what you will do next?"

"He doesn't," Clare said. "That's half the fun." And this time Jarré laughed, showing strong white teeth that made her want to find out who his dentist was. But the kitchen helpers were arriving to prepare lunch and it was time for work again.

Back in the kitchen, Clare watched Jarré prepare sauces for fish and for duck breast. He let her taste his homemade peach ice cream and explained how it was made. Then he had her clean the baskets of wild strawberries, fresh from that morning's market, and together they set up the big table on the terrace for the château party. After that, Clare had to hurry back to the château to change not only her clothes but her persona, from kitchen helper to honored guest.

Promptly at 12:30 Haigh drove Rafaella and Juliette to the village in the Bentley while the younger people walked. Little Blue skipped ahead in her comfortable new sneakers. She stopped to stare at the dogs lying in the shade by the fountain.

"Look, Jake," she called, pointing. "There's Criminal."

He was sprawled with the other dogs, tongue lolling, making like a genuine French street dog. When he saw them, he lifted his head, wagged his tail languidly, then settled down again, making them laugh.

At the café, Little Blue sat, as she always did, next to her grandmother. She propped the woolly lamb that never left her side behind her, sipping her lemonade in a ladylike manner and chattering in what was by now a mix of French, English, and Mandarin, which somehow everyone understood.

A serious Jarré came to greet his guests, pouring the wine from his own vineyard, waiting as always for a sign of approval, even though Scott was missing today, still busy with his harvest. The wind had dropped to a soft breeze that brought with it the fresh scent of the *garrigue*, the stony hillsides dotted with wild rosemary and broom.

They were talking and laughing and eating Jarré's John Dory sautéed simply with a little garlic and tarragon when Jake's cell phone rang. He excused himself and took the call outside. Rafaella's eyes followed him. With wind ruffling his dark hair, she thought he looked like the young boy he'd been when he first came to the château.

He finished his call, made another, then returned to the table. "Sorry, but I have to get back to New York for a few days," he said. He was looking at Franny, and Rafaella knew how much he didn't want to leave her, not now when everything was so new, so sweet, and they were together in the place he loved best in the world. "The plane will pick me up in Avignon this evening," he said. "I'll be back as soon as I can."

They lingered over their lunch and Rafaella caught Franny's eye across the table. She knew exactly what she was thinking, that she didn't know how she would get through the next few days without her lover. She smiled sympathetically—it was a feeling she knew only too well.

55 LATER THAT EVENING, after Jake had left and the others were already in bed, Franny was alone with Rafaella in the small salon. They were sitting opposite each other at a little marquetry card table, playing a game of backgammon. As usual, Mimi and Louis were at Rafaella's feet, while Criminal sprawled by the door, keeping one eye open for trouble, the way he always did.

"You must be missing Jake already," Rafaella said, studying her next move carefully because she liked to win.

Franny sighed. "I didn't think it would be possible to miss anybody this much. I mean, how *can* it be possible? I've known him for such a short while."

"A short while is long enough to fall in love."

"You were in love with Jake's father, weren't you?"

"I was. In fact, I confess, despite everything, I love him still." Rafaella moved her counter and won the game. She sat back, satisfied, and looked up at Franny, feeling the empathy flowing between them.

"I loved him and I lost," she said, with a wry little half smile, "but despite it all I still believe in true love, lasting love. And because I know you do too, Franny, I'll tell you about him."

The fire settled in the grate as Rafaella went to put on a

CD, then she came to sit in the big old leather wing chair, listening to the familiar old song. And for her it was as if Lucas were in the room with her as she told Franny the story of their meeting, and their love affair, how Jake had come to live with them, and how Lucas had sent him away. And from then on, how everything seemed to go wrong.

When she'd finished, Rafaella sat for a while, thinking about the gradual disintegration of love, while Franny watched her silently. "Things were difficult after Jake left," Rafaella said at last. "I was angry with Lucas for turning his son away and I let him know it. In retaliation, he went on to new conquests. Conquering a new woman always made Lucas feel more of a man. But then, I'm sure you've known men like that too, my dear," she added. And remembering Marcus, Franny nodded.

"I didn't know what to do," Rafaella said. "I loved Lucas. I couldn't just leave him. I even told Juliette he was my 'destiny.' But Juliette said, 'Don't you know there's no future in *destiny*? Life is all about your own choices, *ma chérie*.'

"One night a few weeks later I was in bed alone, wondering where Lucas was, what he was doing, who he was with— all the things women do when they are crazy in love with a man. Of course I knew exactly *where* he was, I always did. This time he was in England, playing polo with a prince as well as a couple of dukes, and I suddenly couldn't bear to be parted from him a moment longer. I went to my closet and flung a few things into a suitcase. When I came downstairs Haigh was standing in the hall in his old-fashioned striped nightshirt with his scrawny legs sticking out like twigs in winter. 'You're off to see him, aren't you?' he said. 'So what if I am,' I said defiantly. Haigh told me I was making a mistake, but I was helpless. 'Don't you understand, I can't help my-self?'

"He put the suitcase in the back and asked if I had my passport. He'd given up on the idea of stopping me. 'And what about money?' he said, and I stared blankly at him. Of course I'd forgotten about money.

"He said, 'I knew you would, just as I knew what you were up to when I heard you banging around up there,' and he reached into the breast pocket of his nightshirt and took out some folded bills. I heard him call 'Bon voyage,' but I wasn't even listening. I just wanted to get to Lucas.

"I drove through the night to Paris, then on to Calais, where I took the next ferry to Dover and then drove to London. I was exhausted, I felt terrible. I knew I must look even worse, and I needed to be at my best when I saw Lucas again, so I went straight to the Ritz, where I took a suite. After a long soak in a hot bath, I put on warmer clothes." She looked up at Franny and laughed. "Can you believe that even now, I can remember exactly what I wore—a Chanel pastel-tweed coat with match-ing skirt and a little sweater, because it was so much colder than in Provence, even though it was summer. Then I walked across the road to Burlington Arcade, a street famous for its gentlemen's outfitters, where I bought Lucas a few pretty gifts.

"Quite suddenly I was overcome with fear of what I was about to do. I'd never gone after Lucas before, never dared to show up unannounced. . . . I walked back to the Ritz and sat in the Palm Court and ordered a glass of champagne to calm myself. I looked around the ornate room with its lofty ceil-ings and enormous chandeliers and gilded paneling. I also looked, a little enviously, at the other guests, so happily en-sconced in plush sofas, sipping tea poured from silver pots and eating cucumber sandwiches and scones with strawberry jam and Devon cream. All of them, it seemed, were without a care in the world. Unlike me.

"I tell you, Franny, I drank that champagne very slowly, putting off the moment when I would have to call Lucas at his hotel in the countryside. The smart bags with his presents were piled on the chair next to me, and I tried to imagine the delight on his face when he opened them. Lucas was like a child in some ways. He got so much pleasure from even the simplest gift.

"Finally I went back to the suite and placed the call to his hotel. The desk clerk told me Lucas didn't answer. 'No matter,' I replied, 'I'll be there in an hour or so.' And then I called down to the desk, asked for my car to be sent round, and went back downstairs.

"Lucas's hotel was set in wooded grounds on the River Thames. I can see it still, elegant in a country-manor style with a square white portico and tall Georgian windows curtained in heavy gold velvet, to keep out those bitter English winter winds, no doubt. I remember the desk clerk too. He was about seventy years old, an ex-army-looking man with a bristly mustache and narrow half-glasses. He peered intently at me over the top of them as I asked for Mr. Bronson.

"'Ah, Mr Bronson,' he said. 'I see. Hmm . . . ' and he studied his guest book for a long time, as though it were written in some strange foreign language.

"'He's in Room 23,' I told him, because I knew that from the phone call I'd made.

"'Ahh, yes. . . . Room 23. Hmm . . . Well, I'm sorry, Madame, but Mr. Bronson appears to be out at the moment.'"

"I checked the wooden pigeonholes behind him, where

the room keys were kept, and saw he was right. The key to room 23 was there so Lucas must be out. I told the clerk I would wait and he showed me, reluctantly I thought, into the vast cold drawing room while he went to order some tea.

"However, I'd never been one to wait around, and now I saw my opportunity. Quick as a flash, I was behind that reception desk, unhooking the key from its box. Bags swinging from my arms, I ran up the red-carpeted stairs, saw the sign that pointed to rooms 21 through 25. I was smiling as I inserted the key in the lock, thinking of how I'd be naked in Lucas's bed when he got back. I'd order champagne instead of tea from the fussy old boy downstairs, and I'd spray the pillows with my mimosa scent so it would be exactly like being home at the château.

"I pushed open the door and stepped into the curtained gloom. I sensed heat in the room and suddenly knew I wasn't alone. Lucas was here after all! I felt my way silently around the chairs and little tables to where a massive four-poster loomed.

"'Lucas?' I whispered. And then I saw them.

"Lucas lifted his head from the pillow and for a second our eyes met, then I turned and ran, dropping the bags with his presents on the floor, slamming the door of Room 23 behind me.

"I didn't want to know who the woman was, didn't want to hear his explanations or his professions about how he still loved me. In my heart I knew this wasn't the first time this had happened.

"On the long drive back to Provence, I thought about what Juliette had said about destiny, that it was all about your own personal choices. Now it was my turn to make a

choice—and I knew I had to finish it." Rafaella sat, eyes
downcast, thinking for a long while. Then she said to Franny.
"The only trouble is, I never stopped loving him."

"And you never saw him again?" Franny said.

Rafaella hesitated before she answered. "Oh, yes," she
said. She looked at Franny. "I've never told anyone else that I
saw him again, not even Juliette, and certainly not Haigh. It
was my secret, but now, because I know you believe in true
love, I will tell you that secret."

And then she told Franny a story she would never forget.

56 LUCAS HAD COME BACK to her in the end. No
one knew, not even Haigh, just Lucien and Janine, the *guardiens* at the villa because of course,
that's where they were, right back where they'd
started, at Cap d'Antibes.

Haigh had returned to England to take care of some business, and Rafaella wasn't used to being without him at the
château, so she'd decided to go to the villa. It was just her
and the dogs.

She was sitting on the veranda at twilight, looking at the
sea glimmering like a blue-tinted opal and listening to the
sound of the birds twittering in the pine trees and getting
ready for the night, when she heard another sound. Footsteps
on the lane leading from the gate to the house. Even though

she was alone, she wasn't afraid. She was never afraid at the villa, but she was curious. Perhaps it was Lucien coming back with a basket of peaches picked from the garden, or Janine returning for some other reason. She watched and waited and then he came into sight, a tall man in a white shirt. The sleeves were rolled and his arms and face were so tan they blended into the night. She couldn't make out his features, but she knew that body, knew it as well as her own.

"Lucas," she said in a whisper, but even so he heard her. He stood there, looking up at her, still sitting on the upstairs veranda, unable to stand because her knees had turned to jelly, while in her head she heard that old song being played on the white grand piano on the night they'd met.

"I've come home, Rafaella," he said. His voice was hoarse, rougher than she remembered, and she knew instantly something was very wrong. She gathered her wits and ran down those stairs and through the hall and stood on the front steps staring at what was left of the Lucas she remembered.

He was so thin it was painful just to watch him walk. His step was hesitant, as if he was in great pain. She watched, frozen. When he got close, just a foot away, she looked into his gaunt, drawn face and knew he was dying. His eyes were the same though, sparking with a life force he was unwilling to surrender.

"I found where you were and I came back for you, Rafaella," he said, as though it were that simple. She opened her arms and took him into them, just the way she had in the beginning.

It was obvious he didn't have much time, and they spent those last few days together, as close as they had ever been— maybe even closer. They never left the villa. He slept in her bed and she lay awake listening to him struggle for breath, remembering when he was young and strong and bristling with life and virility. There was never a man like Lucas Bronson. Never.

She fed him the little bits of food he could manage, though she thought he only swallowed them to please her. He didn't really want them, didn't want to prolong his agony. They would sit on the veranda, watching the Mediterranean change from turquoise to sapphire until it melted into the sky, and they sipped wine and held hands and found a contentment they had never managed before.

And he said this to her: "I love you, Rafaella. I always loved you. I never knew anyone who could compare. The fault was mine—I was arrogant and a games player and I had a fatal flaw. Women were mine to take and so I took them. It's no use saying I wish I didn't because now it's all over. But I came back to see you one more time, because you are my enduring memory."

They had five days together, then she woke one morning and he was gone. She searched everywhere for him and finally she found him in a private clinic in Cannes. He died there the next day.

He was a famous man once and his obituary was in all the papers. He'd made a new will in which he ignored his son, as he had all those years, and left everything to a charity for horses. But he had requested that his ashes be scattered among the wild roses at the gazebo out at the château, "The place that always reminded me of you, Rafaella," he'd said.

She had taken care of his last wish.

. . .

As she listened to Rafaella's story, tears trickled down Franny's cheeks. "You are so brave, so good," she whispered. "I only hope my love is as strong as yours."

"Trust me, child, it is." Rafaella patted her hand. "And now I have a suggestion to make. You need a change while Jake is away. Why not go to the villa at the Cap? Take Little Blue with you. I want both of you to see how lovely the Côte d'Azur is. I would come with you but it's too far for me now—my arthritis won't permit it."

This was the second great invitation of Franny's life. The Côte d'Azur was a dream place she'd only glimpsed on travelogues on television, and now she was going there. Rafaella not only had confided the story of her love, she had given her something to look forward to while her own love was away.

She put her arms around Rafaella and hugged her. "Thank you," she said, and Rafaella knew she meant for telling her the story of her and Lucas.

57 Scott Harris was taken by surprise, pleasantly so, when Clare arrived at sundown the next evening, carrying a picnic basket. She appeared in the crushing shed when the machines were going full blast.

"Hey," she said, standing in the doorway and peering into

the dimness. "I brought supper. I figured every guy has to eat sometime, even the superman winemaker."

Scott grinned and brushed back his hair wearily. "I guess you're right. I'd probably have ended up with the same old ham and cheese somewhere around midnight."

"If I had not come to save you." Clare put the wicker picnic basket on the rickety Formica-topped table that already held a laptop and several dozen empty Badoit bottles. "Watch me wave my magic wand," she cried, flinging open the lid and waving an elegant arm at its contents, like a circus performer taking a bow after a particularly difficult stunt.

"Will the magic wand also turn me into a prince?" Scott asked hopefully, and she laughed and shook her head.

"That's asking a little too much, even of me, but I promise it can turn you into a happy man, if only for a brief moment. Look, here's a magical rotisserie chicken—direct from Allier's, and"—she showed him the box—"potatoes roasted in the juices!" She bit into one, moaning with pleasure. "Mmm, oh my god, that's *so* good. Plus"—she waved a baguette at him and took out a bottle and two glasses—"cheap local wine from Mademoiselle Doritée's and a hunk of cheese. Now I ask you, what more could a man want?"

"You," he said, and he kissed her.

She stepped back, surprised but not displeased. "You always thank people with kisses?"

"Only the pretty ones."

She frowned, suspicious. "I wouldn't want you to have gotten the wrong impression."

"My only impression is that you are lovely and that you are also an eater. True?"

"True," she admitted with a sigh. "I love food. That's why I'm taking the cooking lessons. One day I'll be a comfortable fat old lady, still enjoying her roast potatoes and rotisserie chicken at eighty."

"And with a glass of wine, I hope," he said, inspecting the bottle of white she'd brought before opening it. He poured it into glasses and said, "Tell you what. It's too windy outside, why don't we take our picnic into the *cave*? We can light the candles and pretend it's romantic."

"But we don't have to pretend—it *is* romantic," Clare said minutes later, sitting opposite him at the stone tasting table in the candlelight, with their picnic spread out on paper plates.

"What are you really doing here, Clare?" he asked, hacking a hunk of chicken for her with his Swiss Army knife since she'd forgotten to bring one.

She bit into the chicken, chewing silently, thinking. She shrugged. "Like JFK and his famous wife, I accompanied my friend to Paris." She looked up and met his eyes. "Actually, the truth is that I had left my cheating husband and was looking for revenge on the woman he'd been having an affair with. One of the many women he'd had an affair with. I filed for divorce before I left and I made sure to max out his credit cards."

"A woman scorned?"

"You betcha!"

"And what will you do now?"

She knew it was a loaded question. "Now? I'll become a chef, of course, take a job as the lowest *commis* in some smart L.A. restaurant, work my butt off for no money, and eat for free."

"At least you won't starve."

"Would that worry you?" She eyed him, smiling.

"You know I wouldn't allow that to happen."

Clare stared demurely down at her paper plate scattered with chicken bones. "It's nice to know you care. Well, now that I've made sure you've eaten tonight, I'd better let you get on with the crush and go home."

"Home? Is that the way you think of the château now?"

She hesitated. "It's more than just the château. It's the village of Marten, it's here, it's Saint-Sylvestre, it's. . . . Provence." She shrugged. "Of course it's not my home. I have no real home, but this place sure beats the real one where I started out, in the onion fields, working alongside my sharecropper dad. God, I never want to see a Vidalia again."

She was laughing but Scott could tell she was still hurting inside from the hard childhood memories. He helped her pack the remains of the picnic back into the basket, and they walked up the stone stairs and into the grape-scented night.

Clare took a deep breath, standing by the car, the keys ready in her hand. "You could get drunk on just this."

"You'd have to wait for it to become wine first. And thank you for the picnic, it was great." He stepped awkwardly back from her, unsure of whether to kiss her again, but then she did it for him, a quick brush of her lips against his and she was in the car with the keys in the ignition, already turning the wheel and heading across the courtyard to the arched exit.

She leaned her head out the window, looking back at him still standing there, watching her. "You're kinda cute, Scott Harris, you know that?" she yelled, and he heard her laughing as she drove, too quickly, under the arch and back down the hill to the château.

58 CLARE WAS NOT SURE which she enjoyed most, cooking with Jarré or tasting wines with Scott. In fact the "cooking lessons" mostly consisted of the work that Jarré told her would be her lot as a *commis* chef—the lowliest assistant on the restaurant scale.

Clare was enjoying herself. She liked the prickly *frisson* between her and Scott, who was still pursuing her—whenever he could, that is, because after all it was the winemakers' busiest time of the year. He'd sent her flowers, called her, asked her over to share his sandwich, showed her his home, a charming old stone house fronted with an arbor of bougainvillea and fig, the inside of which was a masculine jumble of old furniture, piles of books and horse magazines, with a beautiful old English saddle on a wooden stand taking pride of place in the hall. He showed her his stable and of course his horse, and though she couldn't ride he took her out on a small steady mare, ponying her up and down the rocky hills until her backside could take no more. And she enjoyed it all, though she didn't kiss him again.

But then each morning when she walked eagerly to the village, she found herself looking forward to seeing Jarré, who would be waiting behind his bar to greet her, his innocent black eyes regarding her as though she was the most beautiful woman in the world, astonished that she was here, working in his kitchen. He'd have her *grand café crème* ready, plus now he always had freshly baked croissants. She was aware of him physically as they bumped into each other in the too-small kitchen, and she chatted to him in her newly acquired bastardized French, complete with a perfect Provençal twang, just like his.

Trouble was, she liked both men, she could fall hard for either one. But neither of them was from her world, and she knew neither of them would truly understand where she was coming from. She needed to share her problem with Franny, who was getting ready for her trip to the Côte d' Azur. But first it was time that Franny knew her real background, so Clare decided to tell her about herself. There could be no deceit between friends. Or lovers. Win or lose, it was the moment of truth.

Criminal leaped up growling when he heard Clare come into Franny's room, but then he subsided again, wagging his tail.

"Hi, Criminal, hi Fran," Clare said.

"Oh, hi." Franny shoved the final T-shirt into the bag. "Sure you won't come with us? It'll be such fun, and anyway, how can you bear to miss the Côte d'Azur?"

The moment she said it Clare knew the reason why she couldn't go. It came to her like a revelation, but she couldn't tell Franny about that yet. She'd come to see Franny for a reason, and she'd better get it over with. She plopped down onto Franny's big green-and-white silk-covered bed, staring miserably at her.

Franny looked worriedly at her. She'd never seen Claire

so solemn, not even at the Italian restaurant the night she'd told her about Marcus. Even then she'd been cheery and sarcastic and fun.

"Franny, I have a confession to make." Clare sounded so serious that Franny stopped what she was doing and went to sit next to her.

"A confession?"

"I have not been exactly truthful with you about . . . about who I was. *Am*," Clare corrected herself. "I told you I was Miss Georgia. . . . Well, I wasn't that. I mean I *was*, but in another way." Her shoulders slumped, and her hands dangled limply between her knees as she thought of how to say what she needed to say. "Oh well," she said finally, with a resigned shrug, "I guess the only way is to start at the beginning." She glanced up at Franny, sitting next to her with that look of loving concern in her eyes, and suddenly she wanted to cry. "This is the hardest thing I've ever done in my life," she muttered miserably, then added, "well, not *exactly* the hardest, as you'll see in a minute."

Franny took her hand and Clare took a deep breath. "I told you I was a poor kid. I never had a real home, you know, just that kind of shiftless life, always moving on to new places, new schools, new friends. Most people think that kind of rural poverty doesn't exist anymore because they never come in contact with it. They think it's something from the past, but believe me," she said bitterly, "it's still very much alive and kicking. Anyway, the short version is that I kicked my way out of it." Her eyes met Franny's again. "Just like you did," she said, "only you did it the hard way, getting an education, working nights, all that. I went for the easy version. At least, that's what I thought it was going to be."

She bit her lip, staring silently down at the floor, and Franny sympathetic as always, said, "It's okay, Clare. You don't have to tell me. I understand, really I do."

"No. No, you don't," Clare said tonelessly. "Unless you've been there you can't know. Anyhow, when I was sixteen I ran off to New York. Of course I was broke—hah, broke doesn't even begin to say it. But I was a pretty kid. I lied about my age and ended up dancing in a club, one of the real sleazy ones where every girl was like me, a dropout from their real lives, a loser, desperate in their hearts for someone to put their arms around them and tell them they loved them."

"Oh god," Franny said, and Clare lifted a resigned shoulder. "Hey, it was okay. I liked dressing up in spangles. I liked taking them off and having men admire my body. I'd never known I was pretty before.

"'A gentlemen's club,' they called it, and believe me, it was the saddest place you ever saw in your life. I went by the name of Miss Georgia, and I danced around a pole, taking off the spangles until I was naked, acting like I really loved what I was doing, like I really fancied those guys so they would shower me with money. Then when I was done, I'd have to scramble naked on the floor to pick up all those dollars while the guys laughed at me and cheered."

She looked at Franny. "You ever see a lap dancer, Franny? No, of course not. Well, it's the same old same, faking hot sex while some guy gets his jollies off, and for an extra fee you go in the back room with him and—" she shrugged again "—do whatever he wants to do. I didn't like it, didn't like those guys groping me. In fact I hated it, yet I went on doing it. I didn't know how to do anything else.

"In the end, though, I quit. The other girls looked at me as though I was crazy. 'You're turning down good money, babe,' they said, and I looked into their faces, their *real* faces, the raw, un-made-up, sad faces they never showed to the customers and I saw my own reality behind those faces with the painted-on beauty and the sparky glamour and the hairpieces and the false eyelashes, and I was sick at heart. Some of these women had kids, some had a drug habit. They weren't free to make a choice the way I was." She took a deep breath. "And so I made it. And there I was—broke again. All that and nothing to show for it. I said to myself, I might as well have stayed home and worked in the onion fields.

"Anyhow, I picked myself up, threw away my jeweled thongs, put on a black dress, and got myself a job as a hostess at a restaurant. I also tended bar occasionally—you know, all the stuff you have to do just to stay alive. I worked, dated, made out, got by . . . and then Marcus came along.

"Marcus made me feel good, made me feel he liked me, that I was really someone. I think he asked me to marry him by accident. It just sort of happened—and suddenly there we were in front of the preacher in a cheap Las Vegas wedding chapel. What a fool I was, I still can't believe it. Then of course came the big letdown. Oh, believe me, Franny, Marcus used me much more than he did you—all those other women, all those lives he touched and ruined. But then I met you, and we came here to Provence, and I met all these *real* people and I suddenly realized that I'm in charge of myself and I'm free of my past." She looked humbly at Franny, her eyes pleading. "So there you have it," she said in a wobbly voice. "And if you don't want to be my friend anymore, I'll understand."

Franny opened her arms and reached out for her. "You'll always be my friend," she said. "How could you even think it mattered? I liked you right off, that first night when you came to tell me about Marcus. I shouldn't have liked you, but I did. Because *you* are *you*."

Tears plopped down Clare's cheeks. "I love you, Franny," she gulped.

"I know." Franny stroked back her hair. "And I love you, too."

Clare sniffed. "Speaking of love. . . . It's happened. I mean, I'm actually in love."

"Clare, how wonderful."

"The thing is . . . I mean, he might already suspect, but anyhow I'm going to have to tell him the real truth. You know, about my past. . . . It's only fair." She shuddered and Franny crossed her fingers and hoped Scott was man enough to take this in stride.

"He's a good guy," she said. "It'll be okay." She smiled encouragingly. "Salt of the earth, right?"

"Right!" They high-fived and Clare dried her tears and said she was okay now. She would do what she had to do and hope for the best.

59

THE NEXT MORNING Franny and Little Blue set off for Cap d'Antibes, but the child sitting in the back of the red Fiat was quite different from the one who'd sat silent and frozen on the train to Avignon. In cute blue shorts and a skimpy summer

T-shirt with a straw hat perched on her shining hair, a pair of scarlet sunglasses on her nose, and a smile on her face, she was a normal, eager kid going on holiday, looking forward to learning to swim in the Mediterranean and playing on the beach. "How much longer?" she asked every fifteen minutes or so, the way every child does on a car journey.

Criminal sat patiently on the front seat, tongue lolling, eyeing the traffic with his usual skeptical expression. Every now and then Franny pulled into an *autoroute* café to let the dog run and to buy Little Blue a Fanta orange and a sandwich, because she'd developed an appetite that seemed unstoppable.

Eventually, lulled by the monotony of the Autoroute du Soleil, Little Blue dozed and Franny was left alone with her thoughts, which were mostly about Clare.

Clare's confession had taken her completely by surprise. She was always the perfect lady, perfectly groomed, perfectly self-possessed, perfectly beautiful. But Franny also understood the poor background and her desperation to escape. She didn't blame Clare, she just wished her friend had not had to go that route. But now Clare's life was changing track: her past was behind her and she could look forward to a future with the kind of man who would look after her, a man who would laugh with her and love her the way she was born to be loved. And there was certainly no man more salt-of-the-earth than Scott Harris. He even worked with that earth, made his living from it—and successfully at that.

Waiting behind a retinue of large Mercedes at yet another *autoroute* toll booth, Franny tried to imagine Jake in New York, but she couldn't picture him in his urban loft or the smart offices he'd described to her. Strangely, although she had never been there, she could picture exactly how his mountain cabin would look, and exactly how it would feel because Jake had told her about it so lovingly that first night when they'd dined together. He'd told her it was the only place where loneliness was not an issue and solitude was welcomed, and she'd understood that.

At last, she was off the *autoroute* and on a side road that led to the sea. With its shady pines and secret villas tucked out of sight in rambling scented gardens, the Côte d'Azur was completely different from California's great sweep of rugged coastline and broad beaches with their pounding surf. Driving slowly along the edge of the tranquil blue-green bay, Franny saw the few puffs of clouds reflected in the water as perfectly as any mirror. She woke up Little Blue to look, and the girl and the dog stuck their heads out the windows, breathing in the exciting sea smells, watching the fishermen on flat, wooden boats, like people in a painting by Monet.

Following Rafaella's directions, she drove down a narrow tree-lined lane until she came to a clearing and a pair of large wooden gates set between stone pillars carved with the name VILLA MARTEN.

Little Blue got out to ring the bell, hopping impatiently from foot to foot until the gates swung open. She jumped back in surprise when she saw a tiny old man with a creased brown face and a toothless ear-to-ear smile.

"*Bienvenue, bienvenue, les nouveaux Martens. Je suis le gardien, Lucien. Eh bien, c'est un beau jour . . . Venez, mesdemoiselles, venez, welcome.*" The old man waved them into a sandy pine-fringed lane to a creamy stucco villa, two stories high. A green wooden veranda, overflowing with purple bougainvillea, ran around the entire upper floor, while underneath was a colonnaded patio complete with a carved-stone dolphin fountain. Green-shuttered windows were open to let in the sea air, and on the steps waited an equally old woman in a blue dress and a white apron.

Janine's smile matched her husband's, for she had been married to Lucien for almost sixty years and they had known Rafaella all her life. Now she was happy to greet Rafaella's family, happy to see the old villa opened up again, happy to see a child and even a dog racing around the place.

The old couple no longer lived in the *gardien* house on the property but had a more convenient apartment in the town of Antibes itself. But Janine told Franny that of course they would come every morning, and if Franny wished, she would do the marketing and prepare an evening meal, which she would leave ready for them, though she supposed they would eat at the cafés most days.

Criminal was already checking things out, sniffing his way through the tiled hall and into the kitchen at the back. A few seconds later he emerged, tail wagging, with a leg of lamb clamped in his jaws. Janine shrieked and Lucien came running as fast as he could on his bent old limbs, but Criminal outmaneuvered them. Twisting past their outstretched arms, he ran into the oleander bushes where, safely hidden, he proceeded to demolish their dinner.

"I'm so sorry, Janine," Franny said, trying not to laugh because, after all, Criminal was just living up to his reputation. "*Il est un chien méchant.*"

Still a little put out, Janine showed them the house. It was unexpectedly simple; downstairs were large, cool rooms leading onto the terrace and the gardens, which ran down to the sea and a small jetty, from where Franny caught a glimpse of the narrow La Garoupe beach.

Janine proudly showed off her cavernous kitchen with its rough-beamed ceiling and its ancient stove. Just looking at its steel girth and wobbly burners, Franny sincerely hoped she would never have to tackle cooking dinner on it.

There were comfortable sofas covered in Provençal fabrics, soft rugs, and the smallest TV Franny had ever seen. The massive dining-room table could easily seat twenty, and another rustic wooden table on the shaded patio could seat twenty more. There was also a guest house in the garden, but it had been locked up for many years.

Wild with excitement, Little Blue ran upstairs to choose her room, finally deciding on the big corner one with the view of the bay, while Franny took the one next to it. They unpacked and put on their bathing suits, said good-bye to Lucien and Janine, and set off to walk to La Garoupe beach. Criminal pulled on his lead, wanting to stop every two minutes to sniff, but they were hungry and didn't let him. They stopped at the beach called Plage Keller, where people were sitting under yellow umbrellas enjoying lunch at the Café Cézar. Bottles of wine chilled in frosty silver buckets next to them, and there was the good smell of lobster and pasta, *pommes frites,* and olive oil.

Franny ordered a *salade niçoise* for herself and *calamars frits* for Little Blue, and Criminal slept in the shade. While they waited to be served, Little Blue ran to watch the other children who were jumping off the wooden jetty that stuck out into the water, and Franny sank peacefully back into her chair, letting the sun warm her naked shoulders. A delicious lethargy crept over her. She thought of her soft white bed in the cool shuttered room at the villa and understood why the southern-French took siestas. Eyes half closed, she heard the soft plop of the waves in the distance and the cries of the gulls and the children. She was dreaming about taking a siesta with Jake.

From a table nearby, Alain watched her. He was alone, though several women eyed him with interest. He wore a white polo shirt and shorts and very dark wraparound sunglasses. His hair was blond again, he was tanned and fit-looking and almost unrecognizable from the smart-suited, dark-haired man who had disrupted the family reunion just a short while ago. He ordered another glass of Ricard, savoring it slowly, his eyes on Franny.

Little Blue came running back and Franny sat up, laughing at the child's story. Having fun, Alain thought cynically as Little Blue's laughter rang out. He ordered another Ricard and sat back to watch.

After lunch, the two got up and walked onto the beach, where Franny had rented loungers and an umbrella. The child raced off to the water's edge and Franny, the perfect California girl in a brief turquoise bikini, followed slowly.

Alain eyed her up and down like the connoisseur of women he claimed to be. Not bad, he thought with a satisfied smile. Sometimes life just gave you the right breaks. This time it had given him the only two people who stood between him and his rightful inheritance.

60

WHEN ALAIN HAD LEFT the château he'd known he had no choice. One word from Jake to the police and he was, if not a dead man, then a man looking at a life in jail. Drugs, arms, he'd had a hand in all of them, but he was a petty criminal rather than a grand master, and that fact made him angry. After all these years, he should have been richer than Felix, richer than his mother, and richer than Jake. Fate had conspired against him and that's why, when he'd finally gone to Felix for money and Felix had turned him down, he'd slammed the silver paper knife into Felix's temple almost without thinking. He'd laughed at the shocked expression in Felix's eyes as he died.

He'd covered Felix's bloody body with a plastic cleaner's bag that he found in the closet, so there'd be no telltale blood, then he'd slung him over his shoulder and carried him to the freight shaft. He knew that people falling from high places usually landed on their heads, and lucky for him, so did Felix, obliterating any signs of the knife attack.

He'd known instinctively what to do next. As brothers, he and Felix were alike enough in built and height to make the deception possible. He'd changed into one of Felix's smart suits and a pair of his custom English shoes; they were a little big, but good enough. He'd picked up his brother's briefcase and stuffed his own clothes into it. Then he took Felix's keys, went to the safe, and removed the fifty or so thousand dollars he found there. Knowing Felix, he'd bet no one would know about the money stashed away and therefore it would not be missed, but he decided to leave the watches and jewelry so it wouldn't look like robbery. Then he took the elevator down to the lobby, and with his head down, hurried past the concierge. In seconds he was on the street, a free man.

After the showdown at the château, when he'd been escorted onto Jake's plane by a burly guard, he'd burned with anger that his enemy enjoyed such luxury while, despite his many money-making schemes and ventures, he still had to scramble. They had flown him to Ho Chi Min City, not even offering him a drink or a snack on the long flight. The big bruiser of a bodyguard had kept his eyes fixed on him all the way while Alain seethed with fury. He would get Jake for this, he'd told himself. He'd get back at them all.

They'd decanted him from the plane without so much as a good-bye, and he'd immediately taken the first commercial flight back to Europe. He ended up in Geneva, where he rented a car and drove to the South of France.

The villa had always been one of his favorite places. He used to bring girls here when he was young—guys too. Alain rather favored an orgy. It gave him a feeling of power over women, and he liked that.

He knew that no one ever came to the villa now and that he'd be able to hide there, but first he'd found out the exact times Lucien came to check the property—only a cursory visit on Saturday mornings now.

Alain had gone to the guest house, removed the screen on a rear window, forced the old-fashioned latch, and he was home free. He'd hidden his Vespa in a nearby bamboo thicket and kept the small rented Renault in a parking garage in Antibes. He'd bleached his hair blond again, bought himself some new clothes with his murdered brother's money, and felt like his old self, immune to reality and ready for revenge. His only problem had been how, and now, thanks to fate, that had been solved for him.

61 THE SUN WAS SETTING by the time Franny and Little Blue returned. Standing under the shower, Franny wondered why, after a day at the beach, it always felt like the best ever, so cool and soft and clean against your sun-hot skin. She toweled her wet hair, wrapped herself in a pareo, and went to check on Little Blue, who was sprawled lazily on the bed.

"How about omelettes for supper?" Franny suggested, hoping she could manage that big brute of a gas stove without blowing them both up, but Little Blue said she was too tired to eat, so Franny left her dozing and went down to the kitchen.

She found milk, juice, wine, and a slab of golden butter in the refrigerator. On the counter was a loaf of crusty bread, a wicker basket of speckled eggs, and a deep blue bowl filled with summer fruits. She picked up an apricot, sniffed it appreciatively, then ate it with the juices dripping down her chin. On a cool slate slab in the pantry she discovered a plate of pungent cheeses. She took them back to the counter, hacked off a slab of the crusty bread, slathered it with some of the golden butter, and added a couple of slices of cheese. A glass of cold wine and she was happy.

She sat peacefully at the counter enjoying her meal. Criminal slumped next to her, watching hopefully. Unable to resist those pleading eyes, she tossed him a piece of cheese. He wolfed it down, without even tasting it she was sure, which she felt was a pity because it was so darn good.

Twilight filtered through the kitchen windows, and the bead curtain at the door trembled in the evening breeze. Franny tried to imagine what it was like at the villa in its hey-day, full of happy young people and children and pets. Like the château, the Villa Marten needed to be brought to life again, but she knew Rafaella would never return here.

She got up and went into the garden. The only sounds were the chirpings of the sleepy birds in the pines and the soft crunch of the sandy path under her bare feet. It was still warm and the plants had begun to release their night scents, the jasmine and the roses and sea pinks and the fruits, and she was glad that Lucas had come back to this paradise to find Rafaella.

At last, she went back indoors, locking the big front door behind her. Criminal had found a cool spot on the tiled kitchen floor, where he lay on his back, four paws in the air, sleeping. And upstairs Little Blue was also asleep on her back, arms and legs akimbo, snoring gently.

Leaving the door to the veranda open to catch the breeze, Franny lay naked on the bed. She closed her eyes and, lulled by the night sounds and the warm breeze, she slept, happy in the knowledge that tomorrow would be another wonderful day, and a day closer to seeing Jake again.

She slept so soundly she didn't hear the light footsteps on the veranda, didn't see the man standing at the open French doors, looking at her as she slept naked. Didn't see the smile on his face. In fact, Franny didn't know anything more until she was awakened by the sound of dishes rattling and the smell of coffee coming from the kitchen as Janine prepared breakfast.

62 THEY HAD JUST COME back from another sun-filled day at the beach and were looking forward to a siesta when the phone rang. Franny grabbed it on the third ring.

"I was missing you," Jake said, and she melted at the mere sound of his voice.

"Me, too," she said softly. She felt as if she was alone with Jake.

"I love it here," she said, "but I'd love it a lot more with you," and then she told him about their day at the beach and that she loved him and wanted him here so they could take a siesta together. And he said as soon as he'd finished in New York he would fly to Nice and they'd be taking all their siestas together.

"But there's another place I want to take you to," he said, "a funky little auberge near Saint-Tropez called the Hotel

Riviera. The owners, Lola and Jack Farrar, are such a cute couple. I'm sure you'll like them. In fact, why don't you take Little Blue and try its magic for yourself, just for a night. Trust me, you'll fall in love."

"I am in love," she said softly as he rang off.

The next day they drove to Saint-Tropez. She followed the Ramatuelle road until she came to a flowery sign saying WEL-COME TO THE HOTEL RIVIERA.

Franny followed the narrow lane through the trees, across a tiny spit of land, until she came to an old pink villa whose terrace overlooked the Mediterranean. Lush gardens led to a sandy beach dotted with marine blue umbrellas and sunny yellow loungers, where a few golden people were peacefully enjoying the sun. A small dinghy was tied up at the wooden jetty and, fifty yards out in the bay, an old black sloop swung at anchor.

A pretty woman about Franny's age with a mop of taffy-colored hair stood on the hotel steps smiling at them. "Hi, or should I say *bonjour*?" she called. "I'm Lola Farrar. Are you looking for a room?"

Franny said that she was, and then she introduced herself and told her that Jake had recommended them. "In fact he said we shouldn't miss it," she added.

"Ah, Jake Bronson, the handsome mystery man," Lola said with a grin. "He beats my husband at backgammon every night—*and* they play for money, five euros a game. I swear Jake's never yet had to pay his bill at the end of his stay." She glanced shrewdly at Franny. "You know him well?" When Franny admitted she did, Lola said, "I thought so from the glow." Then they went indoors, where she showed her around and checked which rooms were available.

"I have two," Lola said, studying her book. "There's the Colette and the Bardot. I named all the rooms for French artistes and writers, not that there are many of them—rooms, I mean. Just eight to be precise, but they are all different."

Little Blue came bounding through the door with Criminal tugging at the lead, and Lola Farrar said of course they took dogs, especially if it was Jake's. "He'll probably get along with our own," she said. "He's called Bad Dog for obvious reasons, and I think they've both got the same street-bred look about them. Anyhow, I think Colette is the room for you. It's slightly larger and there's twin beds. Come on, I'll show you."

The apricot-colored room with its brass beds canopied in white muslin, its immaculate linens, tiled floors, and soft rugs was just perfect. Little Blue pushed back the iron shutters with a clang. "Look, oh look," she said, "there's figs growing right outside and I can see children on the beach. . . . Oh, let's go, Franny, do let's go."

Lola told them to go ahead—she would feed Criminal and find him a cool place in the kitchen. So they threw on their bathing suits and ran downstairs, through the terraced garden brimming with blossoming plants and shaded by those wonderful South of France umbrella pines, down the little wooden stairs and over the rocks onto the soft, sandy beach.

Franny left Little Blue safely splashing in the tiny wavelets with a couple of other kids while she swam, enjoying the way the water slid, cool and silky, over her body. She sighed with pleasure, turning to float on her back, staring up at the bluest of skies, thinking of Jake and how they would come here together someday. After a while she swam out to the black sloop. She laughed when she saw its name: *Bad Dog*. Using her old yardstick, she knew Jack Farrar had to be a good guy.

That night she and Little Blue dined on the hotel terrace with the view of the sea and the lights of Saint-Tropez glimmering like a crystal necklace around the bay. Happy and feeling a long way from Your Local Veterinary Clinic, Franny sipped the icy cold Paul Signac rosé wine Lola had recommended, telling her that Signac was a famous artist who'd lived in Saint-Tropez in the early days. They ate grilled *crevettes*, the large ones Lola told them were called *bouquets*, and a rack of lamb from the foothills of the Alpilles and lavender *crème brûlée*, which they said was heaven. Immediately after dinner, Little Blue dived into the bed nearest the window and was asleep in minutes.

Franny joined Lola on the terrace, where she was introduced to her handsome husband, Jack Farrar, who said, "Tell Jake I'll be sure to beat him at backgammon next time he's here, and that's a threat." Since he was at that moment being definitively beaten by a tall, glamorous red-haired guest named "Red" Shoup, that didn't seem like much of a threat to Franny.

She chatted with Miss Nightingale, an Englishwoman who was a dead ringer for Queen Elizabeth, about, of all surprising things, Scotland Yard detectives. It turned out Miss N, as she was known, had been married to one. Miss N also told her the story of how Lola had almost lost the Hotel Riviera to an unscrupulous billionaire a couple of years before.

Her head swimming with wine and stories, Franny slept like a log that night, and she felt sad when they left for Cap d'Antibes the next morning, with hugs and kisses and promises to return with Jake.

.   .   .

ALAIN HAD WATCHED THEM putting their bags in the car and he'd cursed out loud as they drove off to Saint-Tropez, afraid they were leaving before he could carry out his plan. Panicked, he'd climbed onto the upstairs veranda and into Franny's room. He'd breathed a sigh of relief when he saw her things were still there. Then he'd gone down to the kitchen to inspect the stove. He checked its burners, saw that it was fueled by natural gas and not propane, then he'd let himself out of the kitchen door and locked it behind him. He went to pick up his Vespa from the bamboo thicket, drove into Antibes, got his car from the public parking building, and drove at top speed toward Cannes, headed for the casino and the clubs. While the mice were away, the cat might as well play, he said to himself, smiling at the twist on the old saying. Might as well have fun while he bided his time.

63

CLARE KNEW IT WAS now or never. Her future would be decided today. She showered and changed into the simplest thing she owned, a white cotton dress, high at the neck and low in the back, with a soft, full skirt that rippled girlishly around her knees. She put on a pair of wedge espadrilles, brushed her dark hair into a ponytail, and tied it with an orange string left over from the pastry-shop package, where they would tie even a couple of cookies in elegant paper and ribbon. She took a long look in the mirror. "This is it, girl," she said to herself.

Un-made-up and in the virginal white dress, she looked a bit like a darker version of the innocent Franny. She clipped gold hoops into her ears, then decided against them. She dabbed on a little of the lavender scent she'd bought at Mademoiselle Doritée's, stuff made locally and meant for tourists. It cost only a couple of euros, and never in a million years would she have worn it at home, but here, in the countryside, it was perfect. She tried on a straw hat, decided against it, and instead tied a blue kerchief over her head, Jackie O–style.

She picked up the English/French dictionary she'd been studying, plus the little notebook in which she'd written some useful and appropriate phrases, and put them in her pocket.

Still she hesitated. So. Okay. Now she was ready. If she hung about any longer she might change her mind. She grabbed the car keys and ran downstairs, stopping in the hall to see who was there, and breathing a sigh of relief that no one was around to ask where she was going.

She didn't see Haigh peeking from the dining room just in time to see her start up the car and take off too fast down the drive. He wondered where she was going but figured he already knew. Haigh always knew what was going on at the château.

It was just after two o'clock and, as usual in France, everything was closed. The village square was deserted, as was the Café des Colombes. Even the old codgers were gone from the benches, and the dogs had retreated into the cool of the alleys.

Clare parked under the trees, got out, smoothed her white cotton skirt, took a deep breath, then marched determinedly across the cobblestones to the café.

Jarré was mopping his *zinc* when the doorbell jangled. His mustache bristled and his eyes opened wide as he took in the vision in white. He put down his cloth and came out from behind the bar, wiping his hands on the apron slung around his hips.

"Clare," he said, allowing his dark gypsy eyes to express his admiration. "Lunch is already finished, but perhaps I can find something if you are hungry."

By now, Clare's ear was tuned perfectly to Jarré's Provençal twang. "I'm not hungry, thank you."

"*Eh bien,* a drink perhaps? A glass of wine? Ricard? Champagne even?" He'd open his best for her, give her anything she wanted.

Clare thought opening the champagne would probably be premature and she shook her head, "*Non, merci.* Jarré, I need to talk to you."

He gave her a look with those big, sympathetic brown eyes that made her curl up inside. "*Bien sûr,* Madame Clare."

"Clare," she said firmly.

He nodded. "*Clare.*"

She perched on a green vinyl barstool, leaning an elbow on the bar, wondering how to begin. He came and sat next to her, a big man, a warm man, a man with heart . . . *a salt-of-the-earth-type man*.

Realizing that, at this moment, gestures mattered more than words, she reached for his hand. She held it in both hers and leaned closer. "Kiss me, Jarré," she said, smiling at the look of surprise in his beautiful eyes. For such a big man, his lips were gentle on hers, sweet and searching, as though he were tasting a great wine.

"Clare," he murmured, and then he put his arms around her and kissed her again. She slid off the barstool and he caught her and held her close. "Ah, Clare," he murmured again, kissing her some more. Her blue kerchief slipped over one ear and she pulled it off and shook her hair free. Jarré put his hand to her hair, letting the smooth strands slide through his fingers, still looking deep into her eyes. Clare wanted to die of happiness, but she couldn't allow herself, not yet, because after all, that happiness might not belong to her.

"I've loved you since the moment I first saw you," Jarré said in French, but Clare understood it in her heart.

"And I love you," she said.

To her surprise, he frowned. "Clare, you are a rich woman who lives in big cities in America," he said somberly. "I am only a village café owner. I've never even been to Paris. How can I ask a woman like you to marry me? Besides," he added sadly, "I know you are already married."

"Not for much longer," Clare said firmly. "And I'm certainly not a rich woman. And of course you can ask me, but before you do, I want to tell you something."

She stood back from him, arms stiffly at her side, chin in the air, keeping her dignity. "Look at me, Jarré," she said. "Because I want you to understand that what you see is not exactly what you get." She paused, took the notebook from her pocket, and looked up the French phrases she needed.

"Jarré," she said, a little breathlessly because she was very nervous, "when I was very young I was very poor, as poor as the migrant workers here, and I worked in the fields just like them. I couldn't stand it, I needed to escape badly, I just knew there was another world out there, a beautiful, laughing world meant for me. But to escape I needed money." She stopped and looked at him. "And there was only one way for an uneducated, pretty girl like me to make money." She looked him in the eye and said, "So I took it."

Jarré said nothing, just looked solemnly back at her.

Clare went on, half in English, half in stumbling French, telling the story exactly as she'd told it to Franny. She left nothing out. When she'd finished, she took a deep breath and stood, eyes closed, waiting for him to say something— even though she was sure it would be just one word: good-bye. But still Jarré said nothing, and then she knew it was over. Lips pressed tight to stop from crying, she turned and headed for the door.

She felt him behind her, felt his hand grasp her shoulder, but she pulled away from him, fumbling to put on her dark glasses so he wouldn't see the tears that came anyhow. Jarré pulled her around, he looked at her, then took off the glasses and lifted the tears gently away with a big finger that smelled faintly of the garlic he'd chopped for the frittata special that morning.

"I've never met a woman like you," he said in a very quiet voice, and Clare stared dumbly down at her espadrilles. Of course he hadn't. "Women like her" didn't show up too often in small villages in Provence.

"Clare, you're not a poor young girl anymore. You don't dance naked in bars now," he said. "You did what you needed to do then to keep yourself alive. You're a beautiful woman, a woman with spirit. You are who you are *now*." A glimmer of hope dawned in her teary eyes as they met his.

"I love you, Clare," he said, "but I'm a simple village café owner. I tend my vegetables and I cook for our local families and the tourists. It's a simple life and it will always be this way. I cannot ask you to share that life with me." He shrugged sadly. "I have nothing to offer a woman like you."

Her heart plummeted. There, he'd said it again. *A woman*

like her. She pulled away from him. "Good-bye, Jarré," she said, but he stopped her.

"I cannot change," he said, his face just inches from hers. "This is my life, my *world*. Would you want to share that with me?"

She stared at him, eyes popping out of her head, hardly believing. "In a heartbeat," she said, sliding her arms around his neck.

He probably didn't understand what she'd said, but he understood the look in her eyes all right. And when he said, "So will you marry me then, my beautiful, darling Clare?" she said Yes.

64

JAKE DID WHAT HE'D rarely done before: delegated work to a colleague. It wasn't that he didn't care what happened to his clients, it was that his priorities had changed and with it, he knew, so would his lifestyle. He didn't call Franny and tell her he was en route because he wanted to see the surprise in her large blue eyes when she saw him, wanted to hear her little gasp of pleasure, wanted to see that sunny-girl smile light up her face. He wanted every little honest, good part of Franny Marten so he could store them in his memory bank like an unwritten diary of their lives.

Before he left though, he went to Tiffany and bought a

engagement ring. He thought Franny was a true romantic, a "Breakfast at Tiffany's" girl, and he chose an old-fashioned cushion-shaped diamond set in platinum. He planned to give it to her at the villa. He would take her into the garden late in the evening. The sea would be murmuring in the background, and the breeze would ruffle the trees and maybe the crickets would be quiet for once. He laughed, he was becoming a true romantic himself. He'd already ordered celebratory champagne sent to the villa and asked Janine to make sure it was chilled. He'd also arranged for an enormous bunch of Casablanca lilies to be delivered.

Now he was on his Gulfstream IV, somewhere over southern France. Johnny Lang, his pilot and friend for many years, always flew the plane when Jake was on board. There was also a steward and a chef. The plane was his own self-sustaining little vacuum hurtling through the skies back to France.

He checked his watch, then checked with the pilot to see exactly where they were. He sipped yet another cup of coffee and, unable to sleep, prowled restlessly, occasionally eyeing the blue Tiffany box tied with white ribbon sitting on the table. Just the sight of it made him smile. He hoped Criminal was looking after his girl. If not, he'd be in trouble.

BACK IN THE GUEST house at the villa, Alain heard the car returning and the doors slam. The dog barked and their happy voices greeted Janine. He lay back on his bed, hands behind his head, a smile on his face. He had made his plans. In a few hours he would carry them out. All he had to do was wait.

. . .

CRIMINAL'S FAVORITE SPOT to take a nap was on the upstairs veranda, though being a street dog, he always kept an eye open to check what was going on while he enjoyed his evening snooze. Now, with a satisfied grunt, he stretched out, back legs flat, head resting on his outstretched front paws. Then, one eye closed, he dozed.

Downstairs, Franny picked up the phone, intending to call Clare and tell her what she was missing. She put the receiver to her ear, then held it away, puzzled. The line was dead. She shrugged. She would just have to call tomorrow.

She went upstairs to read Little Blue a bedtime story. Hearing them, Criminal ambled in and sprawled next to them, and in no time both he and Little Blue were asleep.

Franny took a shower and she put on a thin cotton robe, then went to lean on the veranda rail, gazing up at the starry sky and the glitter of lights along the coast. The night was unexpectedly humid, and for once the crickets were quiet but over the sea, fireworks exploded in a shimmering cascade of color, starry puffs of gold and blue and scarlet. She watched until the show was over, then climbed into bed and turned out her light. Tomorrow was their last day at the villa then it was back "home" to the château. And to Jake.

JAKE GOT THE PHONE call from his contact in Nice before they began their descent. He was told that Alain Marte had been spotted at the casino in Monte Carlo, where he come out a big winner, thirty thousand euros. That was what had brought him to their attention. His hair was blond again, but it was definitely him. He was driving a white Renault Laguna, but the contact did not know where he was living.

Jake's heart jumped into his throat as he thought of Franny and Little Blue. Where else would Alain go but to the villa? He dialed the villa's number, but the line was completely dead. The hair on his neck prickled. He knew he was looking at real trouble. He called his police contact in Cannes, told them who he was and what he knew about Alain, and that two people were in danger. Then he called a helicopter service and ordered a Sikorsky to be waiting for him on the tarmac. He would pilot it himself.

ALAIN WAITED on a stone bench in the garden until all the lights went out. He'd made sure to leave the guest house in perfect order. He'd even fixed the screen on the bedroom window where he'd broken in. He was sure there was no trace of his presence. In a plastic bag he had a piece of steak. He got up and walked quietly underneath the veranda, praying that the damned dog wouldn't hear, then he flipped the piece of meat up and over the rail and stepped back into the shadows. He heard the dog's claws scrabbling on the deck as he ran, heard him sniffing, heard his satisfied grunt as he took a first lick of the meat.

He took a seat at the long table where, as a boy, he'd eaten so many good meals surrounded by his mother's friends. "Happy times," she'd called them, but Alain had always known he was different. Sometimes he thought it was as though he lived outside his own body, standing back and observing others, mocking them in his mind, ridding himself mercilessly of them one by one in his head until he was alone and master of all he surveyed. And that's exactly what he intended to do now. He had to be very clever, make sure it looked like an accident, though nobody would suspect it was anything else. Except Jake of course. He'd know, and so would Rafaella, but by then he would be long gone and anyhow, as with Felix, they'd never be able to prove it.

He heard the dog begin to choke, then a thud as it slumped onto the wooden veranda over his head. He walked to the rear of the villa and let himself in the kitchen door, using the key that he'd had since he was a kid. He went directly to the old stove and blew out the pilot light. He opened the oven doors and turned on the gas. He turned on all the burners, wrinkling his nose at the smell, then he went back outside, locked the kitchen door behind him, climbed onto the stone bench, vaulted up to the rail, and swung himself onto the upper veranda.

His sneakered feet made no sound as he walked jauntily round to the front where Franny's and Little Blue's rooms were. He stopped and looked at the dog. It was lying on its side, jaws hanging open, eyes rolled back in its head. He gave it a nudge with his foot. It was dead.

He stood at the open door to Franny's room. She slept like a child with her arms straight up over her head, at peace with the world. He closed the door, locked it, and took the key. Then he moved on to Little Blue's room.

She was curled into a ball, her short black hair sticking out like a halo. He thought soon she would be joining the angels, and he smiled. Then he locked her door too and pocketed the key.

He went downstairs, sniffing the fumes already creeping from the kitchen, then he walked quickly into the living room and lit the candles on the mantel. Before too long the fumes and the flames would meet and the Villa Marten and its guests would be no more.

He was out of the house and back on his Vespa heading for Antibes when he heard the clatter of a helicopter overhead and the wail of police sirens. He thought there was no way they could be looking for him yet, but always cautious, he cut off the main road and headed inland. He knew every minor road, every shortcut, every alley in this area.

THE SIRENS WOKE Little Blue. For a minute she thought she was back in Shanghai and she sat up and looked around for Bao Chu, but of course Bao Chu wasn't there. Nor was Criminal, who always slept nearby. And there was a funny smell. *She knew that smell from the gas burner in the apartment.*

"Franny, Franny," she yelled, running next door. "Wake up, wake up, something bad is happening."

Franny heard the panic in her voice even before she smelled the gas and heard the sirens. She was out of bed, grasping Little Blue's hand, rattling the doorknob, trying to get out onto the veranda. *She knew she'd left it open, so how could it be locked?* Fear licked in an icy crawl up her spine. *Unless someone was trying to kill them.*

For a second she stood there, frozen with fear, then she grabbed a shoe and slammed it into the pane of glass nearest the lock. It cracked but didn't break and, desperate, she slammed her fist through it, hearing Little Blue scream as blood spurted suddenly from her wrist. But she had the door open, and they were out on the veranda and tripping over Criminal. They stopped, stared . . . even Little Blue recognized death and she was screaming louder and louder and so was Frannie. And then all the world disappeared in one fiery orange explosion.

65 THE HELICOPTER FLUTTERED above the empty parking lot near the beach and was just settling gently down when the explosion momentarily sucked out all the air, rocking it. Seconds later Jake was out and running.

It was the same nightmare all over again, the explosion, him running, the shattered body of the woman he loved.

He ran until he came to what used to be the Villa Marten. Behind him he heard the wail of sirens, the squeal of tires, voices yelling. In front of him he saw an inferno. He ran toward it.

Voices screamed at him to get back. There was the rattle of fire hoses, firemen running with him, grabbing him, pulling him away. The upper veranda was gone, and flames licked at the remains of the doors leading to the bedrooms where he knew Franny and Little Blue must have been sleeping. He dragged himself free and stumbled forward, calling their names. In front of him he saw a twisted heap of bodies, a jumble of bloodied legs and arms. He dropped to his knees beside them. The medics were right behind him. Franny lay on top of Little Blue, and he could hear the child moaning. He touched her hand gently and said, "It's all right, Little Blue. It's Jake, I'm here. You'll be okay now, I promise." But he still couldn't look at Franny. *It was Amanda all over again.*

"It's natural gas . . . a leak. Better get everyone out of here until we clear it," someone yelled, but Jake did not move. He watched as the medics got to work. "They're alive," one of them said, and Jake's heart retrieved its rhythm. "If they'd been inside that house they'd be dead," another said. "It blew them right off that veranda. The dog, too, only he wasn't so lucky—if you can call this luck."

Jake turned his head. He stared at the grizzled bloody mess that was his trusted friend and companion. He looked away again.

They had Franny in a neck splint. She was on her back now and they were working on her. Little Blue was on a gurney. She was unconscious, but her small hands twitched as though she were fighting someone, something.

He didn't want to . . . he couldn't bear to see it again, not again. He forced himself to look at Franny, and then his mind raced back in time. *He was looking at Amanda and she was lying on the side of the road, her face blown away in the explosion. She was dead and their baby was dead.* He'd blocked this memory from his brain, but now it was happening all over again, only this time it was Franny . . . Franny. Her lips were blue, blue as her eyes, he thought wonderingly, but her face was untouched. She looked peaceful, as though she were just asleep. They put an oxygen mask over her face and now they'd put her neck in a brace and there was so much blood. They had a tourniquet on her wrist, another on a leg. They wrapped her in shock foil, then eased her very carefully onto a gurney and headed for the ambulance.

Jake went and picked up his dog. He walked behind them carrying Criminal. They tried to shut him out of the ambulance but he turned on them so fiercely that, intimidated, they allowed him to accompany them, still holding the dog on his knees.

Half an hour later he was sitting in the hospital waiting room, staring at the clock on the wall as it ticked away the endlessly slow minutes. Minutes that might be the last for Little Blue and Franny. Every now and then some official came to tell him he really couldn't keep the dog there, but he ignored them and eventually they went away.

An hour passed, then two. His pilot showed up with the staff from his plane. They'd heard from the helicopter company what had happened. They brought him coffee that he didn't drink, offered words of sympathy he couldn't respond to, said maybe they should take care of Criminal for him. Jake said nothing, he was still frozen in emotional time—reliving the hell of his first wife's death and the torture of maybe losing his new love.

Hours later, the surgeon came out to speak to him. "We're lucky, Monsieur Bronson," he said, managing a tired smile. "They were not burned. When the explosion happened they were thrown from the balcony. The child is deeply concussed, and we must watch her for signs of neurological damage, though from the scans it's doubtful. She has a broken leg and many cuts and bruises, but she'll be fine."

Jake felt a little lurch of his heart and knew that at least it still beat for Little Blue.

"Mademoiselle Marten took most of the impact of the explosion and she is still unconscious. She has a fracture of the fourth vertebra, which means, sir, that she has a broken neck. Plus she lost a great deal of blood from a severed artery. We've done what we can. The next twenty-four hours will tell their own story."

The surgeon smiled that tired smile again and held out his hand, but Jake didn't even notice.

"She's alive?" he said, as though he hadn't been able to take in what had just been said. "*She's alive,*" he repeated with such a note of relief that the others smiled. Then he buried his head in his dead dog's rough fur and he wept.

66   LYING ON THE BED in his cheap hotel room in Cannes, Alain watched the TV news report. He was not happy. The villa had been destroyed but not the planned Marten victims.

He'd been right, though. There was no way to trace the gas leak to the unlit burners on the stove because everything had been blown to pieces. The villa had not been used for a long time, and it was assumed to be a gas leak, just one of those unfortunate incidents.

He lay for a long time, thinking about what to do next. Finally, he got off the bed, took a long shower to clear his head, then went to get his car. He drove to Le Suquet, the old port area of Cannes, and sat in a bar overlooking the marina with its hundred-foot-long yachts and parade of glossy cruise ships, drinking Ricard and feeling sorry for himself. He'd lost the money he'd won at the casino and was broke. He didn't even have access to Felix's money because Little Blue had inherited his entire estate. He wondered why the fuck Felix had done that. He'd never even acknowledged the kid when he was alive. Of course the real reason was that Felix had never wanted to find out the truth about who was the father because he was afraid it would turn out to be Alain.

Through the years Alain had kept tabs on Felix. He knew where he was at any given moment. Not only that, he'd used his name fraudulently several times, though Felix had never prosecuted. Too proud of the old family name, Alain thought with a grim smile.

He'd gotten even with Felix years ago, though. He'd found the bar where Felix's woman worked. She'd needed to work because Felix had refused to make a commitment to her and she had no money. But Alain made it his business to get to know everything about Felix's woman. He'd kept watch on her. He knew even before Felix did that she was pregnant because he'd made friends with one of her girlfriends who had told him. He'd laughed then. He thought it was amusing, the old story repeating itself—the pregnant girl, him and Felix—who was the father?

He'd called Felix and demanded a meeting. He'd never

forget the grotesque look on Felix's face when, bluffing, he told him his woman was pregnant and the child was not his, that he, Alain, was the father. At first not believing, then maybe half believing . . . then, *no it can't be*.

"She's not pregnant," Felix said in a quiet, deadened voice. How could it be true? He was always so careful when they had sex.

"Ask her," Alain said confidently, "ask her yourself if she's pregnant. Then ask yourself how else would I know, Felix, if I were not the father."

Felix never saw the woman again. He'd paid Alain off, and when the woman died, he sent a small amount of money each month to salve his conscience, and the child had lived in poverty with her ailing grandmother. And that was that.

That is, until Jake Bronson had come along with Rafaella's invitation to the great Marten family reunion, just as Alain was forced to ask Felix for financial help again. When he was refused, in a spate of anger, he'd killed Felix.

He'd gotten lucky that night, but luck hadn't been on his side this time. A big blast like that should have killed anyone in range, yet it had not.

Alain ordered another Ricard, and his thoughts turned to his mother. If only Rafaella had given him what he wanted, just given him the vineyard and the château that were right-fully his, he'd have had enough money to live the lifestyle he enjoyed and none of this would have happened. Rafaella was at the heart of all his problems.

He downed the drink and ordered another. He bought a *Nice-Matin* and as he read the report of the conflagration at the Villa Marten, the rage burned harder in his chest. He sat for a long time at the bar, drinking Ricard and thinking about his life and what to do, until he could bear it no longer. The decision was made. He was going home again. And this time Rafaella would not throw him out.

67 FRANNY WAS LYING perfectly still, but she had a sensation of flying at great speed down a long tunnel. She was weightless, the air against her cheek was soft and there was the scent of lilies.

Her eyelids fluttered and she looked around her. The light was white, sharp, glaring. She tried to sit up but couldn't move. Sudden panic made her tremble, and she wondered if she was a prisoner. But she couldn't be because she was in a garden, she could smell the lilies.

She opened her eyes wider, saw a leg encased in plaster suspended in the air. *Her* leg. She moved her eyes to the right, saw an open window, heard the breeze rattle the shades . . . the same breeze she'd felt on her cheek as she raced through that dream tunnel. She slid her eyes to the left. A great vase of lilies stood on a table. Casablanca lilies. She thought she had dreamed them too, but they were real. She reached out a hand to touch them and pain, sharp as lightning, shot down her back. She let her hand fall onto the sheet, caught the glint of something. She lifted her hand slowly, staring at the pretty diamond on the third finger. And then she began to laugh.

It was the first thing Jake heard as he walked down the hospital corridor. Franny was laughing. *She was back. His girl was here with him again.*

Their eyes met across the stark hospital room. "You might have asked me first," she said in a whisper, hoarse because there had been tubes down her throat and she hadn't spoken in a quite a while.

He grinned. "I did ask, but you didn't answer. But wherever you were, I wanted you to know you belonged to me and I'm never letting you out of my sight again."

"Okay," she said. "Then why don't you come over here and kiss me."

And he did just that. Gently, tenderly, and with love.

68 AS SOON AS THEY had heard about the "accident," Clare had driven immediately to Cannes. All those long days and nights when Franny was in a coma she'd sat stoically at her bedside, and now she was really mad to miss "the awakening." But when she saw Franny, alert and smiling again, she finally cracked.

"Oh my god, I almost lost you," she wailed, sobbing into a Kleenex. "And dammit Franny, I'd only just found you."

"Don't worry. I'm not going anywhere," Fanny said. She was still wearing the big plastic collar meant to prevent her from moving her neck that Jake said made her look like the

German shepherd. "I have a surprise," she said and she showed Clare her ring.

Clare said, "You and Jake were made for each other. That invitation was destiny, it brought you together. And by the way," she added nonchalantly, "I'm engaged too, though I don't have a ring yet to prove it."

"Scott!" Franny's eyes narrowed in a smile of satisfaction. "He's perfect for you."

"Hmm, actually no, it's not Scott," Clare said, looking as demure as was possible for her.

"Don't tell me you're going back to Marcus!" Franny looked shocked.

"*Of course* I'm not going back to Marcus. I'm divorcing that bastard as fast as I can so I can get married again. To Jarré," she added, grinning at Franny's look of astonishment.

"And all the time I thought you were just taking cooking lessons!" Franny said laughing.

"I was. . . . I am. I'm going to help Jarré with the café. I'll be the *commis*, the sous chef, the waiter, the dishwasher— whatever my man needs, I'll be it. Including his lover." Clare looked hesitantly at her. "Truth is, Franny, we haven't actually made love yet." Eyes lowered, Clare inspected her unmanicured hands, adorned with several nicks from the restaurant knives. "I . . . well, I wanted to save that for after we're married. I really want to be the 'virgin bride' for him. I was never that before and . . . well, you have to understand how good a man he is, how gentle, how caring, how . . ."

"*Salt-of-the-earth.*" Franny said it for her and they looked at each other and burst out laughing.

69 JAKE HAD NOT FORGOTTEN what he saw that night. And he had not forgotten about Criminal. He knew in his gut this was no accident. Alain had tried to kill them. He had an autopsy performed on the dog, and traces of rat poison were found in its stomach. It had been dead before the explosion. Obviously Alain had gotten rid of the dog first so he wouldn't bark and sound the alarm.

Jake had his beloved friend cremated. Later he would take the ashes back to the cabin. He would stand on the mountainside and return Criminal to the elements, hoping that the wind in the tossing treetops might catch him and that he would find the ultimate freedom in the place he loved.

Meanwhile, Alain was alive. He was evil. He was dangerous. He would try again. With Alain still alive, nobody was safe. *Especially Rafaella.*

The thought came so clearly into Jake's head, it stopped him in his tracks, as though Alain himself had transmitted it. Alain blamed Rafaella for everything that had gone wrong in his life. Rafaella would be Alain's next target.

Jake knew Alain could not have gone far, and his intelligence contacts along the southern coast—from Marseille to Menton and into Provence—were on the alert, as were the police. Like Felix, Alain was very tall, six-four, thin and rangy.

Even if he changed his hair, wore glasses, grew a beard, there would still be something distinctive about him. It was in the sheer cockiness of his walk, the arrogance of his demeanor. Alain was a man who felt he was better than all others and Jake knew it would be Alain's ego that would prove his downfall.

IT WASN'T LONG BEFORE he got the news that Alain had been spotted near Avignon. He was driving a white Renault Laguna and was holed up at a motel off the motorway on the outskirts of the city. Two hours later Jake was in Avignon, but the bird had already flown. Then the white Renault was spotted winding along a canyon road that led, by a roundabout route, to Saint-Sylvestre and then Marten-de-Provence.

Jake had a helicopter in the air within minutes, piloting it himself. He hovered over the canyon, so close to the rock face that the shrubs and grasses flattened beneath him, scattering terrified rabbits and wild creatures. At last he spotted the Renault, taking the curves like a race car. The window was open and he saw Alain looking up at the helicopter. Obviously realizing he was being observed, he took off, hurtling around curves with a two-hundred-foot drop on one side and a sheer rock wall on the other, winding his way down to the end of the canyon where the proper road began.

ALAIN WAS EXHILARATED by the chase. Adrenaline flowed like heat through his body. He was on flat terrain now, on straight roads lined with poplars. On one side was a railway embankment, on the other a peaceful canal dotted with vacationers' barges. A police helicopter had joined the chase and it clattered low overhead, making giant whirlpools on the canal's still water, sending delighted children running out to wave at them.

Alain swerved onto a minor forest road, then abandoned the Renault in the trees. He climbed the embankment to the railway tracks. A tunnel loomed in front of him.

He ran into it, flattening himself against the curve of the wall. He heard the helicopters immediately overhead, then they zoomed on. He smiled as he started down the dark tunnel. He'd outwitted them again. He knew his way. He'd still get to the château, still get his mother.

Jake radioed the police helicopter. "He can't have gotten far, he's probably hiding out in the woods," then he zoomed in low over the treetops again. The approaching train blew its whistle furiously at him as it entered the tunnel, and suddenly Jake knew where Alain was. And he knew he'd played his last card in the game of life.

70

LITTLE BLUE HAD ALREADY been back at the château for a few weeks by the time Franny was finally allowed to leave the hospital and fly "home" with Jake.

"I don't think I could ever get used to this," she said to him, awed by the Gulfstream's luxury.

"That's good," he said, "because I won't have it much longer." She eyed him, mystified. "I'm selling the business, thinking about finally buying that ranch. How'd you fancy being a country vet?"

"Hmm." She looked away haughtily, enjoying the game of keeping him in suspense. "What, no more fancy SoHo apartment? No more private jet? No more Tiffany rings and world travel?"

"No more," he said. "Well, maybe a ring or two."

"Ohhh . . . well." She pretended to think about it. "Maybe I could handle that. After all, I might enjoy being that country vet."

"Oh, thank god," he murmured, grabbing her very carefully and making her laugh.

Haigh was waiting for them with the comfortable old Bentley, greeting Franny with tears in his eyes and a big hug and triple kisses. As they drove through the village, she leaned out the window and, recognizing her, passing villagers waved. Then the car turned up the familiar drive and she peered eagerly ahead, anxious for that first glimpse of the Château des Roses Sauvages.

And there it was, glowing golden in the evening sunlight, tugging at her heartstrings like a familiar melody from long ago. Rafaella was waiting on the steps with Mimi and Louis. Juliette was there with her Pomeranians, and Little Blue came hurtling toward them, followed by a couple of shaggy, boisterous pups.

And, holding Jake's hand tightly, Franny knew that wherever she was in the world, this old château in Provence would always be "home."

PART IV

Epilogue

Ô saisons, ô châteaux,
Quelle âme est sans défauts?
Ô saisons, ô châteaux,
J'ai fait la magique étude
Du Bonheur, que nul n'élude.

— RIMBAUD, 1874

Oh seasons, oh châteaux,
What soul is without faults?
Oh seasons, oh châteaux,
I have studied the magic of happiness,
Which no one should miss.

A YEAR HAD PASSED. Rafaella stood in the hall looking out at the magical view that had entranced her all her life. A patch of afternoon sunlight warmed the faded parquet under her bare feet, and her red skirt swished around her narrow ankles as she walked to the door, followed by Mimi and Louis and a shaggy brindle pup who bore more than a passing resemblance to Criminal.

She noticed Little Blue's woolly lamb, wrapped in a blanket and propped on a chair, and also her skateboard left on the steps, ready no doubt for someone to trip over, plus her sweater tossed carelessly next to it. Little Blue had learned how to be a little girl, but not without some heartbreak.

Franny and Jake had accompanied her back to Shanghai. For two days they had sat by Bao Chu's bedside while Shao Lan told her sick grandmother happy stories about her new life in Provence.

Shao Lan desperately did not want her grandmother to die. It hurt in her heart to look at her, so small and frail, so tired of life. She had given Bao Chu the woolly lamb to hold for comfort. Remembering what Rafaella had told her about dying, she had looked for the final smile in Bao Chu's eyes.

When she saw it she knew her grandmother was happy, and even though she cried for her, she was glad for her, too.

Rafaella comforted her granddaughter when she came home, spending many hours with her, but it had taken a while for Shao Lan to become "Little Blue" again.

From the kitchen Rafaella could hear Haigh's haughty tones and the child's silvery ones, then a delighted shriek of laughter as a second brindle pup raced from the kitchen with a hunk of steak clutched in its jaws. It ran straight past Rafaella, down the steps, and into the tall shrubbery. It was a true chip off the old Criminal block.

Haigh appeared, a meat cleaver in his hand, his face beet red with frustration. "That damned dog," he roared, "he gets me every time."

"I hope you're not planning on using that cleaver on him," Rafaella said mildly, and Haigh huffed and said he wanted to, but he wouldn't. This time.

"It's about time Mr. Jake taught that dog some manners," he said bitterly. "Or it'll be omelettes every night for supper."

"Don't worry," Rafaella called to his grumpy back as he returned to the kitchen. "We'll go to the café for dinner. I wanted to see Clare anyway."

Clare's wedding had taken place a few months back at the village church. She'd asked Haigh to walk her down the aisle, and he was a proud man that day, resplendent in top hat, striped gray trousers, and morning coat, with Juliette's rich silk vest underneath. And Clare was gorgeous in a simple satin slip dress with wildflowers wound into her glossy dark hair.

Franny was her maid of honor, delicate as a bluebell in that particular shade of lavender-blue chiffon that brought out her eyes. Little Blue was the flower girl in sprigged prim-rose cotton.

Rafaella had seen how Jarré's dark gypsy eyes adored Clare as she walked down the short aisle toward him, and she was glad for their unlikely happiness as they'd said their vows in trembling voices that left no doubt about how much they loved each other.

Rafaella had offered to host their reception at the château, but Clare had said no, the café was their home and they would start as they meant to go on, by doing all the work themselves.

Guests in their wedding finery had spilled from the small café terrace into the square, where trestle tables were set up, loaded with baskets of flowers and bottles of wine. The cele-bration buntings were back up and fairy lights sparkled in the dusty plane trees. The fountain dogs, including Crimi-nal's paramour, who had given birth to the two miniature Criminal look-alikes, had been banished for the night as a potential danger to the racks of lamb grilling on the immense barbecue. Everyone helped themselves from the lavish, never-ending buffet and there was dancing to the local band that went on till the early hours of the morning.

Scott Harris was one of the first to congratulate Clare. "The best man won," he'd said ruefully, and she'd kissed him gently and told him there was no best man, it was just the way the heart went.

Juliette was there, of course, resplendent in a shimmering gold caftan with a bank vault's worth of gold necklaces and bracelets. The Pomeranians wore gold ribbons to match, and even Mimi wore a pink bow on her woolly black head, while Louis sulked, knowing he looked ridiculous in a matching bow tie. For once all the dogs behaved perfectly, though it was observed they enjoyed the buffet more than the ceremony.

Rafaella looked glamorous—in scarlet, naturally—a vintage silk Valentino with a nipped-in waist that she was proud to see still fitted perfectly. The portrait neckline set off her long, slender neck, as well as her ropes of rubies and the ruby earrings sparkled like her happy smile.

Clare and Jarré stayed until the very last guest left, and when Rafaella finally kissed her goodnight and said, "I hope at least you're not going to do the dishes," Clare had laughed and replied, "Jarre's giving me the night off." Then, with a final kiss to Franny and Little Blue, Madame Jarré had walked into her new home on the arm of her new husband.

After the wedding, Juliette returned to New York, but she said she would be back—with the Pomeranians—for Franny's imminent wedding, and this time she was planning on an extended stay. Rafaella would be glad of her company, because soon Franny and Jake were taking Little Blue away. Jake had sold his company and they were happily living the simple life on their new ranch, breeding the horses he loved.

She would miss her granddaughter, but they had promised to return to the château every summer, and in her heart she knew it was wiser for the child to be brought up by young people who could properly be "her parents."

Franny's wedding was to take place next month, in the gazebo at the lake. She'd wanted a small affair. "Just family," and Rafaella smiled, thinking that nothing in the world sounded as good to her as those words.

Was it really only a year ago that she'd stood here in the empty house with the locked dust-sheeted rooms and only the sound of silence thudding in her ears?

The longcase clock behind her ground its gears manfully and struck its flat notes. Six o'clock. All the windows were open, and she could hear birds singing and the sound of pots rattling in the kitchen. Water gurgled in the pipes and happy cries rang from the swimming pool. And surely somebody was playing an old record of "As Time Goes By." Or was it only in her head?

Ah, Lucas, she thought, someday I'll find you again. But this story is not yours and mine anymore, it belongs to the young people. It's about Franny and Jake, about Clare and Jarré, and about my granddaughter's future. Love, as well as family, has taken over the Château des Roses Sauvages. And I am a happy woman again.

Read on for an excerpt from
Elizabeth Adler's next book

THE HOUSE IN AMALFI

Available in hardcover from St. Martin's Press

Lamour Harrington

1 FOR TWO YEARS I have lived alone, not allowing even a dog or a cat to intrude on my solitude. My friend Jammy Mortimer, who I've known since we were little kids, says I'm getting creepy. "All this loneliness is not good for you," she says in her usual forthright manner. "You'll end up a fat, eccentric recluse, refusing to open the door even to me."

Of course that's not true—my door's always open to Jammy. But as far as the weight is concerned, I have to admit I've gotten even skinnier over the past few months. I have a busy life—by day, that is—and eating is a habit I seem to be forgetting. I work as a landscape architect, bringing beauty to other people's homes, creating outdoor "rooms" for them, some small and fragrant, others rambling and wild, but always enhanced by the drift of water, the ripple of a pebbled stream, a simple fountain. I love transforming barren lots with living things: grasses, shrubs, flowers, trees. But most of all I love the trees. Sometimes I ask myself what would life be without them?

Now I think about it, it would be like my own life, barren and empty since I lost Alex, my husband, in a car crash two years ago. It was the second time in my life that I'd lost a man I loved to a tragic accident. The first was when my father died in a mysterious boating mishap when I was just seventeen.

It's my belief that you can never recover from the agony of being rent apart from your loved one within the space of just a few seconds and then having to face the sheer terror of going on without him. My husband was my love, my best friend, my companion. "You just have to pick yourself up and get on with living," friends advised me, after a few months. And I tried. I went back to work all right, but somehow I've never learned to "play" again.

Sitting here now, twenty floors up in my urban Chicago aerie overlooking the blustery windblown gray lake, a cooling mug of coffee clutched, half-forgotten, in my hand, I'm thinking about happiness and trying to remember what it felt like. My dwarf ficus trees out on the small terrace tremble in the chill breeze, reminding me of the pampered lemon trees on Italy's Amalfi coast, sequestered for winter in their cozy greenhouses, emerging again in the spring with a burst of blossoms so fragrant it takes your breath away.

And quite suddenly, because I haven't consciously thought of this in ages, I'm thinking of my father, Jonathon Harrington, who'd named me Lamour after his beautiful but flighty New Orleans great-grandmother, and about the time he took me with him to live in Rome while he wrote his novel.

It was sure to be a success, he told me—how could it not be when he was writing it in a city filled with history, culture, and sex? He didn't actually say the word *sex*; after all, I wa only seven years old. I believe he used the word *sensuality* instead, though I wasn't sure what *sensuality* meant, either. And later, to my surprise, because to me he was just my father, his novel did become a huge success, which he said went a long way to blotting out the pain of the whole writing experience.

Again, I didn't know what he meant, since he seemed to spend most of his time happily in the bar in the piazza near our apartment. Not for us one of those beautiful Renaissance palazzos whose chiseled facades decorate Rome's better streets and whose parquet and paneled, gilded, and mirrored interiors have sheltered wealthy Romans for centuries. Ours was just the top floor of an ancient peeling stucco building with reluctant plumbing and possibly dangerous electricals in what was still the workmen's quarter of Rome known as Trastevere. And for a seven-year-old let loose on its cobbled alleys and squares, it was Paradise.

When we first stepped off the Alitalia flight into the hot sunshine of a Roman summer my father, Jonathon Boyland Harrington from Atlanta, Georgia, told me from now on to call him Jon-Boy instead of Daddy, reasoning it would make me feel more grown-up and him, I guess, more of the "southern writer" and less of the single parent. This was the role he'd been playing since I was three, when he'd picked me up and we'd left my mother because, he told me, of her "drinking and carousing." Again, I wasn't sure what *carousing* meant, but young though I was, I knew all about Mom's drinking.

"I'll never drink and carouse, Jon-Boy," I reassured him that day at Rome's airport, and he gave me that crooked grin and the lift of a black eyebrow that made him more than just handsome and said, "You betcha won't, girl; Italian women don't behave that way." Which I guessed also meant that from now on I should consider myself Italian—at least for the duration of our stay in that country.

We lived at the center of a maze of narrow, winding, secretive streets, more like alleys really, with tall, thin buildings crowding each side. The old gray stone showed where centuries of different-colored stucco had peeled off, and there was always laundry hanging overhead—snowy-clean undershirts and colorful tablecloths and the whitest of sheets. Up on the roofs you could catch a glimpse of scrawny little trees and shrubs sprouting among the TV aerials. The alleys smelled of cats and fresh-ground coffee, of laundry and heat vibrating off stone.

My new neighborhood was far from glamorous, just "homey" in a foreign sort of way. It was certainly light-years from the grassy-lawned suburban street I had called home for most of my short life, and where the aromas were mostly of buttered popcorn or freshly mowed grass. These Roman smells were new and exciting.

My alley was called vicolo del Cardinale, though I can't believe any real red-robed cardinal ever lived anywhere near there. Perhaps he just took a walkabout once and the name stuck. I was usually out on my *vicolo* early, waving to my new friends visible at the windows of their tiny kitchens or already on their way back from the market—in which case knew I'd overslept.

These local women knew, via the grapevine, that I had no mother, and because I was usually on my own they watched out for me. They always asked where I was going and shook their heads disapprovingly when I told them I did not attend the *scuola elementare* and that Jon-Boy was teaching me himself. But they still liked him. How could they not? He was Mr. Charm personified, and he always had time for a chat with them.

In their black dresses and flat-back granny shoes and with their kind, lined faces they were all grandmas to me. I ate homemade pasta in their kitchens, admired pictures of their grown-up sons and their "real" grandchildren, and promised to always be good so that one day I would marry someone like that and give Jon-Boy a grandson of his own. "That would straighten him out," they said, nodding, satisfied at having solved our family problems so simply. How I wish they had.

Still, out in the early-morning alley, with my face hastily splashed with water, a cursory brush of the teeth and my long dark hair in a thick clumsy braid swinging between my shoulder blades, I felt the heady rush of freedom for the first time as I followed the sharp sweet smell of freshly ground coffee and sugary buns until the tall, shadowed alley burst onto the piazza in a shock of sunlight and activity.

The news vendor had already set up his stand and a van was delivering copies of the morning papers and sport magazines that seemed, along with Italian crossword puzzles, to make up most of his stock. Almost immediately behind him, separated by a scattering of small tables with metal chairs that scraped the uneven paving stones with a terrible screech every time someone took a seat, was the Bar Marchetti, already with a few male customers propping up the counter. One foot on the brass rail, they leafed through the early news while knocking back an espresso piled high with sugar.

Across the way in her small wooden hut, Adriana, the flower seller, waved to me from behind a bank of multicolored blossoms, and I made a fast detour from my predetermined route to the bar just to receive her quick kiss. She tucked a pink carnation into my braid and asked anxiously when I would start school like a normal child. I quickly reassured her that Jon-Boy would be giving me a math lesson later that day. This was of course untrue, because Jon-Boy had about as much knowledge of math as any seven-year-old and about as much money sense as your average flea. But that's another story.

Off I sped again, pausing only to peer through the tall wooden doors of the flat-fronted little church topped with a classic pediment and a small verdigrised cross. The plain exterior led into an intriguing ornate gold and frescoed dimness lit by flickering candles. I did not go in because I was heading to the bar for my coffee and *cornetto*, the staple breakfast of every Italian, of whom, after just a couple of months, I now counted myself as one.

"*Buon giorno, Angelo.*" I stood with both feet on the brass rail, elbows propped on the bar. Switching my braid over my shoulder I chewed on the end, smiling my gap-toothed seven-year-old smile at him.

Angelo was in his thirties, a big man, broad shouldered, strong necked and shaggy haired, with a wide face inset with glossy dark brown eyes and long straight lashes, like a cow's. He had a perpetual overnight growth of dark beard from which his teeth gleamed large and shiny white.

I had a kind of flirtation going on with Angelo, my very first. In fact I had not known how to flirt until I came to Rome and sat alongside Jon-Boy in the cafés, watching elegant pretty women walk a little slower as they passed, smiling from the corners of their eyes at him, turning their heads and giving him a long slow look that said whatever was said between a man and a woman. I practiced this new knowledge on Angelo and like most Italians with children, he humored me and allowed me to twist him around my little finger—something I doubt I could do with a man today.

"*Ciao, bella,*" he said, accepting my money and handing me a *scontrino,* a receipt, which I then gave back to him in exchange for my breakfast. This was the way it worked in Italy. Angelo knew my "order" and was already at the hissing, sputtering machine fixing my cappuccino, a drink invented by the Capuchin monks long before espresso machines were thought of, and to whom I shall be eternally grateful.

Angelo piled my cup high with froth, flung a lavish dusting of powdered chocolate on top and shoved it across the counter at me. He picked out the crispest *cornetto,* wrapped it in a small square of wax paper and handed it to me. Next to Italian ice cream and real Italian pizza, this was my favorite thing on earth. I loved the way the crisp layered pastry crunched when I bit into it, powdering my T-shirt with crumbs, and then the soft sweetness as my teeth and taste buds encountered the center. I took a deep slug of the cappuccino, wiped the chocolate dust and crumbs from my mouth with the back of my hand and beamed up at my hero. "Great," I said, forgetting all about speaking Italian I was so lost in my pleasure.

"Great!" he replied in return, and I laughed because coming from him it sounded funny. "*Ecco*, so what you do today?" he said in the kind of simple Italian I had just mastered. (Conjugating verbs was a mystery never to be solved.)

"I'm going to the market in Campo de' Fiori to buy salad for tonight's supper." I patted the money folded in my jeans pocket, filled with the importance of my task. "I'll buy salad and cheese and prosciutto. And bread of course."

"But shouldn't you be in school?" Angelo asked the question I knew was going to haunt my childhood days in Rome. I shrugged it off as nonchalantly as I could, though I admit I was starting to get worried. What if the police came looking for me? Arrested me right here on the piazza with everybody looking on? What if they hauled me off to face the principal at the school in front of all the other kids? The humiliation of that thought left my mouth hanging open—not a pretty sight when it was still half-full of *cornetto*—but Angelo merely smiled and patted my bony shoulder. "Hey, be happy while you can, *piccolina*," he said. "Remember, life is short." And he slid a second *cornetto* across the counter with a wink that said it was free, then went to attend to his other customers, piling in now for their morning espresso fix.

Caffeine was already thundering through my veins, giving a fast lift to my skip as I headed past Pizzeria Vesuvio, my favorite pizza joint, threading my way through a maze of familiar alleys and dodging the speeding Roman traffic that stopped for no one.

I stood for a moment on the corner of the Campo de' Fiori, taking in the crowded square. Awninged stalls were piled high with vegetables and fruits whose scents tickled my nostrils and whose rainbow of colors dazzled my eyes. Wasps buzzed over the peaches and a rattle of female chatter hovered in the air. Smart Roman ladies, long legged in short skirts and heels, perfectly made up, perfectly coiffed, picked over tiny yellow-flowered zucchini and moist dove gray mushrooms as expertly as the local black-clad grandmothers, giving the same intense scrutiny to each piece because nothing less than perfect was good enough.

The displays of flowers near the central fountain put Adriana's to shame. Towering orange gladioli, buckets full of coral roses and banks of greenish-white lilies whose smell captured you at twenty paces, and always the tiny baskets of dense purple violets. I bought one of these to put in my room; then I purchased a single tall white lily. I would present it to my father at the dinner table that night, when my salad and ham and cheese were artistically arranged on plates next to a glass of his favorite local white Frascati wine. It would be a sample of my love, because no girl ever loved her father more than I did.

Dragged back to a cold Chicago evening by a sudden blast of wind that sent the ficus leaves scattering across the terrace, I recalled how I had felt that Roman morning, with the sun hot on my back and my pigtail bouncing. How Angelo's bright white smile had sent my heart racing and the way the sugary taste of the *cornetto* had shocked my taste buds and how Adriana's concerned kiss had made me feel so wanted. I could smell again the lilies in the Campo de' Fiori, and I smiled, suddenly realizing that what I was remembering was that elusive emotion called happiness.

I didn't know it on that sunny morning in Rome, but I had yet to experience *true* happiness. The "real thing" would not come until the following year, when Jon-Boy took me to live in the house in Amalfi. The place where, ten years later, he would die so mysteriously.